IN MEMORIAM

Fein appeared out of the trees. Each carried a glopod or two, emitting soft green light.

Then, from the woods all around, hundreds of ancient fein, all adepts of the Spirit, gave the call, a whisper from many unseen lips.

The susurration slowly coalesced into the lament of the *ay fein*, "those who were left behind." As the whisper reached "Are they forgotten by the mighty?" the pool grew agitated, and tiny wavelets rippled across it though no wind stirred the stifling air.

The Old One dropped the hairs of the departed into the thick humid air above the surface. As each hair approached the water, it winked out of existence. None survived to touch the pool...

Christopher Rowley

THE WAR FOR ETERNITY

A Del Rey Book

BALLANTINE BOOKS • NEW YORK

A Del Rey Book
Published by Ballantine Books

Copyright © 1983 by Christopher B. Rowley

Library of Congress Catalog Card Number: 83-90642

ISBN 0-345-31052-7

Manufactured in the United States of America

First Edition: November 1983

Cover art by Ralph McQuarrie

To Basil and Elizabeth,
who gave me so much

Patientia dea benefica

The fundamental mistake made in understanding both the fein and their eerily ordered world lay in the very human trait of applying human conceptions to systems lying outside human experience. Nothing in human mysticism had prepared the race for Fenrille. Nor had the race yet learned the grace of patience, humility, the application of true objectivity. Of course none could seriously be blamed for failing to grasp the colossal scale of what occurred on Fenrille.

It was only among the inner circles of the oldest colonists, the children of the Asteroid Belters, that any real understanding of the true situation existed, and even there such conceptions were hard to accept. Perception was dim, muffled by the gulf between man and fein.

But how else to explain a world with a continent wrapped about its middle like a ring? A world continent, greater than ancient Pangaea, known to the fein as the *Hokkkh*, the "Knuckle of Delight."

From *FENRILLE: Conclusions* by Pope Bea Paolo XXI

MAHGARA (exodus)

In disillusion with the universe,
Having pierced the veils of the Creator's purpose,
They called for the Mahgara.
To seek for the Creator, to find the Creator, and to die in
    the light that only the Creator possesses
They called for the Mahgara.

Four thousand bahlkwan* were taken to refashion the world,
To move north south and south north,
To solidify the ring around the world,
To grow the forest to cover the world,

For knowing that the universe is but a breath of the Creator,
Cooling inexorably in the dark halls of the All,
Eventually to decay to uttermost nothing,
The Arizel tki Fenrille endeavored to grow out of [through]
    the halls of All,
To sit by the feet of the Creator and bathe in the beneficent
    energy,
To cease existence in bliss.

Bahlkwan is a fein measure of approximately 6,000 Earth-standard years.

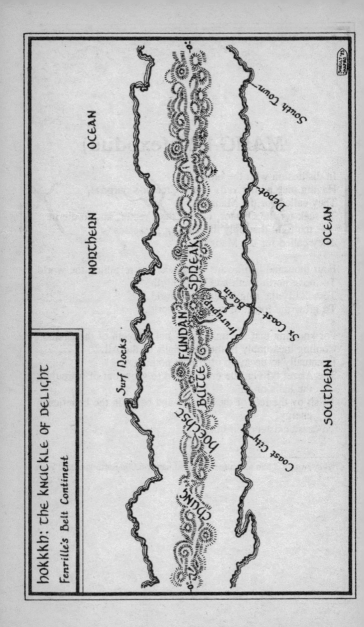

bokkkh: the knuckle of DELIGHT
Fenrille's Belt Continent

OCEAN

NORTHERN

OCEAN

SOUTHERN

Surf Rocks

DUNE

boechse

Butte

FUNDAN

SPREAK

Irrurrup basin

Coast City

South Town

Depot

Sx Coast

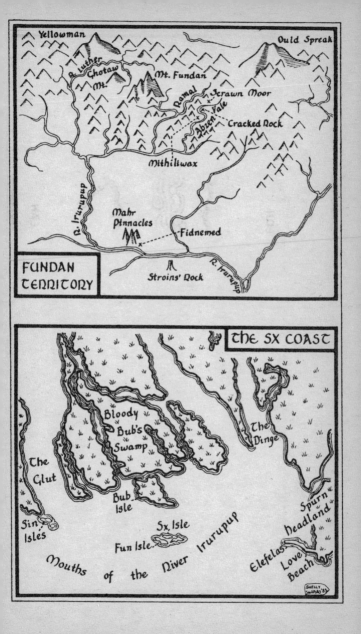

FUNDAN TERRITORY

Yellowman
Ould Spreak
R. Luther
Chotaw Mt.
Mt. Fundan
Pomal
Scrawn Moor
Abren Vale
Cracked Rock
Mithillwax
Mahr Pinnacles
Fidnemed
R. Irurupup
Stroins' Rock
R. Irurupup

THE SX COAST

Bloody Bub's Swamp
The Dinge
The Glut
Bub Isle
Spurn Headland
Sin Isles
Sx. Isle
Fun Isle
Mouths of the River Irurupup
Elefelast
Love Beach

SHELLY SHAPIO '83

1

"Ayoh! There it goes," shouted the fein at the flash of sable on the edge of the glade.

"Spy sourt! After it, we must kill it!" Keen-eyed fein warriors were quickly in pursuit.

The sourt was long nosed, lithe, the mink of Fenrille. On short legs it fled through the wet woods, one thought only drawing it on: "Report! Must report to Bg Rva..." An arrow skewered its thigh, the pain was intolerable.

"Ayoh!" The fein were close, kifkets out, sharp and heavy, for the death-dealing throw.

"Bg Rva." The thought was almost a scream. "Save your sourt!" Desperately it turned toward the riverbank, into the tumblemeadow. Among the boulders was just enough cover to keep a lethal kifket throw in check, but the pursuing fein sprang from rock to rock with a predatory lope that would overtake the sourt in seconds.

"Ayoh!" A fein stood over it.

And suddenly coughed on an arrow in the throat, silent and swift from the dark. Then the second fein took one. The rest found cover and lifted their rifles. On their side of the river! He who dared this was daring indeed!

Bg Rva held the dying sourt in one huge feinpaw. *Live, my sourt*, he commanded, *live a little longer*.

It clung to his fur while Rva sprang out over the swollen river Kayr, a monsoon torrent twenty meters wide. He seemed to float along, as if sidestepping on air, hands outstretched, handling his predator's bulk like a human ballerina.

The pursuit reached the river's edge. One fein pointed to Rva, who was by then almost across, riding metal cleats on the gossamer high wire he'd stretched between two tree trunks.

Ninety-millimeter slugs from Fundan automatic rifles slapped the water, whined off the gray Scrawn, off sandstones, but found no fein target. Rva had plunged into the boiling whitewater.

"Missed, I bet. Stop firing or you'll draw their patrols to this side of the Dognobles positions."

"I excrete on the heads of the Dognobles."

"So do I but they hold the line and the Heavy Impi moves north."

The sourt gave up its message to Rva as he crouched on a rock in midstream below the whitewater. He let it die then and consigned its body to the stream. Then he sent the coded signal to Abzen battle command—their foe's Heavy Impi was on the move at last. Abzen Second Impi must move too.

In the equatorial mountains of the Belt Continent, war came with the tick of the monsoon rains. Raiders swept in under cover of the storms. War raged in the valleys for control of the eternity drugs derived from the chitin insect. War for vast wealth, pitting highland humans and fein against coastal armies, and against each other, too, in a bewildering pattern of treachery and intrigue and slaughter.

In Abzen Valley, a sweeping S-curve extending south of the border of Fundan Clan territory, two battles were underway simultaneously. In Mithiliwax, in the south, human warbands were looting chitin nests while they held off the scattered forces of the First Abzen Impi, a division of aboriginal soldiers mustered by the Fundan Clan, with 5,000 fein and 2,000 human support troops.

In the north, in scrub jik woods surrounding the bare hills of Scrawn Moor, a treacherous invasion by Young Proud Fundan had backed Abzen's commander into a corner. Young Proud, whose own claim to Abzen Valley had never been relinquished in eight years of fighting, had brought his Heavy Impi and two coastal warbands, the Dognobles and the Chevaleers, over the pass from Ramal Valley.

Now Young Proud was ready at last; he would crush the hated upstart, the filthy little creche boy. To the north loomed the bare hills. Scrawn Moor was peppered with scarlet bloodmeknots, flowers of ill-omen for Abzen Valley. Fundan truegenes would at last prevail.

Lavin Fundin, the object of Young Proud's hatred, rested his Impi. Three days of rapid maneuver had kept Young Proud from concentrating against them, but things had begun to look bad. On his front, over the river, were two entire warbands, and behind them somewhere, readying the killing stroke, was Young Proud's Heavy Impi.

To the south, on Lavin's left, lay his communications and the pathway to the only usable airfield. The enemy's Heavy Impi could simply head south and outflank him. Then his only way out would be north, onto the bare moor where a few minutes under fire from modern weaponry would leave a gorging in feinflesh for the jackals.

Lavin had set up the command post in a grove of hobi-gobi, where the big funnel-shaped leaves kept at least some of the downpour off their heads. Around him worked the six young men and women of the Data Net, feeding information to the battlecomputer as it came in from the scouts.

Lavin strove with the battlecomputer in his hand, but the program returned quite monotonously to the inevitable consequence of pitting one Impi, 7,000 strong, against an army of 20,000. While his scouts probed southward for the Heavy Impi, Lavin waited for the inevitable stroke.

Of course Bg Rva, chief of all Abzen fein, had scorned the battlecomputer's predictable analysis.

"He will seek the unpredictable pattern now. That is his way, he can never do the simple thing."

Lavin had half agreed, he knew Young Proud well. After two years in the academy at Ghotaw with him and eight years of fighting him, Lavin had grown to expect the romantic gesture, the unpredictable movement. To Young Proud war was

3

boring unless filled with the improbable. He sought always to bewilder his opponents.

Rva left the post to check for himself. "I will cross the stream. My sourts are good."

"And the Dognobles will catch you and take your fur for a rug for a rich female on the Sx Coast."

"The Dognobles will never see Rva of Brelkilk, nor will they hear him. Excretion!"

Lavin let him go and stilled the fear in his heart. They might all be dead before much longer. And if Rva was right? Then it was best to know as soon as possible. He thought wistfully of how good it would be if he could just get free of the damned Heavy Impi for long enough to take the Abzen Second against the Dognobles, a human supremacist warband that took in the scum of the Sx Coast and brutalized them into soldiers. Men and women alike, they wore huge ID numbers tattooed in their foreheads. They took no prisoners and always flayed fein who fell into their hands.

That Ramal Valley fein would fight alongside such a unit had been a genuine shock for the Abzen fein. The honor of Ramal lay in the dirt for all to see—unless, of course, the Abzen fein were destroyed by Young Proud's stroke.

Even worse was the blow to Clan Fundan. Young Proud had clearly thrown in his lot with the coastal syndicates, shattering the family's united front.

Still no word came from the south of the Heavy Impi. Lavin took a grain of Pharamol, good Fundankristal, and felt the familiar surge of rejuvenation. Seconds ticked by and the hope kindled to a blaze. Could Rva have been right after all? Trust Young Proud to try artistry in place of the simple, clean stroke.

The call from Rva released the tension.

Activity boiled in the Abzen ranks. Lavin split his forces and raced north and west with the bulk of the Impi.

"It was as you expected, Lord," Rva said as they rode together through the jik.

"As I suspected, Mzsee?" Lavin caught the twinkle in Rva's huge yellow eyes.

"He risks the moor with his Impi."

"And heads for Bleilli Valley, to come down in our rear! Which would mean complete surprise and total annihilation for us, except that—"

4

"We will be waiting for him."

"Exactly. Might call it the luck of the Brelkilks once more."

"Brelkilk will excrete on the heads of the Heavy Impi—their honor is lost."

At the Bleilli Valley they set up the command post again, back from the edge of the vale but in sight of the moor above. Cordelia Fundin-9 was worried though. She hooked up her monitor screen and turned to Lavin. "What about the Dognobles and the Chevaleers, sir?"

"I'd say the ancestors excrete on the Dognobles and the Chevaleers. Ng Karoffa and his sept will demonstrate against them, and that'll be enough to keep them in their holes."

"If only we could get the Dognobles on the same side of the river as ourselves," Lucky Fundin said from his post at the communications module.

"If only," Lavin agreed.

"That would be excretion indeed," Cordelia Fundin-9 said.

Lavin's Abzen Impi waited, hidden in positions high above the little Bleilli stream. Artillery dug in, spotters found good places.

Soon the first enemy scouts appeared, advancing with nervous strides, sourts covering the ground ahead with sensitive noses.

Lavin watched impassively. Young Proud risked all on a foolish gamble. He would be made to pay.

Suddenly a dark mass appeared at the head of the valley as the Heavy Impi jogged forth in a dense column. Lavin waited until they were moving well into the valley itself, then he nodded to Lucky Fundin. "That will do. Open fire. Let's give them everything we've got."

The Abzen Second crashed into life, the mass-drive cannon loosing in a volley, their snap-whine shattering the still of the dawn like the bullwhips of some Apollonian god. Puncture cones and accelerated steel shot flashed through the dense ranks by the river.

Incredibly, the Heavy Impi held together. Fein hugged the ground and immediately broke up into small units that attempted to rush the Abzen positions. Smokescreen was released across the field. Lavin grunted. "Those are Fundan-trained fein all right." He smiled bitterly. "But they haven't a chance."

Within minutes Young Proud's Heavy Impi was retreating

up the valley and the Abzen fein were pressing forward, driving the enemy before them, to the moor. The Heavy Impi had hundreds down already. On the moor it could be destroyed.

The Abzen Second gave their enemies no time to recover. Remorselessly they pushed them onto the moor though the Ramal fein clung desperately to the slopes of the Scrawn, fighting for every inch of cover, hugging the ground. At last, though, it was done. The Heavy Impi was left totally exposed.

In a few minutes, after the Abzen artillery was in position, would come death. The Heavy Impi composed itself. The spirits had decided against them, they thought, probably because of the taint of the Dognobles. They had insulted the ancestors and now the fein of Ramal Valley would be flung into the void by their enemies. Stoically they waited, reloading their guns. If death was indeed imminent they would at least take a few more of the excreting Abzen fein with them.

The sun broke through the clouds for a moment and they looked down to the trees and waited for their doom. Minutes ticked by and still no hail of metal fell from Abzen guns.

Instead the quiet was broken at last by a long, sobbing ululation—Abzen counted coup. Brelkilk Village held riffchuss on all Ramal fein. Their lives were spared but their honor was taken.

Now with weary hearts the Heavy Impi got to their feet, dropped their weapons, and trudged north for the pass. They would not fight again until cleansed of the dishonor. Tears ran freely on many faces. Some would have preferred death.

Back on the river Kayr's banks a full-scale assault seemed to be underway. Somehow the Abzen Impi had marched back from the Bleilli as fast as the news had flown by skrin across the moor. Except that it was only Ng Karoffa using his 900 fein and a few mobile guns to deceive the Dognobles into thinking a full Impi was about to attack.

Small parties of fein appeared on the Kayr and the Dognobles' defensive fire grew hotter as armored bridge units rolled forward. Young Proud was in a swoon of hatred as, cursing his own Impi, he ordered the Chevaleers to close up beside the Dognobles. They would concentrate their firepower to the Dognobles' front and annihilate any attack column that sought to cross the river.

Ng Karoffa kept up his demonstration, moving the guns

between salvos, until suddenly, tired, mud-splattered, but triumphant, the other septs of the Abzen Second showed up in his rear. Shortly afterward Lavin and the command team galloped up.

A few minutes later half the Abzen Second Impi, with scarcely more than a few deep breaths after the ten-kilometer run from Bleilli, hurled itself over the Kayr and through the positions of the Chevaleers. By breakfast time the Dognobles and Chevaleers were in full retreat northward. Young Proud, all hope of victory gone, rode out on a Ramal chopper and left the warbands to run for the safety of the pass.

The fein celebrated by getting in a solid breakfast. Rva sat at a fire with close Brelkilk kin and gave serious attention to a plate of jerky patties and waybread. Gwassa, warmed in a fireskin, was passed around and soon picked up everyone's spirits. Replete at last, Rva set out for his appointment with Lavin Fundin. They had another battle to fight, way off in the south.

Rva swung quickly up the path onto the moor. Ahead the walls of the mountains ascended to the clouds so that the moor seemed suspended at the bottom of a three-sided wall, cut off from the world above by the gray ceiling. He belched and spat then noted gloomily that he was covered in mud; hardly fit to visit his mother let alone the sacred glade. However, the timetable was brutal and there was no time for a bath or a brushdown. It was a human timetable, and it was necessary, of course; still, the fein spirit in Rva protested against it. Now was the time for meat, gwassa, and sleep; tomorrow they should go to the shrine.

The clouds were thickening and settling lower and with them came the medical helicopters, returning from Orank, their blades working up a fat *chop* that blurred in the wind and echoed from the slopes.

Rva tasted the breeze, the feinblood on the air, the chemical stink from smokescreen. Yet there was also the taste of victory, a famous one for Abzen, over their oldest and most consistent of foes. For the Abzen fein this was a great day, a day to be hammered into the songs with drums and steel and bronze.

He already had young fein soldiers quartering the field, seeking the dead of both sides and taking a hair from the ear tufts of each. A whistle from behind turned his head and he dodged a mobile artillery team, drawn by fierce-eyed terrestrial mules, wreathed in the steam of their breath. Men in Fundangreen camouflage uniforms jogged alongside. They recognized the tall, brindle fein chief and saluted as they passed. Rva nodded in return. Their gun, a long mass-drive tube atop four balloon tires, bounced past and spattered Rva with a little more mud. He moaned softly, spat, and moved on.

It began to rain again lightly, a drizzle that further occluded his sweep of the gray-brown moor. He welcomed the waters of the wind, let them cleanse him and wash the blood from sawpod and sedge. The rain brought fresh scents, hints of elsewhere, other times. Rva breathed it in and felt renewed.

He paused beside a defile that had become a cemetery for fein from the Heavy Impi. More than a dozen—brindles, blacks, even a gray agouti—were stretched where they had fallen, clustered around a small artillery piece and its two human operators. The fein had fought until the big gun was empty then given the men their own rifles. All had fought shoulder to shoulder to the last, when the Abzen fein overwhelmed them. The bright-yellow skrin feathers worn behind the right ear in the Heavy Impi were all that was clear and sharp in the rain, and Rva counted them before continuing.

He scratched under his weapon webbing and yawned. The casualties had been heavy, but mostly on Ramal's side. Abzen had lost barely a tenth as many. Many fein would be missing from the fires in Ramal forest, many cubs with no one to hunt for them but their mothers, and the blood feuds between Ramal and Abzen would only intensify. Rva could see no end to that aspect of the bloodshed, but he accepted that just as he never questioned the destiny that had set men and fein together against all comers in the high valleys. They held the wealth of eternity in their grip and through its power they survived. So it had been for Rva's people for many generations, and still their numbers were maintained and the villages prospered.

The sound of hooves once more turned his head. Lavin Fundin, wrapped in a long gray-green slicker, a wide-brim hat pulled down against the rain, came up the trail with two staff equerries riding behind him. He reined in beside Rva and his horse muzzled the big fein affectionately. Between fein and horses existed a love affair matched only by that between humans and the swift terran quadrupeds. Rva looked into Lavin's eyes, read the bleakness there.

For a moment the somber eyes held Rva's big yellows in a steady gaze then Lavin spat and dismounted with an air of disgust.

"I notice the hero of Brelkilk is happy with the victory secured today."

"Lord, they were the aggressors. We simply defended our valley."

"But will Young true-genes Proud Fundan ever give up?" Lavin hurled the term "true-genes" into the damp air with considerable venom. "Will we ever be free of this business? His treachery, it sickens me."

Rva shrugged massively. Fein tail flicked in shirrithee, expressing an array of contradictory emotions—anger, disconsolation, loss, mirth. The fein were disposed to an awesomely pragmatic view of existence, accepting occurrences with deliberately unpredictable self-expression. It was better to dance on the curve of now, better to live to the hilt and die in the heat of great passion, better to accept pain and death as inevitable and give them no great importance.

"The Heavy Impi retreat. We watched them go with our heads high. We could have left all of them here, their bones to whiten the moor. The war song of this place is now long and filled with the purples and golds of victory for Abzen fein. Never will it be forgotten by the Brelkilk."

"I wish I could say it would never be forgotten by the Fundans, especially the Proud Fundans." A glance into the defile showed the grim remains of the heroic last stand by a Ramal battery. Lavin grimaced in disgust. "Those were Fundans, fein, men and women, just as you are Fundan fein and I am Fundan man. Fighting among ourselves is just a waste of lives, and I wish an end could be made of it. We have enough enemies as it is."

His mount, a brown mare named Nancy, snorted suddenly, smelling the death-laden air, and would have reared, but Lavin held her head steady and spoke gently in her ear until she quieted. Lavin and Rva scratched under her jaw bone and around the ears until Lavin passed the reins to one of the equerries, a two-headed youth from the Fundan military schools.

"Heck," Lavin said, "take her down to the stables on the

Orank road. When the Impi reforms there I want you to balloon down to Cracked Rock and take three days' rest—that's sleep time, mind you. And take Nestor with you. By the looks of him he's already asleep."

The boys managed a ragged salute and rode away. Lavin turned to Rva.

"And we have much to do, Mzsee—the saddest part comes now." When Lavin pulled back the slicker cape, Rva saw the wound on his left forearm. The flight suit had been cut away below the elbow and a medipad with full biopac was strapped around the forearm.

"Is it serious, Lord?"

"Doc Olanther says it'll hurt for a few days but no bones broken. A stray round, almost spent, I'd say." Pharamol would help it heal quickly, but Rva remained concerned. As body-guard for eight years, the big fein had grown as devoted to the health of his charge as a mother for her cubs. He examined the dressing, sniffing carefully for any trace of rot.

"I will examine it later myself. Likely you need a pultive of midderweed. And another thing you need is a good meal. Have you looked in a mirror lately? You're starving yourself—you're so thin in the face the bones show through. You've had no breakfast, have you? I insist on it. You carry on like the rotid that sips honey, lives on the wing, and dies in the air after one week of life." Rva held up an ominous single finger in front of Lavin's face. "All these potions you take, the drugs, they are not food." Rva's scolding had become so familiar over the years that Lavin merely nodded now and agreed to eat something soon.

"Good, then I will kill a nice young gzan and Ubanquini will brew strong gwassa and we will eat around the fire and tell the old stories again, eh? And then get out the pipe and smoke teosinte together, for this victory, eh?"

Rva painted an appealing picture. A fine dinner in Brelkilk village, in Ubanquini's yard, under the clickholly trees. Time to sit back and consider things while passing the teosinte pipe. And then? Lavin longed just to lie down somewhere and sleep, for a month or so.

But great events were unfolding and he had no time for rest. The Summit Conference between the highland clans and the World Government of Earth would be held the very next day.

10

The Abzen Second, under Lavin's command, had been chosen to provide blanket security for the ambassadors and clan chiefs. As soon as the Impi was reformed, the unit would begin the balloon trip downvalley and then completely out of the mountains to the meeting site.

At the same time the four days of grappling with Young Proud had precipitated a crisis in the lower valley. Mithiliwax forest had been stripped. Billions of credits' worth of Chitin proteins, still attached to the abdomens of frozen Vizier Chitin, was being shoveled into jet transports.

"Yes, Mzsee, we'll hunt together, and we'll feast in yard and cook the liver in the clay oven, too—and you're absolutely right that *that* is what we should do right now, but..." He looked helplessly at the rain sweeping across the moor. Almost absentmindedly he slipped a grain of Pharamol onto his tongue and felt it dissolve, sending immediate warmth through his body. His mind cleared and his resolve hardened.

"We will eat together in Ubanquini's yard the day after tomorrow. If we can save the situation in Mithiliwax by then."

Rva was prepared to argue for the thought of fresh meat and Ubanguini was easily enough to make the big fein stubborn, and he craved a long sleep as much as his commander, but he too knew about the potential disaster in the south.

Chief Neilk Ng Tung called from the far left to report that all contact with the fleeing Heavy Impi had been lost. The Second Abzen was falling back to reform along the Orank road.

The rain began to come down hard, and Rva opened his cape and slipped it on. He pulled the hood over his head. His ears projected from the slits.

"It's the monsoon, old friend," Lavin rasped. "Time's too short and too valuable to waste. Let's get on with it."

They walked slowly out over the moor, and Rva's runners came to them with small envelopes containing the hairs of the dead. Those from fein with yellow skrin feathers were taken by Rva, trophies of victory. Those from Fundan fein, who wore the green flashes, were taken by Lavin. The ID tags he put in the pockets of his slicker, the hairs he carefully filed in a larger envelope.

There were many green, not nearly as many as the yellow, but too many for Lavin's patience and he began to tremble and to curse Young Proud with a harsh terrible whisper. Young

11

Proud, true blood of the line Fundan, so haughty that he could not comprehend defeat. Lavin cursed his full blood true-genes. With each additional packet of hairs, his anger grew so that he soon had to stop himself and try to clear his head lest the horror threaten his sanity.

A few minutes later they encountered two young women bent over the body of Yuin Rva, blood kin of Bg Rva, who was lying near the top of a slope. Forearm and paw severed by a grenade blast, Yuin was weak and close to death from loss of blood. The young medics in Fundan greens worked quickly to attach IVs for blood and plasm stock. The stump had already been bandaged and the bleeding staunched. Yuin pleaded weakly with them for death until he caught sight of Bg Rva. "Cousin, give me thy blade, I would not live like a cripple. Send me to the spirits, Mzsee. I belong in tharyore now."

Yuin's brindle muzzle stretched back in a grimace of pain as he spoke, the white canines stark against the black lips.

Rva looked to Lavin for the nod to use his kifket. Lavin shook his head. This was nothing but temporary morbidity and would pass. Yuin would live to return to Brelkilk and in time an artificial forelimb would be fitted for him.

"No, I'm afraid Yuin must live. Lie still, Yuin, the medics will soon be finished and you'll be on your way home to the yard of Reshishimi. What would she say to me if I let you die? Think of her and her young ones—who'll hunt for them if you are to die?"

Rva moved his hand away from the hilt of the blade. He sympathized with Yuin's wish for death. The fein had a profound horror of dismemberment and amputation, far more than that of humans who were accustomed to it after centuries of advanced medicine. But he also agreed with Lavin and was concerned that one of his blood should seek such an easy death. "You live, Yuin. They will give you a new arm."

Yuin looked stricken. "So Yuin of Brelkilk will become one of the fein with machine's feet. What will the spirits say to that, Mzsee?"

"Be thankful it wasn't your nuts, fool Yuin. They can't be replaced. Lord Lavin is right—what you go dying for? And leave Reshi, and she with three cubs? I think you insult our blood, Yuin. Reshi is kin to all the widepath Rva and I am

12

foremost of them. How can you think to leave her? Did you not pledge to protect her for life? Who will hunt for her?"

Yuin looked away mournfully with his big eyes closed. His body shook itself out as if to enter the death trance. Rva waited a moment, grinned, tail in active shirrithee, "Actually, to tell the truth, fool Yuin, though you are my kin and all, I can think of a few who would gladly hunt for Reshi and her cubs."

Yuin's eyes flew open, his head raised angrily. Rva laughed.

"Who?" Yuin asked. "Name him!" The medics were unable to restrain him.

Rva laughed again. "And you want the blade so you can leave Reshi, eh? You're funny, Yuin, but you won't die. Here comes the chopper."

Rva got to his feet and Lavin directed the chopper down. They watched as the medics loaded Yuin and a dozen other wounded off the moor and flew away.

"This battle was unnecessary. This is a squabble over Young Proud's pride. There's no truth or honor in it."

Rva disagreed, shaking his heavy head. "Aah, but to us this is the best warfare, fein on fein for honor or death. This is clean fighting, with no poisons, no human money, no greed. The other fighting is tainted. The hand of greed lies there no matter what is said."

"But we defend ourselves and the chitin so that we can keep control of the wealth we need to maintain our defenses. As long as we are resolute, we can defeat them and keep the life here as it is. Free, wild, and proud for both the fein and the families. This is necessary war, for if we were to surrender to the coastals we would all be destroyed."

For years they had argued thus as Rva tried to get the young Lord of Abzen to see the beauty of the clean battle for honor and grace. In search of the pure life, beyond the taint of greed or worldly possessions. For the spirits would take the time to read the hairs, and Rva was of the "expansion" creed which held that hairs from human heads would eventually be taken and read in the halls of mystery where dwell the Arizel tki Fenrille. The taint of greed would always be noticed and the spirit infected with it dispersed. The true life, in purity beneath the sun, in clean hunting and battle for honor, that was all that was worth anything in existence. All else was mere illusion. The fein fought to keep the meadows free for the grazing gzan, the forests for the trees to raise their mighty limbs to the sky. Without the pure life it would be better for the ay fein to end their long chapter on Fenrille and return to the All.

For now Bg Rva merely sighed, tasting the wind. The endless philosophical debate around the fires was like that of the bird and the egg. Which came first: the refining of longevity drugs from the chitin or the need to defend the highlands from those who would destroy them for the chitin wealth? The taint of greed was among them, unleashed by the insane pursuit of eternity that so consumed the humans. Now the war against the coastal armies was centuries old and no fein alive could recall accurately how it had all begun.

Lavin spoke into his wrist communicator, and in moments Pilot Gruness brought his stubby VTOL down from the clouds in a whine of jet engines that grew to a throbbing howl as the craft floated down the last few meters.

2

SENATOR IRA GANWEEK LAY BACK IN THE SOFT FOLDS OF THE couch oblivious to everything except the rhythmic movements of the sex object's mouth. His hands occasionally reached down into the brilliant steel-blond frizz that occupied the space between his legs. She was good, well worth the #8,000 he'd paid for her indenture.

His whole body stiffened with the ecstasy....

He rested a moment and Saja rose and prepared a booster of testosterone and protein complex. He rolled over when she returned, and while she slid the needle into his buttock muscle he took a grain of Pharamol and felt it dissolve on his tongue.

Contentedly the senator lay back on the couch and the sex object resumed her allotted place in life. Time passed. The girl was a delight, lapping him with light, delicate touches and occasional hard thrusts. He gripped the sides of the couch and moved his hips slowly from side to side, enjoying each moment of delicious contact. The large rubber pacifier in his mouth was soft and comforting. He sucked on it with all the passion a 178-year-old baby can muster for the nipple.

15

Abruptly the delight from the girl's tongue was finished. An insistant beeping began, annoying him at first on the very outermost fringes of consciousness and gradually growing until he focused on it and it intruded horribly, a sour tone of mechanical civilization invading the unfocused babydom he'd been wallowing in.

He swore, and Saja pulled back with a little cry of dismay as he grabbed for the communicator.

"What is it? It had better be good."

"So sorry, Senator, priority code message. An individual named Termas Hith is here to see you. Says it's urgent."

He swore again. Of all the unlikely interruptions, that was the least likely. But there was no way around it, not if Hith had made it priority code.

As he dressed irritably, Ganweek wondered what Hith might want. The kid wouldn't dare to bother him unless it was important, that much was certain. A breakthrough? Ganweek shivered at the thought.

They met in a small circular room under rigorous security screen. The young man was nervous, his words tumbled out in hurried groups.

"On the final assay of this series we discovered that the Delta proteins were reproducing themselves out of the culture medium, the tonic catalyst was working but not in the way we'd expected. The triplid series turned out to have the highest output, four hundred percent above the first run. All the averages were weighted, the data-9 cross-checked."

"So it works then." Ganweek shut off the projector and the data holo vanished.

The young man shifted uncomfortably in his chair. He nodded vigorously. It did work, and his "crazy" idea of inducing chitin information proteins to reproduce themselves with the aid of an artificial enzyme would increase the supply of such proteins by a factor of ten. Which, in turn, would lead to a vast increase in the amount of base chemicals required for the production of longevity drugs. The Vizier Chitin encoded memory and paths to memory in their fantastically convoluted protein chains, which had proved impossible to copy in the laboratory.

"Yes, yes, it works. At least tenfold increase." Hith wrung his hands together, ill at ease. "Look, senator, the entire human

16

hegemony's going to erupt over this. Everything will be changed, everyone will have longevity within his reach. Think of it! The whole human race will be able to live forever."

Ganweek coughed, cleared his throat. "Or for as long as Optimol or Agunol can keep people alive, eh?"

"Yes, yes, of course, but—"

"Tell me something." Ganweek pursed his lips. "How many copies have you made?" The senator held up a tiny chip of data matrix.

"There are two—yours and the one I made it from."

"What did you do with that?"

The nervous young man became even more unsettled. "I have it safe," he stammered.

Ganweek reached out of the shadows thrown by the senso generator and patted the chemist on the shoulder. "The reason I ask, you see, is that this should remain a secret, for a little while, until—"

"How can you keep something like immortality for the whole race a secret?" Hith was agonized, near hysteria now that his life work had culminated in the most smashing success he could've imagined. Low-grade Optimol would be available to everyone, longevity for all.

The senator's voice grew soft. "Now, of course, it'll come out, it's bound to—I know that. There's a racial hunger out there, a craving that has to be satisfied. And you're perfectly correct, my young friend, this will change many things. This will change the galaxy—this will finally give us the stars."

Ganweek found his own excitement rising and hastened to dampen its reflection in his voice.

"But before we release this thing on an unsuspecting world, we will have to control it, even if only for a very little while. That way your work will receive its proper reward. You've been working how many years—isn't it seven years? Seven long frustrating years on this, and with my backing you've gone all the way. You had no credit, no research grants, and then I set you up with the lab and everything."

"Yes, yes, of course, I haven't forgotten." How could he? Ganweek had saved him. Termas' eyes darted about the room as if seeking an escape route. Debby had begged him for days not to visit Ganweek, not even to let Ganweek know about the discovery. And he was still trembling from the shock of *that*,

17

the enormity of what he'd witnessed as multistranded information proteins replicated themselves in a test tube.

In the end the decision had rested on the pride of the Hiths. They'd never been an indentured family, they'd always kept their freedom. They were second wave but very early second wave, and though they'd never made it, they'd kept their pride. Termas owed the Bablon Corporation for seven years of financial backing and frustration, and he owed Ira Ganweek for the faith the senator had had in his efforts. In the end the thought of running out on Ganweek seemed too contemptible for Termas to contemplate.

"I think you feel, as I do, that you should make something from your discovery. A tidy sum, eh, before you lose all control of it." Ganweek stroked the side of his nose.

Termas' eyes gleamed. So Ganweek would do it right, just as he'd hoped from the start. Bablon Corporation wouldn't try to steal it, indeed why should they—he didn't want all that much anyway, not compared with what it was worth.

A circular magnetic safe was clamped to the wall. Ganweek rose and arranged his purple velvet robe around himself. He opened the safe and removed a slim canister of stainless steel. He activated its security switch and it opened at one end. He shook out a small packet of Pharamol, 100 grains of purple joy crystals in a microsachet, and put the datachip into the tube where it lay on top of a hundred more microsachets.

He gave Hith the tiny packet and wryly noted to himself that he'd have to sell his Pharamol stocks and protein futures as soon as possible. The market might even collapse when the news broke. He'd have to tread carefully. Certainly things were going to change. And Ira Ganweek was going to exploit this advantage to the full. He would be the richest, most powerful human being in the universe. He looked down at the young chemist. He was nervous, had obviously thought of the possible consequences, but hadn't deviated, impelled by that weird sense of honor that motivated early colonials. Ira snorted. "Well, don't just look at it, my boy! Take some—that's top-grade Spreak product, Slade Mountain chitin."

Uncertainly Hith opened the packet and fumbled a grain of Pharamol to his tongue.

"That's just the beginning. You're going to find that Ira Ganweek can really come through for the people who come

18

through for him. From now on it's yours, just about anything you want I can provide. You're going to get a handsome credit extension, I'll make that immediate today. A line right on the Bablon itself. And you're going to need some rest. You've been working hard, I can see it in your face."

Termas felt miraculously calm, almost as if he were floating above the scene. Indeed he did need a rest, a vacation. The first in seven years or more.

"So get on home now and get ready to take the vacation of your life. Where d'you want to go? The Surf Rocks? Or how about Oracle Rock and Hedon's Retreat? It's all been redecorated and it's simply exquisite. Just tell me where you want to go, and I'll set up the credit. The Bablon has hotels in most of the best locations." Ganweek walked up and down impatiently, building momentum into his words. He had the young man in the palm of his hand; he'd do anything.

"Or—I have another idea. Relax here on the Sx Coast. My friend Marcellus Apropriere is trying to sell a sex object that I just know you'll love. He's only had her for three months but already she's exhausted him. I'll get her for you. You can stay in my little waterside villa, my little retreat on Sin Isle. Rest up, get loose again, while I get down to business and make sure we get some good financial openings set up. It's time you were rich, eh? You'd like to be rich, wouldn't you? As rich as anyone in the world?"

Hith allowed himself a smile, his sense of well-being rising as he realized that Ganweek was really going to go through with it, to the hilt. He'd get everything he'd ever wanted. "I thank you, Senator, for everything. You stuck with us for years and years when I often lost faith in the project myself. I'm just glad it's come out so well. I'm a bit amazed by it all, I guess. But, you know, I think I'll just take a quiet vacation. Back home in Coast County, where my family lives."

"Well, if you're sure you'd rather do that than dally with Marcellus' gorgeous blond creature, then by all means. It sounds like a great idea—see the family. But don't give anything away. We don't want to start any rumors yet. We have to keep this absolutely tight from here on. Just for a little while, maybe just a couple of weeks. So you'll have time to rest your voice before we start doing the media conferences, eh? You'd better spend a little time working on your presentation, that's very

19

important. And of course your girl friend, she'll be traveling with you? Is she aware of the need for absolute discretion?"

The girl would have to be found, immediately. Only then could he really begin to think about the unexpected boon to humanity that had walked into his life. He needed time to let his imagination play with the situation, to explore the possibilities.

He wanted to whoop for joy. It'd been such a little thing, just a dabble on the margins of serious chitin chemistry. That's how he'd defended it.

Who would've imagined? What would the syndicate say when he brought this development to them? Now that would be a moment to enjoy. He was suddenly aware that Hith was speaking. . . . "I guess we'll go up home together. Deb comes from the same part of CC as me. We grew up together."

"Good, wonderful. Well, why don't I set you up with fifty grand for the next couple of days until I can get the rest of the credit line fixed into our system here? Leave your forwarding address and I'll be in touch to let you know how things progress. Until then, relax, enjoy! You've just become an incredibly wealthy young man. The universe is at your feet, anything's possible."

Termas' face was pathetically radiant. He looked as if he'd seen a religious mircale. "Thank you, Senator, thank you so much."

When he was alone again Ganweek tapped out a security code on his communicator.

"Yes, sir," a tired, grim voice answered.

"A young man is leaving the pleasure dome now. He has on a light-gray jacket and white athletic shoes. A likeness is now coming on your screen. Listen to me, listen carefully, for this is a very important piece of work, and there must be no mistakes, no mistakes at all."

"I understand."

"Good. Follow him home and kill him as soon as he's inside. Then I want you to arrange for everything you find in his home to be destroyed. Utterly destroyed. I want him to disappear without trace and with no evidence that he ever existed. Dump

20

the ashes in Bloody Bub's or the ocean. Then report back to me."

"The body?"

"*Ashes*, make it disappear. Completely."

Ganweek cut the line and sank back onto the couch.

3

THE GIRL GRITTED HER TEETH AND STEADIED HERSELF FOR another try. She balanced uneasily on a support rod for the solar panel array that girdled the Bablon pleasure domes on the thirteenth level. Below, the walkways of the Sx Coast coiled over the sandbars like pale concrete serpents. The neon lights from the big domes along Fun Beach lit up the early-evening sky beyond the moth trees. The Pale Moon was rising above the distant watery horizon. A light breeze blew off the ocean and she could smell the salt of the sea while tasting the salt of her own sweat as it ran down her face.

Above her head loomed the lower edge of one of the dome's ventilation panels. The panel was pulled open about fifteen degrees, and if she could climb up its smooth metal surface she would gain entry to the ventilation system for the whole dome. It was dangerous, but it was the only way she could be sure of gaining entry to the security-screened upper floors.

The problem was that she could only reach the louver panel's lower edge by standing so far on tiptoe on the narrow solar array that she was sure to overbalance and fall unless she got a good grip with her hand suckers.

"Damn you, panel, damn you, just let me get to you . . ." she hissed then, sucking in a deep breath, launched herself at it and desperately stabbed down with both hands at the panel surface. The right hand sucker hit too hard and rebounded and her hand slipped weakly away. For a nauseating second Armada was certain she would fall to her certain death far below. But the left hand sucker had held. Instead of plummeting to the sands, she hung from the wrist strap with her boot heels dangling over empty air. In near panic she flailed away with the right hand and on the third attempt the sucker hissed as it took a firm grip. She dangled from both wrists.

For a second or so she rested her weight on the suckers and took a deep breath of relief. The sweat stung in her eyes and she shivered again at the thought of failure. With a great effort she hauled herself up until her shoulders were parallel with her hands. She set the elbow sucker on her right arm down and felt it take hold. She released the right hand and moved it farther up and then got a grip with the left elbow sucker. The elbow suckers were mounted in rotating cusps to allow for freedom of movement within a plane. Their suction could be released by a small switch mounted on a ring on her index finger.

Like a huge fly, she slowly crawled, up the fifteen-meter width of the panel. At the top she swung a slim leg over and sat astride the edge. Her shoulder-length red hair had come loose and she had to shake it out of her eyes as the air intake whipped it about. Slightly above her she could see an inspection catwalk inside the dome wall, and she began easing herself along the upper edge of the panel toward it. Once on the catwalk, she made her way into the heart of the dome's ventilation system.

When she halted to consult the circulation diagram again, she found herself trembling. Carefully she removed the suckers and laid them down. The months of planning and preparation had brought her this far; now Armada Butte would extract her revenge. Now they would pay for the agony and humiliation they'd forced upon her.

She knew she was beneath the risers that led to the fifteenth-floor suites with even numbers. She'd memorized the distances and every twist and turn in the air ducts so that now she hardly paused to think as she climbed and crawled toward her goal.

In a couple of minutes, she was crouched behind the small ventilation grille, overlooking the refrigerator in a kitchen. Armada had very little room to maneuver, and the sense of claustrophobia that she'd been fighting ever since climbing into the narrow risers was getting strong. It would be next to impossible to wriggle her way back out of the ducts; but she had to go on.

Carefully she pushed a tiny microphone stalk through the grille. The mike picked up only the mechanical sounds of the kitchen and the hum and whine of distant elevator movement.

Using a jeweler's laser she cut through the four corners of the grille and pulled it back into the duct, sliding it beneath her body. If she could get her shoulders through the narrow opening, she'd be able to rest her weight on top of the refrigerator while extracting her lower half from the duct. To negotiate the turn from the duct to the grille opening, she had to squeeze herself out on her side.

Extending her arms, she began to wriggle out on the surface of the refrigerator.

A door slid open somewhere nearby and feet came toward the kitchen. Armada froze, then hurriedly forced herself back inside the duct. There wasn't time to hold the grille up before the door opened, and a girl with an enormous frizz of steel-tint hair came in. She went to the fridge and took out two bottles of Moka and left again without even turning on the light.

Armada waited a moment or two in the cramped darkness. So there was a new sex object in the house. Nothing changed around there except the sex objects. For some reason the thought brought a grim smile to her lips. Revenge would be so sweet.

Getting out was harder than she had anticipated. Once her shoulders were through, her hips proved the major problem. For a couple of seconds it seemed she was doomed to stick fast in the opening. But the thought of capture caused her such anguish that she found new sources of strength and finally managed to turn herself like a corkscrew and inch her way to freedom.

At last she slipped out of the narrow duct onto the top of the refrigerator like some newly born creature of the building, lathered in sweat like a saline placenta. She was the larva of revenge.

In a second or so she was on her feet, the little jeweler's laser in her hand. Her ears strained to penetrate the silence but no sound stirred in the dark. She checked the time—a full hour before the guards changed shift. She reflected grimly that the guard schedules were burned into her memory forever. She would never forget. In odd weeks Horst had his watch, Leko would be sleeping.

Silently she flitted down the corridor and turned toward the guards' sleeping quarters. Horst's door was open so she knew her memory was correct. She tried Leko's door and it slid open quietly—he had left it unlocked. A foolish lapse for one as hated as he. But, she reflected, the guards had had life too easy for too long; they'd grown soft.

Leko lay sprawled across the bed with his mouth open, a light snore rattling in the back of his throat. One stroke of the laser at cutting intensity, and Leko's head was half severed from his shoulders. The body rose, thrashed once as the spine arched, and blood sprayed across the room. Leko never knew where his dreams became death, where twilight became utter dark.

Armada felt a huge sense of relief and then she noticed with a little horror that she was soaked in her victim's blood. She hadn't expected there to be so much of it; it was all over the bed and the wall, and great splashes had stained her khaki jumpsuit. The dampness of Koko Leko's blood on her skin brought on a hysteric compulsion to laugh or scream, and she had to fight it down by biting on her hands until she broke the skin.

Now she simply waited for Horst, knowing he'd come to wake Leko a couple of minutes before the shift alarm beeped. Something she could remember Leko complaining about frequently in his thick, peevish voice. Then of course Horst had dragged her from Leko's bed by the leash and led her to his own room.... Her resolve hardened. When she caught sight of herself in the mirror and saw the look stamped on her nineteen-year-old face, she was frightened. The intensity was dreadful, implacable.

Eventually Horst arrived, opened the door, and stepped in without snapping on the light. He never saw the noose of elastic

25

flesh that fell lightly around his shoulders, then snapped tight around his throat. He first felt the thing as a slippery grip on his throat and reached for it. It was greasy and hard. He pried for a finger's space with both powerful hands but all the while its stranglehold tightened. Choking and gagging, he scrabbled to find some purchase on the horribly strong thing.

Gasping for air, he sank to his knees as a slender figure emerged from the darkness. She shone a light down on him. He saw her eyes and recognized them and would've screamed except that he would never scream again. The snareworm would keep its grip tight until long after he was dead. Left to its own devices, it would then envelope the body and begin the process of digestion.

She left Horst to die and moved down the hall to Ganweek's chambers. From Leko she'd taken a security card, and she used it to open the locks that guarded the senator's inner sanctum.

Ganweek was half asleep, musing on the new age of mass longevity that he would usher in. They would name the new drug after him; perhaps he would insist that all history from that point on be labeled the Ganweek Eon. He would rule an empire of many worlds, and all its inhabitants would be his slaves. He would reign forever and travel the galaxy with a mighty fleet. It would be a golden age. He smiled to himself at those plans for distant grandeur and settled down for a nap.

Saja watched a video broadcast, late-night All Ball. Watching the big men hammer one another to the artificial matting was at once numbing and vaguely exciting. Thankfully the old pig, as she ungraciously thought of her indenture holder, was dropping off to sleep and wouldn't want any more fellatio until tomorrow.

A forward broke through the defense line of the Cougars and was smashed to the mat by a deep tackle. There was a break in the action as medics rushed on to take a look at the forward, who lay prone on the field. Saja thought she liked it best when there were lots of injuries.

She never heard Armada open the door and slip inside. She didn't even see her sneak past and crouch beside the senator's body on the couch. Armada pressed a tiny syrette bulb against the senator's bare arm and immobilized him with a shot of nerve stun. Ganweek was awake, and she could see clearly the horror in his eyes when he recognized her, but the stun was a

26

massive dose and he could barely move his lips let alone his body. She stood over him and smiled.

"I told you I'd repay you, you filth, and now I will." Her voice cut through the quiet like the crack of a whip.

Saja jumped, squealing in sudden shock. "Who are you?" she said. The intruder was very beautiful, and behind her the senator seemingly lay quite content. "What's going on? How did you get in here? What do you want?"

The girl smiled triumphantly and brushed the long, straight red hair away from her face. Saja noticed the bloodstains on her tunic.

"Let's just say I'm here to settle an old score. A matter of revenge."

"What's wrong with the senator? What have you done to him?"

"Oh, nothing much. He's wide awake, he just can't move a muscle right now. In fact, he won't be able to move for about an hour."

Saja turned for the door.

"No, don't go, there's no point in bothering the guards. They're both dead, and I disconnected the alarms. Stay, watch, enjoy—you're going to see how the fein use one of these to calm the bull gzan for sacrifice. The gzan's prodigious sexual urge can make it uncontrollable in captivity." Armada held up a shining loop of wire.

Saja saw and understood and wanted to laugh out loud. Horst and Leko were dead, the senator would soon have little need for her—she was sure to be sold, a thought that brought only joy to her heart.

"So, Senator, we meet again, as I promised you we would. You had your round, you defiled my body with your filthy, perverse games. You responded to my pleading with scorn and laughter, you outraged me, destroyed me—" Armada was getting excited. She whipped around to Saja.

"Tell me, dear, how long have you been, uhh, serving here?"

"About five months," Saja replied nervously.

"Poor thing, then you've played all this old goat's games by now, haven't you?" The steel-blond frizz nodded.

"Well, just before you came here, your horrible old patron kidnapped me from a party because I beat him at sexarades and then refused to sleep with him. I was a prisoner here for days, and he let those scum out there have me whenever they wanted. Which is why they're dead now and why he's about to undergo a change in sexual status."

"Oh, my!" Saja's whisper hung in the air.

Ganweek wanted to scream.

"What's that?" Armada said, noticing the magnetic safe that lay on the table. On impulse she used Ganweek's security card to open it. She removed the steel canister and glanced inside. Dozens of packets of shiny Pharamol glinted in the light.

"Mmm, I think I'll take this, too." She shook a grain out and put it to her lips. A small datachip lay on top of the phara and she almost flicked it away but decided to keep it instead and see what it was later.

"I deserve some little recompense for my services here, I think." She gave the senator an impish grin. Ganweek's eyes rolled up into his head.

It was over in a few seconds, and the senator fainted before it was half complete. Armada left after tying up the sex object. Using the security card, she took the private elevator to the roof and hailed a flycab. Saja's clothes were a bit of a tight fit but they were clean. Stepping aboard the cab, she spun the card off the roof and watched it flutter down into the surf below the walkways.

4

PILOT GRUNESS FLOATED LAVIN FUNDIN'S VTOL ONTO THE tiny landing area, attitude jets kicking dust off the rocks. Lavin turned and, with a slightly exasperated smile, clapped Bg Rva on the shoulder. Rva was crouched in a ball on the floor—he hated flying.

The fein phobia for jet aircraft always intrigued Lavin. They would willingly risk their lives in combat with just the sharp blade of the kifket, would charge undaunted against rifle fire, tanks, artillery, or anything else, but the first judder of takeoff had them miserable.

The wind up there on the high slopes of Mount Miflin was fierce. They staggered quickly out of the open and into the long, narrow cave that led to the secret glade.

Eventually they skirted the chasm of the Long Dark and emerged in the glade. They were at the bottom of a narrow crack in the mountainside, a pocket slit in the rock. There the ultramontane forest grew in riotous profusion, a tropical microenvironment at 4,000 meters elevation.

Around them blazed scarlet skrin, whistling in alarm. Fen-

29

rille "lizards" gazed at them with yellow-eyed alarm. Small nibbla scampered for shelter. Even the predatory land mollusks retracted into their shells.

The trees were massive, growing over each other's roots, tightly packed together, each twenty meters or more in circumference. Those trees had never been tended by the woodwose, however; bark parasites with exotic blooms were visible everywhere.

Fy'pupe, graycowl adept fein from Ghotaw, Fundan Central HQ, appeared and conducted them forward. Old Fy'pupe's eyes, traced with scarlet, seemed to bore into Lavin; at this ceremony they always did. "The pool is ready, Lord, all await you."

They walked the narrow path, over massive roots, behind the ancient one. It was warm in the glade. Lavin opened his flight jacket and removed his helmet. As always the place seemed to be heated with a warm breath from the living gullet of the world. The humidity was disgusting. He felt the sweat running down freely inside his shirt. The wound in his arm was aching again, the biopac needed changing.

Suddenly he found himself leaning on Rva for support. He would've fallen—another of those little blackouts from too much Pharamol, no sleep and no food—but for Rva's swift grasp. He stood while the nausea passed.

"Now will you listen to me?" Rva growled. "We must stop for food before we get to Brelkilk."

Lavin shook away the nausea, fought down the urge to retch, and slipped a couple of grains of Pharamol onto his tongue. Vigor returned. "Let's get on with it. We don't have much time."

Rva grunted a response tinged with complex accusations concerning health and diet that Lavin refused to consider or discuss.

Fy'pupe whispered, "It is time, Lord. We approach the pool." Then the old one leaned closer, his cowl almost covering Lavin's face. "Tomorrow, Lord, I will meet you on the Lonely Rock. Then Mother Fair will be under our protection. The meeting is very important, she says."

"So it is, Mzsee of Mzsees, and we will make it very safe as well." A soft chime sounded, seemed to reverberate above the dark pool of water that occupied the very bottom of the glade. Ancient fein appeared out of the trees around them. Each carried a glopod or two, emitting soft green light. An adept scattered xanthic petals on the surface of the water. As they settled, the adept carefully marked them. When all had reached the water, he raised his staff above his head.

A sibilance began, a whisper from many unseen lips, that simmered around them in the dark. From places in the woods all around, hundreds of ancient fein, all adepts of the Spirit, were giving the call.

The susurration slowly coalesced into the verse of the ceremony, the general lament of the ay fein, "those who were left behind." As the whisper reached "Are they forgotten by the mighty?" Pilot Gruness felt a familiar moment of awe. Majoring in fein studies at Ghotaw Academy had opened his mind out to the fein and their ancient, ancient history. Some of the events described in their prayers had occurred before there were apes, or even monkeys, on Earth.

Gruness whispered the words he'd memorized at Junior Academy and kept his eyes fixed on the pool. The ceremony was very strictly observed by all Fundan field officers.

The surface of the pool grew agitated, and the tiny petals were swamped in small wavelets that rippled the surface though no wind stirred the stifling air. There was a sense of tension rising, an electric charge growing in the air around them.

Lavin stepped forward to the side of the pool and handed a long white envelope to Fy'pupe. Fy'pupe gave it to the keeper of the pool. Lavin was close enough to smell the sickly sweet carnilla blossom the ancient had eaten for breakfast. In the envelope were the hairs of the dead collected from the fallen on Scrawn Moor.

"Izst," murmured the acoloyte when the last was removed and he held them all in his withered paw. A long moment of silence followed.

Abruptly the old one threw back his head and howled, and the deep-bellied cry went up from all the fein in the trees, until it echoed and reechoed in the rock spires of the mountain above. Gruness and Lavin felt, rather than heard, Bg Rva's basso contribution to the ululation.

It choked off on a long sobbing cry, and in the hush the ancient spread his hands and dropped the hairs into the thick humid air above the pool. There they floated, rocking back and forth gently for a moment before beginning to spiral downward like leaves caught in a slow motion whirlwind.

"Peegav," said the adept, and around him rose the chorus "Nurrum, nurrum, nurrum" in a dense whisper.

As each hair approached the surface of the water, it winked out of existence. None survived to touch the pool.

When the last was gone, all felt as if a vast weight was lifting from around them. A wind gusted through the trees, departing in a whistle of eddies and vortices between thickset trunks. The humidity dropped significantly, the air freshened.

"And so another batch of hairs is gone, dispatched to the Arizel." Gruness shrugged. They were at war, fighting for survival.

"They will be counted, you know," Lavin snapped. "There were too many. There are always too many."

Lavin looked forward to a lifetime measured in centuries, perhaps millennia, in which he would fight bloody battles every half year, dispatching hundreds, thousands, millions of others to violent deaths. Already he'd put in eight years to hold Abzen. His gorge rose at the thought of it and he turned away quickly before Gruness could see his face.

"Let's get out of here," he said at last. "There's a battle at Brelkilk and we should be there."

5

BADLECK RIDGE GLOWERED OVER BRELKILK FROM UNDER A constant drizzle. Conditions were still too bad for effective air attack. Trucks churned the arble groundcover to mud as they whined past yards devastated by days of shelling.

The First Abzen Impi had finally coalesced to face the invaders of Mithiliwax forest. The warbands had been thrown out of Brelkilk and back onto the ridge behind. Beyond the ridge was Mithiliwax forest. But 18,000 thousand warband troops entrenched on the 250-meter heights of Badleck were too much for even the First Impi to dislodge, especially with only minimal air support.

It was too late to wait for a break in the weather, though. The airstrip on the other side of Badleck was covered in cargo jets loaded with a planet's ransom in raw chitin protein, still attached to gassed Vizier Mass. In the morning, bad weather or not, they'd be taking off for the Sx Coast.

Lavin Fundin and Bg Rva rode to the front on a hefty airbed. They passed a few bodies, Flanian soldiers in the distinctive blue-green camouflage, put out by the path.

"Excreting cubkillers," said Ny'pupe, recently promoted chief neilk of the First Impi.

Beyond the yards of the village, in the densely planted common woods, they began to hear the thud of field artillery. Soon, as they pushed the chubby airbed through thickets of glob glob, the sharp staccato of small arms became clear.

"Umpiil holds this sector. They didn't get into the fight yesterday, were held up at the river crossing."

"My old friend Umpiil must be itching for riffchuss today, I can just imagine." Lavin saw Rva and Ny'pupe exchange a grin. Canines flashed. Umpiil and his Marauding Seventh Sept were legendary throughout Abzen—desperate Effertelli, fein from a village of outcasts, males without females. Usually of kintypes of little standing in the yards, they sought honor in glorious battledeath; they would attack anything, almost anywhere.

Incoming fire ripped up the thickets around them so they abandoned the airbed and Lavin set up the command post in a glade among glob glob purples. The command post group set up the Data Net once more.

They considered the holomap. It was an old nightmare. The geography of the valley had placed Badleck Ridge as a wall that virtually cut the lower valley in half on the southern side of the river. An enemy sitting on the ridge held an almost impregnable position. True, the Abzen big guns at Cracked Rock could still zero in on the enemy's positions, but by sheltering in the lee of the ridge one could ride that out, and in bad weather the 150-kilometer range was too far for accurate fire anyway.

"Any suggestions?" Thinking that he must remember the courtesies, Lavin turned to Ny'pupe. *Ny'pupe is young, risen far in just five years....*

"I scouted the saddleback; the battlecomputer suggests the saddleback, too. The Flanians hold it. We pressed them hard yesterday and long into the night. They're tired, and the slope there is easiest to negotiate."

Bg Rva snorted. "On either side they will have particle cannon, machine guns. They must expect the attack there, too."

Ny'pupe's eyes flashed. The old Brelkilk Mzsee rode for riffchuss again.

"On the other hand, the War Eagles hold the flank by the

river. We could attack them by scaling the Badleck Cliffs—I'm sure the Brelkilk would think that approach more suitably suicidal."

Rva grinned. Same old Ny'pupe, stiff as all the Dayini.

Lavin looked intently at the lines. The long slope of the ridge had unimpeded fields of fire below. Beside the saddleback jutted the smooth rock-walled cone of the Wart Rock, 1,500 meters high. Something stirred in his memory so he had the computer project a close-up of the rock.

Normally Lavin would have had the Second Impi with him as well, and the warbands would never have been allowed into that position in the first place. But Young Proud's attack had siphoned off half his forces.

"Their forces in the center are from something called Durgan's Horde," Ny'pupe said.

"Who are they?" Rva looked up from where he honed his kifket on a worn soapstone. He had his slicker over him like a tent. Rain was streaming off at the back.

"Very recently mustered unit," Lavin said. "From the Sx Coast, organized by the Bablon syndicate. A lot of indentured men fighting on three-year leases, plus the remnants of Covey's Raiders. Don't have a battle rating yet."

"Oh?" Rva spat on the silky steel in his hand and pulled it through the cloth. "Rabble then. And right in the middle of their line."

"Yes," Lavin agreed. Something about the Wart Rock continued to nag at him, but try as he might, he could not pin it down. If only he wasn't so bone-weary tired. Five days of action, little beyond Pharamol, beer, and some nutrasoup to keep going on. He concentrated.

Rva noticed the sudden distracted look in Lavin's face. The dark eyes were open but unfocused. Rva knew that look; it was of Ghotaw, the *mathnas* yogas. A memory search. Rva shushed Ny'pupe's question with a wave of his hand.

They waited as the rain fell down harder than ever. Everyone was damp inside the slickers; the monsoon was merciless. Unused to the conditions of decision making at Impi Headquarters, Ny'pupe stared at the commander.

A shell shattered in the thickets to their right, but Lavin sat still as the surface of the Pool of the Spirit.

"Is the commander all right?" Ny'pupe whispered. He shivered in sudden shirrithee.

Rva gestured dismissively, tail high. "This is of Ghotaw, the knowledge there runs deep. Have you ever visited the wind shrine there?"

"I've seen it from below, many times, but few of us were encouraged to visit it while I was in training."

"Well, so you were tutored at Ghotaw." Rva was impressed.

Shirrithee past, Ny'pupe said, "It isn't only the Brelkilk who attend the Ghotaw schools, you know. The Dayin have been going just as long."

"I guess times have changed, friend Dayin. That's not how I remember it. But you know the Brelkilks, eager to hunt, covering the wide path, the first roamers."

"And big eaters, too," Ny'pupe said. Then he saw Lavin stir and sighed with relief; he'd miss Rva's almost endless kin boast.

"They think they're safe up there," Lavin said in a dry, husky voice. He grabbed a water bottle and took a swig. The meditation was over. "But they are very wrong." He gulped down a grain of Pharamol. The high cool winds of phara spread smooth patterns of logic through the problems at hand. His fingers flew over the dirty microconsole of the battlecomputer. The portable memory had a great store of geographical data but the detail Lavin sought to confirm was lacking. With Rva and Ny'pupe in tow, he headed for the airbed where he plugged into the data interface console of the communication link on the bed. The battlecomputer swiftly interfaced with the big database at Cracked Rock Fort and produced the confirmation he'd sought.

They took the bed forward after Lavin had called for a hundred or more horses to be gathered on the left flank, by the saddleback. Ny'pupe was set to finding the hundred best riders in the Impi. They worked their way around the hill that was taking the incoming fire and went forward into Umpiil's lines. Rva knew Lavin was working through the details of a major initiative, but Ny'pupe was mystified. Darkness was falling and there was little to see anyway with the low clouds and mists of rain.

"He has something, be patient," Rva whispered. Ny'pupe pretended he hadn't heard.

Fierce Umpiil trotted out of the murk accompanied by a trio of his neilks. They wore full biowarfare gear, the huge fein gas masks making them look like the monsters of human nightmares. They carried more.

"Antipersonnel mines throughout this sector," Umpiil said. "You ought to at least wear a mask." With that the big, ochre agouti leader of the Marauding Seventh handed them around. They left the airbed and progressed through the gathering murk into the wet undergrowth.

Umpiil had scented an attack impending in the sector and he was eager to be part of it. He happily led them forward until they hunkered down behind the rocks that were jumbled about the base of the Wart. The fractured boulders of the rock jambles were between five and ten meters square. Close to the Wart the stones were piled on each other like giant building blocks.

In the gloom of late afternoon, the Wart was a solid wall that lost itself in the mist of low gray cloud. Creeping through sepulchral avenues between stones that were lined with greenvelvet moss, they followed the curve of the Wart's slope until Lavin spotted a fissure, a crack several feet wide that grooved the rock deeply. They moved carefully there. Visibility was down to a few yards, but sharpshooters above had scopes that could pierce the murk.

They crossed a trail at several points, the tracks of three or four fein in a hurry. "Must have been Effertelli scouts," Rva said, "or somebody who never learned any trailcraft. Look at that footprint."

Umpiil verged on shirrithee, eyes opaque and tongue locked shut. He'd be damned if he'd say anything at all; the damn Brelkilk would twist it anyway.

Ny'pupe made no comment. Handling the Effertelli on an everyday basis was his problem. Careless words now might prove costly; it was a delicate moment.

Lavin broke it by pointing excitedly to what he'd been seeking. "The Wart Rock was pegged by the ancients. The adepts used to climb this rock because a spirit held its peak. As we can see, it was pegged for as many as three climbers at one time—so it must've been an important spirit. The Spirit abandoned the rock thousands of years ago, but the pegging is still in place!"

Peg holes, in pairs, were visible, cut into the steepest rock faces at intervals of between a foot and a meter. Three separate pegged paths could be made out, converging above to use the chimney of the upper part of the cleft and diverging again on the smooth rock above.

"Three at a time we are to *climb* this rock?" Ny'pupe exclaimed incredulously. "To attack them in prepared positions?"

Lavin caught Rva's tiny grin and allowed himself one, too. Ny'pupe would learn.

"The first fein up will take enough pegs with them to peg the whole path. Get volunteers from the mountain villages, fein who've spent their lives pegging up and down the cliffs in pursuit of the mountain byoit." Lavin turned to Umpiil. "And then we'll ask Umpiil here how quickly his gang of Effertelli heroes could climb the Wart if it was fully pegged."

The rain continued to drop from the dark above, but they could see dimly that the peg holes were still smooth. But for a few that were home to nibbla and ground jeers, they were clean, too.

"So we go up there and gut them in the dark?" Umpiil said in a satisfied voice.

"I like it," Rva said. "Those on the rock are in for a shock."

Lavin continued to examine the trails. "You'll have to be as silent as keffir kittens."

"We will be the quietest kittens that ever wore the kifket," Umpiil said silkily, tail kinked and ear tufts tall.

Rinus Van Relt, Commander of the Tri-Syndicate Operation in Lower Abzen Valley, visited the lines of Durgan's Horde shortly after sunset. Van Relt was feeling lucky and looking forward to getting the expedition off the mountain with tons of loot before the night was over. Just let the weather break on schedule and he was away. It would be his biggest success ever.

Yet he kept up his tours of the lines. He'd been over the positions of the Flanians that afternoon. He was particularly concerned there, on the saddleback, a point that he needed to bring up with Lord Durgan. The horde must be prepared to reinforce the Flanians should an attack develop badly on the saddleback.

Van Relt knew of Durgan only from his reputation, that of a loud-mouth braggart, with a big stomach and bigger head,

38

who'd caught the bug to go adventuring and left his safe but boring syndicate niche to take up war for a living. Except that Durgan was one of the wealthiest men on the Sx Coast—a magnate in the chitin trade—so war was to be his hobby, not his trade. His horde was a recently mustered unit, three divisions of indentured men, some fighters who were desperate for a berth, and the last couple of brigades of Covey's Raiders, a band that had been cut in half by Ervil Spreak's crack Black Anvil Impi.

Durgan had enjoyed the raid so far; it'd had some spectacular moments. His position on top of the ridgeline was so impregnable that he'd left his private jet down on the airstrip instead of having a small takeoff apron cleared near his headquarters.

The day before, they'd watched the fighting around Brelkilk which had led to the Flanians' retreat. Durgan had arranged for a few friends, a bevy of attractive sex objects, and several crates of excellent food and wine to be flown in with his baggage. Together they'd had a marvelous day ordering the horde about, making them practice digging trenches and staging mock maneuvers in the dwarf gallipod scrub that cloaked the lee of the scarp. His party had gotten quite tipsy on sparkling wine, and the fein and the fighting down below had seemed far away and quite safe. Until suppertime, when they were joined around their bonfires by a few officers from the Flanians. The sight of those fellows, in dirty uniforms, some with fresh wounds, with eyes lit from the real battle, seemed the perfect touch of romance to Durgan's friends, who toasted the new war leader with helmets of sparkling wine. Gzan from Mithiliwax woods were roasting on charcoal, the fires crackled merrily against the drizzle, and for the inner circle around Lord Durgan there was all the Pharamol you could wish.

In fact, the only complaints Van Relt heard were about the weather, which was generally held to be "quite beastly."

Van Relt, in his faded grays, felt out of place among the colorful sex kittens and adoni that seemed to fill the space around the fire. He and the few officers of the horde who were present were the only ones in military attire. They exchanged looks tinged with a variety of emotions and Van Relt could not restrain a sniff of contempt. None of Durgan's men would have served under him in the old days, in the Kampf Commando.

He turned to Durgan. "Of course the 'perfectly beastly'

weather is making this operation a lot easier than it would otherwise have been."

Lord Durgan was wearing a golden toga and senso halo while clutching the glorious Missy Pompanousse to his side. He seemed surprised by Rinus' idea. "Why in the world is that, my dear fellow? But for the weather we could've gone out and dealt with the enemy on the battlefield instead of clinging to our defensive post. Repaid them for their ugly treatment of our heroic brothers the Flanians."

The Flanian officers were staring at Missy Pompanousse in her silver lamé battlesuit but they looked up angrily at Durgan's presumption.

"We could be leaving sooner as well but for this dratted rain."

"All perfectly true, I have no doubt," Van Relt replied. "Except that the storm kept the enemy from being effective in the air, and it also kept their command busy elsewhere. The storm hampered the fighting in the northern valley."

"But what is this, Van Relt? We were attacked, weren't we? That was real war we watched down there. It was so magnificent," Missy Pompanousse said with a dizzying smile.

"We've been facing the first Impi of Abzen here. They were dispersed when we arrived and were hampered in reforming by the heavy rain. Yesterday afternoon the entire Impi showed up on our lines. You saw what that meant to the Flanians." Van Relt paused to sip the wine. "This is excellent, Messire. How thoughtful of you to bring it up here."

"Yes, yes, yes." Lord Durgan's jowls wobbled. "It's Klevier's Blancs de Blancs, but they renamed it after me, Durgan's Folly. Have some more, but do go on—you were explaining the strategy to us."

Van Relt sniffed again, his long, delicate nostrils quivering slightly from the effervescent wine. "Well, the First Impi has now been joined by its commander in chief. The fighting up north is over, we received word just this last hour. We can expect him to prepare some sort of attack. There'll certainly be some action tonight. Now, I doubt that they'll try anything against our center," he hastened to reassure, seeing alarm spread across Missy Pompanousse's exquisite features. The horde was entrenched above a high steep slope and, barring air attack, seemed impregnable. But just the thought of a sept of fein

cutting through Lord Durgan's HQ curled Van Relt's spine—
it was something he'd almost like to see.

"But, Messire, I do want you to be ready to reinforce the
Flanians should the blow fall on their lines as I expect it will."

Durgan was put out at this. "But we're in a superb, impregnable position. Why should we move *into* danger from
here? Why don't the Flanians move *here* and join us? That
would be much safer."

Rinus was patient. "The Flanians hold the saddleback and
the far side. That way we hold the entire ridgeline and deny
the enemy any avenue for a flanking maneuver. It's very important to hold our line. So if the Flanians take too much
pressure, I want you to put a couple of your units down there
with them to fill up the gaps. We could hold this mountaintop
with two hundred men, and really I'd like to let the War Eagles
extend their line through here while moving all of you down
to support the Flanians."

"Oh, we can't move now."

"Why not? It may be necessary."

"Not now, when we've got such a lovely fire going, and
everyone's having such a good time." Lord Durgan swept a
hand toward the feasting. "It's taken ever so long to light that
blaze and get it going properly—the fools cut lots of green
wood at first. And besides, we're all hungry."

Van Relt sighed. He thanked the immutable gods for the
two useful units he had to command. He had tried for three
entire warbands, knowing that the Abzen raid could be the
biggest of the season. But to succeed his plan had to be carried
out with strength. He'd got the War Eagles—a first-class unit—
and the Flanians, a serviceable, veteran bunch. Then the inevitable syndicate politics had dealt him a weird hand, Durgan's
crazy-quilt Horde. Still, he felt vindicated by the success of
the mission. The transports were loaded down with dynamited
chitin. The backers would realize more than twenty times their
share of the risk capital. He himself would at last retire and
take that comfortable apartment he'd scouted over on the Surf
Rox.

"I understand all that, and I'm not asking *you* to move.
However, it may be vital to keep the Flanians well supported
tonight. If the Flanians were to break under an assault . . . well,
don't let me frighten you unduly, but it's five miles to the

airstrip and we might all find ourselves running for it in the dark. We're entering the most dangerous period of the expedition. Our enemy is awake, he's down there right now working on his plan, and he must strike soon or he'll miss us. Do you understand—you *must* have a brigade on standby from now on, ready to move down on the Flanians at the first moment of need."

Durgan struggled within himself. He disliked the idea of sending a brigade to the Flanians. Or of doing anything to help them. He'd endured rudeness from the senior Flanian officers throughout the trip. On the other hand, the thought of having to flee to the airstrip in the dark was decidedly horrific. But the thought brought further ambivalencies. Might it not be better to fall back to the airstrip immediately if they were in such dire danger? Durgan decided that he would only feel properly comfortable again once he had his own jet in view.

"I think it's awful that we have to take this risk, but if you insist I'll put a brigade ready to aid the Flanians should they turn cowardly and run from the enemy."

"I think you'll find the Flanians will run only when things are hopeless. They're a stubborn crew. I had them with me at the Traif Enclave."

Mention of the great raid by the Super Kommando brought no recognition to Durgan's bland, pink features. Rinus sniffed disgustedly. "Never mind. Just be sure to support them should an attack develop." He sipped the wine and indicated to his staff that they would be leaving soon.

At the front, Captain Shayne made his rounds on the summit of the Wart. So far he had pulled a soft commission, but as an old hand he knew that battlefield luck could change in a remarkably short time. And thousands of fein were out there, under the wet leaves of the forest that was invisible in the dark below.

Sergeant Mengez and his squad were dug in inside their pac-tents, which they'd lined up along the top of the rock so as to get the best view the day before. They had a burner going and were busy fixing supper. Mengez went with Shayne on a quick tour of the rock. Little could be seen because the dark and the endless rainclouds blanketed everything in oblivion. Mengez' position was unassailable by anything except birds, and Shayne and he were soon back at the burner. The smell of fried gzan ribs was irresistible, and the captain stayed for supper and a beer.

Shortly afterward the skies lit up far to the north, near the river. The rumble and thud of artillery undercut the wind and the rain. Brilliant flashes shot up above the distant river. Blue lightning followed.

"What's that, sir?" a youngster in Mengez' squad asked.

"I'd say the enemy is getting ready to have a go at the War Eagles," Shayne said.

Corporal Emo checked the map and called into GHQ. "Sir, that's some kind of missile fire that was falling on the War Eagles' right by the river. They're expecting an immediate attack."

Shayne slipped his headset back on and hooked in on the GHQ circuit. "A full attack's beginning on the War Eagles, there's fighting by the river."

The artillery was in full-throated frenzy. The snapping whine of the mass accelerators was a high chord floating over the deeper rumble of the projectiles' explosion. Ballistic shells from Cracked Fort were starting to drop on the War Eagles' front as well.

Shells were also bursting in the rear, as far as, but not on, the airstrip. The one place the enemy wouldn't shell would be that airstrip, not while billions in Vizier Chitin was sitting on it.

The vulnerability of the Tri-Syndicate operation was also a source of strength, an irony that brought a tight little smile to Shayne's lips.

"Well, if the War Eagles are taking it I guess we're going to be spared. Looks like we dug those slit trenches for nothing, boys." Mengez took another beer.

"I for one won't complain about that," Corporal Emo said.

Flares in bright green erupted somewhere way down the line. Heavy detonations shook the distant ground.

"As long as those accursed War Eagles don't break and let them in behind us," Shayne growled. The others looked off toward the bursts and flashes with renewed interest.

Van Relt was still on the ground near Lord Durgan's tent when the first bursts announced the beginning of the action.

He moved back and took over the radio in the big tent. Anti-personnel missles were already tearing into the War Eagles' positions. Then flares and intense shelling began. Van Relt urgently sought an estimate of the numbers of attackers. If the action signaled the real thrust, he'd be delighted. The War Eagles were his best troops and their position was almost as good as that of Durgan.

The flares and bursts continued and then came reports of actual assaults, small groups of fein moving against the base of the slope, small-arms fire crackling up from the dark forests.

Van Relt was almost convinced, and he prepared orders for a contraction of the War Eagles' line with Durgan's Horde to take up the slack on their left. But he didn't send them. Ol' Rinus smelled a ruse. Following his hunch, he spoke with the Flanians' commander, O'Rorty. No sooner had he told O'Rorty to intensify the patrols on his front than the man was back on the line with the news that heavy assault columns were visible in front of his lines.

The Fundan commander was going for the blow against the saddleback that Van Relt had expected and feared. He quickly pushed the standby brigade of Durgan's Horde to move down slope to their right, to take up position in support of the Flanians.

"Watch the saddleback, Messire. It's about to explode down there. Our Fundan friend here is no fool—one of the best they have, in fact. That stuff against the War Eagles is just a demonstration. His thrust is coming now, against the Flanians."

Lord Durgan gulped, then ordered the horde to the alert. He would have ordered a retreat to the airstrip but for the presence of Van Relt.

Rinus exulted at having caught his foe's plan in the bud. The Flanians would be ready, and supported. They could hold. But he conceded to himself, with just a little awe, that his opponent was nothing if not bold. Fundin's forces had to be stretched very thin in the center. With only one Impi, he could hardly afford to demonstrate so well against the War Eagles, assault the Flanians, and keep anything adequate in the center. If Van Relt could find a way down the mountain, he could take even Durgan's miserable Horde and cut the Abzen Impi in half.

* * *

The word came down to watch the saddleback, and Sergeant Mengez and Captain Shayne did just that as the artillery shifted focus and flares and bursts lit up the slopes below. Parties of fein rushed the slope. Ground fire spattered bullets along the Flanians' lines. An antipersonnel missile went off with a crackling blast and sheets of blue flame.

"God fucking awesome," someone said.

"Do not blaspheme or take the name of the Lord God in vain," someone else said. There was a groan around the fire.

"Someone take Hobbs by his goddamn religious throat and shut him up," Emo growled.

"The Lord will not favor our arms if we blaspheme. It is grave impiety," Hobbs retorted from the dark, unrepentant and secure in his belief as a soldier of Christ Spaceman.

Just about everyone moved over to the right flank to see more clearly the bomb flashes that were bursting all over the Flanians' lines.

"Boy, am I glad we aren't down there. Looks like it's gonna be the real thing."

"Gird up thy loins, soldier, and know that I will aid thee in times of struggle. Thus sayeth the Lord in the wisdom of deep space."

Everyone chuckled at Hobbs. Someone suggested they leave him behind, tied to a tree. "Then he can convert the excreting heathen aliens." They were still laughing at that idea when a scream from the tents turned the platoon around, the hair lifting on the backs of their necks.

Along the edge of the Wart's steepest cliffs was a sight none of them would ever forget. A dozen or more bulky figures in full gas kit were scrambling toward the tentline. Over the lip of the cliff came more. Dangling beneath it were others, like heaving, jumpy bunches of grapes. Before anyone could move two men were down.

A trio of gappling hooks came over the cliff and bit for purchase in the dirt beside them. Someone screamed, "Fein attack, our front!" and they ran for their lives.

Mengez and a few others formed a line, got off a ragged volley into the fein ranks, and then the first attackers were in among them. Energy weapons sliced through rain and struggling figures alike. Grenades puffed and opened pockets in the lines, fein kifket swept a deadly dance through the close-quar-

45

ters work, and the sound of rifle fire punctured the curses, blows, and cries.

When Corporal Emo went down with a kifket through his middle, the platoon broke and ran. Mengez only had time to tell Brigade that his position was hopeless before he took a round through the cerebrum. Shayne found the radio operator dead and tried to raise Lord Durgan on the communications channel but a gas grenade plopped behind him and he took the first strength of it directly. He was paralyzed, still awake, with the sounds of total hysteria from Lord Durgan's tent in his ears.

The sight of what was left of Mengez' platoon streaming by unnerved the subcommander and he ordered his units to fall back on line with Brigade HQ, right beside Lord Durgan's tent.

The fein advanced swiftly, pushing through the brush on the ridgeline, fanning out around the trenches. Umpiil sent his fein in with a roar from three directions at once, and Durgan's Horde discovered that it wasn't really ready for that kind of warfare.

Durgan was so enraged that he wanted to arrest his brigade commanders and have them hanged on the spot. Van Relt restrained the purpling Lord and sent the men back to their commands. Their orders were simple—they must hold their lines at all costs.

Van Relt worked feverishly to get the War Eagles and the Flanians to close up quickly on the center and assist the horde. Neither group could believe him at first; indeed, he himself could not understand how the enemy had sprung a surprise attack straight up a five-hundred-meter cliff and right through his center. The Abzen fein were already close enough that bullets were clipping the top of the tent. At last the War Eagles got units out of line and reserve and onto the ridge trails.

Time was fast running out. Umpiil's Seventh Sept had been joined by Uul Coa's "Ironlegs" Sixth, and together they quickly surrounded the flanks of the brigade and began to peel it from its trenches. Wide-eyed Effertelli fein ran into those flanks with guns blazing and kifkets in hand.

The brigade's flanks were dissolving and Abzen fein units started slipping through the lines, heading into the interior. Men up and down the lines saw the situation was hopeless and began to head for the airstrip, walking carefully at first, as if flight was far from their minds, but running once in the scrub.

In Lord Durgan's tent, amid the ruins of a fine dinner, Rinus Van Relt was losing his voice from screaming at the obdurate O'Rorty of the Flanians. Even worse, the air jocks at the strip were stoned on fein gwassa and Van Relt couldn't get any sense out of them, nor had the War Eagles arrived. Van Relt knew with a sick certainty that the horde wouldn't hold up for very much longer.

A wobbly figure wrapped in a huge brown cloak started toward the door flap but was pursued by three girls in multicolored bodysuits. Lord Durgan had decided to flee to the airstrip incognito. The sex objects begged him to take them with him, throwing themselves at his feet, clutching at the cloak until he kicked them away with desperate lunging swipes of his boots.

A row of bullets suddenly stitched themselves through the wall of the tent, beheading one girl in blue tights and inducing everyone else to dive for the floor. A grenade burst ripped open the rear wall and knocked out the lights. In the dark Van Relt crawled toward the torn section but flattened as two fein, monstrous in bulky suits and gas masks, leaned in and shone a light around the interior. They examined the huddle of surviving sex objects and then shook their heads in wonder before vanishing into the night. Van Relt waited a few moments then slid out the opening in their wake.

Outside was sheer madness. The horde had broken and was packed in a mass on the paths leading back and away from their positions. Those fleeing along the ridgeline ran into the War Eagles and blocked their advance. Those running downhill were heading for the airstrip in blind terror, darting through the trees among fein advance patrols. All around Rinus, squads of Abzen fein were heading at a steady jog over the ridge and onward to the airstrip.

Van Relt felt a mad, searing perplexity engulf him. But his confusion produced only the thought of finding Lord Durgan and killing the fat, pompous oaf. Just then nothing else could be done. The Flanians would have to fall back whether goddamned O'Rorty wanted to or not. It was getting down to every man for himself. Van Relt bounded for cover and sought a way down the hill to the precious sanctuary of the airstrip.

* * *

Once Umpiil's sept started up the Wart Rock, Lavin Fundin set in motion his final blow, the insurance of his victory. A hundred horsefein, mounted on horses from the Brelkilk herds, were ready.

Below the saddleback were the First, Second, and Fifth Septs, readied for a thrust to catch the Flanians the moment they started to withdraw for the rear. The saddleback was a mile wide, and the stream draws on its flank were patched with brush. A stand of Inackaw trees with purple leaves and ripening pods marked the crest. The slope was heavily mined and progress across it would be slow. Oo Pap had sent his advance team—a specialist group and the best in the Impi—ahead and they were now at work in Dyr draw.

Lavin was afraid to trust only in a ground assault up-slope. He had to be certain of routing the Flanians and knew that the best moment would be in that fragile period just after they'd relinquished their fixed positions and begun to retreat. But the septs would have a long way to go to reach the Flanians' lines, and the Flanian men might hold and make the charge extremely costly. Their field of fire was wide and clear.

When Lavin explained the plan to Rva, the bodyguard protested the risk and Lavin's exposure to danger. Lavin brushed the protests aside and climbed into the saddle of a light-gray Brelkilk mare. He led the horsefein on a four-mile detour, scrambling up a narrow hunting trail to Little Thumb Rock, which overlooked the saddleback on the far side from the Wart. The horses were surefooted animals, accustomed to the weight of full-grown fein, and they made relatively little sound as they circled the Thumb and slipped past the patrols on the extreme flank of the Flanians' line.

Once in the glob glob forest on the far side, they immediately began to fan out and grope forward for the outer edge of the Flanian pickets.

Sweat was running down Lavin's face and his skin was sticking to the inside of the gas suit, when they rested for a moment, long enough for Lavin to slip a couple of grains into his mouth. Radio silence was being maintained, so there could be no effective communication with the rest of the Impi. They waited for the advance scouts to probe ahead and listened for the sound of Umpiil's attack.

48

Over the Thumb there were bright flashes and heavy detonations as Oo Pap built up the bombardment on the Flanians. The big guns from Cracked Rock were ranging along the saddleback. Lavin visualized Umpiil and the Seventh Sept crawling up the sheer slope of the Wart and tried not to think of the consequences if they were discovered.

Word came from the scouts. A scattered picket line lay three hundred yards ahead, well back, tucked in close to the main body. The Flanians were not expecting a flanking maneuver, not with the bombardment they were getting and Oo Pap's fein visible on the margins of the forest.

It was time. Umpiil and his mad Effertelli were either slicing into the center of the enemy's line or being shot off the face of the rock by jeering defenders. Lavin waited. It was the crucial moment. . . .

Finally, in the distance, thin, muffled by the booming bursts on the saddleback were shouts, the crackle of automatic weapons, the slightly heavier chug-a-chug of Fundan "peacekeepers."

A scout appeared with news of movements in the Flanians' positions. The pickets were pulling back even farther. Lavin was sure the attack had gone home. Umpiil was engaged, the enemy was anxious at the thought of fein getting between them and the airstrip. He and Rva moved up to join the scouts. They peered into the gloom but saw nothing through the scopes except scrub and hummocks of ground.

"They've gone, completely," a scout said, returning invisibly from the dark.

"Then we go forward, all the way. Let's give them what they deserve," Lavin said. The hundred horsefein occupied a kilometer-wide front, but they moved quickly through the glob glob scrub, eager for the contact.

Rinus Van Relt knew the worst had happened when he started up the final stretch to the blaze of lights on the airstrip and noticed that some of the fugitives were in Flanian uniform.

His own set of Kommando grays was torn and dirty and he was soaked to the skin. The only semblance of authority he'd retained was his command baton, and he'd had to use it already to order men out of his way. A lot of wounded men had hidden in the woods, many with broken ankles and twisted knees suffered in the panicky flight down the scarp in the dark.

The scene at the airstrip was even worse. A mob of former warriors in Durgan's Horde was besieging the transports. The flight crews and the security platoon were keeping them at bay with drawn weapons, but the pressure was building and order wouldn't hold for long.

At least, the big planes were ready to go. The sight of the terrified troops had galvanized the pilots. The first few craft were already idling on the runway.

Van Relt found the security chief and took command of the strip. The War Eagles, summoned urgently, were already on their way. The first planes, loaded with chitin, were to get airborne right away. Though the weather was still terrible, the storm was ebbing. And there was *no* time to wait. Incredibly, Van Relt's great triumph had been plucked from his grip at the last moment, and the operation had suffered a catastrophic defeat.

He looked out over the strip from the little control module. In the lights flaring through the mists, the men thronging the transports and struggling on the runways were a dense mass, like a single remorselessly stupid creature—a dumb, strenuous thing that thrashed and bled. His contempt for them rose another notch and he almost fainted from the nausea it induced. His desire to slay the fat, useless ogre Durgan was more than he could stand.

The ominous punctuation of automatic weapons and a bright burst on the far edge of the strip brought him around. Fein on horseback were firing from the saddle, aiming for the pilots. The cockpit of the lead plane suddenly erupted in flame from an accurate grenade. In despair Van Relt ordered the security details to clear the strip and ward off the fein. Where the hell were the War Eagles?

And then a great wave surged forward, a flood of men in flight—the bulk of Durgan's Horde and the Flanians—weapons gone, clothes torn, fighting each other to pass through the barbed wire into the relative safety of the airstrip. Fein were pressing at their backs, bullets slapped the leaves, whined off the trees. The horsefein galloped for the planes, and all possibility of an orderly escape vanished.

Up and down the strip, pilots taxied around stalled planes, while struggling mobs of men fought to board. Several planes took off with dozens of men hanging from cargo doors, wheels, even tail fins.

Very few aircraft made it aloft; the fein sharpshooters took out the pilots or shot out the tires. Before long full units of the First Impi were on hand to take charge of things and negotiate Van Relt's surrender of the 15,000 men still under his command.

By then Lavin Fundin was already fast asleep in a tent on the saddleback, and Bg Rva was squatting outside, cleaning a freshly killed gzan for the fire he had blazing.

6

FLEUR KEVILLA, EARTH'S DEPUTY AMBASSADOR, LOOKED OUT
the window at the airport terminal that squatted on the tarmac
like a great glittering insect and felt another surge of a by now
all-too-familiar anger. Even after three full years in her post
on Fenrille, Ambassador Blake regarded her as an enemy. A
threat to be neutralized at every opportunity. He was using the
summit meeting at Stroins' Rock as just another occasion to
keep Fleur as far away from the decision-making nexus as
possible.

Blake first announced that he would attend the summit with
just his assistant, Wermil. The idea that Blake and old Wermil
could handle the volume of work at such a meeting was so
laughable that Fleur hadn't even bothered to complain. Instead
she'd organized a mock day's worth of activities, falling into
playing Blake's petty games, and thus made up a few points
on the old man when he was forced to ask her to attend, with
her staff, to handle the load of negotiation.

The man ran the most important diplomatic post in all human
space like a lazy, petit-bourgeois businessman, the owner of a

failing restaurant or a dismal tourist hotel in the back of beyond. He lived like a playboy and shamefully indulged himself in the Pharamol-fueled debauchery in the coastal cities. During the lengthy process of organizing the summit, Blake had read only *her* weekly reports, and he'd finally tried to exclude her if he could.

The anger returned when she thought of the moment when she discovered that Wermil had given the embassy's second jet to his sister for a two-day trip to the Surf Rocks. The first jet was taken by Blake, of course, who wouldn't allow her or her staff aboard. So they had to book a commercial jet, and Wermil sniped about the cost. The man was a snake. She was sure it was his work that had poisoned her relationship with Blake from the start. But Fleur had the feeling that Wermil's infantile hatred of her had been carried too far. He'd overstepped the bounds of administrative spite to the point of actually endangering the Earth diplomatic mission at the summit, the most important meeting held anywhere in a hundred years.

She'd already dispatched a formal complaint and a request for his dismissal, one that had to be sent to Earth for the record. It would take years to get there, of course, although the new negative-space communications system had cut message times since the construction of the transmitter station at the black hole singularity AO 4441, but it meant that even if Blake ignored her protest, as was virtually certain, she could use that as long-term evidence. Her struggle might take fifty years or more.

Nothing would come of it; she was naive to think that it could. She was trapped with Blake as her superior and no redress available. The man was given over to corruption and hedonism. Her hopelessness loomed large; it would be easy to give up the struggle and just let Blake mismanage things the way his paymasters on Fun Isle desired. The syndicates ran things their way; why not let them?

She set her jaw at the idea, blinking back the tears she felt were all too likely to gush. Resolutely she turned away from the hopeless void. She would not cry, she would not give in. She would throw their accusations—implicit since her arrival—that she wasn't fit for her post because she was female back in their faces. If it took a hundred years, she would bring Andrej Blake down.

Of course, there might not be a hundred years to play around with if the summit meeting failed.

The chartered jet was small and noisy but it would at least get Fleur's party to the meeting in time. That was a relief; they couldn't have made it in a subsonic plane. The takeoff did not spare the G-forces and the pilot rode his bird like he was scrambling for combat, taking secret pleasure in squeezing the Earthers in the cabin. At 35,000 feet they pushed through the clouds, and he leveled out at 55 and set their course north and east, into the heart of the Belt Continent.

While they flew, Fleur slipped into revery and returned to the mystery that had obsessed her in the last few days: a coastal girl; a short film clip of a young man called Termus Hith who spoke of a secret that could change the world; a mysterious crisis in the heart of the Bablon Syndicate. She wondered if somehow those things fitted together.

Tan Ubu marshaled the notes before him then turned to Fleur. He saw the boss's expression and, understanding what she was going through with Blake, started to turn away again when she spoke up.

"Tan? What is it? I'm okay, really. This business won't get me down, you know that by now—we never give up."

He handed her a sheet of printout. "The table layout and speaking order are all agreed. Just came over the scope. Blake made a few changes on our side though, look."

"Thanks, Tan. Where're we? Still in the room?"

"You'll be surprised. Something must be up."

She glanced down, absorbed the listing.

"My God!" she exclaimed. "We're right opposite Fair Fundan and Ervil Spreak. Blake's down the end of the table and he's sitting beside the space admiral from the *Gargarin*."

"Finally we'll get to see him, whatever *he* is."

"The rumors have certainly been interesting, haven't they? I'm wondering if this table plan is really Blake's idea. I think I detect the faint but heavy hand of the Space Command."

"Absolutely," Tan agreed with a nod of his boyish, square-cut chin. And she knew that Ubu wasn't just humoring her. The slim African had done five years in the Patrol Space Intelligence before making it into the Diplomatic Corps.

Fleur reflected that Tan was going to be an even more valuable asset during the next few months. The arrival of the

54

Gagarin to bolster the Fenrille Fleet had added new and unknown elements to the situation. The old commander in chief, Admiral Schranz, was said to be approaching rebellion against the mysterious Admiral Enkov. And the rumors about Enkov ran the gamut from obscene to laughable. All she knew was that modern space crew were produced in the Patrol's laboratories on Triton from genes that were altered from the normal human state. "They tell me that they don't really look like human beings," she said, "especially the officers."

Tan shrugged, loosening the collar of his cream-color shirt. He still wore the service uniform issue, another thing that bespoke his conservatism. Fleur wondered slyly if Tan had succumbed at all to the lures of the Sx Coast. She remembered his intense distaste for the coastal society; its flaunting sexuality disturbed him.

"Battle crew have to be able to take high acceleration. Physical stress that's more than human flesh was designed for. But they want to retain human command of warships, can't leave it to the computers. No matter how much you leave to the drones and robots, you still need to have that human factor."

Fleur sighed. "How they hate that, I bet."

Tan turned back into his seat and left her to check the rest of the fresh data. Fundan and Spreak were selected to speak first for the clans at the main meeting. Blake would open the proceedings and act as moderator. No problems there; the summit was gathered under Earth Government auspices and security was to be provided by the Fundans. That meant a lot of fein soldiers would be around. Fair Fundan had mentioned a figure in the thousands. Fleur knew the ancient Fundan matriarch was paranoid about her safety, but bringing a standing army to the meeting seemed excessive to her Earthly sensibility. But Fleur had found that her acceptance of Fundan control of the security arrangements made the task of getting the other clans to attend very much simpler. They were all obsessed with security, but once the Fundans came in, the others accepted the idea.

Fleur was excited at the thought, too; she'd seen few fein since her arrival. They were so beautiful, yet so alien. Like oversized mandrills or catlike baboons with human shoulders and seven-foot statures, fein were rarely seen in the coastal cities except on the horrible gladiator TV shows. The aliens were heavily mythologized, but some of the more extreme political parties called for their extermination as the only way to break the power of the highland clans. The right-wing Intensity Party preached that the fein were not actually intelligent—only very well trained and led by the human clans—therefore exterminating them would not be genocide. On the other extreme were the numerous mystics who taught the fein mysteries and tricks. Mystery cults abounded, many of them advocating a high consumption of the drug teosinte, which induced elation and other effects understood less well.

The summit would be Fleur's first experience with fein in numbers, the highland armies. She looked forward to their arrival with rising hopes and no little impatience.

She noted that Enkov was listed as representative of both the World Government of the Sol system and the Fenrille Space Fleet. So Schranz had been squeezed out entirely, and so soon. She wondered why the World Government had demanded representation on its own, apart from that already provided by the Earth diplomats. Enkov was from the outer satellites, of course, and who could say what nuances of the struggle for power in the home system he carried with him? But she also wondered why they'd had virtually no contact with the new admiral since the *Gagarin*'s arrival at Fenrille, three months earlier.

She frowned, noticing a place set for Quermwyere, the corpulent president of the Chitin Bank and an active member of the Sx Coast syndicates. Their tentacles were everywhere, reaching into every opening, exploiting the shortage of eternity drugs.

Not only was Quermwyere seated, so was Asgood Wythe, leader of the Coast Freedom Party, member of the ruling coalition, which Fleur knew to be little more than a front for the big syndicates like Bablon and Ninevah. "I see Blake has put Quermwyere and Wythe back in."

Tan swung round from the file he'd been studying. "Well, we didn't think he'd keep them out. He'd get in a lot of trouble for sure if didn't admit them."

Fleur put the paper down with a groan, then shrugged. "The families will hate it, but what the hell, at least everybody's going to be there. The way I'm feeling, I think I like the idea that no one can whine later about having been kept out. The issues have to be aired, so it's probably better this way."

It'd taken two months of exasperating struggle and hard work to get the summit arranged and agreed to, but now the die was cast and nobody could tell exactly how it was going to roll, least of all Fleur Kevilla.

7

THRUST LIKE A GIANT CHISEL ALMOST 3,000 FEET ABOVE THE topmost tree canopy, Stroins' Rock caught the early-morning light long before the forest below. Once it had been the lava core of an active volcano, spouting fire and lava during the intense orogeny that formed the equatorial mountains. Long dormant, the volcano had vanished under the abrading hands of the monsoon, leaving only the rocky core.

The rock's flat top encompassed fifty acres, and seizing this natural penthouse above the forest the Fenrille ecosystem reproduced itself in down-size imitation of the pattern that prevailed in the high montane valleys. Here the *Esperm gigans* reached no more than 200 feet, the lyissa vine failed to develop fruiting bodies, and the blood spruip fungi and other such debilitating pests were absent. Most important of all—at least to potential human inhabitants—sheer cliffs on all sides kept woodwose from climbing to tend the trees. They also kept walking trees at bay and discouraged wild chitin. With the break in the fundamental ecological link between woodwose and *Esperm gigans*, the local trees were much afflicted with bark parasites and woodworms.

But freedom from woodwose, fungi, and walking trees made the scrap of land on top of the rock a precious and exceedingly rare commodity on the Belt Continent—potential farmland, or at the least a habitable place in the vastness of the hostile forest. Consequently during the first century the rock was colonized by successive waves of would-be farmers. But the space was too small to produce more than subsistence-level farming and the attempts came to nought.

Eventually the Stroins, an upstart family from the entourage of the Spreaks, seized the rock and attempted to emulate the great families by cultivating the chitin insect for its precious, complex proteins. However, the Stroins were few and they lacked skill with the insect. In time the nests outgrew the limits imposed by the Stroins and secretively hived the land. Instead of chitin farmers the Stroins became chitin prey, and on a night of grim remembrance the entire family passed into legend when the insect invaded their homes and ate them. Soon the unrestrained nests consumed every living thing on top of the rock and eventually died of starvation, their Vizier Mass having grown too enormous to negotiate the vertical rock cliffs.

With the early light, splashed golden on the blue-black rock, came Lavin Fundin and the Second Abzen Impi. His fliers circled in clear skies at 40,000 feet while the transport balloons drifted down from the equatorial mountains, passing over precipitous walls of granite, deep-hidden valleys—many of them never explored by human beings—and torrential mountain streams, swollen with monsoon rains, dashing and leaping on their way down the shoulders of the mountains.

Like a string of huge green grapes, the transports floated toward the shining serpent of the Irurupup River, four miles wide there and still several thousand meters above sea level. In the distance, beyond the river, stood the rock, a dark spire with a crown of gold. Soon they circled it as, one by one, the transports dropped anchor and reeled themselves in.

The Abzen Second hit the ground running. Even as Pilot Gruness brought Lavin's flier down on a bare piece of rock, fein were fanning out over the terrain. Heavy helicopters delivered a bulldozer while Lavin and Bg Rva conferred hurriedly

59

with the advance-team neilks. Sites for the conference dome were examined and one finally selected. Tent accommodation for staff, guards, and auxiliaries was put up. A field kitchen arrived, and Lavin grabbed a much-needed mug of coffee. Soon the men and women of the kitchen staff were serving breakfast for the Impi, sept by sept, of spicy meal cakes, toasted gzanjerky patties, and mugs of steaming gwassa. The roar of heavy engines and the whine of chain saws soon shattered the millennial peace of the place as fein worked to clear the airstrip that would soon bisect the rock's flat top.

As soon as the first few hundred feet of the strip were cleared and rollered, planes began landing. Time was short and security preparations were far from complete.

Old Fy'pupe, with a dozen of his younger acolytes, was one of the first arrivals. Their Ghotaw Schools jet was equipped with sensitive screening equipment to detect unauthorized transmissions to or from the rock during the summit.

With Fy'pupe and the graycowls covering the ground, Lavin knew that Ghotaw School methods would be in rigorous effect, security would be seamless. As soon as the big bubble dome was inflated, specialists moved in, checking every piece of machinery, furniture, equipment, with sharp attentive eyes that sought signs of any disturbance. Once again equipment was taken apart to component level and examined minutely. Nothing was found, however, which pleased Fy'pupe though he gave no visible sign of it.

Things were moving along smoothly. Lavin scanned the skies to the south. Sure enough, the first arrivals were just visible, small dots streaking in across the jungle, Personal Security Teams—three-and four-man units, sent in ahead of the coastal big shots. Lavin's temporary sense of relief now evaporated as tensions arose that reminded everyone that this was going to be a day of trials, sure to test his fein to their limits.

Several members of the professional teams—like Kweegxorn, who scouted for Quermwyere, the chitin banker—were professional gladiators as well. They killed unarmed fein in the killing pits for coast TV. Most such men, and one woman, were semiprosthetic, their bodies extensively rebuilt with artificial muscles, steel-reinforced bones, nerves protected by sheathing. In fein combat they wore body armor and wielded two-handed kifkets. Even so, theirs was a dangerous profession. The 300-pound adult fein they fought occasionally turned the tables; even steel-reinforced backbones could be broken.

The Abzen fein seethed as they recognized many of the faces. They watched the same TV shows as the Coastals. TV was one of the more unpredictable benefits from the great alliance between the fein and the first human colonists, the highland clans.

Lavin had to order Bg Rva to the fein command tent at one point when a surly security honcho tried to push the hero of Brelkilk out of the way. With his advanced prosthetics, the man had bionic power and even Rva's massive chest would have given way, but the kifket that danced lightly in Rva's hand the instant the man touched him froze everyone.

The huge yellow eyes stared, the man stared back, licked his lips. Lavin half expected the fellow's head to be on the floor the next moment and whispered harshly, "Mzsee—no!"

But the blade had appeared too quickly for the eye to follow and the man gave ground, stepping back hastily and turning to Lavin. The fellow wore the insignia of the Human Supremacist League. "Will you order this creature to allow me to pass?"

Lavin waited a moment before replying. "While you're here *you*'ll have to ask my fein to move, and ask politely, understand. This rock is under the control of the Abzen Second Impi, you'd better remember that."

Lavin caught Ng Tung's eye and called a short conference of sept leaders. "Now listen, everyone must cool down. The security teams will be here all day. We have to let them do their job. No bloodshed is permissible. Understood?" Yellow eyes blazed and big hands twitched, but the word went out and the fein did calm down.

Struk Staal of the Freebooters Guild flew in on contract to Asgood Wythe, political boss of the Sx Coast. Staal and Lavin had met before on the coast, at parties and such. Now Staal jibed, "So, still alive, Fundin?"

"Why do you ask, Staal? Was it ever in question?"

"TV said it was a close thing up in Abzen Valley. Syndicates had a very unusual ally this time." Staal chuckled.

Young Proud's treachery was no secret then. Lavin concealed the dismay he felt at the taint attached to Clan Fundan. Instead he smiled. "Might I interest the Freebooters in some indentured men? My slave pens are overstocked today."

61

Staal chuckled. "But not with too many Dognobles, I'll wager. Their bones whiten on the Kirrim, eh?"

Lavin shrugged. "I have others. Would you want War Eagles? Or Flanians?"

Staal laughed, shook his head. "You highlanders are really something, aren't you? But no, the Freebooters are exactly that—*free*. We can't have indentures. It goes against our company charter. You'll have to sell them to somebody else."

"Once they've been castrated, you mean."

Staal blinked as Lavin's lips twisted in a sardonic smile. "What?"

"It's our new policy in Abzen. To discourage others. Full removal of all sex organs, male or female."

Staal shuddered and moved on.

More fliers arrived. One jet brought a couple of blue-uniformed officers of the Space Fleet and a strange little woman, who introduced herself as Epsila, Assistant to the Deputy Ambassador from Earth. She carried several pieces of advanced sensory equipment for detecting microbugs and other forms of espionage. The elflike Epsila sniffed loudly at the sight of a dozen security teams at work, all looking over everything and planting their own bugs wherever possible. It was plant-a-bug chess with far too many players already.

The patrol officers were unaffected types, just doing a job. They seemed to view the summit as a waste of time, thinking the sides were just too far apart.

The inside of the dome was a bare space forty meters across, floored with a single sheet of thick white foamtuf. Epsila worked smoothly and quietly as she examined the surfaces of the simple canvas-back chairs and the flat slab of illuminated acryl that was to be the table. Her microscanner sought for the tiniest eddies in the magnetic fields within the dome. She fed a seeker down under the foamtuf and put several autobiles in motion, crawling over the inner surface of the dome like swift metallic lizards, seeking abnormalities.

For his part Lavin was eager to hear more about the Space Navy's new flagship, the WGS *Gagarin*, which had recently joined Admiral Schranz's fleet in the Beni System.

"Well, that thing is just enormous," said the taller of the two blues, named Hall. "I was on the *Chickamauga* last month when we rendezvoused with it in lunar orbit. Now the Big

Chicka, that's some ship, two miles long, complement of two thousand crew, y'know—but sundust if that *Gargarin* doesn't look about ten times as big. Must be three times as long, space knows how many on board."

The other man, Griffiths, was shaking his head. "Well, let me tell you, I was on leave on the Red Moon when I saw some of that new-type crew they have. No way are those things human beings, you get what I'm saying? I mean, they are too ugly to be human, they're more like spiders. They walk so jerky and they look at you so strange it's peculiar. Give me the old ships any day. May not be so fast, but you don't have to be made of plastic flesh to operate 'em."

Epsila's lizards had found no surviving bugs in the canopy or under the foamtuf. The place was absolutely clean. "Well, Commander, your security people are to be congratulated. A remarkable job considering the conditions." Lavin escorted Epsila and her team past old Fy'pupe to the security tent, where hot coffee and rolls were being served. After he returned to the command post, a stream of VTOL jets bearing highland clan chietains appeared, circling the rock until ground control guided them to landing spaces. A few tricentenarian heads of clan did not take to being asked to queue for landings by a Fundan "whelp" not even in his third decade, but as quickly as possible each plane was brought in and a hastily bulldozed place made available for it. Soon every luxury model of personal jet was sitting on the rough dirt runway.

Ervil Spreak arrived in his gunship, and his own security fein fanned out around it on the apron as soon as its pods touched ground. Spreak would not emerge himself until the moment the conference was to begin; he evidently felt that his presence in a Fundan-controlled zone placed him in danger. With 333 years of experience in such matters, Spreak wasn't inclined to take advice from anyone on personal security.

Lavin carefully refrained from sending Spreak any message other than the simplest welcome. Anything more might easily offend the lofty Spreak dignity and bring to mind unpleasant memories of a raid eight years before.

Meanwhile the air traffic control team, young men and women from Ghotaw, reported the arrival of a half dozen Spreak interceptors high above, where they circled with Lavin's own planes in a shifting game of maneuvers at 50,000 feet.

63

A more welcome sight was that of Rognius Butte, personally negotiating his purple-glazed Starglider to a parking space. Buttes and Fundans were allies, set forever against Spreak and Hoechst. And for Lavin there was the added bond of his wardship of Armada Butte.

"Well, well, there he is, the conquering Fundin. News travels fast, young man, especially when a place like new Brelkilk is celebrating its collective head off. They speak of nothing else on Butte Manor. Everyone wonders how you pulled it off." Red-faced Rognius, bald and as sturdy as a great tree, clasped Lavin's hand with affection. "And they say you took three whole warbands prisoner, including the War Eagles." Rognius adopted a crafty look, eyes slitted. Lavin waited, knowing what was coming.

"If you recall, my boy, it was the War Eagles that took my Lettie in the raid of twenty-nine. They're well remembered among the Buttes." He paused a moment to pick a thread from his purple waistcoat, studded with golden chitin embroidery.

"Well, Grandfather, I ran a test on our captured War Eagles. You'll be glad to hear that five are left on the band that raided Butte Manor in twenty-nine. I'll be shipping them over to you in the next couple of days."

"Excellent. We'll know what to do with them." Rognius' full jowls shook with a nervous excitement at the prospect of revenge after so long. Then the moment passed and another thought surfaced. He laid a fleshy hand on Lavin's arm.

"Armada? Has anyone heard from her?"

"Not for days," Lavin answered wearily. Lately Armada's willfulness had been driving him crazy. "I think I'll have to go to the Sx Coast again to find her, that's where she'll be."

Rognius was disturbed by this. "She's too young to have developed such tastes. Rutting with the coastal scum may be a vice for the older generations, but the girl isn't even twenty yet and her conduct is unseemly. I fear for her—the whole family does. We wish we knew some way of approaching her, of getting her to talk, to explain herself." The patriarch of the Butte Clan wore an expression mixed of incomprehension and the pain of rejection by a much-loved daughter.

"She's a natural rebel, grandfather. It's a common phenomenon at her age. Perhaps she should attend Military Academy with another family. You could send her to Ghotaw. It's not too late." Lavin wished there was a way to bridge the gulf, to tell Rognius the reasons for his daughter's flight from his family. But Rognius, though in his third century, retained the same upright, slightly smug moral outlook he'd formed in his own twenties. He remained a short, stout plant in a garden grown full of strange, complex weeds.

"It's unnatural, this running away from us. She was perfectly happy, she had everything she could want. What more could we do? She had dozens of young people for company, not to mention the entire family Butte. Why this urge to go fornicating across the Sx Coast? Why these awful accusations against my brother Silas? And there's the whole matter of her flight to you. No word from her in explanation, no likelihood of marriage between you though you know that's what we all hope for. And you—what of yourself?" Rognius made a gesture of disgust. "The whole thing's a puzzlement, and I don't know what to think about it."

And there Rognius rested his case. His wayward, wild daughter was incomprehensible to his old mind. Like many of his generation, he was deeply set in his ways, attuned to the rhythms of decades, secure in the mountain fastnesses.

"As I said, Grandfather, the best course is to let her find her own way for now. She's determined to take it anyway." Lavin paused, weighed words carefully. "And she won't come back. As I understand it, she won't go home while Silas lives."

The pain returned to Rognius' face.

"Well, you're probably right," he said at last. "Where did you say? Ghotaw?" He shook his head. Rognius had heard too many things about Ghotaw and the mysteries of its schools. The Fundans had delved deeply into the roots of their world, exploring the lore of the fein, groping for the meanings in the ancient rituals. The Buttes had viewed such things with slight suspicion; on Butte Manor they retained more of the flavor of the old life, the colonial life on the coastline before the equatorial migration and the integration into the ways of the fein.

"If I send her to Ghotaw, what's to stop her turning into a witch? Eh? You know what I mean, boy—our families don't see eye to eye on such things, never have. We Buttes remain Christian, God fearing, and I don't want to say anything against your mentor, but I'm afraid Armada's such a powerfully spirited girl that all that dabbling in fein mysticism will be too intoxicating for her. Who's to say if I send her to Ghotaw that we'll ever get her back, eh?" Rognius paused, then lowered his voice. "Do you know what I wish, m'boy?" Lavin looked up.

"I wish that she'd find some young fellow and marry him in the Christian way and settle down and produce a brood of children. Now, while she's young and her genes are good. When you get to my age you have to abort most of your progeny because your genes are screwed up, won't breed true—you know what I mean. And think what it would do for our families. It's just what we all need. Don't you ever think about that sometimes? Becoming a father, bringing young ones into the world?"

Rognius still cherished the thought of a love match between Armada and Lavin, and Lavin, recalling the day Armada had come to him, seeking refuge from Silas Butte in a plane trailing smoke over the hills, wished he was able to agree, even to announce a marriage day. But he knew it was hopeless, even as he'd known it then. They'd spent a lot of time together then, he listening to her accounts of the Christ and Jerusalem—she was then a fervent convert of the Church of Christ Spaceman—and she listening to his plans and dreams for Abzen Valley and the fortress of Cracked Rock.

But children? For Armada, the idea of children seemed totally alien. Lavin had never met a girl who made love so well but was less interested in love itself. She didn't seem the mothering type.

Rognius stared at Lavin briefly then clapped him on the shoulder and was followed shortly by Ernst Hoechst, who barely nodded to Lavin en route.

A gunship with the arms of the Freebooters Guild landed, and wrapped in a red robe, the immense, dropsical bulk of Quermwyere, the banker, was eased out of the hatch by two hulking geldings whose task it was to carry their colossal master in his chair wherever he went. At the door membrane, however, they set the chair down and small wheels sprouted from it. With a touch of a switch, Quermwyere activated its motors. Lavin felt a surge of disgust. To highlanders such things as gluttony and the ostentatious display of slavery were repulsive, embodying the decadence that they disdained publicly even

66

though many were privately drawn to it like moths fascinated by a flame.

At the door of the command post, Quermwyere beckoned to Lavin. Lavin inclined his head, unwilling to give more than token respect to his enemies.

"You are becoming the new Julius Caesar, young man! They tell me you're rewriting the tactics book. Everyone quotes your maneuvers at Crystal Lake as the epitome of martial skill. What a pity we couldn't get you to change sides, eh? I'm sure Commander Van Relt would agree, eh?" He chuckled wetly.

Lavin allowed a grim smile. "Mr. Van Relt is up for sale like all the rest. Do you want him? I can arrange the details."

Quermwyere shook to a deep guffaw, a minor geological event somewhere in that massive torso, buried under layers of sedimentary fat.

"I think not, Commander, I think not." He rolled into the door membrane and was gone.

The Earth Ambassador and his assistant arrived and were escorted to the dome. Not long afterward a commercial jet made a hard landing and deposited Fleur Kevilla and the rest of the Earth diplomatic team. Fleur saw the rows of parked jets and hundreds of fein, and the tension she'd been trying to suppress rose like a dark cloud to bury her thoughts. The immensity of the task ahead was so overwhelming, the positions on either side so far apart . . . She began to cough on the dust kicked up on the airstrip and had to stop to get herself under control. It was then that she took greater note of her surroundings.

Standing on top of Stroins' Rock was fairly dizzying. The endless green of the jungle was visible, stretching unbroken to the far horizon. It was Fleur's first drop into the deep forest, her first opportunity to see fein in numbers, too.

As Tan and Epsila removed the data terminal and processor from the jet, fein stepped forward to check for hidden mechanisms. Fein were everywhere, patrolling the airstrip in purposeful squads of ten, slipping by singly on errands, standing to stiff attention around the security perimeter outside the dome. She'd never seen so many and never at such proximity, so close she could even detect that faint citruslike scent of their bodies.

Sleek fur, black to every shade of brown and gray, with bands and stripes and even spots; yellow eyes and tall, heavy-shouldered bodies were all around her. For some reason she was fascinated by their tails, ringed and banded and smooth, flicking around or simply held straight down with just the tip kinked or curved. They wore weapons harnesses with green striping, assault rifles over their shoulders. Some wore parts of full camouflage uniform. All bore green flashes above the right ear. Then she saw a few others with different colors and devices above the ears, and then another type altogether with gray robes, hoods pulled over their heads.

Once everything had been examined by green-flash fein, they were escorted along a neatly rollered path to the command post of plasteel plates outside the dome. The young commander was pleasant enough. Fleur barely caught his name but there was something about him, about the relaxed way he held himself and spoke and that shock of unruly black hair, that tugged at her memory. She felt she'd seen him before, but though she groped for it, the memory eluded her in the general excitement. At the membrane the young commander wished her well and she took a deep breath and walked in. And now for the lion's den, she thought.

A moment or two later a jet-black Hermes came in on blasting retros and Fair Fundan stepped out behind the broad backs of three security fein.

Lavin had the First Sept of the Impi on parade in a V, forming a funnel for the Mother Fair to walk down to the conference dome.

Dressed in her habitual white robe with one viridian stripe, she was dazzling to behold. A white senso cloud obscured her feet and trailed behind her like a phosphorescent train, and her face was framed in dark masses of curls in which pale-green senso stars gleamed more brilliantly than any jewels. The faces of the fein in the First Sept were lit up with pride and reverence. This was the Mother of the Clan Fundan, the bringer of salvation and the new life. When she stopped to congratulate Juft Rediz, subadar neilk, on the birth of twins of his mate, Kla, the eyes of the fein in the ranks glowed like hot yellow coals. The whisper said it: "The Mother knows all. Rediz Kla had twins at dawn. Not even Ng Tung knew that."

At Lavin's side, she paused to favor him with a few public words. "Commander, I must say that the First Sept of the Second Abzen are as fine a sight on parade as ever I've seen."

Her voice carried back into the silent ranks while her eyes held his. "With these fein around us, I'm confident this conference dome will be the safest place in the world today."

She waved to them, a small thing, a motion of one arm, but backs stiffened and ears tufts lofted upright even more tightly than before. The honor of the moment would never be forgotten in the sept. The eyes continued to glow long after she'd passed.

For a moment, while they walked alone toward the membrane, Fair spoke. "You seem to have pulled off another of your miracles, young man. Congratulations, although I should tell you that your assault on the Wart Rock was not approved by the Ghotaw computers—much too risky."

"There was so little time, Mother Fair," he stammered.

She enjoyed for a moment the slight confusion she'd aroused. She was well aware of the power of legend and manipulated hers to the full. Her eyes were the longest sighted, her ears caught the sound of a single chitin falling. Her spies were everywhere. She studied him. What a surprise he'd turned out to be, the least like her physically of them all, perhaps, but by far the ablest.

What a terrible shock lies in store for you, my boy, my tender flesh, my General. . . . For a moment the thought brought a sadness to her expression that puzzled him.

Time is short, young man, grow up quickly, be true and strong, for I will have great need of you before long. The crisis approaches quickly.

"And you wound up with lots of prisoners?" she said at last.

"Indeed, Madam, more than fifteen thousand in my pens at Cracked Rock. I have to get rid of them soon; the pens were not built to accommodate so many. I expect prices will fall on the Indenture Market as a result. But we also got a lot of useful equipment. My airstrip is so crowded with jet transports, I'm thinking of holding an auction."

Her pleasure was obvious. She touched his cheek very lightly with a white-gloved hand. "Excellent. I'll send Garth and Inzagawal to bid; we can always use some more transports. Continue, Commander. Farewell."

He snapped a salute but she was already gone, slipping through the security membrane into the dome.

Inside, at the long elliptical table, Fleur Kevilla sucked in her breath. There was enough tension in the air to generate ball lightning. All the chitin clans were represented. The eastern group, the Tammotos, the Robucks, the Chung, the Kuo, and the Kossodo had come; the west's Hoechsts, Clays, and Spreaks, too; and in the middle, dead opposite Fleur herself, sat Fair Fundan, matriarch of the biggest clan of all. Even Iso Rughaugh, the eccentric anchorite of Graveyard Valley, was present. He was engaged in earnest conversation with Ervil Spreak. The two of them, utterly bald, sat together and both had the witch glow of Pharamol abuse under their skins. Together they looked like ancient cadavers, mummified with horrible vigor. Neither had been a young man when the chitin drugs were discovered. Though they had regained vitality, they had not regained their youth.

Fleur noted the absence of senso fields among the clans. The privacy of senso, which was so ubiquitous among the powerful on the coasts, was absent here. Instead the clans favored chitin masks, jeweled antennas, golden scarab chitins, chains of silver chitin—the motif of the great insect was everywhere. Ebella Chung wore a purple chitin mask across her eyes; the antennae were gold and tipped with emeralds. Fair Fundan wore a neck choker of heavy gold chitin.

Fair looked perfectly composed, staring straight ahead, as if her thoughts were a thousand miles away.

Fleur, Tan, and Epsila, with their data terminal, were in the middle of the table. Ambassador Blake and Wermil were seated at one end of the ellipse, beside the empty chair reserved for the space admiral, Sigimir Enkov. Fleur had Epsila ask Blake if there was any reason to expect the admiral to be late as the meeting was due to begin in moments and protocol insisted that all be present on time. A mocking look from Wermil implied that he had arranged the seating to put distance between himself and Ambassador Blake and Fleur and her team. While she sat among the enemy, they would sit beside the space admiral.

She felt the flush in her cheeks and looked down quickly. Damn him! Damn both of them! The occasion was too important for such maneuvers.

"Blake says Enkov will be here on time," Epsila whispered in Fleur's ear, when she returned.

"He's supposed to be here now. What's going on?" Tan

caught her eye. She saw that he had a data link open to the *Gargarin* itself, in orbit above.

"He's leaving orbit now, just unshipped," Ubu whispered.

"Then he's late. This could be disastrous." Fleur looked up and thought desperately for something she could say to head off the explosion she saw coming. Fair Fundan beat her to it.

"I observe that we are all present except for the representative of the Space Forces. Is there an explanation for this?" Fair spoke lightly but there was no mistaking the dark fury in her expression.

Fair Fundan waited for no one! Such an insult was unimaginable now that the meeting time was slipping past second by second. Moreover it was pregnant with a very real danger. The irreplaceable elite of the planet were gathered in one room, vulnerable to attack. Fair had a sudden flush of fear that knotted her guts. What if the new admiral had merely set them up for this? Sitting there like a row of stuffed skrin waiting for a single missile . . . She refused to pursue the thought. The mere idea that her sacred person, her own flesh, should come under such danger turned her heart to ice.

With an oily smile of ingratiation, Blake started to say something so Fleur stopped her own reply in her throat. Let Blake put his head into that guillotine.

"Aah, we believe the admiral will be here very soon. There's bound to be some very good reason for the delay. After all, he is coming the greatest distance."

Fair was not impressed. "We were all advised of the time of the conference. If we can be here on time, why not the admiral with his infinitely greater resources?" Her tone grew menacing. "Furthermore, has it not occurred to you, Ambassador, that the admiral has it in his power to vaporize this piece of rock we're sitting on and that if he did he would eliminate in one stroke the heads of all the clans and the entire Earth Diplomatic Corps?" She paused to let that sink in. "I find his tardiness inexcusable. This conference represents a tempting target, and it was only on your sworn oath that all would attend punctually that I agreed to come in the first place."

Blake's expression was almost comic. The realization that the admiral could, at a stroke, remove most of the key pieces from the board hit home. Wermil hurriedly made for the door and the communications center. Blake struggled to say something and then looked desperately to Fleur. The other high-landers were getting edgy. They were on the point of bolting for their fliers, and once they did, there would never be an opportunity to repeat this unique conference.

Fleur met Blake's eyes. *Now, Andrej, now you need me?* Then she cleared her throat and waded in. "Ahem, why, why don't we begin the meeting anyway? I'm absolutely certain the admiral will be here any moment and will be able to catch up on the proceedings. Since the World Government is scheduled to speak first anyway and present its views, we can presume that he already knows most of what we'll be presenting to you today."

Her classic brows knitted, Fair's eyes bored into hers. Fleur felt terribly self-conscious and clumsy. Who was she to speak up and suggest things? But the meeting hinged on that moment and it might all evaporate. Fleur cleared her throat again, picked up the World Government position paper, and began to read from it.

Fair had considered running for her jet for a moment then dismissed the thought. If they were to die by the admiral's treachery, then it was likely that only seconds remained. A mob scramble to the fliers would not save them. To die like a panicked animal would be infinitely worse than to die calmly, sitting still. She would wait and endure that awful moment of vulnerability, but she vowed to learn from it. Never again would she offer an enemy such an opportunity.

She focused on the young woman dressed in her silly Earth Government uniform, a formal white pantsuit with fake epaulettes of rank. All these Earthers were alike—ignorant, greedy, and sexually incomprehensible. Still the young woman had a few wits about her in comparison to that dullard Blake. She'd been very persuasive in setting up the meeting and now she'd saved it—nobody had left his seat.

"We are all aware of the problem now confronting the worlds of the human hegemony," Fleur began, but the hubbub among the chieftains continued.

Fair spoke. "Perhaps it is time for us to listen to the views of the World Government." Her voice, no louder than Fleur's, cut the hubbub and left a silence.

Fleur looked at Fair Fundan then quickly looked down. She was too nervous even to consider the implications. Fair Fundan had actually interposed herself on behalf of the conference! Fleur forced herself to continue reading from the paper.

"The demand for chitin protein and the longevity drugs derived from it rises remorselessly. The supply is at best static. All attempts to grow or culture the chitin have failed. The insect does not develop properly in any other environment than what it is accustomed to here on Fenrille. The proteins themselves are vastly complicated molecules, assembled in ways unique to Vizier Chitin themselves. All attempts so far to synthesize these proteins groups have failed. It is now believed that Vizier Chitin modulate these proteins with a large and diverse group of enzymes secreted from glands beneath the mouth parts. The enzymes are altogether alien to human biochemistry, and how they work together to alter the immense protein chains is still the subject of intense scientific study. However, the constant inflation in the price of longevity drugs is sapping economic energies everywhere."

There were cautious nods around the table.

"The political pressures imposed by this equation have grown too intense to be resisted. The World Government of the Solar System is united on this subject. The popular demand, voiced throughout the Sol System, is for the outright annexation of Fenrille and the installation of a full military garrison."

Anger flooded many faces. Quermwyere snorted. "Preposterous."

Spreak interrupted loudly. "By damn, there already is a military garrison! What the hell else are Admiral Schranz's cruisers?"

Fleur waited for them to subside. They were aroused, that was natural enough, but thanks to Fair Fundan they weren't stampeding for the exit. She coughed and they sat back stoically to listen to the worst. As she was about to speak, Wermil entered and whispered to Blake. Andrej immediately looked greatly relieved.

"I'm sorry, Messire Spreak," Fleur began when the commotion had died down, "These are the briefing notes with the background information to the specific proposals of the World Government. I believe they envision a much larger fleet and a significant ground force."

And of course that meant that old Admiral Schranz and his three pot-bellied cruisers were heading for decommission and mothballs. A new factor had emerged, and the will of the elite of the home system was now to be exercised by Admiral Enkov.

Spreak toyed with a pencil, holding his anger in check with some effort as Fleur continued.

"There are many things to be negotiated, and the World Government has allowed for some flexibility in its proposals, I believe. However, in essence, they call for changes in the production and distribution of longevity drugs. They calculate that any other course will lead to increasing social instability throughout the hegemony."

Fleur now set off on a detour, reading from her own notes. She had to make them understand how powerful were the forces arrayed against them. It was essential that these proud families, independent of any government for centuries, bend before the wind that was rising and accept a negotiated settlement.

"The population of the home system is now estimated at seventeen billion. Of these, eight billion inhabit the Earth, five billion live on the outer satellites, and the rest are spread over several thousand space habitats, moons, and asteroids. Support for the World Government's position on longevity drugs has allowed the Expansionist faction of the Earth Social Union to gain control.

"New space fleets are under construction. Exploration of star systems deeper within the galactic arm has begun. A more advanced spacegoing race is believed to exist in the direction of Carina. This unanticipated danger has brought greater unity to the World Government than has been the case for centuries.

"It is estimated that more than a billion people in the home system now consume Optimol or one of the other longevity drugs derived from chitin protein. It's fortunate that the dosages required are so small, or so many could never be supported on the current supply.

"Of that billion, some two hundred million, the elites of every world and habitat—are now entering their eighteenth and nineteenth decades of life. Without their daily doses of longevity drugs they cannot live. Thus their desire for these drugs springs from a source familiar to us all, the survival urge. It is fierce, it is passionate, and it will brook no frustration."

Fleur took a deep breath.

"The World Government proposals are concerned with two key areas—the production of the chitin insect and the marketing of the longevity drugs. The World Government believes that the production problem requires a change in the ownership of the means of production. At present it is monopolized by the highland families. Ordinarily the government believes there would be no case for interfering in the affairs of said families, but the control of the source of the longevity drugs on which so many millions of people now depend for daily life has become too crucial to be left in the hands of such a small and unrepresentative section of the human race."

The faces were dark and thunderous. Spreak was pink with suppressed rage, his heavy, thick-fingered hands busily shredding sheets of hardcopy. Hoechst was angrily shaking his head. Rognius Butte snarled something to him under his breath and they both nodded grimly. Fair Fundan, however, just stared straight ahead as if to indicate that she was bored and wanted to get on with the negotiations.

"Therefore the World Government proposes a plan of shared ownership and management of the means of the production of raw chitin proteins. A detailed discussion of the plan appears on pages three and four of the briefing notes. I would like to add that it has already been approved by the Centauran habitats, the Tau Ceti Plenary Assembly, and the parliament of New Zion, Epsilon Eridani. In effect, the entire human race is looking to us for a solution to this problem, the most acute that our species has faced since the early nuclear era."

As they turned to read the details, angry mutterings and explosive oaths could be heard from all parts of the table. Particularly when they read proposals to divest them of an increasing percentage of their holdings year by year.

"In the first year, the families are each to give up one tenth of their harvest. The funds from this will be used to start new schools for chitin talkers. The talker force must be increased so that production can be increased, too. The WG is convinced that both increases must go hand in hand, in part because of an expected unemployment problem on the coasts.

"In the second and third years an additional five percent will be given up. Public managers, appointed from the new chitin schools, will join the families in managing the valleys and working to extend production. A massive research program focused on ways of increasing yields and extending nest ranges will begin.

"In the fourth, fifth, and sixth years, an additional ten percent will be given up and sections of the valleys will be deeded over to the public domain. Compensation will be negotiated with the families affected.

"At the same time the WG program envisions a complete disarmament program for the planet. The warbands in the coastal cities will be broken up and all weapons will be confiscated. The fein armies in the highlands will likewise give up their weapons, and a suitable price will be negotiated with the highland families to compensate them for the cost of these weapons."

The chieftains were sullen, eyes glowering. The syndicate men were equally unhappy. Fleur grimly plowed on, determined to lay it all out before them. No wishful thinking or rejection of the problem would make it go away. It was a hideously painful nettle to be grasped, but grasp it they must.

"In the matter of the marketing of longevity drugs, the World Government finds an even more urgent need for reorganization." The syndicate heads went up.

"At present the system is chaotic. Several layers of middlemen exist between the raw proteins shipped to the coast and the drugs and concentrates that finally go offplanet for shipment to the home system. The supply is diverted for the grossly indulgent uses of the coastal cities. Far too much of this scarce resource is being consumed on Fenrille. One estimate—which I should add is often quoted in governing circles in the WG— puts the consumption of longevity drugs by the fifteen million human inhabitants of Fenrille at fully one third of the entire production. Another fifteen percent is lost to the black market and is smuggled out of the system. Organized crime reaps a tremendous harvest, and in consequence the inflation in the home system becomes uncontrollable."

Asgood Wythe looked upset; his assistants were anxiously scanning the details of the plan.

"The World Government intends to control and police the markets for chitin proteins. Supply contracts will be issued to producers and their deliveries will be made to a WG depot for processing and storage before shipment to the home system. The chitin markets will be closed to all outsiders; the whole elaborate structure of brokers, dealers, and auctions will be dismantled. The WG believes that a saving can be achieved of at least thirty percent of the chitin now lost to waste and the black market. This in itself will help to break the inflationary spiral now gripping the home system."

Quermwyere could contain himself no longer. "When does the World Government envisage this takeover of the chitin markets? Is it aware of the panic that will ensue, of the hoarding that will take place?" The banker's outrage was evident in every quivering inch of his outlandish bulk.

Fleur did her best to sound sympathetic. "The precise details are to be negotiated and agreed upon later. Our job today is to examine the proposals and listen to suggestions and counter-proposals. The WG is aware of the deep differences that exist on these questions but it repeats its warning that the situation impels it to act. There can be no doubt that if it must, it will resort to force to bring about change."

Fair had expected no less; she too understood the dilemma facing the home system governing class. But her understanding did not lead to any sympathy for them or the rest of the short-lived hordes of the home system. Fair's view of the universe had shifted in the course of the centuries of her life, and the future she envisioned for herself and her family did not include the rest of the race.

The tense, angry little conversations now going on around the table were suddenly drowned in a shattering roar of jets and a sonic boom that cracked across Stroin's Rock like a gigantic whiplash. The admiral had arrived.

In the command post, the radar scopes were suddenly fogged with interference. All electromagnetic systems were jammed and probed by heavy sensors while orbital fighters streaked overhead at 7,000 mph, looking down on the circling Spreak and Fundan jets like raptors considering a flock of pigeons. Behind the fighters dropped a stub-nose pinnace with booster jets powerful enough to lift it off Saturn.

Lavin watched the pinnace's heat shield burn a red streak through the upper atmosphere before the craft fired its retros and began to descend on a pillar of flame, cracking the first few parachutes, amid a roar of thunder.

In the last few months before touchdown, the entire rock was shaking from the colossal thrust being exerted by the 150-ton pinnace's engines. The air filled with hot gas and dust and pieces of debris blown out of the jungle. The fein held their ears and turned their faces from the fumes.

For a few minutes after the engines cut out, a complete silence reigned. Even the forest animals had been frightened into an unnatural quiet. The pinnace's upper body was a fat cigar-shaped tube. It rested on a bulky cradle, twice its size, that housed the engines. The heat shield was scorched down to the metal in some places.

A door snapped open halfway up the length of the upper pod. An armature unfolded and exposed several landing lines. Immediately bulky shapes dropped swiftly to the ground on the end of the lines. They bounced oddly on impact, like springs, and though they were humanoid only in general outline, Lavin knew at once what the tall, bulky things were. "Space Marines," he whispered to Ng Tung.

They fanned out in a protective pattern around the base of the ship, and fascinated, Lavin watched them move. The men and women inside the armored suits were having to apply considerable skill in taking very short, almost human strides. The suits were more used to 100-meter leaps and bounds and were difficult to control in an environment of light gravity, no acceleration, and light atmosphere. The marines took mincing little steps, servomotors geared way back and the big power units shut to a trickle.

Above their heads another bulky object was swung from the pinnace and lowered to the ground. This was only the second fighting robot Lavin had ever seen; the first one had been in a museum. It stood more than nine feet tall and was generally humanoid. The cylindrical torso was studded with gunports and other weapon-delivery systems. Three recognizable arm assemblies were folded away into slots on the barrel-like torso. The head resembled a giant clamshell except that the upper surface was spiked with antennas. As the Abzen watched, it swiveled and all the electronics in the command post jolted as aggressive sensors scanned them.

Ng Tung cursed softly. "So these demons are finally turning up here. They warned us of this."

Lavin snorted. The fein disposition to see demons still extended to new machinery, even after three centuries of alliance with humans.

"No, that's no demon, that's just a fighting robot. Deadly

enough—I'll bet it's a lot quicker than it looks. It's got every weapon system in the armory built into it. Those pipes at the back are for laying gas, I'd say, the tubes on the chest are small arms, and so on."

The surfaces of the robot were a glossy black-green, intersected and segmented by its flexons and weapons. The clamshell spun, cameras recording the scene in detail; among the megabytage of other data, the thing recorded the pulse rates of every man, woman, and fein in line of sight.

The fein were just as curious about the machine, and the Space Marines. A number of vulgar ideas began to circulate immediately concerning the thing's reproductive and excretory processes. That it might be dangerous they found hard to believe—it seemed too large and obvious a target to be much of a battlefield threat. More activity above their heads led to the appearance of the naval security detail, which floated down on landing lines.

Sigimir Enkov, First Admiral of the Fenrille Fleet, Captain of the Battlecruiser, WGS *Gargarin*, stepped confidently off the platform and rode down the cargo line behind his bodyguard detail. He wore the simple, dark-blue naval uniform with no decorations other than the pair of silver stars, Order of Chang, which marked his victories at Callisto and Neptune. He wore no senso mask, he made no concessions to the polite habits of the old Solar System. He had no need any longer to hide his real self. Let them all see for themselves.

He floated down into the space right behind the wedge of guards. An odd apprehension had filled in the air. He could sense the uncertainty in the detail—they were uneasy. Crack fighters every one of them, but all Space Marines felt better in the shell. Out in the open, with their crab-white hides and extended skeletal structures exposed, they felt naked and strangely vulnerable.

The source of the unease in the guard was facing them, a full company of fein, drawn up in squads, at ease, and very curious indeed, whispering among themselves despite calls for quiet from the neilks.

So, he thought, these are the fein. At least I get to see them in the flesh. A variety of pelt colors and markings caught his eye immediately and then his attention shifted to the well-worn equipment they carried, the scuffed gunmetal, the dust and grime on webbing and harness. Their stance was relaxed, inquisitive but hardly parade-ground tight. Yet their formation and discipline was obviously second nature, honed and true.

They were magnificent creatures, tall handsome animals. Sigimir thought briefly of the Transylvanian mastiffs that Chairman Wei was so fond of. Extraordinary, he marveled. The tapes and holos had somehow never brought the reality of the aliens home to him quite so vividly.

An officer, a young man in fatigues that were quite as scruffy as those of his fein, stepped forward with a crisp salute. He was joined by two fein, one with a green and white cap and other insignia of rank and another, considerably larger, who edged close behind the man's back.

Sigimir considered for a moment how it would go if he were matched against such a beast. He would be the quicker of the two, oh so very much faster inside, but what of the strength factor? What if the fein were to land a blow?

The young man's face showed shock and disbelief at the sight of the landing party. He'd never seen bioenhanced space crew before. Let them gape, thought Sigimir, let them grow accustomed to their new masters. When the young man had finished introducing himself and his unit, Sigimir replied calmly with thanks.

"I thank you very much for your welcome, Commander. On behalf of myself and the crew of the WGS *Gagarin* may I say that your unit here is a very impressive one. I hope to become more familiar with the fein now that I've finally taken up this posting."

To the fein officer he spoke in halting feiner, repeating the little message he'd memorized. "I have wondered for a long time, over many light-years, what the fein of Fenrille would be like. Now that we have met for the first time I must say that I am honored and that I find your troops to be even more impressive than I'd imagined."

Ng Tung was surprised to hear the admiral-creature speak in the tongue of the ay fein. Few humans knew it well enough to speak it. He replied with ritual courtesy while still faintly astonished by the physical appearance of the new humans.

Their torsos, while humanlike, were elongated, more like the fein, but the muscles of the limbs were bunched tightly around the joints, the hips were narrow, and in general these

80

humans were taller than the types the fein were familiar with. Yet it was the peculiarities of the skin that were most unsettling. Semitransparent but clouded and off-white, blood vessels were visible beneath and a speckling of red nodules formed along chin lines, brows, and around the ears.

Arched ridges and deep, fluted grooves framed the faces, human faces but bleak, hard, minimal, with slits over the eyes and lipless mouths that were drawn tight over beaked jaws.

The bodies of the new humans were filled with enormous tension. Ng read the signs of combat training and something else, something that chafed just beneath a hysteric level of battle lust.

Once the admiral had reached the dome, the bodyguard detail drew itself up beside the entrance and waited at attention. In the command post, Lavin turned to Ng Tung. "Well, my friend, what do you think of the new admiral?"

The yellow eyes rolled and Ng Tung's ear tufts stood on end.

8

THE RIPPLE OF SHOCK THAT ORBITED THE TABLE'S LONG ACRYL
ellipse was amusingly gratifying to Sigimir Enkov. After so
many years of politesse, wearing masks and senso to disguise
his spaceflesh while among the elite of the home system, it
was enjoyable to emerge in his own identity and watch them
shiver.

It took the room a long minute to calm down. Fleur had
heard all the rumors concerning bioenhanced space crew but
the reality of the admiral was still unnerving. For a moment
or two she gazed, open mouthed, at the red nodules and the
white flesh with its hard planes, then she recovered herself and
looked away. Ambassador Blake made the introductions, and
then the admiral spoke. He made no apology for his lateness,
nor did he allude to the shock his appearance had produced.

Recovering poise swiftly, Fair Fundan broke in, decidedly
unamused. "As has already been placed on the record, we
protest your late arrival. The protocols established a precise
time of arrival. All were to be here, without exception, several

82

minutes ago. We deserve an explanation." Minutes of fear, never knowing if the burst would come, bringing death.

Enkov was taken aback. They were all angry, muttering among themselves, shaking the barbarous jeweled masks and helmets they wore. He looked down at Ambassador Blake. A breakdown in communications had occurred, something in Blake's watery eyes and limpid flesh bespoke Funkshun addiction; was he the weak link?

"You were not briefed by the ambassador? The delay was due to an unfortunate problem we had in matching orbits with a supply tanker. I was late into the rehydration tank in consequence—but, Ambassador Blake, you were informed earlier. Couldn't you have briefed everyone?"

All eyes turned to Blake, who wore a rather foolish smile. "Aah, yes, I see. You refer to the message we received this morning. It used a new key. We were unable to decipher it, so we requested a repeat broadcast but your ship was below the radio horizon by then."

A frown creased the thick white skin of Enkov's bulletlike head. "The key was sent to your office three IS time periods ago. I personally ordered it." The admiral's voice had developed an ugly undercurrent.

Blake squirmed, swallowed.

Fresh shock circled the table. Fleur was mortified. The World Government Embassy was left looking utterly foolish by the revelation of incompetence. With a twinge of disgust, she realized that the keys must have been in the top-priority cable that Blake had refused to let her see the day before. *Too busy to distribute the new keys, were you, Andrej? Too damned complacent, too soaked in Funkshun and Pharamol to even know what day it is.*

Blake snarled something at Wermil, who looked for a moment as if he might snarl right back, then he swallowed and accepted the blame. A cold angry moment passed before Fair said, "Well, it appears that communications on the World Government side need to be improved. Perhaps the admiral should launch an investigation into the efficiency of the Sx Coast Embassy. However"—she cleared her throat—"let's forget this matter for now and get on with the meeting. We've heard the meat of the World Government proposals, as laid out so charmingly by the deputy ambassador"—Fleur blushed—"and now I believe it is our turn to reply."

Fair herself was to speak first. She kneaded her temples for a moment, suppressing her rage and concentrating on playing out the hand she held. The currents of fate drew tight around old Fenrille. Many dangers glinted in the shadows. The future of Clan Fundan might soon be in the balance.

"It is more than five hundred Earth years, now, since my grandfather, Dane Fundan, forsook the home system, driven out by the threat of Earth's Space Fleets. The Fundans had always been in the fore of the advance into space, but each time we settled and established ourselves, Earth came after us. In the asteroids we became wealthy, but our wealth was taken by force of arms. We fled to Uranus and built the floating cities like great Barbuncle. We used the energies of the outer planets to build the first interstellar transports and then, with 9,054 individuals aboard, 114 families—including every clan represented here today—we left the home system. We'd had enough of being pushed around by the corrupt Earth government. Our colony was numerous enough to be genetically stable, we sought a new world, far enough away from the old to protect us from ever being attacked again by the greedy home world. That's why our forebears chose to come here, to Beni. Because it was a G-type star and because it was more than fifty light-years from Sol—enough to discourage pursuit. We did not intend to become a colony of Earth; we sought total independence from the rest of the human race."

Heads were nodding, Spreak's very vigorously. Ervil had found a rare moment of complete agreement with Fair Fundan.

"When our ancestors arrived here, they found a heavenlike world but a perplexing one. Innumerable similarities to Earth— oceans and blue skies and great jungles and mountains—but this world has secrets that we at first could not grasp. We tried to tame it, we sought to kill the forest and farm the land. Of course we were doomed. The woodwose killed us, the chitin ate our farmers and our crops, the blood fungi and the sawflies killed even more of us. Even building a fixed structure like a house was dangerous because of walking trees and woodwose. In the end, those of us who'd retained the technology were preparing to move back offplanet, and then we discovered the secret of the chitin.

"The lovely water-planet that Dane Fundan had discovered turned into a personal hell for my grandfather, and he died before the chitin drugs were discovered and changed everything. But we learned, yes indeed, by blood and sacrifice we learned, and we harvested the chitin Vizier Mass so that we could live as long as we might want to. And, indeed, the fein took pity on us and offered us room to live among them in the highlands, and we forsook the coasts and the swamps."

Fair sighed. Born just before the migration, she remembered very little of the earlier life, but her generation had inherited the paradise that poor Dane and the others had so misunderstood.

"We lived with the fein, in the fein way, as hunters and gatherers, and, by the by, we gathered from the highland chitin, which is much safer to deal with than the mature nests of the jungle.

"Our mistake was in communicating the discovery of the chitin drugs to the home system. I fought against it, but younger heads prevailed then. They saw an opportunity of trade with the home system and of improving our technology without having to establish an industrial base. They imagined there might be benefits for people in other stellar systems from longevity drugs. They argued that centuries had gone by—in relative time—in the old system and the Earth's greedy ways must have changed."

The admiral was studying Fair Fundan carefully. The savage clansfolk were remarkable indeed.

"Alas, longevity is precious and the chitin drugs are perhaps the only thing that could have drawn humanity after us so soon. Within a hundred years our skies were filled with ships loaded with newcomers. Their cities rose overnight on the coasts, and armies of greedy, bloodthirsty human predators began to raid our valleys, kill the fein, rob us for the drugs—a hundred other atrocities, until it seemed we must be wiped out, along with the fein." Fair was breathing hard, the hatred thickened her voice.

"Finally when we were back to back in the ruins of our valleys, we armed the fein and developed our own war technology. We turned the tide and drove the vermin from our mountains, and since then we have denied anyone access to them. We have become a society of warriors. Every half year, with the monsoon, they come again and we fight them off or die in the attempt. Our hunting lands are soaked in the blood of our fein and our children."

The chieftains were aglow. Fair had them aroused.

"And so we discovered the secret of the chitin and paid with our lives for that knowledge. To keep out the raiders we have waged war for centuries. We are linked to our lands through blood. Except that now the home system puts forth its strength once more and demands that we give up our sacred land. Demands control of the chitin harvest. Demands that we surrender to Earth's authority again—and for what? So that the same corrupt elite of the home system that drove us out so long ago can control the chitin for its own ends."

Fair paused. Fleur thought she looked like an empress about to send a would-be usurper to the block. Then unexpectedly she softened.

"However, my answer to your proposals is not entirely negative. We live in the real world, too. We have traded chitin for survival for centuries. There are things we need, and there is chitin which you need. Perhaps we can increase the yields. Certainly we'd be glad to help in policing the coastal markets and ending the horrific wastage that goes on there. We might deal directly with the World Government and thus bypass the chitin markets altogether." On this note she finished.

Quermwyere grinned, his jowls quivering slightly. They all thought they could get along without the marketplace, thought they could fix the price of eternity just like *that*. Thought they could keep the corruption at bay. To himself he sniggered delightedly. What fools they were, what monstrous, utter fools!

Fleur was also delighted, but for very different reasons. Fair Fundan was clearly out to see what play there was in the current situation. She would negotiate! That in itself was an enormous step forward from the original clan positions. Fleur looked down the table to where Blake sat. He seemed uncomfortable with the close company of the admiral. Andrej wasn't having a good summit meeting. Publically humiliated, he'd retreated into a Funkshun trance. He and Wermil had made some bad miscalculations, the admiral had plainly been something of a surprise. There didn't seem to be anything corruptible about the new Space Forces commander.

However, Andrej had also forgotten his role as moderator.

Fair Fundan had finished speaking, and he was sunk in reverie. Hurriedly Fleur cleared her throat and jumped into the breach.

"Well, we must thank Fair Fundan for presenting her proposal. As she pointed out, the roots of our current predicament go a long way back into history and we should bear in mind that history is really a record of negotiations between groups seeking solutions to their problems. Indeed it is the World Government's belief that compromise is possible, here as in so many other apparently insoluble confrontations."

Fair looked relieved that someone had taken the initiative. That fool Blake was incapable of action. Fleur thought to extend a further courtesy of protocol. As the admiral had been late, perhaps it would be wise to offer Spreak the opportunity to speak next.

"Messire Spreak, have you anything you would wish to add?"

Ervil Spreak was in the act of absentmindedly slipping a grain of five-star Pharamol, valued at around #3,000, onto the end of his tongue. He let the grain dissolve and enjoyed a surge as it rejuvenated his ancient nervous system once again.

"I would only care to add certain specifics. For instance, the things that we need are mostly in the realm of advanced technology. For far too long we have been planetbound, and currently we are denied direct access to space. Having to go through a host of middlemen to get a load on a shuttle is not only expensive but frustrating. We need shuttles, that's definite. In fact, we need to rebuild our spacegoing capacity. In the area of defensive equipment, I could give you a list in a few moments of the items we would be interested in negotiating for, in particular orbital fighters." Ervil rubbed his big hands together, grinned like a shark. Fleur thought how odd the human hand was without fingernails. How simple and direct it was. Ol' Ervil doesn't want that much now, he just wants orbital fighters. And then what? Battlecruisers? NAFAL transports? One thing the WG was determined to keep was the edge it held over the chitin families with control of the spacelanes. Those remarkable people weren't about to be allowed loose again. The WG wanted them brought to heel, firmly and speedily.

Quermwyere was signaling his desire to speak next. It would further change the agenda, so Fleur looked to the admiral for an objection but found none. Indeed Enkov was eager to hear more views from the table, especially after Fair's preposterous account of her bandit family's flight from justice in the home system. Sigimir wasn't really sure yet whether these people were serious. They were certainly fanciful. He hadn't seen such a show of ostentation in decades.

"Messire Quermwyere," Fleur said. The banker looked up, piggy eyes like bullets in his huge head.

"Why, thank you, Deputy Ambassador," he began, directing another clear snub to Blake. "I would very much like to reply to some of the accusations that have been so wildly thrown around here although in truth I have to agree with the accuracy of some of Lady Fundan's descriptions of the past. However, the situation is one that has been repeated over and over again throughout human history, and those of us who take a long-term view"—he paused and looked around the table for a moment—"believe that control of the means of production is inevitably going to spread out as more of the human races comes to be represented in this vital area. However, there are problems—not only with the sharing of production control but also in the markets where the prices and supplies are determined. In fact, there are problems in every area. But at least we have a system that delivers a great quantity of longevity drugs. Not enough, we're told—increase the supply. Do away with the middlemen, clean up the system. Has anyone considered for a moment what the economic effects on the coastal cities would be if the markets were closed? Or if the Chitin Banks were closed and the war bands forcibly disarmed? Why, the very least of your problems would be an outrageous unemployment problem. The economy would be shattered and the whole delicate fabric that keeps those remarkable cities glittering and alive on the edge of Fenrille's implacable eco-systems will come tumbling down. Without the coastal cities, how will anyone refine and export the chitin proteins? Are you aware that on the Sx Coast alone twenty thousand laboratories are involved in advanced chitin research, seeking the synthesis. In the highlands there are, I believe, no more than fifty such establishments. And, without the banks, who will provide venture capital? Who will supply the highland clans with all those things they need but cannot make for themselves? Everything from bandages to aircraft comes from coastal factories built on sandbars or vertical cliffs." The banker let them think about that for a moment and then in a lower voice he continued. "And perhaps most important of all, who will take care of those millions of active men who now belong to the warbands?"

Indeed, Fleur thought, who will take care of them? The elaborate social structure of the coastal cities depended on the chitin just as clearly as did the highland clans. If the summit were to be democratic about it then it would obviously have to be the clans that gave ground. They were only a few thousands. Not even as many as the population of the Sx Coast. But of course they were not going to be democratic about it. Fair Fundan and the others were neither democrats nor fascists, republicans or socialists—they were aristocrats and quite content with the title.

Pull out the rug on the warbands? Again Fleur wondered if it was possible. How did the admiral envision enforcing such directives? And essentially, Fleur knew, it would all come down to that. Could the *Gagarin* and the Space Marines handle the coastal cities and regulate the trade? Or were they more likely to take on the clans and pit Space Marines against the fein armies? If the WG took control of the source of production, it took control of the problem.

That was all Fair was waiting for, the earliest signs of which way the blow would fall. Fleur realized this in a rush. Fair was desperate, the clans were in a deadly trap. The status quo had long been threatened by the sheer weight of numbers on the coasts and suddenly there were Space Marines to contend with as well.

The other chieftains had their say, Rognius Butte lowering a finger at one point to aim at the admiral like a weapon while he roared. "Anti-Christ, you represent the godless communistic Earth! We recognize you for what you are—a representative of Satan."

Fleur reflected that the clans did have some justification in feeling abused. During the wars of resources their ancestors had been harshly treated. It was now their tragedy that the drugs which made them so powerful drew the World Government after them once more.

Finally it was Sigimir Enkov's turn to speak. "I have absorbed the data presented so far, and I will deal with their proposals in a moment. But first I will address the problem of the antisocialist noises we have heard here. These antisocial whines have been heard before, of course, but that has never stopped the fulfillment of the expressed will of the people of Earth as laid down by the World Government, the people's instrument. The World Government is the supreme representative of the human race everywhere. It is nonsensical to suggest otherwise."

Ervil Spreak exploded. "Then by hot bloody damn you can tell me what use that is. I get no protection from your World Government when the warbands attack. I've never seen your damn ships around then."

Admiral Enkov waited a moment, shifting mental gears, ignoring Spreak. "We are engaged in a program of military buildup made essential by the discovery of the PBL lifeform in Carina. Since the stars associated with the PBL lifeform are more than one thousand light-years distant, we do not expect contact within the next couple of centuries. However, the PBL lifeform is definitely advanced and expansionist. We have just enough time to get our economy on a less inflationary track and arm ourselves before that inevitable clash occurs. The inflation must be broken, the supply of longevity drugs must be increased."

Gavin Ofgarbade, a slender hawklike chieftain, interjected. "So you're telling us that because of a supposed threat from an alien lifeform more than a thousand light-years away, you have the right to steal our lands, bring in the coastal scum, and slaughter the fein? The fein are an alien race as well, intelligent, much older than humanity, with much to teach us. They will be destroyed because of your fears of another alien race far away? This is madness."

Gavin's eyes were blazing, his big hands bunched into fists.

"We digress, but I will respond." Enkov cleared his throat, looked up. "We have no intention of destroying the fein. If necessary, they will be put on reserves, but they need not be killed."

Nobody in the room believed him. They'd all lived with the reality of human ways, they'd seen the rugs of fein fur, the gladiator shows on Sx Coast TV.

The admiral was oblivious to the tide of feeling around him. "So, to increase the supply there must be changes. You've been given our proposals. They are hardly ungenerous—indeed they are so liberal that it was a tremendous struggle just to get them accepted in the World Government Council. There will not be summary takeovers of the highlands. Nor will there be arrests for war crimes alleged by the citizens of the coastal cities."

That was a bad mistake. Fleur saw the hackles rise.

"Property will be paid for," the admiral proceeded as if describing boat drill. "Each year there will be a larger public share of production. We will control the chitin throughout the cycle, we will deny the waste that now so heavily depletes the offworld supply. As the WG share grows, the capitalistic markets will wither away. Eventually, of course, the clans will lose control of the production process and indeed there may have to be dispersals and relocations from the valleys. However, the World Government has authorized me to construct the technology required to alter the environment to allow clearance of sections of the forest and the establishment of agriculture and a more rational form of society than now obtains on Fenrille."

"Hot damn!" Ervil Spreak said, which summed up the feeling among the clans exactly.

"But, as I said before, the clans will be compensated and will be able to buy new lands from the clearances and begin an agricultural pattern of life. They will exchange their present precarious position for the solid, dignified joys of farming within the humanly uplifting socialist system."

Rognius Butte was purple with rage, but "Godless communistic scum" was all he could splutter.

Fleur flicked a glance toward Quermwyere and Asgood Wythe. They seemed equally devastated by the exchanges. The admiral wasn't winning many friends. She looked over to Blake and Wermil. They looked helpless, like cadavers, flesh already whitened on the coffin. Then she knew the meeting wasn't going to hold together, it was too fragile for the heat of the passions being unleashed. Enkov's bluntness was coming much too soon. The admiral was probably the hottest thing to happen in planetary space war since it began, but at diplomacy he was less than adequate. Unless his lack of subtlety was deliberate . . . The thought that he might want to sabotage the negotations did not bode well for the future. The loss of months of painstaking work was disheartening, too, and the thought of how hard it might be to convene another meeting was not something she even wanted to contemplate.

Fair Fundan was still curious though, and she broke in since Rognius was too upset to continue. "Ah, Admiral—earlier on I mentioned that there was a certain amount of flexibility in our position, and this remains true. I wonder if you would give us some reaction to those proposals. If we can increase the production of chitin proteins, what form of negotiation might be open to us? For the matter of trade, can we negotiate a direct contract? What are we being offered for these increasing percentages of our crop that are to be taken by the World Government?"

Again Admiral Enkov seemed to ruminate on the questions before replying. "The most convenient method would be for the Fenrille Authority, which has been authorized and set up by the WG, to distribute deeds and titles to the new lands that will be cleared for agricultural use. These will act as bonds, assuring the holder that the land will be his or hers when cleared. Thus the firm agricultural future of the clans will ensured."

"Does he think anyone's buying this?" Tan Ubu whispered to Fleur. She shook her head sadly. There was a general sense of unreality around the table.

Fair wore an amused smile. "Let me get this straight. You're offering us notes of promise on jungle land that you intend to clear of the natural forest and turn into farms. And we're to become sturdy yeopersons of the soil and accept our lot? I see. You realize that that's not exactly the sort of thing we came out here to hear from you. You do, don't you?"

Enkov attempted to sound a cheerful note. "Whole provinces of corn and vines will be planted. Fenrille will be a garden world for settlers."

"There'll be woodwose at the bottom of your gardens, though," someone said and there was a titter of mirth.

"I think you've forgotten a whole lot of things," Fair said in a cold hard voice. "Very good reasons account for why no farmers exist on this planet except for the coastal scum who cultivate fish and kelpweed. If you keep on this course, you'll discover why there's no farming here, and that may be a hard lesson. The ecosystems will resist you; they are implacable. To survive here human beings must coexist with systems that have been in place for a very long time. Don't think for a minute that because this world resembles the Earth that it behaves like the Earth. A magic runs deep within this planet's heart that is unlike anything in Earthly experience. You see, Earth is a young world, our race is in its infancy. Fenrille is old, very old indeed. If you delve deep enough and damage the environment it will awaken, and then heaven itself could hardly save you, or us, or the entire human race. You tamper with things here that you do not understand. Until you do, I advise you most strongly to do nothing."

The admiral interrupted with a dismissive wave of the hand. "There must be changes to accommodate the growing populations here. We estimate that Fenrille could support several billion human beings even with only partial forest clearances. Preserves for wildlife and the fein would be set aside. Of course the ecosystems were too much for your grandfathers. They failed because they were disunited, working alone or in family groups. If we look back to the thought of Chairman Mao Tsetung, great socialist inspiration of the twentieth century, we can see how the common idea gave great strength to the people's efforts to free China—a vast area of the Asian continent—from drought and flood. Before the application of the people's entire effort, they were only able to drill shallow wells and erect small dams. The communes drilled deep wells and built enormous dams. Never again were drought and flood great. So it shall be with the jungle here. My ships will position lunetta reflectors in orbit above the forest to starve the trees of light. Our people will work together to cut the forest and clear it of pests and wild beasts. Then we will plant together in peace."

Fair stifled her impatience. She still hadn't heard the one thing, the telltale sign. "Excuse me, all that's all very well, but what if we say that we don't want to know about your pieces of paper for your proposed agricultural clearances? What if we say we want technology, in particular we want boosters, shuttles, spacegoing vessels?"

"That is a foolish request." A cold look entered the admiral's eyes.

"Foolish or not, *that's* what we want to talk about. If you're prepared to deal with us on a sensible, rational basis, then we're prepared to cooperate to eliminate the waste you complain of in the coastal cities. We'll funnel our production to you directly, and you'll control the market. What you do with it then is your business, but we'd at least expect some help in suppressing the warbands that attack us so relentlessly. That should increase the offworld supply by a hundred percent." Fair found a smile to go with her offer, a considerable effort.

Quermwyere snorted in disbelief and earned a withering look of contempt from Fair. *Slug!* Didn't he see what turned on the moment? The future of worlds, of galaxies, most certainly the future of the human race. Fair suppressed a shiver. This was the great crisis foreseen, the time of their flight into the shadows, as prophesied by the acoloytes of Distant Claw. Danger stalked the family's footsteps; great care was necessary.

"Your offer of cooperation has been noted. However, the earlier plan which was mentioned—extension of control in production matching extension into the market—is the one we have chosen to proceed with."

Spreak erupted. "What d'you mean 'chosen to proceed with'? We're here to negotiate, but you've laid your demands on the table and now you're saying 'that's it; accept them as they are.' You don't sound to me like you're negotiating."

Admiral Enkov appeared to digest this, but the hard lines of his face were stretched in an unhappy frown. "Changes have to be made. The program has been stated. There has been discussion, and now the program shall be implemented. What more can be said?"

"You have to be joking with us, eh?" Ernst Hoechst said. "This can't be your serious proposals, just this bare bone of promised lands in the never never, when you can manage to clear the jungle and kill the *gigans* trees. Actually I can't believe that the World Government would wish to insult us so openly."

"Yes, tell us it's all a joke," Fair said, appearing to fall into the spirit of things, sure now that the blow would be against the clans.

"No, no, no joke is intended. My pardons if I haven't made myself clear enough. Perhaps it's the wild unreality of your beautiful world. I'm more accustomed to shipboard reasoning, if you see what I mean. I meant no joke—the program has been evaluated thoroughly. It originated in the Social Technology Institute and it offers the maximum benefits to the greatest number of people while compensating the highland clans and removing the corruption of the capitalistic drug market. So"—Enkov leaned forward and spread his big hands; the red nodules were stark against the crab skin—"it is a good plan and, as has been mentioned, we are empowered to put it into effect. In fact I would like to get started on it right away. Can we move on now to discussion of other aspects of the proposals? For example, I would like a schedule set up today for the deployment of observers and intelligence officers in your valleys at the earliest possible moment. There is much to be done, a lot to absorb, the data flow will be enormous."

Spreak was laughing openly. Hoechst joined him. So, Fleur noted, had Quermwyere. They were almost hysterical. She groaned inwardly. All her work, the months of painstaking negotiations, was gone now. Lost, foundered on this unknown factor, the ponderous space admiral and the brute inflexibility of his positions. The demands in themselves might have provided the basis for initial negotiations, leading slowly to cooperation with the clan families. But *this*, this, she saw bleakly, was the end.

Now Fair spoke while stabbing the table in front of her with an angry index finger. "Well, this is no joke either. We completely reject your proposals, they are of no use to us whatsoever. You have our offer of negotiations, and you know the areas that would be mutually interesting to discuss. But we—at least I—have no intention of remaining here at intolerable risk to listen to any more of this nonsense." She rose to leave. Spreak and Hoechst and the others were also getting to their feet.

"Halt! No one is to leave the room. The meeting is not finished. It is forbidden to leave the room," the admiral yelled at parade-ground volume. *"Anyone leaving the room will be arrested."*

Fleur gasped and the clansfolk looked around in alarm. Spreak's hand suddenly sprouted a tiny steel needle, which he held at the ready. Fair pulled away from the table hurriedly and made for the exit.

"Stop, no one is to leave," Admiral Enkov bellowed.

"I'm sorry, Admiral, but I don't think anyone is listening to you," Fleur said quietly.

He snapped around and there was a dreadful malevolence in his gaze. "This meeting was a mistake. Harsher measures will be necessary, I see. I repeat my order: No one may leave or the Space Marines will arrest them and take control of the area."

"There are more than four thousand armed fein out there, Admiral," Fleur spoke in a hushed voice. "Do you think a dozen Space Marines can handle that? Think about this very carefully before you say anything more."

The clan chiefs moved to the exit and ripped the membrane open. The admiral's face betrayed a fierce internal struggle that ended abruptly. He got away from his chair and left right behind the clans.

"You did your best, Fleur. In fact, you may have helped unseat old Blake at last."

"Thank you, Tan, but I'm afraid of this admiral. Do you think he's had to play a diplomatic role before—you know, handling delicate negotiations, that kind of thing?"

Ubu laughed, his African lips framing a set of immaculate white teeth. "I'm afraid not, except in the sense of demanding and receiving unconditional surrenders. The admiral is gifted in the control of warships."

"That's what I was afraid of."

Outside the farewells were brief, and the air around the rock was positively dangerous for a while as jets jockeyed for the departure slot.

The Space Marines and Admiral Enkov were retrieved on the same hooked wires they'd descended on. The pinnace burst loose from the rock in a shattering blast of thrust and then was lost in the sky. Way above their heads something became visible, a bright daytime star that closed rapidly along a line of intersection with the bulleting pinnace.

The Earth diplomats were among the last to leave. They said good-bye to Lavin Fundin by the edge of the airstrip. Fein were already dismantling tents and equipment. Lavin noticed that the Deputy Earth Ambassador was looking decidedly depressed.

At the sight of him, though, she brightened. "I know where it was," she said, holding her chin.

"Where what was, Deputy Ambassador?" Lavin nodded to Tan who gave him a cool glance.

"Where it was I met you."

"Met me?...." Lavin smiled. He visited the Sx Coast occasionally, but he didn't recall the deputy ambassador, attractive as she was in her wide-shouldered, stately way. Her face was beautiful, with patrician features, delicate nostrils, wide, languid eyes, and a generous mouth with an easy curve to her lips.

"Perhaps you don't remember, but it was at a certain rather unusual, rather wicked party on Mimi Zimi's yacht... a harlequin minx?" She saw the memory slide into place behind his eyes.

"*You* were the harlequin minx?" There was a note of genuine wonder in his voice.

"I've never danced so long or so strenuously in my life." She amazed herself. Though she'd just seen the work of months go down the drain, she was feeling positively lightheaded.

"Yes, I remember. And we exhausted ourselves on the dance floor and later you gave me a card with a number to call. But you know something?"

She grinned.

"The ink disappeared when I turned on the light."

"That's an old trick of the harlequin minx, I'm afraid."

"How does the Deputy Ambassador of Earth come to know Mimi Zimi anyway?" he said, voicing a question that'd been on his mind from the start.

"Ah, well"—she had a full, warm smile, he noted—"we'll have to talk about that some other time. It's actually quite a long story, and right now I don't think I'm up for long stories."

Lavin understood. He'd caught the sense of the meeting from the anger among the clan elders when they'd emerged like a herd of stampeding gzan.

Now the dome was coming down, deflating into a limp nylon bag.

"Nothing much was accomplished then," he said. "From what I heard things ended badly." She nodded and Tan shifted uncomfortably on his feet. He was anxious to get away, and he was always uneasy around the highland bucks. He'd seen too many of them on drunken rampages on the Sx Coast. That his boss had odd tastes in terms of recreation he knew, but that she'd found a highlander commander to her fancy surprised him. All those guys knew was battle maneuver and how to kill. They were like trained attack dogs on a military leash.

"I can't imagine how we're ever going to get them around the table again, but we have to." She looked over to Tan. What a help he'd been and what a waste it all was. She felt a hysterical need to either laugh or cry. "But we have to because there's really no other solution. There has to be a negotiated settlement."

She felt Tan's impatience but she lingered a little longer. Any contact with the clans was valuable. And she surmised that Tan was restless because of his exaggerated dislike of military types. Tan hadn't adjusted well to the Space Navy. Besides, the young commander was good-looking in an intense sort of way, and she knew he could dance like an angel. And his eyes were so like Fair Fundan's it was uncanny. He had the same high cheekbones, too, the broad face, thick eyebrows. Were all the Fundans so alike?

"But how can we negotiate when one side just lays down demands and refuses to consider anything else?"

"That, my friend, is exactly our problem. How do we negotiate in such conditions? I was very encouraged by the flexibility that came up on the highland side. A good sign for progress that was, and I hoped to build on it, but..." She trailed off. "We must get them back together, somehow."

"What if there isn't *any* solution?"

She looked puzzled. "There has to be. Otherwise there'll be war."

"So?" Lavin shrugged. "We have war all the time. So we have more war, what difference will it make?"

Tan disliked the easy assurance in the young officer's tone. He broke in sharply, barely concealing the irritation he felt.

"There may be a lot of difference, especially once you have Space Marines and fighting robots dropping out of the sky. There'll be orbital fighters up top and don't forget the heavy stuff. The *Gargarin* is built on a scale to allow for the reduction of planetary fortresses. They'll be pouring everything they have down on you. It won't be like fighting the warbands."

Lavin nodded; he was realist enough to have already submitted a plan to Ghotaw in which he'd addressed the factors involved in withdrawing to the deep forest and fighting a guerilla war. "Yes, I'm afraid you're right. It won't be easy to beat them, not when they have control of the air and orbital space. However, they may find us a tougher nut to crack than they think if there really is to be war."

Talk of war depressed Fleur. "We must avoid it," she said numbly.

"It won't be easy," Lavin said.

"And that's an understatement," Ubu added, seeing Lavin with fresh eyes. This one didn't seem quite so arrogant, nowhere near as obnoxious as other clan members he'd met. Fleur felt a certain awkwardness. It was time to go. "The day's scarcely begun—can you believe it, it's early afternoon. We've got the whole day ahead of us, and I feel like I've been through two full days already."

"Good-bye then. Perhaps we'll meet again, harlequin minx?"

"Perhaps we will, Commander. I think I'd like that." She turned away and caught up with Ubu.

9

IT WAS DARK INSIDE THE WIND SHRINE HIGH ON GHOTAW
Mountain. The monsoon brought complex breeze patterns to
the shrine and the stone shell moaned, its intricate windways
seizing the airflow and producing a range of fluted tones. The
fein adepts had opened the intake ducts to maximum for Even-
song and now played the delicate higher passages. The fein
moved through the narrow adits in subtle patterns to add new
tonal suggestions and shadings to the windsong.

Several Fundan operatives had been summoned to the shrine
by the Mother Fair. Now Suella Fundan strode the spiral stair
to the highest level, to the circular chamber about twenty feet
across that capped the shrine, which spread out beneath like
the expanding shells of a colony of giant snails.

In the almost total darkness, Suella could see the glow of
the chitin in the flesh of the Mother Fair, that same glow that
Suella saw in her own skin during the dreadful night-long
examinations of her body in her Sx Coast apartment, when she
wept at the sight. Her second century dawned, but her hair and
nails were gone and soon her ovaries would die as well.

Fair sat naked in a high chair of carved stone. Without wig or false nails or any sop to modesty. The Mother Fair had the appearance of a woman in late middle age; her breasts had sagged and been tightened by her surgeon, her belly was wrinkled, she was slightly gaunt in the face. Suella felt the old, primordial fear of Fair—Fair her mother, and more than mother. Then her anger welled up again and she took a seat, feeling normal once more.

For a long time when she'd first known the truth, she'd thought Fair was insane and perversely cruel. But that period had passed. Fair simply could not be judged by the standards employed for other people.

Fair whispered, "Suella is here now. I heard her coming, that third tremor from the sump pipe never lies. Good, all my spies are here, my keenest eyes and ears. Where nothing can be overheard because of the windsong."

Suella saw little of the other faces, though she knew that if she could see them they would all look uncannily alike, all dark-haired women with brooding eyes, just like Suella herself . . . just like the Mother Fair.

Fair reached out to grasp Suella's hand. "Ah, my flesh, my most beautiful experiment of all. You are well? Recovered from that little immigrant adventurer at last?"

Even in the dark Suella felt her face flush. Fair knew everything, even her disastrous affairs.

"Never mind, my dear. I still love you as much as always." Fair released her and flicked a hidden stud and a bright holo sprang into view. Suella saw first a tall man with very broad shoulders and an odd way of carrying himself. Then the scene shifted to a closeup, and she winced at the strange streamlined face, so hard and tight and speckled with scarlet nodules. It dissolved to a group of similar men drinking at a bar on the Red Moon. Suella, a high-class prostitute for a century or more, knew every establishment of the kind in the Beni System.

"What are these, Mother Fair?"

"These creatures have become an interesting factor in the situation facing Clan Fundan, my flesh. Listen carefully. We must study them. I want to know everything about them, everything. . . ."

After such a disastrous day Fleur found it surprisingly easy to succumb to Tan's request that they go out to eat, drink, and try to forget. She let him entice her to the Golden Crawbowl with the words "toasted soysteak, *real* crawfish flavor, you'll love it...."

They had some incredibly expensive wine, grown on an orbiting vine satellite, but Fleur didn't care about the #33 tag on the bottle. As long as the liquid eased the pain.

But they'd barely finished the main course when she was paged and brought a phone. The call was from an occasional agent of hers based way out on the peninsula of Elefelas, in a slum called Love Beach.

The message was enough to pull Fleur and Tan from the Golden Crawbowl and send them running first to the embassy and then to the Mass-drive Transit station. In minutes they were whirring through the transparent tube, stretched ten meters above the waves of the Irurupup estuary. Tan stared out at the dark water hurrying past under the light of the Pale Moon and wondered what it was that was dragging them out to Love Beach of all places. He could still taste that crawfish soup.

Ahead loomed lights, the crowded dome suburbs of Elefelas. The train decelerated with a whoosh of compressed air then eased into the first stop. Elefelas people got off, mostly cooks and house servants going home to dome apartments, and others got on, folks seeking pleasure at the Anome-Zone Dome at the end of the line at Spurn Head.

Five more stops, each one in a more densely packed dome zone, brought them at last to Love Beach. When they left the car, the first thing they saw was the Woodwose Wall, 150 meters high, rising right across the peninsula, blocking out the jungle beyond.

The station was perched on a concrete pylon with escalators connecting to the walkways. These were crowded, filthy, and covered in teen-gang graffiti. Underfoot was a dusty layer of litter. Below the walkways, Fleur could see a dense warren of shantytowns spreading around the big domes from side to side of the peninsula.

"Ugh!" she exclaimed. "No air conditioning?" Despite her years on Fenrille, Fleur was amazed at the idea of anyone's surviving the sweltering tropical climate outside the domes.

"That's Death Wish City, boss. No air conditioning and no laws, only place the dispossessed can run to."

Fleur's nose wrinkled at a foul odor on the air. "Kelp farms and the fisheries," Tan said.

The walkway itself was damaged here and there. Twice they had to cross stretches where the concrete had been replaced with rickety wooden bridges.

"What's happened in this sector? The warbands haven't been fighting here, have they?" she said.

Tan looked at her for a moment. For someone as well informed as his boss, there were surprising gaps in her knowledge of the city she lived in. "Woodwose break in. Just a couple of months back."

"What! I don't remember that."

"Didn't get much media play. The Senate ordered it suppressed. Six adults got over the wall, casualties were pretty high."

The thought of woodwose running loose inside the wall made Fleur shiver. She tried her best not to think of the nightmare things that lived out there, in the jungle beyond the wall. "I'm glad I live on an island," she muttered.

At last they reached Dome 125C, at the end of the line of domes that made up Love Beach. Beyond 125C were just the two and three-story structures of Death Wish, all the way to the foot of the wall.

"How can anyone live out there?" Fleur's face filled with revulsion.

"Don't knock it, boss. For some it's the only life they know."

They found Barty's Bar on the ground floor, next to the elevators. The storefront next door was burned out, the ruins covered in teen-gang scrawls. Barty's sign was melted at one corner as if by a blaz tube.

"A rough neighborhood all right," Fleur murmured.

"Good place to hide," Tan said.

Fleur agreed, hoping desperately that this might be the line she sought, to the mystery of Termas Hith and his girl friend, Debby, who'd brought her that little film clip and then vanished.

"Ira Ganweek is in the hospital," she said. "That suggests a few possibilities to me already."

"So there's a price of a hundred thousand credits on her head. Big reward, eh?"

Barty's was a dreary place filled with beat-up tables and chairs, lit by a pair of flickering fluoros and smelling faintly of urine and alcohol. The crowd was mostly kelpies who stank of manure. Three men in filthy overalls were getting seriously drunk at the bar, which ran down the right side of the room. Pulz pop blared from hidden speakers, throbbing in the murk.

Fleur took a seat on a rickety barstool. She watched a pair of coarse-looking whores, in late middle age, trying to work up a trick or two from the tables.

"This is where the folk who don't make an Optimol plan come to die," Tan said bitterly.

The barkeep wore a tattered military jacket and was missing one arm. Fleur noted that he wore the insignia of the Flanians warband over the heart pocket.

"What's your pleasure?" he asked gruffly. Clearly they didn't get too many ladies dressed like Fleur Kevilla in Barty's, and the barkeep was overcompensating somewhat.

"What's the popular drink here?" Fleur asked, trying to be diplomatic.

"Most go for a chug-a-lug, twist of sea kelp." Fleur eyed the bottles of 120-proof vodka behind the bar and shuddered. Tan stepped into the breach.

"We'll have two Mokas please." He slapped a #5 on the bartop.

The brews appeared, condensation dripping down the bottles' sides.

"Uhh, you want glasses?" the barkeep asked surlily.

"Correction, we *need* glasses," Tan said in chill reproof.

Glasses duly appeared, and they sipped the cold Moka quietly while Fleur watched for any sign of Barty himself. She noticed a sign saying "Office" at the back and was about to ask the barkeep, when noise erupted on their left.

The three kelpies were having a falling out. Too drunk to figure out who ought to buy the next round, they were arguing viciously. The bartender moved down to quiet them, but one was just too crazed to shut up. When told to leave, he pulled out a stubby automatic and let fly.

There was a wild commotion, and Fleur and Tan hit the floor as bullets zinged overhead. Fleur looked up and saw the man, face slack with booze, eyes alight with rage, struggling to aim the gun at her, his mouth framing the word "bitch." She thought how absurd it was to die there like that.

Then a blaz tube made ozone of the air in the bar and burned the gunman's head off.

10

A STUMPY LITTLE MAN WITH A HUGE HEAD AND AN OUTSIZE blaz tube in his hands had appeared. Tan helped Fleur back onto her feet. Her suit was ruined, bar grime on knees and arms, Moka stains, but she was alive.

"Thank you, Messire. I believe you just saved my life."

The stumpy man looked at her for a second. "Hell, lady, I'm sorry about that, but I had to wait for Jake to take a good video of the creep before I blew him away." He turned, the big head moving on that neck like a tank turret, and bellowed at the bartender.

"What in the name of kelpshit took you so long, boy? I almost lost the lady there. What were you doing?"

Jake wore an air of injured innocence, but Fleur was left wondering if perhaps the surly barkeep had wanted her to get shot. "I can't help it, boss," he said defensively. "The switch on the camera is unpredictable, sometimes it works and sometimes it don't."

"Well, I got my eye on you, Jake—remember that, remember I'll be watching you. Any more damnfool mistakes and out you go, you got that?" Barty shook his heavy head and slipped the safety back on the blaz tube. Fleur looked briefly at the remains of the drunk kelpy and had a sudden, desperate need to get to the washroom before she threw her #20 soysteak *au grande* over her shoes. She made it to the dirty blue door of the john, and as it closed behind her she heard Barty talking to a cop.

When she reappeared she was still shaking a little but the queasiness was gone, along with the remains of dinner. Tan was waiting for her, the body was gone, and the barkeep was mopping down the floor with a dirty-gray ammoniated mop. He had an air of resignation about him. "Fourth time we've had to do that this week. Y'know, I should quit this job. Every time he yells at me about that fucking camera and I tell him what's wrong with it but does he ever get it fixed?" Jake seemed to have few doubts about whether that camera was ever going to get fixed.

"Barty's waiting for us in back. Are you okay?" Tan said.

Fleur nodded. "Yes, thanks. I think I'll make it. It was the shock more than anything else. I really thought I was going to get it there."

"You weren't the only one."

They threaded their way to the back and through a door marked "Private—No Admittance" to find Barty's office.

Barty was sitting behind a big, metal-top desk in a swivel chair that squeaked as it turned. He had on the closed-circuit TV monitors, giving a flickering view of the bar outside, and the blaz tube, which had seen a great deal of use, rested on the desk near to hand.

"Once again, Lady, I must apologize—I don't know what gets into Jake. He freezes up sometimes and forgets what's happening. But I hate to blow someone away before we gets the video evidence to give to the police. They don't like it much if we shoot someone without clear reason, makes too damn much paperwork, upsets the computers something terrible."

"Mr. Barty, let's get to the point. You called me with some interesting information concerning a red-haired girl."

"Exactly, Lady, that I did. That girl that's wanted by the syndicates so bad they're turning over every heap of shit from here to South Town. The description is someone with long red hair and very good looks. A little wildcat highlander sounds like."

"Yes, Mr. Barty that sounds like the one exactly."

Barty put his palms together. The chair squeaked. "Well, now, you know that I always give what information I can to the Earth office. I'm from the homeworld myself and I reckon it's my bound duty, being a patriot and all that."

"Yes, Mr. Barty, your information has often been useful to us. We value your assistance; I have mentioned you in dispatches on a couple of occasions."

Barty's face lit up. "Well, now, you did that? Mentioned me in dispatches to the home world? Why, that's wonderful, yes, sir, that's what we expect of each other, us Earth folk. Right?"

Fleur smiled. "That's right, Mr. Barty. Tell me now—do you have any proof that you've seen the girl here?"

Barty opened his desk drawer then flicked a photo across to her. One glance at it was enough to confirm that they were on the right track. Although she looked dumpy in a brown kelpy suit, the girl was slender, beautiful, but it was her red hair, tied up behind her head, that Fleur checked first.

In the silence, Barty was thinking. "This girl, they say there's a helluva reward for her. The syndicates want her real bad. I've heard figures mentioned that are simply mouth-watering, you know what I mean?"

They knew clearly what he meant. Barty's patriotism for distant Earth was one thing, 100,000 credit units in the hand was another.

"Well, the syndicates are very fond of offering big rewards," Tan said slowly, shifting in his chair, "but everyone knows they're not so good at paying them. It's so much easier to make someone disappear if they refuse to take what they're given and shut up. It's got to the point where it's getting counter-productive—people are too scared to try and collect."

Fleur knew that Tan had put his finger on the precise point that worried their informant. He could go to the syndicate, but what chance was there of actually collecting a reward from them and living to spend it?

"Believe me, I know what you're saying. I hear all them stories, too."

Tan privately doubted that Barty heard anything like the

same stories, not having a large network of informants spread out over the Sx Coast. Fleur's dedication to the building of that net had been one of the things that'd most impressed him about his boss, that and her unfailing honesty.

Then Barty said something that made them both sit up in their chairs and exchange looks of concern. "Oh, hell, I almost forgot. Right after I called you and you said you were coming out to see me, I got a call from someone at your office—someone who wouldn't give his name."

"Really!" Fleur said, alarmed. "Why did he call?"

"Said he wanted to know what I'd called you about. Said he was some kind of superior officer or something."

"What did you tell him?" said Tan.

"I told him I only deal with the lady, she's been good to me and I don't trust too many people in this world. Y'know how it is, and I asked him his name and he wouldn't give it so I hung up."

She frowned, looked to Tan. "Wermil," she breathed.

"How did he get a bug back on our phones? I cleaned the whole system down last week."

"Sounds more like a tracer on the outside line. He couldn't have got the call but he could find out where it came from."

Tan nodded, face grimmer than usual. "If Wermil knows where we are, then who else will know by now?"

Fleur turned back to Barty, who'd been watching this exchange with interest. "Messire Barty, if I offered you ten thousand in cash right now, would you take us to the girl and then take an immediate vacation on the Surf Rocks?"

Barty's face lit up at the mention of cash, but his features hardened as he considered the implications of his need to take an immediate vacation. Tan Ubu looked at the boss with concern. Ten thousand was going to blow a hole through the department budget big enough for a woodwose to walk through. Why was Fleur so desperate to get the girl?

"You mean this is going to be dangerous for me?"

"I'm very much afraid that it's already very dangerous for you."

"What'd I do?"

Tan looked at him with contempt. "C'mon, Barty, you know how it is. The syndicates are the ones who make the rules, and they break them as they please. But with ten thousand in your pocket, you could hide out for months. When you get back things'll be changed—I doubt they'll even remember your name."

"And," said Fleur, "perhaps we'll be able to get you some more money by then, another little lump of real money, not syndicate promises."

"Yeah," Barty said, fearing that invisible barriers were moving into place all around him for reasons he couldn't begin to guess at. A single phone call had gotten him into more trouble than he'd bargained for. "That caller then, who was he?" Barty was ready for the worst.

"No friend of ours, I'm afraid," Fleur replied. "I think you'd be wise to accept our offer. In fact, I think we ought to move quickly, all of us. Every minute may count."

Barty grimaced, threw his hands up in the air. "Sheez! The syndies are coming here then, after me?" He was out of the chair and tearing open a cupboard. He quickly filled a small bag, stuffing the blaz tube in at the last. "Lady, I hate to ask you, but that money you mentioned?"

Fleur was ready for him. She counted out ten big, pale-green #1,000 notes drawn on the Chitin Bank.

"Okay," Barty said, grabbing the bills. "Let's go. It's on the ninth floor, directly above this office. She's staying with a kelpy supervisor name of Squibb. Apartment eighty-eight B."

The ninth floor was barely lit by a pair of flickering fluoros, one at either end of the long, barren corridor. Graffiti and evidence of attempted burglary marred every door.

Tan knocked firmly on the door of eighty-eight B. Fleur prayed that someone would be in. Tan knocked again, more loudly.

This time the door snapped open and a peeved voice growled, "What the hell d'ya want?"

"Are you Squibb?" Tan asked.

"And what if I am?"

"Then, Mr. Squibb, we want to talk to you about a financial bequest that you have been made the recipient of."

"What's that?"

"It's a matter of a thousand credits, more or less."

The door opened and Squibb, an ugly, muscular man with pale-brown skin, stuck his head out belligerently.

"What're you shitting me for?"

Tan looked at Fleur, who nodded; there was no time to waste. He hit Squibb twice, once in the solar plexus and once across the side of his throat. The man went down in the doorway without another sound.

They moved into the squalid little apartment cautiously. It was a mess, with papers and junk and yards of kelp wrappers lying everywhere. The kitchen was thick with flies, the sink piled with dirty dishes and glasses.

Fleur pushed open the door to the bedroom and then froze as a force beam cutter was pressed against her throat.

"Who are you?" somebody female and desperate said.

There was no point in lying or beating around the bush. "I'm Fleur Kevilla, Deputy Ambassador from Earth. I'm looking for a red-haired girl that the Bablon Syndicate wants so badly it's offering one hundred thousand credits."

"Since when have Earth diplomats been bounty hunters?" the voice asked. Fleur couldn't turn her head to see the speaker, for the force cutter was pressed tight against her skin. One slip and it would take her head off.

"Not seeking the reward, trying to save the girl. We need contacts with the highland families. She's a highlander and in a hell of a lot of trouble too."

"Oh, as simple as that, eh?"

Fleur swallowed, wondering if it would be her last. "Yes, really, we've no other option. But there's little time, the syndicates will be on our trail already."

Holed up in this fetid burrow with only one door, the girl had little choice but to think things over. After a few seconds of silence, she snapped. "Show me some ID." Fleur fumbled for her card, thanking the fates for her decision to get a new photo taken the week before.

"Mmmm, that's you, all right. What can you do for me?"

"We can take you to my office. You'll have diplomatic immunity there until we can figure out a way to get you home."

"What's this *we*? Who else is here?"

"My assistant. You can trust us. Honestly, we mean you no harm, we really want only to help you."

Armada made a decision. If the Earth diplomats could find her then so could the syndicates. It was time to move. She was sick of Squibb, too, and the stink of kelp and garbage. "Okay, let's go."

11

THE RIDE BACK TO FUN ISLE ON THE MASS-DRIVE TRANSIT had been a nightmare. Armada was wearing kelpy khaki fatigues and her giveaway hair was tucked under a forage cap. Still, the quality of her skin, her good looks, and the softness of her hands declared to anyone who looked that she was no kelpy. Moreover Fleur and Tan were easily recognizable by their uniform.

When they finally reached Fun Isle after an eternity of skimming over the wavetops in the tube train, Fleur insisted they stop at a late-night boutique and buy Armada some new clothes. She chose a wide-brim hat with a blue veil to hide the girl's hair and a black silk pajama suit with matching mules. She dumped Armada's kelpy's bag and bought a new one of fine-cured nachri hide. Ten minutes later they were out of the store and on their way down the promenade to Fleur's dome. Fleur was impressed with the speed with which the girl had switched wardrobes. She evidently had a practical streak.

Once inside the dome and under dome security Fleur relaxed

a little. They reached her quarters and, after checking all three security systems, they slipped inside.

Inside her apartment, Fleur poured herself a drink. Armada joined her and mixed herself a huge chug-a-lug but looked in vain for a twist of sea kelp.

"No kelp?"

Fleur smiled bemusedly. "My, isn't that a bit of a snort?" she said, feeling suddenly motherly and dumb.

Armada gave her a withering look. "My day started a long time ago and if you hadn't bothered us I'd have had several of these by now. You should try working on the night shift on the kelpy beds—that's when the bloodsuckers are out. It's hard to see them in the water."

"Oh," said Fleur. "Well, in that case. But you can tell me a couple of things. First, your real name, and then what it is that someone as young as yourself has done to get that sort of attention from the Bablon Syndicate?"

Armada chugged down her drink and then made another, which she took to a window seat. "I took something from Senator Ira Ganweek, do you know him? You do—yes, I suppose everyone knows the old pig. Anyway, I took something rather precious to him."

Fleur concealed her disappointment. "So you're a thief, a young beautiful thief from the highlands. What family? What's your name?"

"Why do you need to know?" Armada's glance was cool to frosty.

"It would certainly ease my mind if I knew who it was I'd rescued from Senator Ganweek—at no small cost, I might add." That #10,000 for Barty had been a gesture she could live to regret. But she'd had a hunch from the first moment that this business with Ganweek was something to do with the other mystery she had connected to him, the murder of a young research chemist called Termas Hith. In a safe, sunk in the ceiling of her office, Fleur had a tape of a young lady, a friend of Hith's. It made disturbing viewing. Since getting the tape Fleur had lost contact with the woman, who seemed to have disappeared. Fleur had been making discreet inquiries ever since. Now it seemed she'd guessed wrong. The girl was just a superior sex object of some kind.

"Well, I don't agree. I don't know you, so I feel no reason

to give you my name. We're not on the same sort of social footing anyway—aren't you an Earther?"

The girl said "Earther" with a disdain that curled her lip and brought a flush to Fleur's cheeks.

"Her name is Armada Butte, a daughter of Rognius Butte and the subject of quite a solid little file in the memory banks," Tan Ubu said as he stood up from the console behind Fleur's ornamental purple lyissa vine at the far side of the room.

"Well, that's good to know. Armada Butte; how do you do, Armada, I'm glad to meet you. I'm sorry to be such an unworthy friend, and an Eather in the bargain, but that's the way of it and we'll just have to get along. If you don't like it then you can always go and make out your own deal with the syndicate."

Armada sniffed. The woman was transparent in her desire and she wore makeup to reduce the disharmony in her rather gaunt features. She obviously thought Armada was some petty thief. So let her see the proof. "Get me my bag," she said in a tone of command to Tan, who stopped dead, halted by her voice. After a moment's hesitation he fetched the bag and gave it to Armada who took it without acknowledgment. Tan raised an eyebrow.

"Earthers," Fleur mouthed.

Armada fished inside and produced a small leather pouch, marked around its circumference with lines of green and ochre stain. It was tied together with a scarlet thong. Fleur immediately recognized the fein markings. The bag was a kuilowee jui-ji; it contained evidence of a great coup. By the mark of the thong, scarlet for blood, Fleur knew it was a very important coup indeed.

"If you like you can look inside that. I've blessed it so no demon can attack."

Demons? What in the world was the girl talking about? "What's in it?" Fleur was reluctant to touch it or to lower herself in any way that might be considered "Earthish."

"Senator Ganweek's balls."

Fleur stared at her. After a smile she spluttered, looked at Tan, who was fighting to repress a sick chuckle. Ten thousand!

"What did you say?"

"You heard me. That old pig defiled me, with vile treachery, so I gelded him in revenge."

"No wonder the senator's in the hospital," Tan said with a straight face.

Fleur choked. No wonder there was a hundred grand on the girl's head.

After a moment's surprise Fleur got a grip on herself. "Then our big problem is just getting you home alive. Right now I'm not sure exactly how to go about that. The Bablon Syndicate has a long reach in this city."

Armada sighed wearily. "Don't I know it? I should have killed him, that was a big mistake, that and leaving a certain little sex object alive, who must've raised the alarm on me. When I got to the airstrip I found they already had a guard on my plane."

"That does sound like a mistake," Tan said dryly.

"How on Earth did you do it—I mean, get to Ganweek?" Fleur said. Everyone knew how well those old monsters in the syndicates were guarded.

"On Earth did you say, Ambassador?" Armada gave a sharp laugh and then gave them a brief account of her entry to the dome and the slaughter of the guards.

"Why did you choose the kelpies to hide among?" Tan asked when she'd finished.

"Because it was the only place left. The commercial flights out were all covered, the whole airport was swarming with Bablon guys. So I wound up taking the transit tube, and after I got out at Elefelas I checked out the fishing boats. I was thinking of making it over to South Town, but I realized the boats were covered, too. So I thought about hiding on the fish farms, but since everyone knows the syndicate controls the price of fish..."

"That they do," Tan agreed, impressed with her story. "Have you seen the price of meatfish lately?"

"So I knew there'd be plenty of syndicate contacts down there, and I had to avoid them. I just kept going down the line to Love Beach. I would've gone right on into Death Wish except that I met Squibby and he hid me on his kelp detail. The syndies aren't much interested in kelp, the price of kelp stays low, the labor is even cheaper. There's nothing there for them."

Fleur's thoughts were in a whirl. The girl had nerve! She was fresh from slaving on the kelp beds after castrating a mafia

115

overlord and she was looking down her nose at *them* for being "Earthish."

"So you hid out as a kelpy?"

"For the last eight days, and every night I had to take care of Squibby when I got back to the dome."

"Ah, yes, Squibby was the big belligerent sucker I had to lay out, right?" Tan had fixed himself a drink, tonic on ice. It'd been a long day and now it looked like getting even longer.

"I hated him, he was stupid and gross, but he was easily controlled." The way the girl said "controlled" gave Tan goose-flesh. The gorgeous young creature spoke with the authority of a wanton ten times her age.

"Well, now it seems we're in the same soup as you are. The syndicate won't rest until they get their hands on you. Thank goodness we can take you to the office—that's diplomatically neutral territory, you'll be safe there." Fleur was trying to think of a way out of the mess.

"Perhaps we should get her offplanet?" Tan suggested.

Armada's pretty face crumpled into a scowl. "No way will you drag me off this world. My blood belongs here, my bones must lie on Butte Mountain if I ever die."

"It might only be a temporary measure, honey," Fleur said. "Just boost to the orbiter and then drop down again to your home. Look at it this way—it'd be the quickest way to make the journey, eight minutes going up, ten minutes going down, and half an hour in between."

"Certainly sounds better than jetflight. My behind is still aching from that workout today."

"I will die before I leave Fenrille," Armada stated flatly.

Fleur shrugged. "Well, let's examine all the input and talk about it later. Perhaps there's another way." She looked at the time. It was close to midnight.

"I think we should move over to the office. We'll sleep as best we can there. It's been more than an hour since we left Barty's. Time enough for them to have pieced together the whole story. And we'll be secure at the office, which we can't be here."

They packed a few things. Tan passed Fleur a small energy weapon. "Stunner, very short range, just for emergencies. You never know what we might run into out there."

116

Fleur looked at the weapon with distaste—had it come to this, this small silvery egg with its brainscrambling field?

The lobby was empty but the elevator was not. As the doors opened Fleur found herself gazing into a familiar face.

"Mr. Barty!" she said before Barty fell forward and hit the carpet with a thud. Other elevators were coming.

"Quick," Tan said, "the firestairs at the rear of A Deck. Down to the garage."

They ran through the corridors of the deck suspended within the dome's vast interior. Fleur found her shock suspended. Barty was dead, and she couldn't understand why. "Why, Tan? Why did they do that?"

"To panic us," Tan said, "drive us back into the apartment— means they're not here in strength yet. Maybe Barty tried to warn us."

They pounded down concrete steps. Fleur's deck was one of fourteen interlocked floor plans at that level, and there were ten levels below. It would take them a minute or two to make it, time for the elevators to go up and down again. It would be a close thing.

After the maze of fire tunnels they emerged into the garage tunnel. A glance up the passage showed someone waiting outside.

"There's only one."

"I see," Fleur whispered. "Let's use two cars."

They ran to the parked autos, small four-passenger vehicles leased to dome residents. They were unlocked and always kept fueled. Armada got in with Fleur while Tan gunned his machine to life. With Fleur right behind he raced up the ramp. They converged on the syndicate man waiting there and he barely managed to avoid their wheels before getting off one shot, which went wild and high.

On the autoways, sunk below the walkways in concrete troughs, speed and travel were computer regulated. Population density on the Sx Coast was much too great to allow for independently controlled vehicles. They were soon slotted in on the route to Fun Beach, a mile or so away, where the embassy was located.

Armada watched the concrete sliding by above their heads and on both sides with dismay. Their route was just as claustrophobic as the air vent she'd crawled through to get at Ganweek.

"I hate to be closed in. I hope this ride isn't going to last long."

"It's less than a mile now. Just grit your teeth, shut your eyes and pray."

"Pray? I thought you Earthers were all atheist, antispirituality, even anti-Christ." Fleur was surprised again. The girl was clearly religious in some way, a strange characteristic for such an amoral child.

"Oh, yes, well, it was just a figure of speech."

A red light appeared in the tunnel, and the car began to slow.

"Uh oh, what's the hitch?"

The cars stopped. The red light was nearer.

Tan jumped out of the front car, Fleur and Armada pushed open the doors. "Repair vehicle, they must be ahead of us." Tan was already running back down the tunnel. They followed him to a maintenance ladder that led to the walkway above. They scrambled up it.

"Let's just hope the door isn't locked on outside," Fleur said while silently thanking her gym classes as she monkeyed up the iron rungs.

It was. Ubu wrestled with it but the mechanism had been sealed above.

"How could they be so damn stupid as to put in one-way locks on these things?" Fleur said with a despairing snarl.

"Hold it, there's no problem. Let me get past you." Armada was already scrambling around them. She produced a force cutter and aligned it with the hasp of the lock. A fierce bluewhite light seared the darkness, and the metal began to disintegrate.

Down below the repair vehicle had lifted their cars off the roadbed and was clanking down to the bottom of the ladder.

"I hope you're gonna get through that pretty soon," Fleur said nervously.

Tan had his stunner out but he felt terribly exposed, perched up in the maintenance well.

The vehicle ground to a halt with a huge sigh of heavy hydraulics. Footsteps clattered in the road. Two men in Security Police uniforms appeared below, blaz tubes in their hands.

118

"I hate to mention this, my dear," Fleur said quietly to Armada, "but we have company."

Armada spat and held the cutter against the lock. "Not for long," she said as it broke at last and she heaved it open. They scrambled through the hole and appeared abruptly on the well-lit promenade of the Bablon dome walkway.

"This is not where we want to be," Fleur noted gloomily.

"Back, hoof it to the turn-off and go around through Nebudchadnezzar Gardens. Cut through to the transit stop behind the Theban Dome." Tan was already moving and they ran, with frequent backward glances, ignoring the disapproving stares of the promenaders. They reached the turn-off just as the maintenance door opened again and dove between rows of potted glob globs whose flowers were at their brightest yellow.

Nebudchadnezzar Gardens was filled with the usual crowd of sybarites and whores and criminals. Several plutocrats were being carried along above the throngs on the shoulders of heavy-set indentured men. A woman dressed in a glittering costume of fish scale was haranguing a small crowd on the benefits of burial at sea. A peddler of unusual nerve tonics barked his wares and was echoed by a chorus of children trained to bark on tonal scales.

They pushed through the throngs as quickly as they could without attracting attention. For a minute or more they were stuck behind a carnival procession as several dominants paraded sex slaves on long leashes while a glittering samba band followed behind keeping up a steady rhythm.

Eventually the procession reached the fountain of De Sade, an elaborate rococo work in ferroconcrete set amid rose vines of steel, and a gap appeared through which the three fugitives plunged. Fleur stepped forward too soon, however, and a pair of naked men sprang toward her. But their angry growls became gasps as they ran out of leash.

An angry dominant, a powerfully built woman with an over-ripe bosom and flaunting buttocks in a skintight costume of black silk, glared at Fleur and used her whip to get her slaves back into line.

"Trying to ruin our procession, are you? What are you?" she yelled. "A saboteur from the Whip Demons?" Clearly outraged, the woman yanked on the leashes bunched in her fist and moved on, the slaves barking around her.

At last they cleared the gardens and ran down a path to the small transit dome.

The trains weren't crowded, but there were enough people around to make it unlikely that they'd be attacked directly. Two stops on they reached Fun Beach and emerged on the other side of the walkway from the Westwind Dome, in which the Earth Embassy was located.

The walkway was filled with strolling couples and there was no sign of syndicate stake-out. Nervously they started toward the dome. Halfway across, Armada gasped as a small dart stuck in her veil. Fleur saw it and looked around. Some of the strolling couples had converged on them, another dart shot by.

"Run for it," she yelled. Armada pulled her laser and fired it in the direction of the syndies.

A dart caught Fleur behind the ear, just a couple of steps from the door. Coming behind, Armada saw Fleur's stumble. The girl accelerated, caught Fleur under the arms and bore her in on sheer momentum, past an amazed Tan Ubu. He let the door slide shut as their pursuers pulled up not twenty feet away. Darts clattered against the glass.

"Upstairs, quickly, we've got to find out what was on that dart." Armada let Tan take Fleur's legs and together they rushed her to the elevator.

At the embassy door Tan opened the lock with a touch of his thumb. Epsila appeared, groggily clearing her eyes of sleep. She had the late shift and had been napping by the switchboard in the lobby. At the sight of Fleur being carried in by Ubu and a strange young woman in a black silk suit and veil, she gaped and then got herself into motion.

The embassy was a quarter-floor suite on the twentieth floor of the old but distinguished Westwind. It had several residential suites, unused for the most part, a small refectory, a corridor lined with offices, and at the end of the corridor a small laboratory. As soon as Fleur was arranged comfortably on the lab table, Tan busied himself in scraping the tip of the dart and getting down to an analysis. Epsila read Fleur's vital signs and took a blood sample; she conferred briefly with Tan, then hurried back to join Armada, who was checking the doors, windows, and walls.

"Where's the most likely place for them to try to break in?"

Armada asked the very thin, short woman in the white pantsuit uniform of Earth's Diplomatic Corps.

"Oh, they won't break in here." Epsila laughed. "Whatever it is that they're angry about, they wouldn't dare to break interplanetary laws completely. An outright attack would be a virtual declaration of war, don't you think?"

"I suppose you know what you're talking about." Armada looked dubiously at the closed-circuit screen in the reception module.

After a minute or so of pacing about the lobby Armada announced she was going to take a nap, and did so, stretching out on the lobby upholstery and pulling a cushion over her head. Epsila was left to keep an eye on things. She checked with the dome security force and then went back to see how Tan was doing.

"Do you think you can find out what it is?" she said, leaning into the little lab.

"It's easier without interruptions," Tan said irritably. "Sorry, but this part of it is painstaking work. Soon as I get a sample fit for the analyzer, we'll get some idea. I'm just hoping it's not going to be something complex."

"Isn't it pretty bold of them—I mean astonishingly so— for the syndicates to do something like this? What are we going to report to the Space Forces about it, for instance?"

"As little as possible, I hope, Epsila. With any luck she'll be able to tell them herself." And explain that #10,000 to Barty. Tan was beginning to suspect that this business was going to torpedo his boss's career. Blake was afraid of her, so there'd be nothing but hostility from that quarter. If she'd unwittingly got herself mixed up in a blood feud between the syndicates and a highland clan, that would present a source of political embarrassment that could become a lever to get her transferred or dismissed. Janks Wermil hadn't clawed his way to the top, to sit beside Blake, without gaining a well-deserved reputation for ruthlessness. Suddenly Fleur had too many enemies.

Ubu still couldn't begin to understand the reasons for Fleur's intense interest in the girl with scarlet hair. So there'd been a heavy reward on her head, but many fugitives in the past had had syndicate rewards posted, and Fleur hadn't indicated an urge to find and rescue them. But as soon as the word reached her—even though the soysteaks at the Golden Crawbowl were the best on the coast—she'd acted as if it was a matter of interplanetary importance that they find the girl.

He knew Fleur would have reasons. In the years he'd worked for her he'd come to appreciate her obsession for information and for making moves based only on the best information. She was dedicated to her career in a way that he understood and respected for he shared her feeling toward the diplomatic effort they were engaged in. In a way he had never expected, Fleur Kevilla's seemingly natural enthusiasm for the direction of human affairs had affected him. His own profound disillusion with life, his self-disgust after the years in Naval Intelligence had given way before her vision. She converted him, as if to a religion, to her patrician view of their posting and responsibilities. Of course, Kevilla was the daughter of the first female interplanetary ambassador, and it was no freak accident that secured her this job, the most sought-after post in the service. But Ubu had been inspired nonetheless, and he was genuinely concerned for her. The undying enmity of the Bablon Syndicate was not something she could survive easily.

After fifteen minutes, he had a reading from the analyzer that provided a dose of relief. It was a simple chemical, most likely the commercially popular Stunguard used in hundreds of automatic safety systems by the rich and security conscious. The dosage was small, and the effects would wear off within an hour. However, they had no antidote.

Fleur was already lying comfortably with a cushion for a pillow. Tan left her to recover and headed for the lobby. He arrived just in time to pick up a phone call that was blinking on the board in front of the dozing Epsila. "Yes?"

"May I speak to the deputy ambassador, please?"

"I'm afraid she can't come to the phone right now."

"Yes, I thought you might say that. Well, in that case I will speak with you." Tan flicked on the recorder and started tapping into the computer for an analysis. There was no visual signal.

"By the way, this call will not be traceable and my voice is being distorted so I shouldn't bother to be the efficient little spy that you are."

"Who is this?" Tan said, half mockingly.

"That is irrelevant. There is only one relevance—the girl. Send her out to us and do it now. We will not wait very long."

"That sounds like a threat. Are you threatening the Embassy of the Earth Government?"

"Hah, I like it! Yes, damn right we are. Get the girl out here or face the consequences."

"You realize that this office is diplomatically neutral ground, that such actions and threats could be construed as a declaration of hostilities."

"So call the police. See if they come. Then open the door, put the girl and her possessions on the elevator, and we can all forget that any of this ever happened."

"I think you're forgetting that there's one dead man in this and that the deputy ambassador has been attacked and wounded."

"Are you trying to stall me? Don't give me that obvious shit—just let me know whether and when we get the girl. No, let me change that—just tell me when we get her, because, my bully young man, we *will* get her. But hurry up. We've never been very patient, and we're long past patience now."

"Are you Senator Ganweek?" Tan was getting angry. There was silence . . . it continued . . . Tan waited.

"Do you want to die, young man?" said the voice.

The warning throbbed on the phone line. Tan felt it and wavered, the words frozen on his lips. He was almost alone. They just might launch an attack on the embassy itself. And Armada Butte's act had certainly set her in blood feud with the Bablon Syndicate. The Brothers of Marduk were a pitiless enemy.

There was another silence. Tan felt a pressure billowing down on him. Closing around him in a vise, ready to prize his head from his shoulders. There would be no escape for an assistant to the deputy ambassador, especially if the deputy ambassador was disgraced.

And if he was disgraced and fired, what then? The syndicates had every aspect of economic life covered except the kelp beds and the chitin valleys. How long could he last down in Love Beach or Death Wish? All he had to do was give up the girl. He looked around wildly. The silence on the phone continued. He could kill Epsila, tell Fleur that they were overpowered, and nobody would ever know the difference.

He hesitated, began to think there was virtually nothing else he could do—it was so hopeless, how could they stop an army of syndicate fighters?

"Well," the voice said, "we can't wait much longer."

"What are you asking me to do?"

"Just put the girl on the elevator. That's all, then go back and wait for your deputy ambassador to revive, which will take about fifteen minutes. Then explain to her that local politics is a rough game, that sometimes there just aren't any rules. She's a very intelligent person—very career minded—she'll understand the inevitable, that you'll be doing what you have to do. You made a mistake, that's all—you put yourself into a situation where diplomatic mice aren't needed."

Tan tried to ignore the sinking sensation in his guts. "What you're asking is diplomatically impossible. It violates the whole fabric of diplomatic relations, ignores the right to asylum, can't you see that?"

Tan was just playing for time. The voice knew that. It grew disgusted. "That's your answer then? All right, you were warned hero boy. Too bad you have no significant brain, eh?"

The line clicked off. Tan put the receiver down feeling a little weak. Then he roused Epsila and Armada.

The Butte girl sprang into action with an alacrity that surprised him. Tan's opinions of the highland aristos didn't usually take into account the nonstop martial training they all received from age five.

They immediately lowered the steel shutters around the windows of the offices. The door was barricaded although Armada argued that instead they should control the whole floor and take the elevators as control points. But Tan thought that too ambitious for the three of them, and he and Epsila were both loath to consider the integrity of the wall of the embassy. Neither of them could still really believe in their hearts just how serious the threat was.

Then the TV monitors from the lobby ceased sending signals. They heard the elevators moving. They checked the ammunition in their weapons. Tan had opened the embassy armory and equipped them with .38 revolvers and manstopper plastic ammo. There were also gas grenades and masks. Epsila went to check on Fleur and fit her with a mask, too.

They waited, listened at the door, and waited some more. Armada grew restless. She hated to be on the defensive, having to wait for the blow to fall. After a minute she got up and went to prowl along the office walls, listening intently. There was nothing to hear.

She got back to the lobby and as she did so something began to work away in the back of her mind, gnawing insistently. Try as she might, though, she couldn't pull it out of the chaos.

"Hear anything?" Tan asked.

"No . . . but something's going on and I just can't quite pick out what it is." How hideous they all looked in gas masks, like robots, or giant insects. She looked down at her grenades. When they dropped those grenades the air in the whole system in the building would—"Of course!" she exclaimed. "Just like I did, they're coming through the ventilation system!"

Tan jumped as if he'd been stung. Gathering the grenades, he ran for the office corridor. "The main shaft goes right through here, above the offices."

They ran for it and got there in time to hear a soft curse echo from somewhere deep within the duct.

Armada swiftly unbolted the grille, then Tan armed a grenade and rolled it into the duct as Epsila threw the air-conditioning switch to VENTILATE to expel the air from the corridor and keep the gas out.

Muffled in the metal walls they heard a sudden burst of noises, shouts echoing, distant cursing.

Satisfied that a surreptitious entry through the ventilation ducts was out of the question for a while, they returned to the door. Tan noted that the door might be destroyed with blaster fire, so they pulled desks from offices and stacked them across the entrance to the corridor. This meant they would give up half the embassy if the door was breached, but because the corridor was at a right angle to the front door they'd be safe from fire from blaz tubes. For a while at least.

Epsila went to check on Fleur again and found her just awake, groggily trying to sit up. She had almost removed the gas mask. A few minutes later Fleur rejoined them, a cup of coffee in hand.

Tan explained the situation to her and Fleur managed a weak chuckle when told of the foiled air-duct ruse.

"So they don't think interplanetary politics is a rough game? We softies from Earth don't know about playing rough, eh?" Fleur looked as disgusted as she felt. Diplomacy, as it'd been practiced in the Kevilla family for generations, depended on the idea that embassies were inviolate.

"All the wild regimes of history that violated the security of embassies fell by the wayside. It's a mark of social decay and instability."

A blaz bolt seared the door. Pieces of wood and the security screen flew into the room.

"The Sx Coast syndicates don't seem to have read their history books," Tan commented with a brittle smile.

Fleur saw that Armada was flushed with battle fever. The highlanders were nothing if not eager for battle.

"Don't worry, Deputy Ambassador, they'll have a time getting in here."

"Yes, my dear, I'm sure they will. But have you also considered that we're going to have a time of it getting out?" She turned to Ubu.

"Call Blake, he has to put a stop to this."

"Of course." He hesitated. "What if he won't?"

Fleur dismissed it. "Of course he has to. He's the ambassador, it's his mission that's getting shot up."

Tan dialed and got Blake's answering robot. He tried Blake's club and found the ambassador was "not to be contacted" while visiting the yacht of the illustrious Lala Pmoor, who was entertaining an intimate party for the night.

A call to Janks Wermil produced only an answering machine as well. Further calls were rendered academic when a heavy blast shook the dome and threw them off their feet. Smoke and dust blew down the corridor.

"What the hell was that?" Armada sprinted down the corridor. At the end she threw open the door to an outer office. A gaping hole in the outer wall of the dome was surrounded by vapor as the room smoldered. A chopper was visible through the wall swinging in to discharge an assault commando.

Armada steadied herself, took aim as she'd been trained to at Butte Manor, and put six bullets into the cockpit, hitting the pilot. The chopper banked away, disappeared from view. "I got it!" she yelled delightedly.

Another explosion, a heavier deeper blast, occurred down below.

"You certainly did," Tan said with just a note of wonder in his voice.

"What do they think they're doing?" Fleur screamed. "Blasting holes in the dome is surely going too far!"

"Not according to what I was told," Tan said.

Thick black smoke was billowing up from where the chopper had impacted. Cautiously they pushed through the rubble of the room to the edge of the blast crater. The torn tissue of the building confronted them with fibrous pipes and snapped steel channel amid burned surfaces. Armada, pressing ahead too soon, burned her hand on a stanchion to which was stuck a gob of smoldering liquid-plastic insulation.

Eventually they worked around to one side and looked down. The chopper had struck the base of the dome and flames were billowing from the ground floor.

Sirens wailed in the distance.

"If the dome's well alight below us, I think we're going to have to move. I hate to bring everyone down with this idea, but there's no way around it," Armada announced cheerfully. Fleur had seen Armada's grimace of pain from the hot insulation and decided to forgo the trip to the blast hole. Still, the smoke billowing up was voluminous. Obviously a lot more than just the helicopter was burning.

"The fire department's coming."

"That'll give us a chance to get out of here then," Armada said. "Good. I want to move, I hate being trapped like this." Seeing Fleur's face cloud over, she added hastily, "There doesn't seem any point in being here, does there? There's no sanctuary for us on the Sx Coast, don't you see? We've got to get out of the city."

Fleur faced the incredible thought. Diplomats of the Earth mission were actually in danger of being slain in a blood feud arising from the castration of a mafia chieftain.

"I find it hard to believe." Fleur's whole universe, one based on law and reason, governed by negotiation, seemed to be slipping away.

"Well, look at that hole and tell me again how safe we are here."

Fleur was still confused when a shout from Epsila stung them into action. They raced back down the corridor, to find the front doors taking a battering.

"One last charge! They're desperate to get us before the fire department comes. Get ready, and if the door breaks fire in volleys." Armada had the fire of the Buttes in her veins. She'd reloaded and was handing around gas grenades.

Fleur grimaced. She had pushed her mask off her face so that it looked like a weird hat. "Do we really have to use those things?"

"If we have to, why not? They're not lethal. They may be very useful outside in staying ahead of the syndies—you can always clear a room with one of these."

The door was giving. Fleur took a revolver. She looked at it and shuddered. "I can't use this," she said in a flat, emphatic voice.

"What do you mean, you can't use it?" Armada asked in bristling tones.

"I can't kill another person, I'm a pacifist."

"This is not the time to be a stickler for pacifist ideas if I may be so bold," Tan muttered.

"I can't help it. I was raised in a certain way, and that way did not include the firing of guns that kill people."

"You can't be serious?" Armada sounded close to hysterical. She wanted to start shooting, and the way she was feeling Fleur might easily be her first target.

Fleur nodded. On the subject of guns she was as serious as could be.

"They're going to kill us all, you included, I would think, after all this. In fact, you know something? I bet that if you'd left me alone out in Love Beach with Squibby I'd have managed to take care of myself a lot better than you have. Why in all saints of godless communism did you have to come and screw everything up?"

Fleur groped for an answer to that.

"They're going to kill us all, and that means me, and you caused it. Now you won't even help us save our own lives. What kind of honor do you operate on anyway?"

Epsila, practical to the last, gave Fleur a long-range stunner, an unwieldy thing needing both hands to keep steady. "It won't matter if you fire a stunner, will it?"

Fleur snatched at the straw offered. "No, not at all—it's just that those revolvers are so crude. They fire bullets!" Fleur had seen what bullets could do to human beings.

The door finally gave way. There was a moment's lull and then a rush by the commandos.

Armada barked, "Now!" They rose as one from behind the desks and fired, three revolvers emptying in a roaring, effective fusillade and one stun beam, which took an attacker square in the face and effectively saved his life.

The commandos were caught squarely, the intensity of the fire not only unexpected but almost overwhelming. Nine men were down in the first few seconds and with bullets slicing through the doorway the rest wavered, crouched behind whatever cover could be found, and then pulled back outside the defenders' field of fire.

Tan and Armada slung gas grenades through the ruins of the door. Confused movements could be heard in the hall outside following the crackling detonations. Meanwhile, with an energy that Fleur found almost distasteful, Epsila reloaded the guns.

They waited for a second wave but it never came. The fire engines were already in place down below. The commando unit could not risk a confrontation with the fire department— if anything was sacred in the Sx Coast, it was the fire department.

Not even the Bablon Syndicate would risk wounding a fireman—on the Sx Coast, where so many people were squeezed into such a small place, firefighting was regarded with a reverence normally reserved for the tenets of a religion.

If the commandos were trapped in the dome until the fire was put out, their presence would be impossible to explain away, and the level of real political damage would rise enormously.

Everything had gone wrong for the syndicate. It had taken twenty casualties, lost a chopper—the whole business had become agonizingly frustrating. Ira Ganweek had to be heavily sedated when they finally brought him word.

However, the fire was spreading and the victorious defenders of the embassy would have to make a break from cover— they couldn't stay where they were. Once out on the walkways again, in the darkness, the syndicate would close in.

Armada had set her mind to separating from the Earthers and leaving the Sx Coast.

"You people won't even be at risk if you just leave me alone. I'm going to go my own way. At least I know how to survive and stay out of trouble."

Tan was still smarting at the girl's superior performance in combat; he found her skill with a handgun hard to believe. "And where will you go? Back to Love Beach?" he sneered.

"Look, I was doing all right there until you came snooping around. What the hell does it have to do with you anyway?" Armada hefted her bag and trooped out through the shattered doors.

Indeed, what the hell does it have to do with us? was an unspoken thought that Tan wanted to bring up but couldn't. Not yet at least. Fleur wasn't going to let Armada go, so she and the others were forced to follow.

The elevators were out and smoke was beginning to fill the upper corridors. Armada marched to the far side of the building, where she opened the fire exit and started down the narrow catwalks of the fire stairs. The Westwind Dome was one of the earliest generation of second-wave structures; its fire stairs were exterior and in none too secure a state. Fleur, who had a horror of heights, had never felt so vulnerable or exposed in her life. Each flight of rickety metal slats was an agony of suspense. To look down to see where her feet were going meant looking through the narrow slats to the ground far below. That brought on a vertigo that threatened to send her toppling into the empty air.

As they finally approached ground level they ran into a party of firefighters, who were charging up the stairs with shouts of "move it over there," and "you folks shouldn't be on these stairs, y'know." But the firefighters passed without incident and Armada and the others left the fire escape in the dome delivery access area. For a moment they stood confused, unsure what to do.

"Well, no one seems to be waiting for us down here at least," Fleur said, trying to inject a note of brightness. She'd had just about as much of being chased and terrorized as she thought she could stand.

"I'd say it's too early to be sure of that," Tan remarked as he looked around cautiously. "They've had us covered most of the way. I wouldn't expect them to give up so easily."

Armada scouted around the exit gate and returned with the news that the walkways around the dome were clear but for firefighters. "They've got five engines and a cherry picker round front. It must be a big fire." She gestured toward the gate. "I don't know about you folks, but I'm getting out of here now. If we hang around they're sure to pick us up."

"I have just one question," Epsila said in a small, bleak voice. "Does anyone have any idea of a place where we can hide? I'm scared. I can't think of anywhere that they can't find us."

Fleur considered the problem and her face fell. Epsila had raised an awfully difficult point. The list of places that Fleur could crash at so late an hour and expect sanctuary from the Bablon Syndicate was limited.

"Yes, you've got a point there," Tan said slowly. "With the syndicates aroused to this extent we have to assume that nowhere's safe for us. Who the hell can we go to for help?"

Armada had her hands on her hips and was staring at them wide-eyed. Her anger finally got the better of her. It was a tense situation after all.

"So now instead of your rescuing me, it's up to me to rescue you!"

"I never said that." Fleur was stung.

"You don't have to, Deputy Ambassador. I can see with my own eyes that you people don't have a clue as to what to do next. All this sort of thing's a little out of your line, I'd say. But I suppose I should forgive you and stay and help you."

"*Forgive* us?" Tan bridled.

"Of course. I'd be perfectly safe out in Dome One Twenty-five right now if it wasn't for you fools. Why in all the names of hell you had to come out and blow my cover I can't imagine. Born meddlers, that's what they say of all Earthers."

"Uh oh, we're back to *Earthers* again. Now, I know your opinion of the home planet is pretty low, my dear, but you know we all come from Earth, one way or another—even you. And we're all in this together. Why don't we concentrate on our problems and forget the bickering and the name calling?" Fleur was breathing hard. She was also eager to do something, go somewhere. She agreed with Armada that lingering was likely to prove suicidal. The problem was, where could they go?

After a moment Epsila, in a small pained voice, spoke up. "Well, I live in the old Gomorrah, that's on the Sx Isle. It's only a little place but maybe we could stay there."

"How long have you lived there, Epsila?" said Tan.

"Oh, for ages. It doesn't have a view of anything, but the rent's very light. Of course it's only three rooms and a micro-shower, but that part of the isle is so secluded, you know?" Epsila's voice had taken on the eagerness of the low-rent house proud.

"Forget it. All our home addresses are on file and the syndicate seems to have plenty of access to critical data coming out of the embassy." Tan stared gloomily at Fleur. A horrible sense of helplessness was beginning to creep up on him.

Epsila was looking at her, too. The thought that her little lovenest on Sx Isle was now desecrated by syndicate hitmen, possibly waiting to kill her, had brought angry questions boiling to the surface.

"I'm so sorry, Epsila," Fleur began, seeing Epsila's expression.

"Hold it—I've got it," Armada interrupted. "We'll hide in the A-Z."

Ah-hah, Tan saw it all now, it was a plot by somebody to totally degrade them forever. The A-Z, the absolute nadir of the Sx Coast.

"The Anome Zone, of course!" That settled their fates.

The first stop was to a senso outlet in a nearby retail precinct. On the Sx Coast senso rigs were on sale every hour of the day.

"All we'll need to do is last through the night. At dawn I've got it all figured out," Armada said. The questions multiplied in Tan's mind. Now submerged under senso fields and behind holographic yellow plate armor, they rode the Mass-drive again, looking for all the world like a senso combat team en route to the A-Z. Other people gave them wide berth. The four knights in fuzzy yellow armor were eventually riding alone. Tan looked out gloomily at the waves hurrying below. The Irurupup, in full flood from the monsoon, had risen a few feet closer to the Mass-drive tubes suspended above. To Tan, their flight from the syndicate seemed just as unplanned and disorganized as the torrent below. They'd been off balance from the start. Since Fleur first got the idea of finding the girl, for whatever peculiar reason that was.

At the end of the line, inside the huge pleasure dome, one floor of which housed the Anome Zone, they left the train and rode escalators to the A-Z lobby. They were surrounded by other people in senso rigs. Every imaginable disguise from imitatory statuary to simple cloud forms was employed, and others were in combat senso, too.

At the portal they were admonished by the A-Z Holdings Corporation that under Sx Coast Law they would be beyond all legal restraint or concern of either that corporation or the city government.

The hologram tech spied the Pharamol container in Armada's small pack and demanded an inspection. Fleur and Tan held their breath while Armada opened it. The guard inhaled abruptly at the sight, and Armada bribed him at his next breath and then, five grains lighter, stepped through the security membrane. The guard never even got as far as discovering the components of her revolver, scattered about her person along with the ammo.

The others followed, bunched together inside. Tan gasped, Fleur was rocked for a moment, and Epsila held a hand before her eyes. It was dark in the zone, except as it was lit by a raging array of neon and holos and huge TV plates across which hurtled innumerable advertisements describing things unimaginable.

The dome floor was covered in a warren of three-, four-, and five-story modular structures. Here and there larger establishments shouldered upward another few floors and thrust up colossal casino signs that flashed full-color coverage of events within.

The blare of advertising was intense. Drink in complete Safety at the Hows-a-Sham Rok, security guaranteed—*Yumba yumba, bondé-a-buns, you've never liked it before*—200,199—Safe Drinks 100%—Go, Go, Go, Go!

Electronic Game Saloons, offering total-game environments and big cash payouts for lucky winners, were crowded in one alley. Winning there brought jackpots, but losing meant pain—laser burn or broken bones. And then you had to make it back out of the A-Z, past the slavers who lurked around the doors. Still, business was brisk, and where else could you pick up #3,000 by beating a dumb robot at space war?

Blaat the Almighty is here again! Watch Blaat kill the unwary! Tonight just #600 gets you in to see the horrific Blaat dispatch ten of those he snatched today from the combat mazes. In luxurious surroundings, with full bar service, over two

hundred booths for sexual privacy available. Safe drinks in
secure surroundings—the Towerlite—the Power is in the Tower!

They hit the Hows-a-Sham Rok and Tan was grateful to
have his hands around a drink. Armada laid out the rest of her
plan. Tan had another drink and laughed bitterly. It was madness. "Look, it's seven thousand klicks from here to your home
in the mountains. It's wishful thinking."

"It's been done before, almost," Armada snapped. "I can
do it. I've flown those things several times before."

"But not across a continent." Tan went back for another
drink. "Chug-a-lug, twist of kelp," he told the bartender.

Armada scowled after him then went out to take a look
around. Outside she turned her senso down and mingled in the
crowds. Other establishments were crowded around the big
Hows-a-Sham Rok bar complex. Boxee Dee Sade's Fun n'
Torment was situated next door. Armada looked in. On the bar
a young naked man sat in a cage. He was pleading into a
microphone. Heavy electronic music accompanied his cries.
An audience wearing heavy senso masking ignored him.

Back on the street, Armada cased two rather simple-looking
brothels, another couple of small bars, neither very secure
looking, and then slid back to the Hows-a-Sham Rok.

At the entrance a group of four figures in combat senso
discussed something with a waiter. A manager appeared. He
was being shown an image.

The x-ray tech at the door must have blabbed about scanning
a girl loaded with Pharamol. Armada searched for a side entrance and rejoined the others.

"Quickly, they're checking for us at the door."

They followed her to the side entrance and headed deeper
into the A-Z, toward the full-combat zones.

There was no immediate sign of pursuit but Armada remained wary. They entered the third-level zone. A combat club
took up half one block, Shock-Doktor Combat Lounge blazed
the sign above.

"Sign for a hundred-credit bout, but sign for Level B. That's
vital," Armada said in a reassuring, confident voice.

"Why?" Fleur said. There were several short lines leading
to admittance booths for combatants.

"Because in Level A the house selects your opponent. On
B it can only choose the weapon."

"Why didn't we sit upstairs and watch instead of going in and making fools of ourselves?" Epsila said. "This is awful. I don't want to fight anyone. I don't know how to fight."

"You can use a gun."

"That's different."

Armada was impatient. "Just regress. Use a force baton or whatever they choose."

Epsila's expression was matched by those of Tan and Fleur. Personal combat had hardly been something they were expecting from the night.

Fleur reached the booth and suffered the scrutiny of a young female medic. "A bit scrawny, for this sort of thing, aren't you, dear?" the medic asked.

"None of your business," Fleur said. She was shaking a little as she received a tag.

"Insert the tag when your number is called and you will receive your weapon assignment and combat time."

They waited with dozens of others in senso and watched wall screens showing the bouts in the lounge. The galleries were full, a big crowd in evidence. The combats were of every sort, from kick-boxing, lethal and sublethal levels, to the use of a variety of sublethal weapons often very ingeniously employed for joke bouts. One favorite was mixed-sex bouts with padded rubber staves as weapons. The male participant was drugged to slow his reaction times.

They had pretty high numbers, the end of the night's intake. To kill time, each adopted his or her own strategy. Armada explored the area of the club open to combatants, then examined the competition in sublethal kick-boxing, for which she had entered herself. Tan stared at the competitions, trying to analyze the movements necessary in padded-stave combat while Epsila stared dumbly at the screen as tears welled up in her eyes. Fleur stared at the floor and thought desperately for some way out of this ghastly morass.

Armada was called first. She entered, was placed in a three-corner kick-boxing combat with a slim young man and a heavy-set woman. The young man incapacitated the heavyset woman with a brutally swift combination of left- and right-foot face-smash. He tried for the offensive posture with Armada, too, but she used a low kick to damage his knee. When he rose he was wary, and the bout grew boringly defensive. People even

135

began to groan and boo. The young man attacked again and Armada parried his kick and got in a risky one to his lower abdomen. Winded, he was helpless, and the bout was called dead.

Tan was next and took a drubbing in a four-cornered padded-club combat. He dispatched one man but was immediately struck down from behind by another opponent. He stayed down, too, quite content to be out of the bout with no more damage than bruised shoulders.

The wait grew longer, hours passed. Fleur dozed off and awoke when Armada pushed her in the ribs.

"You're up next. Here—take a grain of Pharamol, it'll really help." Fleur gazed at the criminal purple chemical. A fortune in longevity drugs in every grain. "No, I couldn't."

"Don't be an idiot, you've got to—you've got to win. You've drawn boob worms for weapons."

"What?" Fleur cried in disgust.

"You're in a joke bout, but if you lose, the worm will use you to host its eggs."

"Ugh." Fleur squirmed at the thought of being host animal to the boob worm—a nonlethal coelenterate that ate sludge but needed a warm-blooded host to bring its eggs to term.

Armada shook her by the shoulders. "Come on, lady, wake up. You've got to remember, keep a grip on your own worm. Don't let it sting you by accident."

"Oh, no—I don't know if I can do this." Fleur sounded desperate.

"You have to," Armada said fiercely. Fleur clutched at the Pharamol.

All too soon Fleur found herself in the ring, surrounded by three galleries crowded with jeering spectators. She and her opponent, another woman, were both naked, "a scrawny old pair of witches" as the compere announced so gleefully.

"And now fellow members, the coup de grace for our combatants. Boob worms, full adults, captured this morning in the waters of the Dinge. If you could feel them, you'd know they're heavy with eggs."

An expectant giggle shook the audience.

Fleur found herself hating them, the people who paid to watch such events.

She grabbed the big worm firmly around the nonstinging

136

end, but it fought her grip, trying to pull itself free to bring its stingers, clustered around the pink, nipplelike end, to bear on her skin. Fleur fought down the shivering revulsion that threatened to send her screaming from the ring. As the worm struggled, Fleur remembered and looked up. Her opponent was waving a worm at her and mouthing an insult.

A chime sounded, the crowd roared, and the other woman advanced. Instinctively Fleur held up her worm, clamping it as tightly as possible in her hands. At once she realized that the test would be to see who could keep her grip on her own weapon the longest, because the worms were horribly strong and hard to hold. One slip and she'd be paralyzed while the worm crawled into her intestines. Having a boob worm in your guts was a nonfatal experience but one that few victims could ever manage to forget. It was frequently described as "unbelievably disgusting."

The gaunt-faced woman, with stringy blond hair, was in range and with a practiced move stepped away from Fleur's outstretched arms and inside, then slashed at Fleur's shoulder. Fleur jumped back on reflexes she had never realized she possessed. Then she recalled the Pharamol she'd taken and blessed Armada. She kept retreating from the outstretched worm.

That became the pattern. The blond woman strove to get close and Fleur retreated desperately. It could not last for long. Fleur tripped on her own feet, sprawled headlong. The crowd rocked with laughter but she held onto her worm. The blond woman closed in, a smile frozen on her face, worm held out for the stroke.

Fleur scrabbled away but there was no time to regain her feet. One touch of those stingers and she'd spend the next three days wishing she'd never been born.

The woman lunged and in desperation Fleur did the one thing they always told you not to do, she threw her worm. In the air the worm instinctively tucked in its stingers and so its venom did no harm to the blonde. But it did drive her back with a squeal of horror when it struck her shoulder. She rubbed the spot.

Fleur got to her feet. The released boob worm groped around it for a suitable host animal to sting.

The blonde advanced again, and again Fleur backed around the ring, keeping an eye on the other worm, which now occupied one corner. Soon she was caught between them. The woman lunged and Fleur ducked and instinctively punched her in the solar plexus. The worm missed Fleur by a hairsbreadth and then her opponent sank backward and sat directly on the other worm.

Laughter rocked the galleries. Fleur jumped away as the woman lost her grip on her own worm and immediately suffered its sting as well as that of the one she'd sat on. Both eagerly sought an orifice to enter.

Fleur flew from the ring and ran to the shower room. It took ten minutes for her to stop shaking.

When she rejoined the others they greeted her warmly.

"I don't know how you did it." Armada threw her arm around Fleur's shoulders and hugged her. It was like being squeezed by a young bear. "You did everything wrong, but you did it. Congratulations." Armada toasted her with Restorade. "You should drink a lot of this. It's superrich in vitamins and we'll be needing that."

Epsila's face was etched with anger and fear. Armada stared at Epsila's combat slip. Epsila had drawn boob worms as well.

"I don't know why we're here and I don't much care. I don't know what any of this has to do with me. And I don't want to know about having one of those horrible things inside me." Epsila sounded bitter.

Fleur tried to organize her thoughts, to explain her hunch that Armada, the red-haired fugitive, was somehow connected to the Hith case, but then Epsila's number flashed up on the screen.

"Your turn, Epsila," Armada said. "Have some Pharamol." She extended a grain to Epsila, who took it and then went out the door. However, Epsila didn't enter the ring and after a couple of minutes Armada cursed and began to reassemble her revolver. Not long afterward it was functional once more, fully loaded, and tucked in her waistband. Tan Ubu was left to marvel again. The highland children were given military births as well as funerals, they grew up with guns in their hands.

"Epsila is gone, probably will try and go home," Armada said. Fleur nodded. "So we have to get out of here, too. They'll get her in the station or maybe even at the security membrane. Either way there's not much time and we need to take an elevator."

They left the combat club unopposed and started for the security membrane while Tan protested. "You're talking about seven thousand kilometers over a jungle that you cannot land in, with nothing but a sunsoarer—a glider—nothing more than that. It's insane."

Armada was adamant.

But two security guards stepped forward with drawn force batons. Protesting, the fugitives pressed into an elevator car. The guards entered and the car rose swiftly.

"Where are you taking us?" Fleur asked. "I demand to know."

"It's all right, Fleur. They're taking us to the top floor. I think I can imagine why, too."

Quermwyere and Asgood Wythe were waiting. They greeted Armada with a pair of pitiless smiles.

"Ah, excellent. At last we are reunited. The little hellcat is trapped."

"You grotesque worm, you shouldn't call anyone names. Remember, I've seen you, Quermwyere!"

The banker's fat face split in a jolly-seeming smile. "Yes, my dear, that's true, I remember the occasions very fondly. Old Ira Ganweek has always been good to me."

Armada spat suddenly and the security guards grabbed her arms and bound them behind her.

Wythe reached out and plucked the Pharamol tube from Armada's little sneak pouch.

"Ira will be glad to have this back safe and sound."

"A pity about the other items, isn't it?" Armada sneered.

Wythe flushed. "When they finish with you, girl, you'll have many years to wish that they too could be restored. Messire Ganweek has prepared such thorough, almost extreme methods."

Armada now proceeded to faint, toppling into Tan and falling, forcing him to grab her and hold her in his arms.

"My hip," she whispered. He helped her to her feet and felt the butt of the revolver in her waistband. The guards had not expected weapons. The gun was out of the holster in the next moment and pressed between Quermwyere's eyes.

"That will be enough of that sort of talk," Tan said firmly. ease her!" he shouted at the security guards. "Hurry, man, or he gets it first and then you get it, too."

The guards unfastened Armada, who took their force batons and handed one to Fleur. Then she backhanded Asgood Wythe across the face with the other and sent him into the corner.

She searched him while Fleur held a force baton over his head. Armada removed and pressed to Wythe's head the sleek little snub-nose automatic she found.

The security guards then bound Quermwyere and Wythe under Armada's watchful eyes and then were bound themselves with the same nylon handcuffs. Armada completed the job with four improvised gags.

Armada put the Pharamol back in her suit before she, Fleur, and Tan headed for the roof. There they took the small elevators and rose to the galleries in the cliffwall above, where sunsoarers and other gliders were kept by the Sx Coast Sunsail Club.

A security guard met them at the top and demanded ID. As he examined Fleur's, Armada put her gun to his back and they tied him up and left him in an open hangar cave.

The caves were dug deep into the cliffs at that level and housed an assortment of strange gliders and short-range powered aircraft. A concrete launch apron extended from the cliff. Retrieval was from water landings up a cable system running over the top of the dome.

It was still several minutes before dawn and the place was deserted but for the sole security guard. They had time to break into half a dozen hangars in search of the right kind of sunsoarer. From one cave they pulled two machines that impressed Armada—until she saw the holes in the wing of the bigger one. The other, a yellow-and-black-painted hornet, was a racing club glider and built for speed and distance.

Armada continued to search and then found just what she wanted. She wheeled out a much bigger but equally lightweight glider, a two-person machine with an eighty-foot wingspan and cranks for powering the propellers should the solar-drive motor's storage batteries run down.

"This is what I was hoping to find. It's a real long-distance machine, a deep-sea fish spotter."

Fleur examined the plane with something less than enthusiasm. It looked so flimsy she imagined she could punch holes in it. The pilot positions were thin strips of foam padding on which they'd have to lie, facing forward, side by side under the wing. In front was the tiny, high-efficiency electric motor that drove the big prop at the rear. There was no space for provisions other than water. Armada filled some two-gallon containers and clipped them in place under the pilot pads.

"This is all very well," Tan grumbled, unable to take it all seriously. "But what are you planning to eat? Fruit snatched from the trees? You can forget that—there's only one kind of tree out there and it doesn't bear edible fruit."

Armada dismissed this dietary concern with a cheerful gesture. "Hey, don't worry—I still have at least thirty grams of Pharamol. We'll divide it; that'll keep us going for a couple of weeks at least. We won't need food, although we'll lose a little weight."

Tan recoiled. "You're planning to live on Pharamol and water?"

"Well, it could be worse." Armada shrugged. "Come on, what's the matter with you? Rather stay and fight the syndicates to the bitter end?"

Tan hesitated, a picture of indecision. "This is insane. I can barely believe this is happening to me. A few hours ago I was a well-respected diplomat, holding down a great post. Now I've got to risk my life in that thing." He was getting angry. "Look, it's seven thousand kilometers, you'll never make it."

"Tan, enough!" Fleur snapped. "What else is there to do? They'll kill us, they made that perfectly clear. We're too dangerous to them now to be allowed to live."

"We could go to Andrej, ask him to get us offplanet. We could go down and get the Mass-drive right now. Before Quermwyere and Wythe get loose."

"Something makes me think that Blake won't help us. And we'll be in danger every moment of our lives afterward even if he did and if he could protect us, which I doubt. No, the only safe place now is out of the Sx Coast, and this seems to be the only way to go. I'm going to try it anyway. I know it sounds crazy..." It sounds crazy to me, too, she finished in her head. It is crazy, but what else can we do?

"Are you ready? The sun's up. An early start is essential. They'll be out searching for us later. We need to get a few hours on them."

Fleur shed her senso rig and everything else except a single layer of clothing. "Which one am I going to fly?" she asked.

"You fly with me in this one. He can take the hornet."

141

Fleur opened the fragile hatch and worked her way into the narrow, foam-lined cradle in which she would have to lie for at least a week. Armada shut her in, freed the chocks from the undercarriage cradle, which would stay behind on the ramp, then wheeled it to the launching point. From there extended the jump down which they would pick up speed before launching into the air.

Tan watched them, put a hand to cover his eyes from the new day's sun. "Aren't you coming?" Armada asked as she looked back.

Something seemed to snap at last inside him and he growled, "No, I'm not." He turned and stalked back up the gallery toward the elevator. Armada watched his departing back for a moment then glanced down at Fleur, who was cinched in, gripping the control bar so hard her knuckles showed white. Armada shrugged then set the bird rolling, jumped into her cradle, and pulled the hatch down over her.

The sunsoarer rumbled down the ramp and up the jump then wobbled out into the air. They were airborne with the wind whistling past and the ocean far below.

Fleur shrieked a little at the sight, but Armada pointed to the propeller, which was already turning, the engine humming busily. Soon the huge gossamer-winged machine picked up a little speed, lifting into the sea breeze. They swung around in a huge arc over the water and headed inland. The onshore morning breeze picked up their speed a little more and soon they were making a respectable seventy klicks an hour and maintaining an altitude of two thousand meters.

"Where's Tan?" Fleur asked after a while.

"He stayed behind, didn't get in his plane."

Somehow Fleur had expected that. Since it was too late to go back, she forced herself to dismiss it. If she survived what lay ahead, she'd come back and look for Tan Ubu, but just then he was on his own.

At the elevator shaft on the cliff face above the glider terrace, Tan watched as the big graceless soarer turned over the ocean and disappeared inland. He checked his gun and felt the weight of the ammo in his pocket, then started down in the elevator.

12

IN THE GREEN OF LATE AFTERNOON, THE SLEEPY CRY OF THE calanther echoed across the bush draws of the riverbank. The bloodmeknots, the monsoon flower, were out in scarlet profusion, drawing vibrant patches beneath the glob glob and jik scrub.

In the groves of liskal the blue-gray blossoms were thickly massed on the branches; insects buzzed about them; shiny green-banded chitin foraged on the meadows. The olive-tinged light of Beni shaded the few wisps of high cirrhus in an otherwise cloudless vault of blue-green. It was a time of regeneration, refreshed with the monsoon waters. The nibbla were mating beneath the roots of trees; with the dusk, the sarmer mackees would begin to mate. The mountains were like dark outlines in the sky, stark in the clear air, backdrop to the quiet.

Through the liskal orchards they tracked the gzan, a kin pod of six adults and as many pups. The blue-gray blossom filled the air with its musky, fruity scent, but Bg Rva, with occasional pauses to sniff the ground more closely, followed the faint trail of their quarry. They'd found the droppings two kilometers back, along the riverbank where the gzan had paused to drink. Now the hunters closed in swiftly, slipping quickly across the clearings, hesitating only moments behind each tree.

Rva caught a hint of motion ahead. He gave a signal and Lavin, a clip of quarrels loaded in the crossbow, shifted crab-wise off the trail beneath a twisted little jik tree. Rva faded back into the scrub on the other side of the trail.

The chief of the kin pod, the premier bull, trotted into view farther down the bank. He was nervous, sensing that danger lay close at hand. He paused to taste the air, but he was upwind of the hunters. He was a fine specimen; his spine plates were fully developed, with purple spines, and the nose crowns were heavy, the mark of the successful harem lord.

They waited; they had no intention of trying for the bull, a two-ton behemoth that they had no use for. Ubanquini had specified a pup, a nice fat calf pup, no than two hundred pounds, so that the chops would be perfect for toasting at her special fire.

The group ahead had six youngsters to rear, something that slowed the pod and made the bull understandably nervous. Taking one would make the lot of the others easier. Perhaps two would survive to mature after the next monsoon rather than just one. Thus Bg Rva had calculated before setting out to trail the kin pod.

The bull disappeared in the glob glob of the next draw along the bank. "He'll be in ambush now, waiting for us to appear."

Lavin nodded and took to the water, slipping over the edge into the stream to float silently, like a great sarmer mackee, holding the crossbow and his communicator out of the water.

Rva took the higher path, going around the bull where it waited in the thicket, impatient for enemies to appear that it might charge and trample.

Beyond, on a meadow enclosed within a loop of the stream, they found the pod.

Five females, two of them fat-bellied with young, grazed while pups gamboled and charged. Rva slipped into the deeper thickets to cross the pod's line of retreat. Lavin took up a position by the bank, hidden in marsh reed, bow at the ready.

Rva burst from hiding with explosive speed, a streak of dark fur over the arble. The gzan reacted with instant flight, but

144

toward the riverbank, where they were forced to swing sharply to their right, cutting back as Rva closed.

It was over in a moment. Rva reached close enough to scratch the flanks of the lead female and then slacked his pace, content without a kill, satisfied with just the knowledge that he could have taken the gzan—without even the kifket—if he'd needed to.

But the kin pod was less one calf pup. A small male lay still, near the river. Three quarrels jutted from its throat and flank. Rva noted that it was the plumpest of the litter, the tastiest and also the least likely to survive the nachri and were-cat. He also noted the accuracy of the shooting. As always Lavin Fundin found the mark.

An hour later they broke out of the brush, their packs laden with the dressed flesh of the pup, and found Pilot Gruness dozing beside the airbed where they'd left him.

"Well, Pilot, do you care to join us for supper? After enduring the boring part of the hunt, you've earned your place in yard."

Gruness, who had actually enjoyed a peaceful afternoon in the woods, was glad to accept. Fein feast in yard was a privilege extended to few humans.

"Well, Rva, d'ya think Ubanquini will mind a pilot in her yard?"

Rva feigned distress. "I think she will be much too happy to see one. She will want to know all about planes, so she can pester me to get her one. Maybe she will want to learn to be a pilot, too."

Lavin chuckled at the thought of Ubanquini, a matriarch in her fourth brood, wanting to fly in a VTOL jet. Even Rva was terrified of the things, didn't even like to ride the Impi balloons.

They took the bouncing airbed back into Brelkilk village, which more resembled a parkland forest than any human habitation. Ubanquini's yard was fenced with dark clickholly trees through which they wound until they reached the newly constructed long hut. Since the summit meeting at Stroins' Rock, Rva had been building a whole new set of yard shelters and storerooms. He built in the traditional manner, cutting and fashioning jik wood beams and wall posts while the cubs wove mats of barkfiber and glob glob frond that were then daubed with clay and heated rock-hard over the embers of the fire.

145

The effort of keeping Ubanquini's fourth brood, three wild little males and a pair of arrogant females, hard at work had been enough to give Rva fits. Yet the hut had risen, almost on schedule, as had the shelters for Ubanquini's horses and the storerooms. The old ones had been fed to the fire.

Ubanquini had called many of the Rva kin together for the feast and she and her cubs labored all day in stripping a vast variety of seeds, nuts, and fruits and combining them in salads, or preparing them for various methods of cooking.

She inspected their catch with a critical eye, squeezing the flesh of the thighs and opening the lip to glimpse the teeth. There was nothing to find fault with. Indeed she praised Bg Rva for an excellent choice. Immediately therefore the pup's flesh was butchered and trimmed for the fire. Gruness was invited to smoke teosinte and drink fiery gwassa draughts with the elder Rvas as they lit the fire with the usual ritual and banter. For the occasion the males were wearing the full-length hide apron called the dmembl, and each carried the special kifket of his name and kin place. The sheaths of these were elaborately decorated and emblazoned with ritual fetishes.

Surrounded by the taller, heavier fein, Gruness felt like an elf among giants, but he accepted the teosinte pipe as it was passed and he took a swig of gwassa, after a moment to nerve himself for it. He got it down, too, and felt the immediate warmth spread in his stomach as it was absorbed. By then the teosinte smoke had taken hold and he began to understand the jokes and cheerful insulting banter being passed around among the males.

Somebody asked him why humans were so often vegetarian and Gruness struggled to reply, acknowledging that he was a vegetarian himself. His answers hardly satisfied the Rva fein, and they each brought forth some sally or other concerning the mystery of human ways.

The fire blazed while they drank gwassa, and when it died down somewhat Ubanquini and Bg Rva laid the gzan in chops, steaks, and cutlets over the embers on a circular grille. Enough salad and vegetable dishes had been prepared for any vegetarian, and Gruness soon filled a plate before rejoining the group around the fire.

Ubanquini then held court from her place by the gwassa jug, the traditional seat for the female in whose yard the feast

146

was held. She thus monitored the flow of gwassa and protected the notorious drunkards from overconsumption. Lavin Fundin sat next to her, a place granted as a mark of courtesy and respect.

Groz Rva, Ubanquini's oldest uncle, Mzsee to everyone else, was consumed by something he'd seen on the television set that his daughter Fiullili had received from her lover. He called across the fire to Lavin.

"It is a truth that for the fein to understand the human is much more difficult than for humans to understand the fein. Ours is the true life, as it has always been, and thus we hunt as we were meant to, and our numbers are small for there are but two hundred bahlkwan fein in all the world, or as you would put it, a little more than a million. Our life is simple, but the humans live what the adepts call the life of 'shadows,' penned in stalls, cut off from the sky. They live out of the light, they travel in the great dark between the worlds, they exploit the world for gain, excepting of course the fein-friend humans with whom we live as kin.

"I have read that humans were once hunters, possibly like ourselves, and I should add than I am the tenth in line of the Groz Rvas who is able to read, another thing brought to us by the humans though the adepts say that once the fein could read, or decipher ancient texts of lore. But with the Mahgara—the Exodus—all these things began to fade, and so long has our footprint been laid upon the world that we have lost all trace of such things. For the real life, the life of the soul, should always be the life of the trees and the stars. To walk beneath them and to gaze upon the glory of the evanescence of the Creator."

Bg Rva coughed. Groz Rva was a notoriously longwinded Mzsee of Mzsees.

"Yes, well as I was saying, I have read about the human love of hunting, but now I have seen this thing they do in the forest near the coast that they call hunting but what it has to do with hunting I cannot tell. My little Fiullili has one of those devil boxes that they get over in Ghotaw and I have seen this; the humans go out into the forest in machines and use modern weapons to kill animals like the nachri or the gnirr, even the woodwose. They take only trophies from the prey. There is no edible flesh from these creatures, nor are they worth the trouble

147

to hunt for none of them would think to hide from an enemy. So I wondered and I wonder now, why do they do this thing which seems so unnatural?"

Many tails were in shirrithee, the idea of attacking the wood-wose was so alien, so strange.

Ubanquini spoke, her voice hushed. "We remember when they came here to hunt the fein and to kill them and take the skins only. Nor did they hunt within the grace of the world but always with their modern weapons. They were the antilife, the destroyers of grace and desecrators of the All. But thankfully other humans were already here, the fein friends, the long lived, they who stand beside us."

Gruness swelled with pride. Ubanquini's wrinkled face and muzzle, the clear yellow circles of her eyes, flickered in the firelight. Fat spattered as the chops roasted. Meat was handed round and Ubanquini allowed another jug of gwassa to circulate.

Old Groz came out of shirrithee later than everyone else and said in a loud voice, "They have aided us with their weapons and their blood, and between the fein friends and the coastal humans there is only hatred and death. As I have said before, and will no doubt say again, it is a truth that the fein must struggle to understand the human; for the human it is easy to understand the fein."

Lavin set aside the rib he'd been chewing and wiped his lips. Old Groz, vying just a little with Bg Rva's supremacy among the Rva kin, wanted a public reply.

"It is a truth, Mzsee, indeed it is hard to comprehend the humans for they are like the great Irurupup, and the fein are like the river of Abzen near the spring at Gray Rock where you can step across in one stride. The fein are but one-colored thread on the loom of the All, but the humans are a million bahlkwan colors, and each is different yet all are the same.

"Now this so-called hunting that the coastals do, this is something that must be seen in the context of the whole human race. It is not the way that all humans would hunt, nor have there been humans who live the true life, the life of the soul, in the manner of the ay fein, for hundreds of years. And yet that is not even a single bahlkwan—six *thousand* years—for the human race is a torrent, a great river bursting with floodwaters, whose components cannot be numbered for they are many,

many times a bahlkwan, and then again and again. Even then you would not approach the number of humans alive. But though humanity is vast in numbers, it is tiny in age. Our years are few, for the fein have lived more than ten thousand bahlkwan while humans have lived on their home planet but five hundred bahlkwan.

"The humans are the children of sentience, with great power but little self-control. In this they are the opposite of the fein, and they know little of themselves. But it is true that once we hunted as do the fein, just for food. In itself hunting and trapping were but components in our lives, much as it has always been with the fein. In this I myself believe we see a sense of order that transcends the distances between worlds. Forms develop employing the same elements, guided by common principles, sharing identical processes and following similar tracks. But always, within the All, there are differences, too. Humanity's urge has been to expand and explore the universe and find new worlds. Here on Fenrille some humans became the fein friends. Now there are the other humans, but they bring the way of life of the human worlds and know nothing of the fein or Fenrille. Because they are hemmed in, because they exist only for the longevity drugs, there is no soul in their lives, their cities exist only for pleasure and for murder. This so-called hunting is just another form of escape. They call it a sport but it is nothing, it is certainly not the way all humans would hunt. I find it pathetic, a mockery of the true hunt."

There was no doubting the sincerity in Lavin's voice. Gruness almost wished he wasn't a human being at all, the ways of the coastals were such an abomination.

Then Lavin spoke again, with less anger audible in his tone. "Now there is another side of this, though, for some humans go out to hunt in the deep forest with just the bow or a rifle. They brave the hand of the woodwose to hunt the nachri and the gnirr, because those animals are so powerful, so strong and fierce that they represent a challenge. The humans are a young race and they can still remember the thrill of the hunt. But how many fein, if they were men instead, would care to hunt alone in the great woods?"

Eyes widened. Old Groz looked a little uncomfortable.

"So you see they take a great risk for what they believe to be glory, and perhaps in that there is a truth."

Of course every cub longed to hunt in the great forest with just the bow and kifket. Disparaging the dangers' Obwode, Ubanquini's eldest in the fourth brood, broke in. "What's to fear from old longlegs woodwose? He cannot catch the fein."

Lavin chuckled. "Obwode has yet to run from longlegs in his home. I want to be there when Obwode comes walking impudently through the treeyards of old longlegs and has no fear."

Ubanquini laughed, thanking the lord Lavin for his gracious handling of Groz' attempt to secure riffchuss. "That day will come soon for my fine, fat Obwode and he will run from longlegs, you'll see him striding inside the monsoon year. Maybe even before the rains come. Certainly he pesters the females enough for one who should already have been to the forest."

Bg Rva now brought out a barrel of Ubanquini's homebrew and distributed a round.

Lavin was just finishing his first pot of brew when his communicator shrilled on the alarm mode. He tuned in the message, relayed from Cracked Rock Fort by the battlecomputer on the airbed.

Space Marines had landed in Spreak Valley, heavy fighting was taking place around Spreak Hold. Elsewhere orbital fighters hung overhead in full squadrons, powerful sensors were probing computer defenses; war was breaking out across the continent.

The word quickly passed around the fire. Lavin made his apologies to Ubanquini and left with Gruness and Bg Rva. Other Rvas, neilks in the Second Impi, began to slip away soon afterward, eager to rejoin their posts.

13

WAR CRACKLED IN THE HIGH EQUATORIAL VALLEYS AS THE Space Forces probed for weaknesses in the highlanders' defense.

The contestants were mismatched, or so it seemed at first. The thirty-first-century technology of the Space Fleet so obviously outclassed the clan armies that the High Command aboard the *Gagarin* looked forward to a brief, salutary conflict. Their warships assumed low orbits to deploy and retrieve flights of orbital fighters. The *Gagarin* launched scores of Space Marines' pods on commando raids in the valleys.

Throughout the operation, a vast quantity of microelectronic probes, sensors, and transmitters was dumped over the highlands. Soon a torrent of data was being processed by the computers aboard *Gagarin*. Simultaneously the ships directed powerful particle beams to claw out defensive electronics and blind radar eyes. In some valleys the power of the beams and the quality of the Space Forces' intelligence gathering were an unwelcome surprise. Computers, radar, communications equipment, all were soon chopped to shards of smoking plastic.

Performance on the part of the Space Marines varied widely from place to place. In the Purple Valley of the Chung, Im Ten Chung was caught squarely in the open with his Twelve Winds Impi. Eleven pods of Space Marines dropped on him in the classic "falling square" manuever. Intense suppressive fire from *Gagarin* and a flight of orbital aerodynams kept the concrete clamshells shut on the great Chung fortress of Bolun Mountain.

Without artillery support or air cover, the Twelve Winds Impi was forced into a brutal firefight with the Space Marines in dense jik thicket. A heavy toll was taken before the battered Impi, hundreds of fein down, managed to stagger away and hole up in the Glay Caverns.

The victorious marines formed up and in 100 meter leaps marched their armored suits to the small fortress at Tilay, which served as Im Ten Chung's headquarters.

The defenders spun the clamshell but orbital fighters appeared and strafed them until they shut it again. The marines broke through a thin screen of fein outside and reached the ferroconcrete walls. They scaled the outer blastshields and laid shaped satchel charges against the turret collar. In a few minutes it was all over. The shell was cracked, the turret collapsing in on the mass-drive cannon. The marines took many prisoners and then pushed on to the grouping area at a more leisurely pace.

Shortly afterward the eastern sky bloomed with a harsh new sun as a massive booster shuttle dropped toward them. While another flight of orbital fighters skimmed over, their sonic booms cracking like giant whips, the marines boarded quickly and shuttled skyward at twelve gees.

At Ghotaw Mountain a major battle was fought between the Third Space Marine Battalion, 650 strong, and the Ninth, Tenth, Fourth, and Twelfth Ghotaw Impis. At times during the hour-long struggle the front was more than fifty kilometers long before the marines finally broke contact to escape a slowly encircling net of fein units and artillery backup. The marines regrouped on North Uip Moor, out of direct range of the mass-drives on Ghotaw Mountain.

On the third day of the fighting the *Gagarin* veered slightly south of the equator and scoured Abzen Valley for unshielded radar. A scatter of clean nuclear warheads was detonated just outside the atmosphere, sending EMP surges groundward faster than lightning and zapping all unshielded electronics on the voltage surges.

Then the *Crecy* hurtled over the horizon and launched a squadron of orbital fighters that coursed down Abzen at forty percent of orbital velocity and left a trail of orange fireballs, sonic booms, and spiraling smokeclouds lifting from the valley floor.

"Brace yourselves," Lavin Fundin said as the clamshell spun on Cracked Rock Fortress to present the eight-meter-thick blast shield to the incoming fire. The fort shuddered, the whole structure rocked slightly under the impacts, shifting upon the waterbearing at the bottom of the shaft and discharging much of the received energy.

Assault pods were already leaving short streaks of fire in the upper atmosphere. Soon the chutes of Space Marines and fighting robots were freckling the sky over Abzen. Radars exposed vulnerable dishes to scan the descending cloud of parachutes, chaff, and decoys. A flood of data kicked the Cracked Rock computers into frantic activity as they dug through the mess for real targets.

High above the computers, buried in their cocoonlike Faraday cages under hundreds of meters of rock, Lavin Fundin watched the orbital fighters pass overhead for the last time and begin their climb back to orbital space. Instantly he spun the clamshell. The motors groaned briefly and the 3,000 ton mass of sculpted ferroconcrete turned smoothly while the outer blast shield rose like a helmet's visor to expose the heart of the fortress, the multiple barrels of the mass-drive cannon. The magnet gates whined like rock demons in the great central shaft and the hydraulics smoothly lifted the cannon into the turret.

Only the high-speed impacts of the charged delivery cups betrayed the firing of the guns as they accelerated steel shot, canister, and puncture cones, under the direction of the computers, into the descending enemy ranks. So rapid was the fire that for a few seconds the delivery cups made a roaring sound as a million impacts were compressed into a second or less.

Another wave of aerodynams arced over the wall of mountains and missiles leaped from their belly bays. The ferroconcrete shell spun once more. Detonations rocked the structure, shaking it from shell to shaft. By the time it could be spun again to bring the guns to bear, the enemy would be on the ground. Lavin and Bg Rva sprinted for the elevators. On the airstrip Pilot Gruness had the motors running and within a minute they were airborne. Four pods of Space Marines were down in Orank Woods, close to Ebble Meadows and the major radar and communications station of Bitaraf Shoals.

As Gruness held the craft low over the treetops, he kept a sharp eye on the radar for any hint of orbital fighters. He had no protection against their deadly heat seekers. Lavin examined the situation at Orank with mounting concern. The Space Marines' robots were jamming communications very effectively while employing false orders in attempts to confuse Fundan listeners.

"There's only one target they could be after. The question is, how did they find Bitaraf? It's completely hidden, under rocks, a classified secret."

Rva grunted, muzzle agape, mocking him. "You forget the devices I showed you, the little spy eyes. They are everywhere."

Lavin nodded glumly. It probably had been from such ubiquitous electronic surveillance. It presented a poor omen for their future. How could they keep any element of suprise under the constant monitoring of a million microelectronic cameras, many of them mobile, creeping around like little metal insects and beaming images skyward every other second. The techs at Cracked Rock had promised EMP emitters to destroy them, but it would take several days for the workshops to turn out a sufficient quantity. Lavin had made it a top-priority item nonetheless.

The dark leaves of the jik forest flashed past below them. Lavin turned to Bg Rva. "Well, what units do we have in the area?" Lavin's tone betrayed his considerable apprehension.

Bg Rva hastily inquired of the battlecomputer, his big, brown furred fingers tapping delicately on the small square keys of his hand module. He read out the data as it presented itself on the screen.

"At the stone bridge below Bitaraf Shoals we have the First Sept, Second Impi. They guard the bridge and are dug in there. In Bitaraf Woods there's a screen of pickets from the Ninth Sept, Second Impi. In close support of Bitaraf there's also a section from the Third Artillery; three guns, an eight-person team. They're in North Ebble."

The radio was still almost useless; all frequencies were a riot of static and enemy transmissions of enormous power.

"Who's in charge of those guns?" Lavin snapped, brow furrowed as he pictured the terrain at Bitaraf.

"Glor Fundan, Second Lieutenant, third year."

Lavin's eyebrow rose. "Young Glor, is it? Well, let's hope that her true-genes have brought her enough wit to see our peril. We need those guns."

They skimmed the waters of the river Abzen and then the tall arble of Ebble Meadows. The trees of Ebble lay ahead.

"So, is that it? That's all we've got to put between four pods of Space Marines and our second-most-important radar station?" Lavin's exasperation was audible.

"Well"—Rva swallowed—"there's a band of chitin talkers and a battalion of trainee technicians. They're on their way back to Cracked Rock from mountain training. They've been up on Kirrim since the day before we caught Young Proud at Scrawn Moor. They're bivouacked at Bitaraf with the chitin people."

Lavin pursed his lips, nodded sourly, then he settled down to think. The plane, Rva, Gruness, everything else faded away in his mind as he concentrated on the terrain and the forces at hand.

Five hundred young, doubtless weary trainees fresh from the Ghotaw Schools and an extended mountain trip. They weren't much, but by a stroke of fortune they were in the right place, and if the chitin team realized what was happening then there was just a chance. An accident of the terrain might give them an outside chance.

He glanced at the chronometer. They had less than fifteen minutes before the Space Marines could be expected to be in range.

Gruness brought them in with a boom of motors by Ebble Bridge. Distingi of Fuflafu, Neilk of the First Step, Second Impi, was waiting. A tall, black-furred fein with the genetic rarity of turquoise eyes, Distingi greeted Lavin with a detailed battle plan and a list of actions already underway. Lavin found his own plans anticipated. Already the bulk of the First Sept was upstream with the picket line in Bitaraf Woods. All units

155

had caught the alarm and enemy position coordinates. Furthermore, Distingi and Glor Fundan had conferred and Glor's three guns were en route to Bitaraf.

"I always knew there had to be a reason why Distingi of Fuflafu was rising so rapidly in the ranks," Lavin said as they roared off again on howling boosters.

"Distingi is still in fourth molt, a mere stripling and already he has sept udars running for him. Who would've thought it possible of a green eye? And someone from Fuflafu, of all places."

Lavin chuckled at Rva's yellow-eyed prejudice. "Ng Tung will have to watch for that one in a few years. He'll want riffchuss."

Rva made a wry face. "Today's youth are a strange lot. Maybe it's the time we live in but still they're strange to an old Mzsee of the widepath."

"Yet efficiency is something to be encouraged. We survive by it."

"Lord, imagine being a Sept Udar in Distingi of Fuflafu's sept. Those green eyes peering down at you every morning, scrutinizing for every detail, criticizing everything—riffchuss, you mention riffchuss? Bah, I'd rather hunt a sick gzan."

Lavin turned over in his hands the pair of electronic creepy crawlies that Distingi had handed him. Each had been disabled with a kifket chop. The sept had worked hard in the early part of the day to clear the woods around the bridge of electronic spy devices. Slow work considering the scale of the problem— there were literally millions of the things, in many different kinds, scattered over the valleys. The ones he was holding, for instance, were the size of his thumb, moved on four spiderish legs, and carried a bewildering array of sensors.

"What's the chitin team at Bitaraf?" he enquired.

Rva read it from the screen. "The Quixotic Cavaliers. A mounted group, in the ninth percentile."

"Excellent, I know them—an enterprising crew indeed. Came in third last year in the chitin trials. Defeated the Brelkilk Bullions in the quarter finals if my memory's correct." Lavin grinned slyly sideways but Rva pretended indifference to the name. The Hero of Brelkilk wanted to forget the fortune in horseflesh he'd lost in wagering on the Bullions.

They landed to find the Cavaliers awaiting them, a band of

twenty men and women in traditional chitin talker garb—leggings, loose shirts, caps with marks of rank and skill. Bold, suntanned people, with the ease of those used to life in the open and the confidence of those with millions of credits in the bank. At the first sounds of attack they had roused themselves and the youngsters of the tech battalion. All chitin crews carried weapons and had access to the hidden cache system that spread ammunition and small arms all over the valley. The techs were now well armed, drawn up in marching column.

"We recommend moving to Bitaraf overlook. There are clear fields of fire there," said Lynn Styngely, the Cavalier's coordinator, "clear all the way to the crossing."

"Exactly. Carry on," Lavin agreed. "We'll join you. The enemy landed quite short of their target but they'll be along soon. I suggest double time. Let's hurry." They moved forward. Lavin had taken an assault rifle, Rva hefted a Kelchworth .90-caliber machine gun and a box of ammo belts. Pilot Gruness remained behind in the clearing with his VTOL and waited for the orbital fighters overhead to pass.

In clearings all over North Ebble, other VTOL jets were waiting for the signal to attack. Microwave tightbeam receptors were strung in the trees.

They reached the path above Bitaraf in time to catch sight of the artillery teams pounding along ahead with their mules, ears up stiff and mad.

Glor Fundan saluted crisply enough as she jogged by with the others.

"Wide separation please, Lieutenant," Lavin called as she passed. "I want those guns well spread out."

Behind the brush that fringed the open slope above the crossing of the Ebble, they took their positions. Lavin and Rva set the trainees out in two long lines, six paces between each man, along the edge of Bitaraf Overlook. Two hundred meters away the shoals cut the swift Ebble into a myriad white sheets of water.

The First Sept was coming into position on their left, reinforcing the pickets who already filled the woods. The Space Marines would have to cross there, where the Ebble broke over the shoals, or leap downstream to the bridge. Lavin was sure they'd take the direct route. Of course any lesser streams they'd simply jump, but the Ebble was in spate and was already a wide, deep river at that point, hurrying in a torrent to join its sister, the Abzen.

Lavin calculated that they simply had to hold the Space Marines for a few minutes. By then his aircraft would be overhead as the orbital fighters were forced to lift out of the atmosphere for retrieval to refuel. The marines would face annihilation if his planes caught them in the open.

"Here they come," Bg Rva announced. He was dug into a hole behind a tree, the Kelchworth .90 projecting its twin barrels from under a coiling root. Suddenly, dazzling metal figures could be seen, soaring on long, leaping bounds just above the foliage on the far side of the river.

Lavin passed up and down behind the trainees at a trot, ordering them to hold their fire, encouraging the gunners, and casting a keen scrutiny on each young tech's position. With no time to dig a foxhole, they had to use the terrain as well as possible. As he passed them he felt the intensity of their gaze. It was a warm, sunny day, but explosive death was only seconds away. The tension gripped them all like a charged field.

"Steady along here now," he cautioned in a quiet but effective voice. "Hold fire until you have a clear shot at faceplate and neck collar. Those are the weak points. Conserve ammunition—what seems like a lot at the beginning of a firefight can seem all too little by the end."

His firm voice steadied them, and they renewed their determined stares westward.

"All right, take good aim now, they're advancing straight over the shoals. They must bunch at the keyhole rock, so concentrate your fire there."

The Space Marines lurched forward from the concealing vegetation. In the open, treading carefully over the slippery rocks of the shoals, they were for once slow and vulnerable. Then the defensive fire cracked down with a roar, punctuated by the deeper chatter of the Kelchworth machine guns and the air bursts of canister shell from the mobile artillery.

There was considerable surprise among the marines. So swift had been their progress without opposition that they had not expected resistance until they reached the target itself.

The incoming fire was heavy, though, and each direct hit from an assault rifle at that range felt like a kick from a mule. Very quickly their armor was pocked and scored from impact and ricochets. The .90 slug of the Kelchworths was even less pleasant and could disable a soldier even inside a Shnyss body shell.

The marine officers quickly assessed the situation while dense fire from the slopes ahead and above whined off the rocks and impacted frighteningly on armor. They hunkered back under the trees and called for aerial support. Then fighting robots began to mortar the Fundan positions. But at least 1,200 seconds would pass before one of the capital ships could provide orbital fighters. Long before that the defenders would have VTOL aircraft overhead and progress by the marines would be cut to a crawl.

Once again the Marines drove forward, firing rifle and grenade ordnance to suppress enemy fire. However, at the first crump of the robot mortars, Lavin had pulled the techs back from the battle edge, leaving only a few spotters. Only when the marines reached the keyhole rock in midstream did he order the techs back.

Once more the defensive fire grew intense. When finally the marines won through to the far shore, the mobile mass-drive cannon began to accelerate puncture cones and steel shot at them. If they caught the right angle, puncture cones would crack a suit's body armor like eggshell. Two marines were struck so in the shoals and died instantly. Another took a Kelchworth round through the faceplate. Yet another missed his footing and fell into the stream and was washed down to quieter waters before he could right himself and move along the riverbed. VTOL aircraft were approaching in numbers.

With four dead, one missing, and two more with defective suits, the mission commander was forced to order a retreat to the secondary collection zone. The marines were forced to crawl along below the tree cover as the Fundan jets then controlled the air. Progress was slow but eventually a frustrated, battered commando assembled to watch the flare of a daytime star bloom in the western sky as the *Gagarin* launched a booster shuttle to collect them.

Lavin watched them go with mixed feelings.

"Lord?" Rva said questioningly.

"We held them here, but we were lucky." Lavin indicated the cheering crowd of young techs. "What if these kids had been one more day in the mountains?" Lavin said. He didn't voice his other, grimmer realization—if the enemy had had better air cover, they'd all be dead now.

The tech brigade ran up cheering and chanting his name, and Lavin let them whoop for a few minutes.

A dull boom, followed by ground-trembling thunder, announced the booster's lift-off while orbital fighters once again pounded the clamshell of Cracked Rock.

Lavin held up his hands. The techs gradually grew quiet.

"Okay, we won today here at Bitaraf Shoals. But let no one deceive himself—it could easily have gone the other way. We were fortunate on two counts: the terrain and their lack of air cover. Furthermore, we had three artillery pieces; that was our decisive edge." He glared around at them, angry for the loss of lives, even though their casualties had been slight.

"This struggle has just begun. We must guard our optimism and keep our weapons ready. Now, at double time, to the bridge at Ebble."

In moments he was airborne again, streaking back to Cracked Rock.

14

NEWS OF THE FIGHTING SENT THE CHITIN EXCHANGE ON THE Sx Coast into a roaring panic. As soon as the doors opened the next day, the floors were jammed. All contracts were off, all long bids canceled, nobody was selling chitin for any price. Stocks and shares in public companies, warbands, syndicates, fell precipitously. By noon, the sweat pouring freely down his face, Quermwyere was sitting in John Freeman's office above the howling mob of brokers on the floor. The President of the Exchange had a deathly expression on his face. In a century of operation in the so-called New Building, there had never been such a panic. His personal fortune in warband shares had been wiped out. He was ruined. Quermwyere struggled to reach the president, lost somewhere in a mental morass. John Freeman had to act before everybody was ruined.

Rex Songbird and Asgood Wythe entered past Freeman's protesting assistant. They sat with Quermwyere and together they strove to put Freeman back together again.

At five minutes to noon, a shaken Freeman walked out to the bell outside his office and the exchange was closed. Brokers scuffled with exchange officers as the doors were shut and the day's business came to a premature halt.

A tangible pall of unease hung over every coastal city as ubiquitous as the TV news broadcasts that updated the story throughout the day. Nobody could speak of anything else.

The sun set through a distant haze of upper latitude origin, vapor drifting south from the vast volumes of exhaust generated by shuttle boosters and orbital fighters. Beni sank like a scarlet ball into a flat red shadow and was lost within it. Blood shadows flushed the cities, and many people shuttered their windows and abandoned their balconies.

The security channel crackled with the code phrase "The Mother Aloft," and Suella went into action. The Space Marine she'd picked up in the Pleasure Palace was dozing. She stuck the nerve-stun syrette bud into his neck and though he came awake long enough to reach for her, he was unconscious before he could more than bruise her neck. It'd been closer than she'd expected though and she was shivering a little when she slipped into the shower and reached for the steam tap.

For Fair's human security team it was a rare opportunity to excel—the first time they had guarded the person of the Mother Fair in sixty years, since her last personal visit to the Sx Coast.

She was dressed for this as any other well-to-do Sx Coast matron might be. A pantsuit of green and white linen, a white veil starred with green shimmers. She kept a subtle senso operating, an enhancement of the veil. In various guises the team had shadowed her progress, from the airport to the spaceport terminal and then to the shuttle. Now they clustered around the arrivals tube aboard the Red Moon.

Team leader Frick Fundin was wearing the gray overalls of the orbiter Customs Staff, which allowed him to wear and use the walkie-talkie prominently displayed on his shoulder.

Gay Fundin was working on the innards of an information display terminal while wearing the blue and white uniform of the Orbiter Maintenance Corps.

Lucy Fundin was traveling in the same group of passengers as the Mother Fair, and she had picked up the syndicate tail during the early moments of the flight. His face had spurred her memory, and suddenly she found a particular name in the long lists of such names and faces that every security officer memorized.

When they disembarked from the shuttle she signaled to Fair to wait a crucial few moments, thus forcing the syndicate man to disembark first. Lucy's alarm call reached Frick at the same moment. Lucy then moved ahead of Fair, to the rear of the syndicate tail.

The tail turned when Frick tried to detain him at the customs point and ran back down the tube. He met only Gay Fundin, however, Lucy having shepherded Fair out through a maintenance exit. Gay Fundin caught the syndicate man, disarmed him, and stunned him. Then he picked him up, took him to the maintenance airlock, and discharged him into space. The word sped around the team in code, from point to point around the orbiter city.

Suella opened the door after the fifth carefully measured knock. Fair was wearing typical tourist clothes, like some dowdy Coast County aunt. Suella suppressed a smile. Fair slipped inside accompanied by a girl from the security team.

"Greetings, Mother Fair," Suella whispered, accepting Fair's embrace.

Fair was visibly excited. "Do you know, child, I haven't been offplanet in two hundred years. I was so excited I couldn't sit still, even during that acceleration. Ugh, that's one thing that doesn't improve with age." Fair did, however, find the half-gee orbiter gravity relaxing; she felt ready for anything.

Suella indicated the technical data she had accumulated from her sessions with a number of Space Marines.

"But that stuff is nothing. Wait'll we talk to this one. He's a low number in Communications, that's the equivalent of Ghotaw Command, I'd say. All their tech staff is numbered from one to a hundred. Below that are junior ranks."

"My dear, you must have witnessed some marvels." Fair pulled her veil away from her glossy black wig. Suella smiled. She had hardly expected such enthusiasm from Fair, who as far as she knew hadn't even stirred from Ghotaw Mountain in decades.

"Well, I guess you could say that." She motioned awkwardly toward the small doorway to the sleep space. "He's in there. I stunned him a little while ago. Do you want to take a look, or would you like a drink first?"

Fair thought about it a moment. The security girl was un-packing some interrogation tools. "Look first, drink afterward," she said. Suella popped the door and Fair examined the stunned Space Marine. "Drink," she said and turned back for a closer look.

When Fleur Kevilla shifted out of unconsciousness again it was to the world of pain. She ached everywhere, and every part of her body that was in contact with the sodden foam padding was bruised. Her legs were so tired they trembled and ached with a dull, constant throb. She wished she could've slept forever, to stay in the dark away from the pain. But it was morning again and Armada had to sleep. Armada was haggard enough to be a witch, and if that was how a girl of twenty had become on the endless flight, then Fleur didn't even want to imagine how she herself must appear. She fumbled two grains of Pharamol to her mouth and eagerly awaited their effect.

When she forgot the pain, it was only to remember the thirst, the hunger. The hunger was the worst; they still had a little water. By staying dormant most of the time, they'd con-served water well. But the hunger was always there, gnawing at her reserves, burning somewhere in the shriveled pit of her belly.

She lay in a pain machine, suspended forever beneath the heavens and the endless green and brown of the forest below. A hell of infinite ordered space, always tantalizing, curving away over the horizon.

The Pharamol took effect, and she felt a slight renewal of energy. Armada was already asleep, arms hugging her elbows, face turned toward Fleur.

They maintained a steady 2,000-meter elevation, passing from one group of carrion gurns to another, where they spiraled in the jungle thermals. The gurns would give a flap or two to swing themselves over to inspect the giant intruding flyer, but after deciding that the sunsoarer was neither dangerous nor edible, they would lose interest and ignore it.

It was their eighth day in the machine, and still the horizon mocked them with no hint of the mountains they so desperately sought. Fleur felt the controls shudder slightly as a ripple of wind took them sideways. The computer realigned the wing surfaces slightly and took advantage of the wind.

The eighth day of hell. Fleur marveled that they were still alive, then recalled the first day. It hadn't been all that bad. In fact, there'd been an exultant sense of novelty that'd kept them both in high spirits. They'd flown steadily into the interior all day under scattered clouds. Syndicate search planes never found them. Within the first few hours they'd left behind all trace of humanity. The very last testament to the colony was the immense stone cross erected by Arvad Butte to perpetuate the memories of the two-hundred-odd Buttes who died in the area in the early years.

"My great uncle built that," Armada had noted laconically, as they flew slightly to the west of the 2,000-meter-high cross of locked concrete cubes. Each had been airlifted into place by skillful balloon teams.

Fleur had tried to put it into perspective. The early settlers had been accustomed to molding asteroids. They'd traveled between the stars. But they'd failed on Fenrille, defeated by an implacable jungle. Arvad had sought to overawe the jungle with his final, crazed gesture. And yet, although it was enormous, the cross was dwarfed by the endless forest expanse. Moreover, the lower half was already wrapped in a dense network of creepers. The jungle reached up with green fingers to tear the arrogant intrusion down.

Later she'd dozed off for a couple of hours. When her eyes opened it was to gaze on the gray-green mudflats that heralded a loop of the great Irurupup River, here at its widest extent in the tidal reaches. The river itself might as well have been an ocean; for more than two hours they flew steadily over nothing but brown water as it moved inexorably to the sea.

While they flew they practiced flying the soarer on pedal power and found, to Armada's considerable relief, that high-efficiency gearing allowed them a good measure of thrust upon the prop.

The sun had been slipping toward the fringe of forest that awaited it on the western horizon when they crossed the last of the mudflats and had trees beneath them again. They found a last, dwindling thermal and circled with some gurns over a long-dead volcanic stump. As they rose in slow, stately circles, the forest below echoed with the hoots of sarmer mackees and the shrill whistles of the litypups. They'd passed gurns who turned long necks to regard them with beady black eyes beneath wattles of pink and purple. One or two clacked incarnadine jaws at them as they rose and then night had fallen and Armada had tested her skills at gliding in the big, cumbersome, but gossamer-light flyer. That night there'd been a long, surging tailwind and they'd not only maintained elevation but gained many kilometers. Only in the hours just before dawn had they lost the wind and finally been forced to use the batteries until Beni rose. The solar rechargeable batteries were good for four hours' flight so they had been well within the safety margin.

During the long drowsy hours of daylight, they fell into conversation about their lives. Fleur tried to explain her motives in leaving Earth and migrating the vast distance to Fenrille. Armada in her turn had discussed her own career prospects.

"Now that I've cleansed the stain on my honor, I will have to find a more serious pursuit."

"Does that mean you'll settle down somewhere and farm the chitin?"

Armada laughed. "No, I'm afraid one doesn't "farm" chitin; one has to learn to lie to it." Fleur's expression of puzzlement sent the girl into another giggle.

"No, I'm no chitin talker—I found that out when I was just a kid and I failed to get into the Butte Manor chitin school."

Fleur was surprised to hear that the redoubtable Miss Butte could have failed at anything.

"Oh, yes, I'm afraid I just couldn't tell lies well enough, nor did I have the true empathy for the insect that is needed. You see, the chitin must be coaxed to give up its Vizier Mass to the talker. The nest thinks that the human is its slave and that it will help the nest to found new nests with young queens and some Vizier controllers. The nests are very neurotic about founding new nests; it's very difficult and dangerous for them in the wild. So the talker must learn to love the insect and to betray it at the same time, but of course the nest must never learn about that or it will kill you—and to die in a chitin nest is horrible, no worse death exists."

Fleur was astounded. "You mean the chitin talkers actually get inside the nest?"

"Of course, how else can the talker 'love' the Vizier Mass? You have to go to the nest every day and take little gifts—

things you know the Vizier and the Queens will like. The nest intelligence is very arrogant—after a while it gets used to the talker and eventually it will decide to make use of the human to help in founding the next generation. Of course as soon as you can get some Vizier out of the nest, you kill them and take the information proteins from their bodies."

Fleur gasped. "And that's how all the longevity drugs from chitin are obtained?"

"Of course. This is the secret of Fenrille. One we keep close. I suppose I shouldn't even have told you, but perhaps you can be trusted."

Fleur was quiet for some time after that, pondering the bizarre secret of chitin production.

When the stars appeared they'd come in a rush and seemed to blaze in the vault of the heavens like a desert of jewels set in remote velvet. To keep warm, to pass the time, Fleur had identified some of them for Armada. Fleur's interest in astronomy went back to New Baghdad and Tuesday nights at the city Astronomical Society. She'd joined initially just to look at Beni through the society's twelve-inch reflector, but the star-watching bug bit and soon she was turning her interest to other stars and the planets of the Sol System.

Of course, the stars blazing so clearly above Fenrille were in different locations and all the constellations were different and there were stars, like nearby Monar, that were brighter than any star in the night skies of Earth. However, Fleur had spent some time with a telescope on Fenrille and had learned how to track down Sol. When Sirius rose she'd pointed past the distant bright star with its hard, white light. To one side and below, past the nebula, lay Sol, small and yellow and hard to see with the naked eye.

Inevitably thoughts of the home world had come to the surface. Armada cursed the Earth and Fleur asked why.

"Because it betrays us, because it always comes after us. I used to read about the Earth and I even wanted to go there. I thought it would be like Fenrille, only with more different sorts of places to live, without the forest. Then I saw the videos of what it's like now that the Communists have taken over and everyone's bred like nibbla and covered every square inch of it with buildings. It looked awful. There wasn't room to breathe. I couldn't stay to watch all of it."

"It's not totally covered in buildings," Fleur had exclaimed, taken aback by Armada's vehemence. "And I don't know what you mean by Communists. There aren't many of those—real Communists have been an endangered species for the last two or three hundred years."

Armada replied coolly and reasonably, as if confronting a stubborn child. "You can't fool me. I know a Communist when I see one and you're a Communist yourself. Admit it. Anyone who works for the World Government has to be a Communist."

"Ohmigod," Fleur had spluttered in disbelief, bringing down Armada's immediate wrath.

"There's no call to blaspheme either. I know what you are and I know you don't even believe in God or the Spirits. You're like the stupid coastals, not that you're so stupid—just one of those among the Godless." Armada had flashed her sunny smile. "But that's okay," she'd said, "I like you anyway, even though if you were really clever you'd have left me where I was on Love Beach."

They'd laughed together then. A strange bond had already formed between the young aristocrat of Butte Manor and the skinny diplomat of humble Earthly origins.

Later Fleur tried to defend or define herself, she wasn't sure which. "You know, you ought to get this right, I'm a Socialist, not a Communist. There is a difference." Armada shook her head but Fleur continued. "You must remember it's a question of extremes. If you like, it's the degree of coercion to be applied to the property-owning class to ensure a workable distribution of what people need for their lives. I've always supported the idea of a mixed economy, with some overall supervision by elected authorities. The state-run centralized economies that I think you're referring to passed away a long time ago. They were only workable in war time because they crushed initiative and human rights in the name of necessity. This stifled their progress. No, I believe in political freedoms, private freedom, and some public control of some vital economic sectors."

Armada's eyes had gone round as saucers. "You really believe in freedom?" she'd said in such a wounding tone that Fleur had reflected bitterly to herself at just how vast was the ignorance gap that had grown up between the coastals and the highlanders.

"Yes," she finally said in a weary voice, "I believe in freedom. Even though my views are under attack in the home system now."

Armada was surprised to hear that there'd ever been ideas of freedom, especially political freedom, among the slave masses of the Social Union of Earth. Certainly that wasn't how Earth was described from the pulpit of Rognius' Kirk of Christ Spaceman on Seventh Day at prayer time. Finally she said, "Well, if there had been freedom like you say, why is it being attacked now?"

Briefly Fleur explained the World Government's crisis over chitin protein supplies.

Armada's response was all too typical of the highlander way of thinking. "Then why don't they ration it fairly, or give it up entirely and just be themselves? There isn't enough for everybody to live forever, nor can anyone get more chitin out of the nests than we do already. We've been at maximum production for centuries now."

After Fleur responded to that, Armada had brooded long into the night. There would be war with the Space Forces, maybe there already was war and her family and people were just an obstruction to the rest of the race, a tiny group standing between enormous populations and the longevity drugs they were determined to have.

The wind bucked the flyer, the wings wobbled and shook Fleur out of her reverie. Soon—too soon—the Pharamol euphoria faded and Fleur felt her strength drop. There could be no water until her next watch, so there was nothing to wet her parched mouth with. She let the air flow into her face, seeking whatever moisture there might be in it but there was none. *My skin must be ruined, completely dehydrated,* she thought, and mocked herself for worrying about wrinkles when she would surely be dead in another day. *Too weak to make it now, and we must be off course. Should've seen something by now surely...* It hurt, it was almost a physical pain when she thought of the maddening, elusive mountains. Where were they? Were they retreating, moving away from them around the curve of the world?

She opened another packet of Pharamol and took another grain.

It was such delicious stuff, no wonder it caused the problems it did. She recognized how quickly she'd come to anticipate the time for the next grain. The smooth, elegant feeling of control and well-being and strength returned as the Pharamol moved quickly into her bloodstream. Once again she forgot the pain and hunger. But still the old accusations came back, funnily enough with an image of Tan Ubu's face and pointing finger. She shrugged them aside more easily now. To survive she had to take the little purple grains. There was no other way.

By the fifth day the journey had really become a torture. Armada and Fleur were exhausted, the straps and the pads holding them in were torments to the flesh. Armada had sores on her shoulders and thighs from chafing in the confinement. Fleur felt too weak even to move the controls—she left it all to the computer. That night they found no evening thermal to get a good start on the nighttime gliding. Long before dawn they were forced to drain the batteries to stay aloft over a vast body of water that they saw revealed below by moonlight. They were forced to pedal, urging tired legs and drained bodies to give their utmost.

The first glimmers of dawn light had found them wallowing over the treetops of a hill. The terrain was altering but, in the predawn murk, it was hard to tell how. Ahead another hill and a group of prominent trees thrust shaggy heads through the surrounding upper cloud canopy. As they pedaled toward them in the cool, damp air, Fleur had become convinced they were going to snag on the high branches. A dark outline, dooming them with its topmost leaves, thrust three hundred meters from the forest floor. The black branches waited to seize them. Fleur had felt her heart freeze in her chest. Together they'd pumped the pedals. The slightest touch of those branches would bring them down.

Then had come the awful realization that Fleur had used up her strength. Not even the Pharamol could keep her legs going around, and, though Armada was moving the prop, they weren't gaining altitude, they were just holding their own, and that would not be enough.

Fleur had found a growl, defiant if somewhat high-pitched, coming from her throat as she reached for hidden reserves she'd never dreamed existed. Armada's howl joined hers, and, shrieking like fighting wildcats, they somehow built up speed.

The trees had approached and at the last moment a sudden tail wind gave them a critical meter to spare.

Once over the trees, they'd crossed the gorge of an immense tributary of the Irurupup where it slipped through a notch cut in granite. The sky had brightened and soon began to activate the solar panels on the wings.

All day on that dreary eighth day Fleur kept an eager eye on the northern horizon, seeking some sign of the mountains. But she found nothing to see but forest and nothing to think about except the throbbing where her weight lay on the stinking padding. Shift and turn as she might, it was impossible to feel anything less than a constant ache. Hanging there, awake, asleep, and more often somewhere in between, Fleur felt the horizons mock her. She was in a prison cell too small to let her touch her toes or scratch her calves, even to roll over on her back, but the bars of her cage were fragile enough to be torn apart with her bare hands, and the whole endless green world beckoned just outside.

As Beni set once more they sought out a column of carrion gurns circling in an updraft. Once again they rose into cooler air with the waning light, and when they topped out of the thermal Armada noticed something bright etching the northern horizon with light, still reflecting the rays of Beni.

"Look," she whispered hoarsely to Fleur who shuddered from the cold, feeling weak and sick. "It's the summit of Mount Fundan, at last—we're almost there."

But the distant sparkle was gone when Fleur raised her head and the north was illuminated only by the wan light of the Pale Moon, now riding high in the east.

On the tenth day their water was finally gone, and the Pharamol was half gone, too. Both women were virtually unconscious. Fleur could no longer raise her head, and Armada, considerably the stronger of the two, was increasingly concerned that the older woman would suffocate with her face pressed against the padding. But Fleur could not be woken, and Armada had no strength to spare for anything but the controls.

They were dying at last, having kept fate at bay with Pharamol for days. The mountains, those beautiful wrinkled ramparts of white and blue, had finally ceased to mock them from

171

the distance, as they'd done for the whole of the terrible ninth day, floating always on the interminable, hazy horizon. They were visibly growing, rising to form the vast wall of the equatorial range where peaks like Ould Spreak and Mount Stanley cut the thin atmosphere at 54,000 feet.

By noon they flew between outlying, jungle-clad ridges and Armada wondered where she should try to land. Neither woman had had a drop to drink in twenty-four hours, and with no food in ten days they were too weak to forage for water once they were down on the ground. Armada resolved to fly to the water they needed if she could keep awake and alive long enough.

In midafternoon they flew through a bank of mist and emerged over a dramatically altered landscape. The endless jungle was now broken by bare rock, like claws of the world itself, protruding through the fabric of the forest. Sprawling ridges, steep slopes, and rockfields began to appear. They were entering a broad highland valley, its rocky walls sloping away above them to merge in high ridges of rippling stone beneath the blue.

15

IN THE DARKNESS OF THE WIND SHRINE NO SONG WAS SUNG that night. The adepts called from every valley in the equatorial highlands were crowded tightly together by the main pipe. Illuminated by glopods, Fair Fundan stood before them. Behind her were representatives from the other clans.

She spoke. "Within the compassing of the world and under the beneficence of the Arizel tki Fenrille, our families have settled here and prospered, side by side with the ay fein. In truth we are one with you and this world." She paused. There was a general murmur of agreement.

"But now we face a grave threat. A power greater than our own fills the skies and will soon ravage our valleys. I have been to the Red Moon itself"—there was a gasp and a current of murmurs—"and I have studied this power that threatens us all. Having seen it, I have concluded that we would be foolish to stand in its way if we do not absolutely have to. We are not strong enough militarily to defeat it, and thus all that remains for us is to die fighting, to submit to this enemy, or to flee."

There were further whispers. The adepts' eyes were the

bright yellow stars in a thick firmament that focused on Fair's slender figure at the center.

"Only our pride, human and fein, could force us to stand and die in our valleys, and if there were truly no other way out then I would choose to stand and die. However, such grievous loss of life is unnecessary. If we remove ourselves from the valleys and take shelter in the deep forest, the enemy will find no targets to strike at, and in time, I believe, they will have to negotiate with us for a settlement."

She took a deep breath. "Accordingly, I am sending out the order tonight to all Fundan Valley commanders. We shall withdraw into the forest." Her voice rose, challenging her listeners. "In forty days we meet at the Mahr Pinnacles. Will the fein be with us?" There was no hesitation. The adepts keened their acceptance, trilling and echoing within the pipe.

The South Mithiliwax chitin team were on their way back to the grouping area after another dismal day spent undoing the damage caused in the great warband raid. Many established nests had been destroyed, dynamited open so that machines could dig out the bulk of the Vizier Mass and freeze it. What remained in the nest was then gassed, to cut down the danger to human operatives. The blasted nests were left like open sores in the verdant valley fabric.

The team, clad in the traditional leggings of fine gzan skin, with green-striped cotton shirts, had worked mainly in planting new nests, implanting young queens of Slade Mountain Green chitin, a variety that'd always done well in the mixed forest of Mithiliwax. But it would be years before the queens would produce the vast horde of progeny that it took to maintain a full chitin nest with all its castes of workers, warriors, and thinkers.

They'd also had a few dangerous moments in suppressing old, damaged nests, where the queens had survived and gathered the warriors around them. Here and there they'd also found nests that the raiders had missed altogether, nests that had observed the carnage wrought all around them by men and were suspicious to the point of paranoia. So there'd been several of those moments, the supreme of their craft, the ones that old chitin talkers loved to relate to awed novices. Of going naked into the nest, down the main hole, vulnerable to an agonizing death at the whim of the slow, brooding nest intelligence, and striving to rebuild empathy again and regain the Vizier group-mind's trust in humans.

It was the queens, though, that made the task so difficult. Vain, arrogant, subintelligent but separate in consciousness from the larger nest mind, the queens could be vicious indeed. The Vizier group mind was addicted to stability and a certain, fierce relentless egotism that was extremely narcissistic. But not even the most craven flattery could sometimes keep a queen from willfully extracting a few gasps of pain from a trapped chitin talker.

To be covered in warrior chitin, each with inch-long mandibles and stingers, put the talker very close to an indescribably unpleasant death. Out of such desperate plight only the experienced talker—who with guile and craft soothed the insect mind via the empathic, near-telepathic link that had to be developed in prolonged training—could hope to survive. To bring the Vizier mind around, the talker had to use love and gentle caresses, and praise and flattery, and promises of delicacies, jik blossoms galore, and ripe glob glob fruits by the bushel. The talker had to know when to press forward, reaching to stroke the Vizier, to offer fruits to the queens, and when to hold back, beseeching the arrogant insect for its cooperation.

The South Mithiliwax team were all veterans, among the best. Paid in Pharamol increments based on a percentage of their production, each member had already cached enough of the eternity drug to live for another thousand years. Some of them had ambitious plans for eventually giving up the work and emigrating to the stars. Others, more modest, planned to retire and live out their days in one of the uninhabited high valleys. For a talker with a dozen nests to his or her hand, the future was not only bright but endless.

As the team crossed the Layr Stream, they observed a slow-moving object heading up the valley at an altitude of no more than 300 feet. With Space Marine raids expected to resume at any time, they were galvanized into action. To get a better view they climbed trees and saw it go down in the woods on the far side of the river Dimpl. They radioed the news to Cracked Rock, and an alert was posted and fein teams dispatched to comb the woods for spies.

Not long afterward a helicopter was summoned from Cracked Rock. On its return to base, Lavin Fundin left the control center

175

to visit the emergency room on the medical floor. The two women brought in from the downed flyer were unconscious and painfully thin. Doctor Olanther, stern-eyed, tall, like a stoop-shouldered heron, was amazed.

"By rights they should be dead. The dehydration is very advanced and I don't think they've eaten for a week or more, but it's the dehydration that worries me most."

Lavin held up the steel canister, the only other cargo in the sunsoarer that'd been found snagged in a glob glob grove in Dimpl. "This has about 13 grams of Pharamol still inside it. I presume this is what they were using instead of food. It's certainly a lot lighter."

Olanther nodded, stroking his salt-and-pepper goatee. "Yes, exactly—they exhibit many of the signs of acute Pharamol poisoning. Possibly that thing was full when they started out. If we assumed it held a total of twenty-eight grams—about one ounce in the old measures—that would account for some of the effects. Of course, they've had about a thousand times too much of the stuff in that case. Funny thing is, Pharamol poisoning may be helping them survive the dehydration."

Armada's sudden appearance, from out of the wild blue nowhere, had been yet another shock for Lavin. He'd begun to assume that wherever she was, she'd stay until the fighting was over. That she should turn up alongside Fleur Kevilla, the Earth diplomat, was astonishing. Try as he might, he couldn't think of a more unlikely pair of companions.

After Olanther finished taking Armada's pulse, he attached a water feed and an IV drip. "Of course, the girl's built like an athlete. She's always been as strong as she's willful." Olanther had never shown Lavin the report on Armada's condition on her previous return from the Sx Coast. "I suppose she'll live, although probably only as long as it takes her to get back to that godawful city."

Lavin nodded, a grim expression creasing his face.

Olanther covered Armada with a sheet, folded his arms. "You know, I pity you, young man. This girl is too wild for anyone to control. You have a hopeless task before you—why don't you send her to Ghotaw Schools now? Now, before it's too late?"

Lavin shrugged. Armada would do whatever she wanted to do. Nominally he was responsible, but Olanther was right, she was ungovernable. However, Lavin was young enough to sympathize with her wild spirit. He too felt the call of the Sx Coast and the society of human beings outside the rigid confines of Clan Fundan. Sometimes he too slipped away and spent a day or two kicking back on Fun Isle, or cruising in Mimi Zimi's yacht. Besides, there were no longer Ghotaw Schools to send her to even if she'd agree to go.

"How about the other?. . . " They looked down on the wasted form of Fleur Kevilla. She was mere skin and bones, the skin stretched tight over her skull and cheekbones in a deathly grip. Olanther read from his medical computer's screen.

"Well, this patient is considerably older, in her physical late thirties. Has a small birthmark behind her left ear. Considering her age, her general condition is rather better than might've been expected. However, I can't say whether she'll recover. She's been in a coma for at least twelve hours."

"When can they be moved?"

"Not for at least forty-eight hours, and then only in case of extreme necessity."

Lavin paused for a second, looked past Olanther to the rest of the ward. There were several other patients. "You've heard of the new general order from Fair Fundan?"

Olanther nodded. "Yes, I was informed. We are all to leave within three days. I called the medical staff together this morning and briefed them. The Medical Corps of Cracked Rock fortress will be ready on time."

"We'll leave these two until the last then."

"Certainly. They need as much bed rest as they can be given. You know, I've practiced medicine all over this planet, in the coastal cities and up here in the high valleys, but I've never been to the deep forest. I must say I'm torn between a strange excitement at the thought and a certain amount of trepidation. However will we survive in the jungle?"

Lavin smiled. "We will learn to be careful. There are ways of surviving down there. We shall have to be as cautious as the gzan and as fierce as the gnirr. The adepts will assist us in winning passage from the woodwose."

Lavin turned and left Doctor Olanther to his work.

However, when Armada opened her eyes again, a few hours later, they fell on Lavin Fundin, who stood at the foot of the hospital bed. Hunched over the small computer, he studied its diagnosis with intense concentration. In his stained camouflage fatigues, his belt festooned with weapons and equipment, his boots scuffed and dirty, he was the most reassuring sight in the world.

She was alive. Confirmation of what she'd dimly suspected before, from the odd sensation of lying on her back somewhere, from the soft contact of the sheet. Not only was she alive, they had made it to Fundan territory. They hadn't drifted off course after all! She tried to whoop for joy, but her lips were like rolls of rubber and her tongue was stiff. All that came out was a mournful sounding croak.

It caught Lavin's attention, however. He whirled around, eyes bright.

"Ah ha, there she is, awake at last and at my mercy. The coholder of the intergalactic, transcontinental, solar-powered flight record. We shall have to notify the Guinness Institute on Earth."

He was angry, and he wanted to be stern with her, she could sense it immediately. So she waited, closed her eyes. He would get over it in a minute or two, he always did. As predicted, when she opened them again the storm clouds had faded and only a genuine puzzlement remained on his face.

"Well? Is there perhaps something you'd like to tell me?"

"Please, Lavin, not now." It was a trap. Couldn't he understand that it was an effort to say anything right then?

He reached across her and put the water drip into the corner of her mouth. He gave her a morose glance, the single dark eyebrow furrowed.

"Please," she said, "I don't want to talk about it."

"Ah!" He slapped his palms together and marched around the room. "You don't want to talk about it. Very well—but I do. This is easily resolved. You listen and I'll talk." He whirled around and pointed at her. "So, you take a jet again, without permission, and fly down to the Sx Coast. You're gone for weeks, I hear absolutely nothing from you despite all your promises. You might be dead, you might be sailing on the deep blue sea for all I know. Then you suddenly reappear, three quarters dead, flying a sunsoarer with Sx Coast Sunsail Club markings. And you think you can get away without talking about it?"

Armada would not let herself be depressed, it was just too

wonderful still to be alive. The single green Fundan stripe on the doors, on equipment, on the nurses' uniforms, was like a beacon of freedom.

"I know it sounds awful but . . ." For a moment she allowed herself just to radiate affection toward him, he was so wonderful to be so concerned about her. And yes, she admitted to herself, she was so unworthy of all his concern.

"You can explain? Oh, yes, I'm sure you can. In fact, you'd better have some good excuses this time. You realize what your little jaunt has meant, don't you? Not only do we have a full-scale war on our hands, so every plane is vital, but I've had your father on my neck every *day* wanting to know where you are and why you haven't been in contact and when I would have some idea."

It was time to appear contrite, so she suppressed all appearance of glee. "I'm sorry, Lavin, truly I am. But I had to go. It was a matter of honor, you see—and nothing is more important to the Buttes than honor. But it's all over now, and I don't ever have to go back there again."

The eyebrow twisted up.

"Honestly, I had to go. You'd have done the same thing in my position."

He smothered a grin. "Somehow I find that hard to believe, but let's forget it for now. I give in, I'll be reasonable. Just tell me why you took out after the solar flight record and where you came up with your copilot?"

"Ah . . ." She paused. There was so much to tell, and he must never know the real reason. "Well, you see, there was no other way out. We had to take the soarer. The syndicate was after us and they had the airports covered. Anyway, her name is Fleur Kevilla. She told me that she knew you—is that true?"

He nodded. "It is."

"Well, the syndicate had us trapped, so the only way out was to steal the soarer from Spurn Head. Fleur didn't want to come at first, but she turned out very well in the end. I probably couldn't have made it without her. She's too intelligent to want to die, I think." The words tumbled out and she knew it wouldn't make sense to him. But she recounted as much as possible of their flight through the city until she coughed and had to settle back on the water drip. Lavin still wore a frown. Then she remembered what he'd said in passing and rose back on one elbow. "But what was that you said about war? Is it the war that she told me about?"

"Yes, I'm afraid it is, and it's not the kind of war we can hope to win."

"What's happened? How could they lose, the chitin lords of Fenrille?"

"Oh, nothing all that spectacular, just a continuous pattern of Space Marine raids and constant bombing. Just small strikes, local damage—they're destroying all our equipment, piece by piece. The Space Marines move so fast we rarely get a crack at them, and they have so much air power that we daren't offer battle beyond the reach of the main guns. Some places have been badly hit, some forts destroyed. There's been a lot of casualties."

"But why? Why are they doing it?"

"They want the valleys, they want full control of the chitin, and they don't want us."

"And the fein?"

"They are with us. Fair Fundan asked the adepts of Ghotaw to poll the fein. The fein see little chance of their survival under the control of the World Government. They remember the bad years under the coastals. They will help us escape into the deep forest and leave the highlands to the enemy. With no further supplies of chitin on the market, the World Government will have to negotiate rather than make war."

"I see, so we'd better get well very soon. How is Fleur? Is she awake?"

Lavin shook his head. "Not yet, still in a Pharamol coma. Olanther is worried about brain damage."

"Oh, I pray not, she was so brave. She did so well, when we thought we were lost." Armada tried to sit up but fell back; she was much too weak.

Lavin tucked her under the sheet. "You must rest while you can. Olanther says you came close to acute Pharamol poisoning. You pushed it to the limit, but she may have gone over the limit entirely. An ingenious way to travel, I called it, but I don't think the doctor would agree."

A sudden thought sent her fingers to her neck for the kui-lowee pouch. It was gone. Her eyes widened. He was grinning at her.

"Don't worry, at Cracked Rock Infirmary we take an inventory of every patient's belongings. Since the kuilowee pouch was virtually all you had with you in the way of luggage, I'm sure you'll find it's been stowed under your cot. As for the small fortune in Pharamol and that memory chip we found, I put them in the fortress safe upstairs in my quarters. You can have them whenever you want them, though Olanther thinks you shouldn't touch Pharamol for at least a year. Of course there is the question of how you acquired so much—there were thirteen grams in that tube. I hesitate to put an exact figure on it since the market's been in chaos for days, but it must be in seven figures."

The grin infuriated her. "Damn you, it's important to me that I live in honor."

"But did you have to go that far? I mean, I know passions can rise and all that . . ."

"Damn you, damn you, leave me alone." She was crazy, always had been, and still amazingly beautiful even if reduced to skin and bones. He bent down and picked the little kuilowee pouch out of the locker and gave it to her. She clutched it defensively. At least she had done it, she had dealt with Ganweek. They would never forget the Clan Butte in the Bablon Syndicate.

A bleep from his communicator turned his head. "Yes, Fundin here."

A tiny voice read ominous news; seven pods of marines plus fighting robots and small VTOL fliers were operating in Ramal Valley, virtually next door. Young Proud Fundan was under heavy attack.

"I'll be up to Command right away. Get hold of Ng Tung for me, and hold a line open to him." He broke contact. "Young Proud has trouble, more than he can handle, I'd say."

"Will you go to his aid, if he calls you to under clan rules?"

Lavin hesitated, then chuckled. "I think Young Proud would rather die than call on me to help him, but if he does I'll consider it. Hell, I don't think the Brelkilks would stand for it if I passed up that sort of opportunity—enough riffchuss superiority to keep the whole pack of them in the air for a year."

Once in the command center Lavin quickly ran through the data coming in from Ramal, which seemed to have been selected as a weak point, suitable for a massive attack. A landing

181

in strength had been made following a heavy bombardment. The marines were marching on Proud Tower under a screen of their own VTOL jets.

To contest the issue Young Proud had put the Ramal Impi in the path of the enemy. A fierce, inconclusive struggle had taken place in the thickets of Ramal but with their own jets to ward off Young Proud's air force, the marines were able to maneuver fairly freely and slipped through the fein concentrations and ambushes with only minor casualties. Young Proud was holed up inside Proud Tower with the Heavy Impi, a unit still rebuilding itself after the stunning defeat on Scrawn Moor.

From deep inside the massive concrete shelter of the Keep at Ghotaw, Fair Fundan responded to Young Proud's call for aid with the suggestion that he simply remove himself from Ramal and hasten into the forest where they were all bound anyway. Since the Space Marines were too few to surround him, he was free to melt away down the valley.

Young Proud spurned this advice and called instead for Impis to be sent to oust the invaders before he left Ramal. He refused to be "chased from my home like a nibbla put out by a were."

Fair Fundan reiterated her general command to all Fundan Valley commanders: full evacuation at once. Combat with the Space Marines was to be avoided since it was too costly in lives and had become irrelevant. The crisis would change in dimension once the clans and their chitin talkers were gone. Already the panic on the Sx Coast had sent the market for longevity drugs into a seizure. Prices doubled in the first ten days, and they looked set to double again. If inflation from shortages of longevity drugs was the problem in the home system, it was only going to intensify. Admiral Enkov would have to negotiate.

In Ramal events took a tragic turn. The defending forces were gradually hemmed in by skillful work on the part of the Space Marines. Then atomic satchel charges were used to crack Proud Tower's huge blast shields. Young Proud's air force was shot from the sky by marine VTOLs with advanced missiles. The marine jets could strafe the fortress, destroying the guns.

Shrugging off the attacks by the Ramal Impi in their rear, the marines fought their way inside Proud Tower over the bodies of hundreds of fein, men, and women. They would have taken Young Proud along with the other prisoners if he hadn't managed to escape in a hidden VTOL jet.

Proud Tower was leveled and the air strip destroyed, and then *Gagarin*'s big booster shuttles landed to collect the expeditionary force and hundreds of prisoners. When last heard from, Young Proud had collected the remnants of his Impis and headed south and west, into the sanctuary of the Irurupup basin.

When the news of Young Proud's disaster was brought to Old Proud, he broke down and wept. Later he grew morose and uncommunicative. He refused to listen to his subalterns. In alarm, his valley commander, Decius Fundin, called Ghotaw and agreed to submit the forces of Fintral Valley to the central family command.

In her report Fair Fundan announced, "This disaster to our family arms is the most grievous we have suffered in two hundred years. However, from it has sprung a tender shoot of family unity. We are healed into one unit once again; Fintral has returned to the fold. Our clan is whole again."

Fair glossed over the obvious fact that Young Proud would never be brought round, even if Old Proud agreed to submit. Yet it was important to stress unity in the face of the disaster of Ramal.

For Fleur Kevilla, waking up in a Fundan military hospital was but the first of a series of new and astonishing experiences. Finding herself alive was in itself a sort of miracle. Her memories of the end of the flight were dim. But she had suffered no significant brain damage and her memories were unharmed for the most part. Doctor Olanther pronounced her recovery a medical miracle, and as soon as she was able to submit to interrogation he began a further investigation. When Olanther discovered that Fleur, as a poorly paid diplomat, had no previous experience with Pharamol, he concluded that she had probably had the luck of the innocent. Her body had been able to absorb a lot more of the drug than was possible for systems that had long accommodated themselves to its chemistry.

Fleur and Armada were on an intensive protein-rich diet to build up their strength. But Fleur was still too weak to walk when the order came for them to be moved down the valley to the base camp, so she was carried out of the fortress on a stretcher by two orderlies. Armada walked beside her. The girl's color had returned and she was rapidly regaining her natural weight. It was a brilliant day, and the short trek along the sun-drenched ridge that connected great Cracked Rock to the rest of the mountain was a marvel for Fleur. The views were magnificent, even if all she could see of them were occasional glimpses past the hurrying figures of men, women, and fein who bustled back and forth to the helicopter pads.

They saw Lavin very briefly when he clambered out of a helicopter that he'd just landed. Though he was caught up in a frenzy of activity, for a moment he stopped beside them where they waited to be loaded onto the chopper. His sunshades were pushed up on his head and his flight suit was soaked with perspiration. It looked as if he hadn't shaved or changed clothes in forty-eight hours. And he hadn't. Organizing a disciplined withdrawal from Abzen Valley into the deep forest was as difficult logistically as a battle on two fronts.

Fleur was loaded into the chopper, Armada and Doctor Olanther got in beside her. Lavin reached in to wish them well, then he waved and returned to the whirl of decisions and orders. The chopper's blades picked up speed and they lifted off, the fortress dwindling beneath them until it looked like a smooth white mushroom growing on the side of the mountain.

As they flew, Armada worked deftly with needle and thread to alter a suit of basic Fundan greens for Fleur. She took in the waist and used a cloth stapler to attach a weapons belt. She'd also brought a pair of wide-brim bush hats, waterproofed on top.

Armada had brought a small satchel with a few absolutely necessary possessions. She'd packed a .38 revolver plus a box of ammo. There was a hairbrush and toothbrush, paste, cleansers, shampoo, plus her Butte Bible and a small portable audio kit with earphones and a pack of five music chips. Armada's tastes in music were simple, cleft in twain. While reading her Bible or while meditating, she enjoyed old terrestrial organ music, religious works, especially J. S. Bach. The rest of the time she played loud, rhythm music, especially the pulz sound.

When she'd emptied Ganweek's stainless-steel Pharamol tube, she checked the contents of the white-bordered chip and found a complicated mass of chemistry notation. Armada had no use for the data, but her conservative Butte instincts told her to keep it, so she dumped the contents into the mainframe memory bank. Then she recorded pulz rhythm music into the chip.

Now she had six chips, and indeed the white-bordered chip had a larger capacity than her blue music chips. She would be able to record new sounds, from the same stations on short-wave, and that would be a blessing since the march ahead of them was sure to become oppressively boring before too long. Music might be the only thing to keep her sane.

She repacked the Pharamol into two small grain dispensers carved from jik wood to look like crouched nibbla. She gave one to Fleur, who returned it immediately, saying she didn't want "that stuff" too close to her.

From the window bay of the chopper Fleur watched the valley slide by, and for a moment she felt a shattering sense of déjà vu. Once more she was flying, in the pain machine, trapped in the center of the sky. Then the feeling passed and, trembling, she closed her eyes and remembered she was alive. They'd made it to safety.

Or at least she hoped it would be safety.

16

![decorative ornament]

FAIR FUNDAN'S MEETING HALL IN GHOTAW KEEP WAS IN-
tended to impress anyone who entered its cathedrallike space.
A natural cavern, part of the chain of karst limestone caves of
Ghotaw, it had been widened at the base by Fundan engineers
and cleared of stalagmites for the most part. The floor was
polished, and the stalactite-studded ceiling was used to great
effect by Fair's senso engineer.

On this occasion, the senso was turned off and only Fundan
Valley commanders were in attendance. They had no eyes for
anything except the relief hologram in front of Fair, which
depicted the northern part of the Irurupup basin.

Fair addressed them from a dais. "We've all compared notes
now and we've all come to the same realization, that we can't
fight the Space Marines without destroying the fein. The fein
are our sacred charge. Any serious harm to them, any threat
to their continuation, would bring down the wrath of the Arizel
upon us all. Now, we can always endure a blow to human
pride." Her eyes glittered around her—all knew how proud
the Fundans were. "And though it hurts, we must remember

that Clan Fundan has more important priorities than the simple maintenance of pride." How grim seemed the emphasis on pride then with Young Proud on the run and Old Proud broken in spirit.

"We can always come back from the forest, and we can always rebuild forts, and we can replant nests. But we cannot rebuild the numbers of fein so easily. So we must change tactics and become guerrillas. We shall swim in the ocean of the forest the way fish swim in the sea."

Her manner changed, she closed her palms together. "However, we must move quickly. The fleet has not attacked since the destruction of Proud Tower yesterday. We are engaged in a diplomatic effort to prolong this cessation of attacks, but we cannot hope to see it last much beyond midmorning. That means that tonight we must move everything we can, everything possible, out of the valleys and into the base camps. Tomorrow we must complete the process and move our people into the forest. As you've seen from the briefing notes, we have had parties of adepts clearing safe trails for us, and the adepts will precede us throughout the march to be sure of maintaining good relations with the woodwose. Now unless there are important questions, I will say good night and farewell until we meet by the Mahr Pinnacles."

On his way to the exit Lavin was handed a note by an ancient graycowl fein. He was "invited" to visit the Mother Fair in her own quarters! He quickly rode a security elevator up through 500 meters of mountainside to reach Fair's apartments, which were perched on a north-facing spur of the mountain. The elevator deposited him before a circular steel door that opened slowly as he approached. Once through the door he found himself in a large, airy room, painted in white with green trim, the illumination entering from a skylight. On the polished wood floor fine rugs glowed and on the walls were tall embroidered panels depicting moments in the history of Clan Fundan.

Security men and fein were everywhere there, and one of them motioned for Lavin to follow him through a pair of high wooden doors. Lavin followed the squat security man down a spiral corridor past a series of rooms with both east- and west-facing windows. The wide reaches of the Luther Valley were the foreground. Beyond them, in a ring surrounding the lesser

187

peak of Ghotaw, were the true giants of the equatorial range, Mount Fundan to the south and east, Ould Spreak due east, Yellowman in the north with Mount Dane and the tallest of them all, 64,000-foot Mount Butte. Buttressing each giant were several smaller mountains in the 25,000- to 35,000-foot range. From Ghotaw, a minor peak set in the middle of the great sweep of the Luther Valley, it seemed as if one were at the bottom of a vast bowl, the sides of which were brushed white with snow.

The rooms were a series of contrasts, some stark, almost bare, while others were stuffed with sumptuous furniture, colorful paintings and tapestries. Lavin could only deduce that the Mother Fair used each room as the mood took her, that she had many moods, and that some of them were pretty extreme.

At the end of the corridor another pair of doors opened and they entered a large room, filled with the buzz of conversation from dozens of guards and advisers. Fair Fundan stood alone, however, wrapped in thought. She wore a simple white gown, the veil frosted with tiny green points. Lavin was announced and for a moment she studied him, her head inclined slightly to one side. Then she dismissed guards and advisers and ordered some tea brought.

The empty room revealed a spartan sensibility. Besides a table and two stiff-back chairs there was only a plain white rug and a small table holding a communicator. Out the window Mount Fundan loomed in the middistance, a titan of white tipped with dark stone above the snowline.

"Greetings, Lavin Fundin, my hero of Abzen Vale. The news of your success at Bitaraf Shoals comes hot on the heels of the victory at Badleck Ridge. With great bursts of light and hope, you continue to shatter the darkness imposed on us by our enemies."

She was studying him intently. Her gaze prompted a wariness within him. She sat then indicated that he should sit facing her across the polished wooden table.

"This is much too formal for what is an occasion of family business, but the fortunes of war dictate our circumstances. We shall have to make do. As it is there is little time and I prefer that we take an entire evening, over a meal here in my quarters. There is much to tell you. Indeed I may have been remiss in not telling you before, but there's no point in regretting what's not been done."

He was confused and sensed a tension in her voice. This was not the Mother Fair with whom he was familiar, who had led him all his life in various forms, the guiding figure of the nursery to the center of High Command, Fundan Forces.

She lifted her veil. Her dark eyes were intent, they bored into him. What did she seek? he wondered.

"Tell me, young man, what do you think of my plan? My grand strategy? Remember, now, I'm not on a dais addressing the family. You may be frank—in fact, I expect you to be."

Her lip trembled slightly when she looked upon him. A difficult, bitter mood of purple melancholy had settled upon her, which, strive as she might, she could not budge.

The crisis was moving toward the focus she dreaded, the nexus point foretold by the Adept of the Wood, Izzyma Taa. For a century and a half she had worked to avoid that, but despite her efforts the prophecy was coming true. "Well?" she said, disliking hesitation.

The hundreds of training films in which the Mother Fair had inculcated generations of children in Fundan creches had primed him for her tone. Hesitation, like the other ultimate bugaboo, inefficiency, was a trait that could only lead to failures. Yet there was something eerie about sitting across a table from the personage who had shaped his life, who he had venerated and, in a sense, fought for all his years. That she was also a human being was somehow hard to accept.

"The plan makes excellent sense. I'm glad that we can at least remove our personnel from further harm."

Fair removed silver skewers tipped with chitin masks of emerald from her wig and pulled away the veil. The long, dark hair fell out around her shoulders.

"So you do approve! Good, I'm glad. I was concerned, but only a little, that you might not, you being the most combative of my commanders."

Lavin was quick to try to correct her. "Actually, I wouldn't describe myself as combative. I've found that we can often do as well by maneuver and negotiation. You must be thinking of Young Proud. Now, there's a truly combative person."

She chuckled. "Spoken like a true Fundan, a cautious Fundan—the best kind.

189

"My dear, it gives me great pleasure to tell you that you have it, the true Fundan skill, the thing that has made this family great and prosperous, and that is flexibility. With flexibility comes the ability to avoid rigid, linear thought and to achieve tactical surprise, to find the true dynamics in any situation. With flexibility comes the ability to listen truly and to analyze. To see the situation as it really is, not as one might wish it to be."

She paused, then continued. "Once our ancestors were faced with the choice between fighting the home world or fleeing battle against a superior enemy. Clan Fundan might have stayed to die for the Principate of Asteroid Fundan—most of the other belters stayed and they were crushed. Again, after the emigration to the outer planets, a lot of other belt families decided to stay and exploit the hydrogen resources. They set up in grand style—there were the Oxygen Kings of Europa, the Ten Families of Hydrogen, the Barbuncle Empire of Neptune—why, all the snowballs of the outer Solar System were awash in wealth and imperial dreams. But the Fundans knew better, we knew that the menance from the inner planets would only grow again until it was ready to reach out and take what it wanted. We liquidated our resources, joined with the other pioneer clans, and built the interstellar ramscoop. They sneered at us, just as the belters had called all the families who fled cowards, but what happened to them? What happened to Grand Barbuncle, the red jewel in Neptune's gas clouds? Now we can look up and see the military might that was developed by Earth to crush the spacers and the Lords of the Snowballs."

A female orderly in tight Fundan greens brought tea and served it to them in china cups of delicate Ghotaw white and green.

"So, you see, it is *that* quality, the ability to see the long term, that we search for in our schools. With it we survive—it's as simple as that." Still the melancholy moved within her, but she shrugged. It was time to begin the process of self-realization within him. He had much to learn, but she felt he was stable enough and secure within himself.

"But now I must tell you something very important, something that you have never known, and I must welcome you to the inner family and explain something of your real place here.

"You remember Junior Academy, of course?" Lavin nod-

190

ded, memories floating up from some deep buried resource. He was lying on a battered cot in Dormitory Five and watching a hologram film of Mother Fair as she demonstrated how children should tie a pair of laces and taught them the shoelace song. When the film ended Nurse Fundin switched the projector off and instructed them to sing the song and then go to sleep.

"Now I know that when you were young you probably received no end of drubbings and demerits in my name—please accept my apologies for all that, but our creche system has been the heart of our recruitment program and there is no other practical way of raising children to become efficient parts of the family. I bet you must have grown very tired with the Mother Fair."

He laughed. "Everyone does—about the age of nine, I think. But I got over it, and I can still remember the shoelace song."

She smiled, felt the melancholy pierced to its heart. "Good, but tell me, when you were young, did you ever resent the true-genes? Did you hate it that you were Fundin and not Fundan?"

He hesitated—did she possibly test his loyalty?—then dismissed the thought as absurd. "Yes, I did, but only later on, when I joined the Rangers. Until then the difference never meant anything. We were all equal in Junior Academy."

"There is equality in the Ranger youth, too, isn't there?"

He shifted in his seat, shrugged. "Possibly, but not in Young Proud Fundan's section. Under his command the suffixes were rigorously applied. Fundins shined Fundan boots."

Her eyes had tightened slightly, she acknowledged the curse of the Fundans. "Alas, I'm afraid it's true what you say. The system is open to abuse. Ovula Butte's excesses, for example, have their parallels among the Fundans. Pride, overweening pride, that is our undoing.

"However, injustices aside, would you have lived your life so differently if you had had the choice? What would you most prefer to have done, what are your dreams of the future? For instance, would you consider leaving Fenrille?"

The Mother Fair questioned him about his dreams? And if Clan Fundan were dispersed? Broken up and driven from Fenrille?

"Well, I have known no other life except that of our valleys, but my education was not confined to the arts of war. We were made to read widely, to understand our position in the universe, in human culture. I think that yes, I would have preferred a life of peace but it was not my lot. It fell to me to hold Abzen Vale for Clan Fundan and I will do so to the last."

His sudden vehemence surprised her. "We must avoid undue morbidity, my young general. . . . Such thoughts are a romance that we cannot afford. We must be clearheaded if we are to find the way ahead where all avenues are filled with the murk of possibility and danger.

"But, you have spoken honestly! Good, I expected as much, Lavin Fundin. I, too, would prefer a life of peace, but before that can come about we must pass through this crisis. I believe that on the far side we shall find that peace we all seek, and an end to the conflict. But what are your feelings toward the true-genes now? Do you resent us?"

"Some. I resent Young Proud's obstinacy and aggression, plus all the lives he has cost me."

"Of course, but you don't hate all of us, or at least there are some of us that you approve of?"

She sensed the questions forming in his mind, but the time was short, she must begin. "What would you say if I told you that you were born of Fundan genes? That you are in truth Lavin Fundan—true-genes Fundan—that your suffix is false?"

Lavin stared at her. The suggestion went against everything he had ever believed about himself.

"It's true, my dear, you are true-genes. But you had to be hidden, for there are more enemies in this world than just the coastal scum. So your birth was kept secret and your real parents never acknowledged you. To do so would have been fatal. In fact, I can tell you that your predecessor was murdered in his first year at Military Academy."

A pall of unreasoning fear rose in his heart like black smoke. He had never dreamed that he could ever know his parents. He had always assumed that his ancestry was lost and that he could only look to the clan, to the Mother Fair for the source of inspiration. Now those foundations were shaken, the world turned topsy-turvy. "My mother, my father, who were they? Are they still alive?"

Her eyes fell. That was yet an area that he could not be told about. "Unfortunately the circumstances do not yet allow it, but in time all will be made clear to you, and then perhaps you will understand and perhaps you will forgive us. You will see why these steps have been necessary."

He smiled then, bittersweet, as he felt tears well deep within. Something wet was on his cheeks, he could barely see.

"You seem troubled by this news. Is it so hard?"

"No." He waved a hand. "I should thank you, I know— it's just that this changes so many things, I . . ."

"Here, have some more tea." She poured another cup for him. They had all gone through this scene, and for some it had been harder than for others. But it was essential, the second phase before the ultimate realization could be allowed. Yet she would try to steer him through those shoals even though time was precious. She recognized that he might prove more fragile than the others. His very directness—the quality that distinguished his military career—and acuity like the honed blade of a kifket, that quality that allowed such intense powers of concentration, could threaten him. He could bring the question into such powerful focus within himself that it might tear him to pieces if he sought answers where none existed. At least none that could yet be given him.

Yet Fair had planned well and much remained to be done, enough to keep her most ambitious human project too busy for introspection. She pressed a holo stud and projected a map of the southern valleys. "Look closely, there is much I must tell you. . . ."

17

EVEN AS FAIR CONFERRED WITH LAVIN ON GHOTAW MOUNtain, the vast complex of tunnels, forts, and paths around them was boiling over like an angry chitin nest. The chitin schools, the Military Academy, the industrial and scientific complex, all were being emptied. Light equipment was packed up along with machine tools and computer memory cores to be buried in secret. Everything else, even the magnificent horses of Ghotaw, would be left behind.

Long columns of fein and humans marched southward. Many were quite glad for the adventure, eager to see the great forest. Most were bitter at the thought of leaving their possessions to unknown enemies, yet they consoled themselves with the thought of the stories they would have to tell their descendants, unto the umpteenth generation, of the great march of Clan Fundan. The elan of the Fundan military organization was still healthy, a current of confidence welled throughout the ranks.

The steamer *Luther Fundan* met them with a string of barges behind her and then began what might be her last voyage down the river Luther.

The refugees went west and then curved southward and soon reached the falls at Madelina, the end of the *Luther Fundan*'s ride. There the river fell in a series of rapids to its confluence with the Irurupup. Above the falls the forest was ultramontane, jik predominated, and glob glob thickets.

Below the falls things were dramatically different. Surrounding the permanent plume of spray was a grove of shaggy titans, each 300 meters high, occupying the sky with millions of heart-shaped leaves. Farther downstream these were the only trees that grew. From the mountains to the distant ocean, the ground was covered by their massive roots. They were the *ayeirl*, the "world" tree of the Knuckle of Delight, and all of them were tended carefully by the giant tree shepherds, the woodwose.

Fleur had to be carried for the first two days, but on the third she donned the Fundan greens Armada had taken in for her and took her first tottering steps. She set her green rain hat at a rakish angle and did her best to saunter, rather than stagger, outside their tent.

The next day she did much better although she felt even weaker and sicker than she had aboard the NAFAL starship *Hermes* during that first long, awful acceleration period. She walked for most of the morning and rode only after Doctor Olanther sternly ordered her to. Doctor Olanther also constantly urged her to eat fresh meat, of which there was an awful lot at every meal.

"Once we're in the great forest it'll be jerky day after day, so you should get your fill of meat while you still can."

"Actually, Doctor, I'm a vegetarian," Fleur bleated weakly.

Olanther's haughty gaze trembled for a moment. "That's all very well but I'm talking of your health. You need protein, and while you can get it from vegetable foods, you won't get enough quickly enough to restore your health. And the medical environment down in the forest will be harsh. We'll be taking Alvosterine every day, of course, just to keep off the spruip blood fungi. That particular pest can kill you in less than a day. Flies will be biting, of course. Fenrille flies can even bite through a layer of clothing so no matter how well you protect yourself, you'll still have to battle off native bacteria and viruses. Fortunately we have good supplies of the drugs to deal with all that and the human body can even be trained to produce good antibody, too, but that'll take time, and at the beginning you will still be very weak. So you must eat meat."

Fleur attempted a slice off a thick gzan chop that Armada brought. She could smell the animal grease on it and the fibrous flesh, filled with what she could only visualize as blood, turned her stomach. She barely made it out of the tent and into the trees.

So Olanther had her eat a nauseating concoction of yeasts and curded beanpod instead. It was less than appetizing, but it was easy to treat it as medicine. Meat was not something she could bring herself to consider.

At last they reached the southern extension of jik forest, the point where the Abzen Valley joined its parent, the Irurupup's immense drainage basin. *Esperm gigans*, growing taller with every ten kilometers of southerly progress, were now visibly crowding out the jik, the mindal, all the ultramontane trees. With the gray-green shag of *gigans* forest canopy knitted together just ahead, they camped for the last time in Abzen.

Nearby the youngsters from the Abzen creche were camped. They were under the guidance of Fy'pupe and a dozen young human officers from Cracked Rock in addition to the creche staff, which was headed by Doctor Rollas Fundin. Fleur visited the creche, a family cum school of two hundred boys and girls. All the children were Fundins, even those who were orphans taken from the Sx Coast poorhouse. The place was in uproar, and the creche campsite was hardly a model of tidy efficiency. Everything seemed more like a family, just a very large one, with loosely applied rules that were often ignored. The young officers yelled a lot but this appeared to have very little effect on quelling the constant, unceasing activity of two hundred kids. Rollas Fundin, a matronly woman whose few gray hairs betrayed the advanced age at which she began taking Pharamol, was more effective, just a quiet word here, a tweaked ear there. Fleur observed that Rollas herded the children constantly, keeping them on the move, breaking up fights, imparting education, applying bandages. She was plainly superhuman. Her energy never seemed to flag and Fleur came away amazed, sure that even one of the little monsters would have been enough to leave her weak every day.

That night they labeled and repacked medical supplies. Fleur propped herself in a chair and wrote out labels. After an hour Lavin Fundin and Bg Rva appeared suddenly by their fire.

Everyone stood and saluted, which surprised Fleur until she recalled that she was with a military unit and Lavin was its commander. Lavin returned the salute and took a seat beside her. Rva produced a bottle of gwassa and offered it to Fleur who took it, thinking helplessly that it was the first time a lion had ever offered her a whiskey.

She took a swig. It was strange stuff, not alcoholic, made from some tree root or other as she recalled. Then she felt the stimulating effect.

"Thank you," she said to Rva who flashed an enormous, fanged grin and shook her hand. She was slightly amazed that a being with hands so large could be so gentle.

"Once again we cross on the paths. Ahead lies the widest. I drink to that." The Hero of Brelkilk took a mighty swig and passed it on.

Lavin took up a pen. "I'll write labels, too." He smiled.

"Here, do some more Alvosterines," Fleur said. "We need ever so many."

He grinned. "Vital stuff from now on. Hope you've got your suppositories."

"Every orifice must be protected—yes, I know. The doctor lectures me about fungi or sawflies every day."

Piles of labels mounted in front of them. Medical crates were broken down, and fein appeared regularly from the dark to take away small medipacks. One fein turned out to be a close relative of Bg Rva, young Yuin of the Brelkilks. Lavin spotted him first, in the line, and called out, "Well, well, is that a ghost in the line for medical? Mother, better call the cubs in to chase it away. Fie the old ghost!"

Rva greeted his cousin with a massive embrace and then took the mechanical hand in his. "So, Yuin, the machine-foot fein, eh?"

The metal-and-nylon prosthetic had little cosmetic appeal but Yuin moved it enthusiastically. "It has the direct biolink with my arm, my nerves control it. It is much stronger than the old one."

Lavin's eyes fell for a moment. "Ah, Yuin, but you were more beautiful to me with just your old paw."

Rva was chuckling. "I think Reshishimi must be glad to

have Yuin to hunt for her again. Looks strong enough to hold a bow, all right."

"Oh, yes, Mzsee, very strong, and with Reshi," his voice dropped to a sly whisper, "it is a wonder. Never have I known my Reshi so eager for the private hut at night. We'll be a couple of cubs heavier in yard before long."

A ripple of laughter ran through the line of fein.

After a while the gwassa got the fein to singing. The songs were the old, old ones of the ay fein, sung for countless millennia.

Fleur's grasp of feiner wasn't good enough to let her catch more than an occasional phrase, but Lavin explained the songs to her.

A new one began, with a counterchant of three lines concerning the "wise young fool." "This is the Efellessa Ummulteeze, the story of Efellessa of the mythic village of Brel. It's a Brelkilk specialty of course, and Efellessa is always claimed to be the first of the Brelkilk kin. Anyway, he was also the first fein to walk right around the Knuckle of Delight. He circumnavigated the northern shore."

Fleur started. "Why ever would anyone want to do that?"

"Oh, Efellessa was an adventurous type, very 'widepath,' as the fein would say. He disagreed with the orthodox view in his village that the ancestors had flattened the world out and stretched it between two poles situated at infinity. In vain he had pointed to the movements of the objects in the heavens. The cultists refused to believe the world was round. Efellessa proved them wrong."

It was a magical moment, but when the Pale Moon rose Lavin saw that Fleur had fallen asleep in her chair.

Armada appeared. "She's not really that strong yet, you know. She should be in the tent by now."

"Yes, yes, I forgot—or maybe we both did. I was afraid that I'd bored her to sleep."

Armada smiled. "No, cousin, I don't think the ambassador would ever be bored by you."

When Fleur next awoke she was on her cot in the tent. Beni was already well above the horizon and camp was breaking up. Before she'd even finished getting her greens on, Armada appeared with a bowl of tuber curd and a patty of spiced gzan jerky.

Fleur found the curds perfectly delicious, something like the consistency of ice cream but with a flavor more like that of a nutty custard. The gzan jerky was more of a problem. She stared at it, trying not to think of its fleshly origins. It didn't help to watch Armada wolf hers down with unconcealed pleasure.

"Going to have to eat a lot of jerky on the trail. It's light, easily replenished, and highly nutritious" was all Armada would say.

Fleur struggled with the jerky, got it to her lips and tasted the saltiness, but for the moment her revulsion was too powerful. She left it on the plate.

Once again they formed up behind Doctor Olanther and the fein advance guard then moved off under the jik trees. The fein were commanded by Sept Neilks R'pupe and Pepaz, a tawny golden-brown pair from Brelkilk village. When introduced, Fleur watched her hand vanish into their enormous paws and reemerge miraculously undamaged. She tried to note distinguishing marks. R'pupe was less brindled than Pepaz and his tail was less strongly banded, while R'pupe had more wrinkles around the eyes and muzzle. She was beginning to differentiate among the fein faces at last, each as different as human faces are.

The path was all downhill and she rashly confessed to Doctor Olanther an urge to walk all day. He peered down and gruffly warned her not to waste any energy and to be sure to eat her jerky.

"It's vital for you to get enough protein. We'll be traveling too fast from now on to forage for much vegetable food. We'll have to live like the fein, and that means we'll live off the gzan."

Fleur faced the prospect with some concern.

Then they reached the Garzzen gorge, where the river Abzen dropped through great rapids to the Irurupup below. The jik forest vanished and was replaced by a lush, wildly tropical flora with giant glob globs and hobi-gobi towering over a dense mat of vines and stagga brush. Swarms of honey feeders clouded around big glossy vineflowers of yellow and purple. The trail became very steep for a while then they rounded a curve and drew away from the mists and jungle and found spread before them an immense vista of limitless forest.

The gray-green leaves of *Esperm gigans* covered the world under Beni's rays. Fleur felt odd memories return and saw Armada's shaky smile.

"I had the same feeling, just for a moment. Déjà vu."

"We've been here before," Fleur said.

18

SOON THEY'D LEFT THE FOOTHILLS OF THE MOUNTAINS, AND all around them towered nothing but *Esperm gigans*, the trees growing mightier with each step downward. Over the forest floor writhed a maze of immense roots, many of them more than five meters thick, snaking along the ground like natural walls. In places the roots locked together between competing giants and overlay each other in a tangle of frozen aggression.

The trunks of the trees were titanic. Fleur estimated most to be at least 100 meters in circumference, and the topmost canopy leaves were 300 meters or more above their heads. Fleur felt like a mouse in a land of giants.

The trail they followed wound beneath roots that made arches over their heads and in places formed long tunnels that had to be negotiated in a back-breaking crouch. The light of Beni was now filtered down to a green dimness through hundreds of layers of leaves, and the smell of the forest, the damp, the wet ground, the slow rot of tons of dead wood was strong in Clan Fundan's nostrils. Fleur wondered just what sorts of creatures might exist in the eerie jungle habitat. Whatever they were, they had to be comfortable in gloom, she decided.

Not long afterward, some visible evidence of the lower forest fauna appeared. By the trail lay the hulk of an assassin crab, a tree-root mimic with great clutching pincers. Small arrows, the type the fein customarily tipped with poison, had punctured its carapace in the joints at the base of the pincers. Armada showed Fleur where the fein had cut open the crab's abdomen and removed the soft, tasty flesh. The convolutions on the shell were brown and black, the eyes were red dots on black stalks. The whole thing would be invisible when clutched to the bark. It was as big as a retriever.

At another point they found a fein adept, wrapped in gray, sitting calmly beside the trail. The ancient was dining on a xanthine blossom, leisurely chewing each petal down to the seedpod. He was stationed to warn them away from the path of an aroused and hostile chitin nest that occupied the next clearing.

Fleur's party skirted the area indicated, following a new trail already well trod by thousands of Abzen folk ahead of them. To mark the trail, phosphorescent blazes were daubed on the roots. When at last they halted for lunch, Fleur was very glad to sit down and drop her pack. She eagerly wolfed down some travel biscuit and split a tube of spiced beanpod with Armada.

"Are you having second thoughts, Fleur?"

"What, about coming with you?" Fleur shook her head emphatically. "There's nothing for me to do back on the Sx Coast, except maybe get killed by the syndicate. Since the shooting war started, my role is pretty much over. I think I might be more useful if I travel with the Fundans, then should there be further opportunity for negotiations, I'll be right on the spot."

She waved at the trees. "You know, it seems much quieter than I remember. When we flew, a lot of sound sometimes came up from the jungle. But down here it almost seems like a sepulcher, it's so still. I thought it would be like the rainforests on Earth—they're filled with sounds."

"Well, at night the forest floor does get pretty noisy, but most of the daytime creatures here are silent. At night we'll climb the trees for safety from predators and to protect us there the adepts must persuade the woodwose that we will not harm

202

the trees. During the day, the noisy animals are concentrated in the upper canopy. At night while they sleep the predators come out and they're all silent, whispery types, completely the opposite of those that live on the forest floor. It's almost as if they lived in different worlds."

The spiced beanpod was fast becoming Fleur's favorite highland food. She enjoyed the creamy nuttiness, but the spice was unlike anything she'd ever tasted before.

"Now tell me, why were we warned away from that chitin nest? Since we have so many chitin talkers, why didn't they befriend the nest? I thought that's what they were going to do anyway."

"Not every nest is approachable. You're forgetting that the nests down here and the nests up in the highlands are different—the highland nests are always immature. Because the temperatures are cool and the food supply is limited, in the highlands they never reach full adulthood. The adult nest is very difficult to control, they're too suspicious. Some nests live for hundreds, maybe thousands of years. They replace the queens as they wear out and just keep building up their Vizier Mass until they have enormous memory reserves. But such old nests regard everything that walks or grows as potential food and nothing more."

"How did anyone discover the chitin could be controlled, could even be communicated with? It must have been terribly dangerous in the old days."

"It was," Armada said matter-of-factly. "Of course it was. In the beginning it took years to build up a level of trust with a nest, and even then it was fifty-fifty whether you'd ever get out again once you went in. Haven't you ever heard the story of Old Henry McGinty?"

Fleur confessed she hadn't.

"Well, Old McGinty was one of the best of the early talkers. He gave up his family and his farm and went into chitin talking full time. He became very wealthy, of course, because he was good. Then a farmer asked McGinty to talk with a nest that was raiding his crops and devastating the fields. So Old McGinty went out there with all his tricks. He fed the nest interesting little sweetmeats and offered it essences that are known to give the Vizier a pleasure just to touch and smell. He carefully worked his way in, taking plenty of time—he'd seen friends die in a nest and had no desire to follow them. And the nest let him get close. He'd lie all day just outside the main vent and stroke the warriors and any Vizier that might come out. Eventually he was sitting right over the queen chamber and was thinking about going inside when the nest sent out workers to build a little wall around him. A circular wall marking the spot. McGinty was charmed. He went back every day and sat there stroking them and singing to the nest and they kept building the wall higher. Eventually it was five feet high and there was only a single narrow entrance. One day he went in and then found the exit blocked by warriors. They walled him up and built a roof over him. After that he was kept by the nest and fed by the nest and studied by the nest the whole time. The farmer noticed that McGinty hadn't been around for a few days and called in some help. They went in with gas and managed to dig him out alive, but he'd completely lost his mind. He was a gibbering wreck for the rest of his days."

Fleur shivered uneasily.

"Now, of course, those were the old times, things were hard. You must know about the old history." Fleur nodded, so Armada rushed on. "Well, the colony nearly failed. The farming was hopeless, much too dangerous to be practical, and our robots couldn't cope with the woodwose any better than we could. When desperate people like Crazy Augustine, the one they called the Saint, learned that it was possible to walk into a chitin nest and walk out with a young queen in their hands and an army of trusting Vizier trotting along behind them, well, they were ready to risk it. Of course it took skill, and years of trying—unless you were a natural empath like the Saint—and lots of those early chitin pioneers died as a result of their inexperience. But the survivors discovered the best strategies and the clans survived and moved to the highlands."

Fleur listened and reflected that the process of changing from failed grain farmers to incredibly wealthy chitin ranchers had been very Darwinian, a quite brutal expression of the survival of the fittest.

After an altogether too brief one hour's rest they were back on their feet and off again down the narrow trail winding through the colossal root systems. The fein, in family groups, generally walked ahead of the medical team, but a screen of fein soldiers followed behind as well. As the afternoon wore on, the medical team lagged behind farther and farther because Doctor Olanther and Fleur found the going harder.

Late in the day they came to an abrupt break in the terrain, emerging at the top of a steep, faulted cliff wall. Hundreds of meters below was a rift valley half filled with the gray-green foliage of *Esperm gigans*. The sudden exposure to sunlight hurt their eyes when they first emerged and it took a few moments to adjust.

The cliff was matted with brown vines, and Fleur was examining one when she looked down and saw several move. As the movement was repeated, she made out the outline of a creature with a long, central tubular trunk, many times the size of a man, that was moving up the cliff on enormously elongated arms and legs. The thing was covered in a shaggy mat of fuscous brown fibers that blended into the creeper background so well it was invisible except when it moved.

She knew instantly what it was and felt her heart freeze. She pointed.

"What is it?" Armada asked. Then she followed Fleur's finger and gasped.

The woodwose was now about a hundred meters below their position and another hundred back along the cliff wall. Fleur could clearly see the wide triangular head that surmounted the cylindrical torso like a tank turret and could even make out the seven round black eyes that dotted the upper surface like glassy buttons.

Udar Pepaz, noncom in command of the fein rearguard, put in an urgent call to the front party, more than a kilometer away by then, to learn if the wose had been approached and pacified by adepts. It was the first they'd seen and Pepaz was concerned because wose that had been approached would have concealed themselves from intruders. The adepts had been working along the trails for days, but woodwose territories were often quite extensive and one might have been missed.

Fleur watched in fascination and terror. The wose was searching through the creepers for small treepests. When it found something that started away along the vines, the long arm would reach ahead of the prey and scoop it up with a motion too fast for the eye to follow. The prey would be held up for scrutiny, sometimes to be thrown away again, at other times to be thrust whole into the vast yawning mouth that opened right across the triangular head.

"It's seen us," Armada whispered urgently. "Fall back! Quickly now, it's coming." Everyone ran for the trees. No living thing except the adepts of mystery would willingly face the woodwose.

They were behind and among a gnarling root system when the woodwose clambered over the cliff and assumed its bipedal stance. Fleur glanced back. The thing had missed them momentarily since they were in the shade and its eyes had yet to adjust from the sun. She watched aghast as it raised enormous hands—the creature was easily twenty-five meters tall—to shade its eyes while it peered after them. And then it stepped quickly toward them with a clockwork gait of uncanny swiftness that made Fleur think of an enormous insect. Then she was running again, jerked almost off her feet by Armada.

A loud crashing sounded in brush off to the right. For a second Fleur thought they were already caught and she raised her hands to her head, but Armada pushed her on, exclaiming, "That's just a pride of nachri, we startled them. Hurry, the wose is coming."

Pepaz had found a narrow burrow under a trio of great roots and they frantically dove into the space. It was warm and stank of animal droppings, but they scrabbled in and joined the others.

"Pray that Umpiil brings an adept back in time," Pepaz said. They all listened, crouched together, six fein and the nine humans of the medical team. Jane Fundin-22, one of the orderlies, was on the edge of hysteria and she stuffed her hands into her mouth to stop herself from screaming. Doctor Olanther scrutinized her briefly with his flash and reached immediately for a sedative hypo. But before he could get it into her, she emitted a single scream of hysteric terror that penetrated the dark and seemed louder to Fleur than even the alarm klaxons on the wose wall at Elefelas.

A massive tread, one step and then another, disturbed the ground outside. Fleur gripped her head in her hands and pressed down against the muck. She found herself mumbling half-remembered words of prayers, to Allah, to Jesus, to Krishna, to the Gods she'd never been in need of before.

With a precise motion almost too quick to see, a long arm ending in an eight-fingered hand tipped with diamondlike claws swung under the root complex and fastened unerringly on poor Jane Fundin-22, who vanished from their midst with a last dopplerized scream of horror that lasted for a chilling couple of seconds and then cut off abruptly in wet, pulping sounds.

Fleur was on her belly, scrabbling at the mud, praying to be spared. She didn't want to die this way, not devoured like that.

The fein drew their kifkets and formed a knot in the entrance, linking arms. The woodwose would not eat them, but if it was aroused by the human presence it might still kill them.

The hand came back again, smashing fein aside, ignoring kifket chops that took off foot-long sections of the incredibly tough, fibrous hide. It seized a medic, plucked him from the root he clung to as if he were a berry on a vine. Rohrbach's death shriek was mercifully brief.

They waited, pressing their bodies into the soil of ancient Fenrille, begging for life, flesh frozen in fright, like nibbla trapped by a were.

There was silence. The wose seemed to be waiting for something. Was it reconsidering? Or just playing with them? Either way, it didn't jibe with what Fleur had always been told concerning the woodwose, whose response to intruders was said to be immediate, total, and unrelenting, as automatic as the human immune system.

There was a sound, a long soft hoot, as if a trumpet had been blown into velvet. It was repeated, but this time it was unmistakably closer.

"Another wose," Armada whispered. "Perhaps—" But Fleur blotted out the rest, stuffing mold into her ears. A second woodwose was coming, drawn to the feast.

Thus she never heard the exchange of hoots, low and mournful mingled with higher tones, some comically similar to a steamboat's whistle, that took place over their heads. When it was over Armada reached to hug Fleur, but at her touch the Earthwoman writhed into a fetal ball and fainted.

When Fleur opened her eyes again she was outside, lying on her back staring up into the canopy so far above. She jerked to her feet, amazed to be alive. The others were a short distance away, gathered in a circle around a cairn of stones. She drew closer and Armada saw her and brought her into the circle under a protective arm.

As she watched, Doctor Olanther finished inscribing the names of Jane Fundin-22 and Doctor Rohrbach on two stones, which he then put into the cairn. They said a short prayer for the departed then returned to their packs and belongings. While they marched, Armada explained what had happened.

"The wose that came after us was new to this area, it hadn't been approached by the adepts. The other wose had been and it came over to save us. They know what their fellows are doing—some of the adepts speculate that they are telepathic. Anyway, they had a long hoot session and then both of them tramped off together to clean a sick tree."

Eventually, exhausted, still in a state of near hysteria, and soaked in perspiration, they halted for the day. Biting flies were abroad and their whine was a constant irritant. But the fein found a tree marked with a phosphor blaze, indicating that the woodwose which tended that grove had set the tree aside for them to sleep in.

"Why should they be so particular about a tree for us to sleep in? Why does it matter to them when there are so many trees here?" Fleur quizzed Armada.

"The trees exist for the sake of the Arizel spirits. The wood-wose are charged with tending them. No one knows why some trees may be climbed and why others are prohibited. All that is certain is that if you climbed the wrong tree, the woodwose would sense it and come for you immediately. The trees are as sacred to them as their own flesh, if not more so."

"I see," Fleur said. Without another look at the other trees she followed Doctor Olanther as he climbed the *Esperm gigans* selected for them. The bark was very thick and rough textured, providing many natural footholds. Every few meters the fein had driven in dagger thorns to serve as pitons. Still the climb was an effort that Fleur had not expected to have to make and her strength soon began to ebb away though at least thirty meters remained before the first branch on the tree. She gripped the bark, rested her forehead against it, and refused to consider looking down. After a moment she found the resolve to continue and resumed the climb until finally, when her arms were trembling uncontrollably as she clung to the tree, powerful hands seized her arms and hoisted her smoothly the last few feet.

The light of Beni was already so dim and murky that the forest around her seemed like a gargantuan temple, each colossal tree trunk acting as a pillar to hold up the vastness of the vault above. The branch she stood on was fifteen meters thick and more than a hundred meters in length, yet she could see that it was only a small branch, far down the trunk of the tree. Above her head, another fifty meters away, were the first major branches, each twice as thick and many times as long.

She and Armada found a place to stretch out beside their packs. The sarmer mackees down by the riverbanks began their uproarious mating surge and the twilight dimmed rapidly into dusk. The sarmer mackees could have been screaming right below the tree and Fleur would still have fallen asleep the moment her body was horizontal.

She awoke, it seemed, only moments after she'd gone to sleep, but Armada was insistent. "Fleur, here's some food. You must eat to keep up your strength."

Stiffly Fleur sat up and examined the bowl. Armada was right, she did feel weak. "How long was I asleep?"

"Several hours. The moons are up now." Armada gave her a bowl of tuber curds tossed with green string-fruit.

"What are these, Armada?"

"Sipispirr spirrs—they're very rich in essential vitamins. Heavy on the C in particular." Although the tuber curds were cold, Fleur soon emptied the bowl. Armada produced a stick of gzan jerky.

Fleur grimaced. "Oh, no, I'll throw the lot up if I eat any of that just now."

"Come on, Fleur, you have to have protein. Doc Olanther insists."

Fleur held up a hand weakly. "I will, I promise—just let me get this lot down first." Armada frowned.

"Please?"

"All right, Fleur, but you must try to eat some before you go back to sleep." Armada set out a pair of freshly plucked glopods. "The light will increase if you squeeze the bulb beneath. It's enough to see your way around if you're careful."

Fleur was finally taking notice of her surroundings; the food had kindled a warmth in her belly that was most welcome. She soon found herself considering some more of the tuber curds, even reconsidered a little gzan jerky. Then she noticed the little glimmers and blurs of light down below.

The nighttime forest was a phosphorescent world of fantasy.

Aglow, insects and poisonous creatures wishing to advertise themselves scurried through the dark. And the trees themselves were crusted, especially about the roots, with lustrous nodes. They shimmered with a cool nachreous light. For a while Fleur thought her eyes were playing tricks on her, but on closer inspection she decided that the little flickers she saw in the tree bark itself were for real. Odd sparkles of gold and short-lived flickers of greenish radiance. Intent, she examined the bark beneath them. In the deepest crevices nachreous maculae glowed; tiny flickers of gold seemed to scamper beneath them.

"What causes that, Armada?" She was fascinated by the little eldritch glisters. "Is it phosphorescence?"

Armada smiled, ghostly in the light of the glopod. "No, silly, I told you before, the trees conduct energy for the spirits."

Still awed by the transformation of the forest into a wonderland of soft lights and sparkles, Fleur decided to take Armada's advice to heart and go for seconds of tuber curd. She strolled inward along the branch, past the sleeping figures of humans and fein. Near the trunk she found the cooking station. The fein females had prepared several days' supply of curd and used portable cooking irons to heat the dried blood and fruit mixture called surree by the fein. Fleur took some more curds but passed on the surree.

The three watchfein, lead by Sept Udar Pepaz, walked over to sit with her. Pepaz had already told the others of Fleur and Armada's epic sunsoarer flight. Now they brimmed with questions that she tried to answer between mouthfuls.

Abruptly they were interrupted by a sound from below. Hard scrabbling notes, heavy claws digging into the bark. Pepaz grunted, the three grabbed their bows and strung arrows.

A harsh, coughing growl broke the night and into the pool of light by the cooking station bounded two powerfully built nachri. Each was two meters tall but built more heavily than a fein. The creatures' orange eyes glowed with feral curiosity. They sniffed the air vigorously, drawn by the scents of food. The fein gestured with their bows, intentions plain.

The nachri moaned unhappily and roared and waved heavy paws. Unperturbed, the fein motioned with their bows again. Pepaz drew the string, took aim.

With a hiss like escaping steam, the nachri retreated and descended to the forest floor.

Sobered by the sudden intrusion of the nachri, which would eat a man as soon as look at him, Fleur said good night and returned to her place to sleep.

19

THE CONTROL CENTER OF GHOTAW MOUNTAIN WAS HUSHED, as empty as the rest of the huge complex. As empty as the valleys themselves. A single TV monitor was on, screen blank, a square of light that cast shadows on the far walls and sent gleaming spectra rippling over the armor of the Space Marines as they cautiously pushed their way in.

"Empty, like all the others." The captain strode over to the command module, a circular ring of consoles and monitors with a dais in its exact center. "Everything's in working order, I'll bet. It's as if they intended to come back tomorrow."

"No chance of that," Sergeant Innes grunted. He was still awestruck by the size of the fortress they'd occupied so easily. "Imagine having all this stuff, just one goddamn family. This place has more armament than all the pirate cities of Triton put together. And they just got up and walked away from it all. I wonder where they went."

He flicked a few switches on the board and monitors snapped on bringing more views of empty rooms and corridors.

"Beats me, but I'm sure glad we didn't have to fight our way in here."

"Hell, Captain, I don't think we would have. High Command would've nuked this place and just left a crater. Trying to fight our way in, the casualties would've been crippling."

Captain Storm nodded absentmindedly. Innes was probably right. Admiral Enkov couldn't afford to waste any marine personnel; the supply was limited and casualties had already been much too high. Storm investigated the boards, located the computer section, and tried to activate the mainframe machinery he knew was buried somewhere closeby. The screens offered only a short message, for the main memories had been removed. After another futile stab he turned away and put in a call to *Gagarin*.

The news was brought to Enkov where he sat across a table from Quermwyere, Asgood Wythe, and Ira Ganweek, the most powerful men of the Sx Coast syndicates.

"Excellent." Enkov clapped his hands together. "Gentlemen, great news. We are in possession of Fundan Headquarters, too. We now have control of every major highland nerve center. The highlanders have given up the struggle."

"You have taken prisoners?" Ganweek said.

"No need—the families have fled, they and the fein, all of them. They've abandoned the high ground and we think they're now traveling in the forest regions adjacent to their previous territories. Clearly they prefer lives as nomads or guerrillas to surrender. So, let them. Now that we have possession of the source of chitin protein, we can begin our program."

"Except that now you'll have no one to supply you with chitin protein," Asgood Wythe whined.

"If you recall, my dear admiral," Quermwyere sniped, "this is precisely what I warned you they would do if they could not hold their own against your marines."

Ira Ganweek, fresh from his hospital bed but several steps ahead of the others, glared at Quermwyere—it was not the time to anger the monster. He had to be cozened then drowned in his own desires. And only the sweetest of honeys would do for the red-banded wasp....

Quermwyere sensed the senator's mood and cut his complaint short. Since the "accident," Ira had been very irritable and twice as tyrannical as before. The man was driven by a new urge, one so powerful that to Quermwyere it seemed certain to be affecting Ira's judgment. Quermwyere sympathized. Sexual release was one of life's profound pleasures, but there were other contentments, and to make of this matter such a crusade, such a drive for vengeance was unbalanced.

Quermwyere had risen far in the world by trusting to Ira Ganweek's decisions, and time after time he had seen those who'd turned against Ira go down in ruin. He would wait for others to turn coat first.

The admiral, however, was oblivious. With his usual indifference, he continued, "The only important question now is how to quickly step up production. What can your people do?" He seemed confident.

Ganweek was rocked. *There* was a void large enough to drive a bulldozer through, but it was also an opportunity of solid gold. Yet there was almost no possible way to seize it. Or was there? Ira's brain spun and he spluttered for a moment until Asgood Wythe chipped in, "The clans went with the fein—that means they took the chitin talkers with them. Without chitin talkers you can only get Vizier Mass by killing the nest. This gives you good production for one season but then you have to wait nine years or more for the Vizier Mass to grow again in a new nest."

The admiral blinked irritably. The damn situation had more factors sticking to it than a four-orbit problem with gogoplectar numbers. In an uncharacteristically sour voice, he said, "It was perfectly clear that our strategy would produce early results. Frankly I'm tired of all this criticism from people who've done little but profit from the corruption in longevity drugs that has caused so much havoc in the home system. All computer projections suggested that the clans were so combative that they'd offer battle and, once soundly defeated, they'd surrender and accept our terms. This agreed with both the psychological profiles and the economic statistics we considered. They've stored away a great deal of wealth—the fleeing columns must be really rich in Pharamol, for instance. Now we have these new developments to consider. They're determined to stay outside the reach of World Government law by living as nomads in the jungle. Well, we will let them. We will occupy the valleys and take control of the means of production."

"But—" Quermwyere began in desperation. Why could the

fool not be made to see sense? There were no successful chitin talkers—or barely a handful—outside the clans. No talkers existed but those who'd passed through the clan schools and learned the techniques, the arts of gaining the cooperation of the carnivorous insect.

"No buts," Ira Ganweek said. He sat up and placed his hands on the table, taking charge and silencing Quermwyere. "We shall immediately begin to raise an army of chitin talkers on the Sx Coast. There are thousands who'd gladly risk the dangers for the chance to share in the output of nests they might control."

The admiral was instantly pleased. *That* was more like it, sensible progress at last.

Ganweek suppressed his own smile less it give away too much of his real feeling. The admiral was out of his depth. He was helplessly bound to the limited and remorseless logic of space war, all that endless matching of orbits, a chess game limited to curves and orbits and governed by numbers. It was all very well outside the atmosphere with a space cruiser under you, but such straight-line logic and brutal instruments of war could be of limited effect in human conflict on the planetary surface.

Enkov was buoyant. The sudden surrender of the valleys, just when his own casualties had begun to raise serious doubts as to the feasibility of the campaign he'd undertaken, had lifted his spirits. And he felt he might have found an ally at last down there on the Sx Coast. That fellow Ganweek was the one to deal with. He made sense, he could get things done, and, most important, he knew how to listen. Listening was the most important ability to watch for in potential subordinates. Quickly Sigimir sketched the details of what they would need as he imagined them. Taking their cues from Ira's quick glances, Wythe and Quermwyere settled back in their chairs and held silence, their eyes occasionally meeting, questioning, in the dark.

Ira Ganweek proved to be correct in his estimation of the potential supply of people who would sign up as chitin talkers. Within hours of the advertisement's first appearing on Sx Coast TV, long lines formed in front of the Bablon Dome. Thousands who'd lost all hope of anything better than a shack and a short life under the shadow of the wosewall flocked to apply from Death Wish.

When he heard that they were taking anybody, without even ID checks, Tan Ubu quit his job as bookkeeper in a Death Wish bordello, said good-bye to his grubby room, and went along to apply himself. With luck, he thought, he could make enough credits to buy some good plastic surgery. With great luck, maybe he could even make enough to buy a syndicate pardon.

Sporting a thick beard and wearing worn, torn clothes like everybody else from Death Wish and Love Beach, Tan wasn't concerned about being spotted by the syndicates. Since the war had started they'd been much too busy trying to keep a lid on the coastal cities. The potential for hysterical chaos was lurking just below the surface of the sea of social inequity that the syndicates floated on.

At the Bablon Dome, as he was young and intelligent enough to pass the oral and written tests, he was quickly processed. With another fifty trainees, mostly young and desperate types, he underwent "training."

After the second day of training he began to suspect the truth. All day long they'd studied dissections of chitin types. There had been a lecture from a professor of chitin biology on the relative merits of different species of chitin. Another lecture by a female doctor with a profound knowledge of chitin chemistry had completely overwhelmed the trainees in methoxy-gluranate transposition series and aldehyde megagroups.

On the third day his suspicions crystallized when the trainees spent the afternoon learning how to dig holes in the ground with everything from small mechanical shovels to the old-fashioned, hand-held kind.

The very next morning they acquired as Senior Instructor a stout, florid young woman wearing a brown warband uniform. The students were outfitted with a uniform of their own, a suit of gray sycloth that came in awkward sizes. Then they were drilled for an hour by the stout young woman and another warband officer, a male sergeant major. The drilling was just old-fashioned square bashing, presumably designed to wield the trainees of Unit 47 into some sort of cohesive group. To Tan it was very mild treatment compared to what he'd been through years before at the academy, but some of the trainees were obviously hopeless.

At the end of the drill they were marched to the refectory in the basement of the Bablon Dome. Tan listened intently to the conversations around him while they served themselves fish stew and soycurd. None voiced his suspicions. Perhaps he was wrong, but he doubted it.

While still digesting lunch, they were marched out of the dome and into choppers that took them to the airport. Twenty minutes later Unit 47 was airborne in a big warband jet transport and plowing northward over the limitless forest.

Tan sat with another dark-skinned Earther. They traded banter. Such encounters were rare.

"You American roots, too?" Transford Jay asked.

"No, African," Tan said. "East Africa. I'm pure Kikuyu. Nairobi."

"Oh." Transford Jay was taken aback. Tan smiled. It was always the same with brown-skinned Americans. Meeting an African African brought out complicated emotions, something almost ritualized within the Americans.

But gradually the trust between them grew more solid and Tan ventured an opinion. "You have the feeling at all that they perhaps don't really know what the fuck they're trying to do?"

Transford thought about it for a moment, then shook his head, puzzled. "I don't get you, brother. How do you mean they don't know what they're doing?"

"Well, we've studied everything about the chitin that they know in the last few days, including all that stuff about protein chemistry that I couldn't follow."

Transford grinned. Hardly anybody in the unit had understood a word of the chemistry lady's lectures.

"But they haven't told us a thing about chitin talking, about how we're supposed to walk in and get a nest to open communication with us."

Transford nodded slowly, now thoughtful. "Well, they did give us all those sugar cubes as treats."

"Uh huh."

The flight continued and neither Tan nor Transford wanted to chat anymore. Ten hours later they touched down at Ghotaw Mountain. Tan emerged from the plane into the brilliant, supernatural light of the high valleys and gaped at the colossal vista of white-walled mountains that surrounded them. They were at the bottom of a bowl 30,000 feet deep, in a great green valley of arble and jik.

That night they were quartered in what had been a school of some kind until very recently. The buildings were all low, dugouts of poured concrete construction, set into the ground. Standing in the center of the Ghotaw complex of schools, factories, and laboratories, all he could see were the ornamental trees, the flowerbeds, and the arble-covered low roofs of the buildings that never rose more than a meter out of the ground. The interiors were spartan indeed. The Fundans had removed everything that wasn't bolted down.

After breakfast the next morning, they were marched out to the woods equipped with shovels and small mechanical diggers. Everyone had a big bag of sugar lumps.

Chitin nests were everywhere. Tan saw the brown masses of hard-packed earth rising in every direction he looked. Each represented the ventilation system of a nest and marked the main entrances. Some of the fin-shaped ventilators were three meters high.

Captain Votts, the stout woman with the florid face, ordered them to select nests and to approach them in three-person teams.

Tan, Transford, and a buxom strawberry blonde who called herself Jessilou Rick formed a team and walked off a ways to find a nest on its own. They found one and approached it. No chitin were in sight, in fact there was a watchful silence—not a thing seemed to be moving. They shifted on their feet, considered the sugar lumps and the shovels. Then Transford started giggling.

"What is this, man? What are we supposed to do now?"

Tan grinned, chuckled. "Was I right? Or was I right?"

Jessilou wore a puzzled expression on her pinched little face. "What are you two guys laughing about? How are we supposed to get this chitin under control with you two giggling around?" She planted her hands on her hips and gave them a cross look. Tan found this even more hilarious, but eventually he quieted down and they looked over toward the nest they had chosen.

"Well, we have to make contact, I guess," Transford finally commented. They slowly stepped toward the cluster of irregular brown dirt columns and hillocks. Five central pipes projected under the radiator fin, so it was a big nest, in its second century.

218

It knew the tread of every creature that walked and in particular it knew the tread of man.

The nest sat in the center of an area worn bare of vegetation. The circle was some thirty meters wide. When they stepped onto the bare ground holes behind then opened and warrior chitin poured out.

Transford was the first to notice their new escort. "Well, would you look at that," he said a little hollowly. A patch of ground five meters wide and a meter deep behind them was covered in a carpet of brown and green chitin. The insects advanced toward them. There was no mistaking the wishes of the nest—they were to approach more closely. As they moved near the brown dirt towers, more and more chitin poured out and surrounded the path. All that was left was a narrow trail leading right to the central opening.

"What do we do now?" Jessilou said. Transford wore a strange uneasy expression. Tan was sweating. The warriors were four inches long and each had mandibles up to a quarter of its body length. They had a choice of two acids, as well— one mildly reactive, which caused puffy swellings in the victim's flesh, and the other a venom that produced nerve fire in humans, frequently blinding them.

"Well, we have to try to communicate with the Vizier in the nest. That means we have to make friends." Transford got out some sugar lumps and bent down and put them out before the warriors. Several darted forward, ignoring the sugar, and snapped their mandibles, producing audible clicks. Transford jerked back.

"Make friends?" Jessilou's expression was getting panicky.

They stopped, the insects stopped. A long moment of silence ensued and then, from out of the nest, came a dozen or so other shorter chitin, fat, bumbling creatures with iridescent abdomens that glittered with the colorful proteins embedded there.

"Vizier chitin, they're coming to meet us."

The Vizier marched confidently up to Transford who bent down and offered a hand. One insect climbed into his palm immediately. Transford held it up and lightly scratched its back.

"Doesn't seem so hard now, does it." Transford continued to stroke the three-inch-long insect that sat on his palm.

The warriors moved forward and closed up behind Transford. When he didn't move, the leading warriors nimbly climbed over his shoes and bit him around the ankles. Transford yelped from the pain and jumped forward, warriors pushing in behind in a carpet of rustling brown. Tan and Jessilou were left surrounded by a ring six feet deep of warriors.

Enough to kill us if we try to escape. Tan could feel the sweat running down his back and from under his arms. But he did his best not to seem too terrified to Jessilou.

Soon Transford was almost out of sight, in the middle of the brown columns, but he kept reporting on events in a high, nervous voice. "Oh, boy, get this—they're all climbing onto me. Dozens of 'em, but these are different. They're much smaller, only an inch long and they've got small mouthparts. Hey, guess what? They're chewing up my clothes! Can you get that? They want my clothes off. Man, this nest is hot for ol' T-Jay. Whoo!"

Tan did his best to sound encouraging. "Right, that's part of the ritual. You've been chosen to enter the nest. Do you see a big hole? One wide enough for a man to get into?"

Transford's voice, a little shaky now, shot back, "Yes, sir, I do, there's something like that right here where they made me come. Now they've got my pants. Hell! They're chewing through my shoes, too. One thing for sure, they chew fast."

"Okay, now you've got to get into that hole, T-Jay, that's where you have to interface with the Vizier Mass."

Transford was quiet after that.

A long, sobbing scream floated over the trees from off to their right. It went on for several seconds and ran up and down the octaves sending shivers through Tan's spine.

"What the hell was that, man?" Transford asked quickly.

"Get in the hole, Transford," Jessilou said.

"Well, I don't know exactly that I want to do that. I didn't think we were going to get quite so intimate quite so soon, if you know what I mean. They got all my clothes and now they seem to be waiting."

A moment later he yelped in pain. "Okay, okay, I'm in the hole, man. Oh, God, I don't know if I can handle this. Get me out! Someone get me out! This is too much. This hole's deep too, real deep. Uhh, oh, no, oh, God, no! They're making me go down into the hole, right into it. Oh, God, and the hole is full of them, there's millions of them down here and it's dark and, oh, no, oh ugh. They're crawling on me, man, they're crawling on my body, they're on my face, hundreds of 'em."

"Take it easy, Transford, just try and relax. You have to let it examine you, it wants to check you out. So just stay still as you can and relax," Tan said, feeling useless and redundant.

At this point of business a trained chitin talker would be empathizing with the nest with all his or her might, stroking the Vizier, making little love sounds, little clucks and moues, trying to radiate a torrent of love and warmth toward the cold, brutally selfish nest intelligence.

But such knowledge was not widely known outside the highland clans. Certainly Transford Jay knew nothing of the arts of insect love, and if he had he probably would've been disgusted by them.

For its part, the nest soon tired of the cold, unresponsive human it had received. Briefly it considered eating him, but then it remembered the Warm/Love female who always brought the sweet berries and knew to tickle the underside of the abdomen first, where every Vizier wished for more pressure. Warm/Love female would be upset if the cold human was eaten, the nest memory confirmed this. There were several precedents from the past.

A path cleared magically above Transford Jay. The Vizier retired into deeper tunnels. Warriors bit his feet and drove him out with cries of pain and desperate lunging strides.

The circle around them faded away and all three ran for the trees.

Transford had dozens of puffy red chitin bites on his feet and legs and enough dread in his heart for ten men faced with imminent death. "I ain't ever going back into no goddamn chitin nest," he said emphatically. The others agreed they weren't about to either.

Back at the Ghotaw complex they found a turbulent scene. The warband officers, including Captain Votts, had guns in their hands and were standing together in front of the central building. Facing them was a mob of gray-uniformed chitin trainees demanding to return to the Sx Coast.

The officers refused and raised their guns. The mob threw stones and the officers opened fire, shooting a number of trainees. Then they retreated inside the building while the mob ran to the airstrip and commandeered the planes.

Tan Ubu ran with the rest of them and managed to force his way onto the second plane to take off. At the Sx Coast, they found an armed reception committee of warband troops, but nobody had thought to order their arrest and detention. Tan quickly got rid of the gray uniform and rode the Mass-drive out to Love Beach. His old room in the hovel on the beach in Death Wish was still vacant and he moved back in at once.

Tan and the others of the first recruitment group were lucky— those who didn't get eaten on that first day of operations. The second recruitment group found that things were considerably different. The syndicates had found a few quack chitin "talkers" who were now teaching their methods of communicating with the insect. At least the quacks did know that the reward method was the basic platform to the art of "talking." They gathered glob glob fruits unripe and bitter and they sent the trainees to fetch nuts and garstang flowers. Some mixed sugary syrups and poured them over soybread.

The second recruitment group was then escorted to the nests by Space Marines and ordered to enter the nests. Anyone refusing was shot.

20

ON THEIR SEVENTEENTH NIGHT IN THE DEEP FOREST, THE ABZEN medical team came close to death once more. This time it was the kind of blind, incidental death that had given the forest some of its reputation for elemental ferocity, a world where humans were powerless.

Their tree for that night was an ancient giant, so old that its bark was festooned with moss colonies and several of the upper branches had died, killed by a fungal disease beyond the remedial powers of the woodwose. Soon, the wind whispered, the tree will fall. They climbed once again, 100 meters or more, to the lowest branch, where they spread their sleeping rolls and made a quick meal.

It had rained most of the day and, for the most part, they'd trudged in silence, through an endless jungle of scrub glob glob and satursine vines. Fleur was desperately glad to grab even a bowl of hot jerky stew and then throw herself into a notch in the bark and fall asleep. Under Olanther's keen eye and with her diet massively supplemented with vitamins, minerals, and high-quality protein, she had mended steadily, even while marching thirty to forty kilometers a day. Still, in the evenings she found it easy to fall asleep each day.

Since it was still raining, no one felt like sitting out with a glopod and some teosinte to talk or sing. Everyone slipped into his roll and tried to ignore the damp and the dripping rain. Fleur was soon dreaming of the southern ocean, the yacht under full sail and spinnaker, bowling along on a westerly breeze. It was bright and sunny, trees were nowhere in sight.

She awoke to a violent commotion and general alarm. The branch she lay on trembled. Something unseen cracked the air like a giant whip. Then she saw a tentacle two meters thick leap in the dark then slam down and across the branch not two meters away. It struck like a falling tree and the branch jumped under her. Where the tentacle fell it tightened like a huge organic spring, thickening and bunching. Another two meters and she would have been crushed like a grape upon an anvil.

Armada was on her feet, grabbing her pack. She peered over the edge for a second then turned and pushed Fleur before her. "Go, Fleur, run, for your life, run. A walking tree's coming, and it's moving fast."

They ran out along the branch away from the trunk and soon came to one of the thick tentacles. It was covered in something that looked like a glossy bark, with whorls and rings raised up all over it. As it gripped the branch, it flattened enough to let them clamber over it and continue outward. Fein were there, and Doctor Olanther, and together they scrambled way out to the end of the branch.

Then the branch bucked and heaved and they clung for their lives. Twice Fleur was jounced a foot into the air by the violence of the motion, and each time the breath was knocked out of her when she regained contact. Then, mercifully, the gyrations ceased. The branch continued to quiver, shaking, small branches waving wildly, but gradually slowing. Eventually it ceased to move and they regained their feet.

The fein gazed anxiously upward.

"What's going on?" Fleur asked.

"The woodwose must have found a walking tree—you know, the tree parasite that looks like a branch. They chased it but it found our tree and climbed. In the trees it would have the advantage over the woodwose for speed. Unfortunately we were in its way."

Fleur felt ill—the shock had been so sudden. Nausea swept over her and she lay down again and waited for it to pass. Armada sat by her.

Abruptly the fein shouted alarm. "Grip the tree," they called, and they sprawled flat once more.

With a cracking like a bolt of lightning, an upper branch, dry and long dead, sheared from the trunk and went crashing down, snapping off lesser boughs wholesale in an avalanche of thousands of tons of wood and leaves and hapless animals. Their branch took a momentary blow from the tumbling mass. Though it jumped beneath them again, it held.

The impact far below was still echoing through the forest when they heard woodwose hooting and the sounds of violent struggle.

"A branch broke under the weight of the walking tree. Now the woodwose will tear it to pieces." Armada fished in her satchel for a flare and detonated it in the dark below. In the brief burst of light, Fleur saw the walking tree, a fat trunk ribbed and beaded with nodules atop great snapping roots, curling and coiling like tentacles. There were no branches, however. The trunk ended in a bulbous digestive sac. Around the thing were six or seven woodwose. They attacked in unison, evading the lashing roots and tearing at the walking tree with diamond-tipped claws. Then the darkness returned and Fleur could only guess—from the tumultuous noise that built to a climax after a few minutes and then died away to jubilant hooting from the wose—that the tree shepherds had succeeded in killing the most hated enemy of their trees.

On the thirtieth day in the deep forest, Lavin Fundin, Bg Rva, and the fast-marching First Sept of the First Impi caught up with the medical team. They stopped to brew tea together and break out travel biscuit and cold jerky.

Lavin seemed fit and well, less harried and tired than he'd seemed at the base camp. He had plenty of news of Abzen for he and the First Sept had stayed behind to gather information for Fair Fundan and the family central command. They had worked to cover the retreat, taking pains to obliterate the trail, sowing quick-growing satursine seed behind them.

But it was their encounters with the woodwose and the

225

walking tree that seemed more important to him. He listened with an increasingly grim cast to his features.

"Why so down, Lavin?" Armada inquired at last. Weren't they at least still alive, wasn't the plan working?

"I'm sorry, I was just thinking of all our losses. This has been a hard time, but as long as we learn from these lessons we can probably prevent such things in future."

They spent the night gathered around a fire lit in a portable brazier. The fein sang songs and stripped down the carcasses of a pair of gzan. Soon the flesh was being pounded and laid out briefly on racks over the flames to dry it out for jerky.

Lavin and Fleur spoke together of the war and what the future might hold, until the Pale Moon rose. Finally Lavin clambered to his feet. "I'm exhausted," he admitted. "Good night"—he paused, their eyes locked—"harlequin minx," he finished in a whisper.

Her smile went before him to his sleep sack and comforted him through a short night's sleep. In the morning, by the time Fleur was up, the First of the First and Lavin had already left.

"Don't worry, Fleur," Armada said with a sly grin, "we'll all be meeting up again at the Pinnacles of Mahr. In a few days time."

Two days later Fleur climbed down from another branch, high on the side of another giant tree, and found another group of Fundan refugees standing in a mass on the far side of the trail.

She knew instantly that something was very wrong. Sept Udar Pepaz was decidedly on edge, tail out stiff and tight, hands by his weapons. His fein were equally alert. On the far side was a large group of fein, a hundred or more, with yellow ear flashes, bandoliers, and assault rifles in their hands. Backed up a short way was a sizable group of humans, all in Fundan camouflage kit but all bearing a single yellow flash.

"Ramal forces, Young Proud Fundan's army," Armada whispered as she stepped down beside Fleur. Fleur looked back with a blank face. So why were they standing like this, the fein eyeing each other like cats and dogs before a scrap?

"Young Proud is Lavin's blood enemy. The Proud Fundans have never accepted Lavin in Abzen Vale."

Fleur understood. An in-family blood feud—there were

226

dozens of them in the undying ranks of the highland clans, some stretching back centuries.

"Will they fight?" she asked, almost unable to believe it possible.

Yet Armada merely shrugged. "Who can say? Young Proud is prone to dangerous moods, unpredictable action."

"Would they kill us, too?"

"Yes, of course."

Fleur looked back over the trail at the opposing fein—who were still holding rifles but not aiming them, not actually even looking at them—and imagined what it might be like to be attacked by them.

Commands rang up and down the Ramal column and the yellow-flash fein suddenly formed ranks and trotted forward, moving past Pepaz and his fein without making eye contact, and on down the trail. Behind came the humans, technicians, and medical people.

Fleur commented on the downcast eyes of the Ramal fein to Udar Pepaz.

"They are of the Heavy Impi. Their kin blood watered our valley not long ago. They must fight us again or die of shame in an unholy state, but they have no riffchuss with us and cannot attack such a small party with honor. To meet our eyes would have asserted riffchuss and forced a fight, so they were ordered to pass us with eyes low."

She was glad that Pepaz had them wait by the trail for a while before they started on, allowing Young Proud's group to get far ahead.

Late on the following afternoon, they entered the rendezvous region, the Mahr Pinnacles. A great sequence of ancient granite pinnacles and puy domes jutting up from the forest floor, the peaks were aptly named. The pinnacles were clustered along the leading edge of the upfaulted plateau that the Abzen population had traversed. Beyond them the land dropped sharply again into the river basin. Fifty kilometers away the great Irurupup coiled across the land.

As they reached the first outposts of bare rock, they met another group of Abzen fein, escorting a hundred chitin talkers, members of the Abzen Rangers. The two parties fell in together and soon found that, by comparison, the rangers had had an uneventful trek—"boring" was how they described it. They had suffered only one injury, a man who had slipped and broken an arm falling from a tree. Fleur's account of the walking tree and its destruction brought sharp exclamations from the rangers.

Soon they encountered more groups on the trail. Some were Abzen forces and others were from other valleys. Fein with purple, aquamarine, and orange ear flashes, men and women in every imaginable variation on the basic suit of Fundan greens.

At the head of a long, narrow glade, a command post had been set up, a tent with a long table beside it. As groups came up they were assigned campsites and direction.

The trail, which in truth had been many trails, braided together through the trees, now split, bifurcating like a river delta and spreading the Fundan forces throughout the region of pinnacles and granite outcrops.

The medical team found its campground on a boulder field covering the shoulders of a steep granite crag. Around them green pennons proclaiming sept identities fluttered over gray-green tents placed between the blocks of granite. At the western edge of the field, the land dropped away in the precipitous slope that marked the fault line.

After they'd pitched their tent, Fleur suggested to Armada that they climb the crag to its highest point. When they finally clambered to the top of the rock, the sun was setting in the west in a riot of deep red and gold.

"Look to the east and south, more east than south, though. Can you see anything?" Armada looked but saw nothing except the line made through the forest by the distant river. Fleur produced a pair of high-power binoculars she'd borrowed from Doctor Olanther. Carefully she scanned the horizon until at last, far, far away to the southeast, she found it, a narrow column or rock, catching the last light of Beni. Stroins' Rock! Excitedly she pointed it out to Armada.

"Well, Madam Ambassador, this particular neck of the woods seems to draw you back now, doesn't it? We must have flown across the river somewhere about here on the ninth day."

Fleur sighed. That rock was where she'd first met Lavin Fundin—at least where they'd really met, as themselves, not apparitions for parties.

"The great forest of Fenrille. Who'd ever have thought that I would wind up here?"

228

"Fleur, the spirits are guiding you. Perhaps it was decided for you." Armada seemed serious.

Fleur smiled. "I suppose it doesn't matter either way." She felt an odd contentment.

The sarmer mackees were surging; it was time to leave. They scrambled back down the rock.

21

BY THE END OF THE THIRD WEEK OF THE SYNDICATE EFFORT to restart chitin protein production, it was clear to everyone that the attempt was an unmitigated disaster. Morale in the so-called Chitin Corps was at zero. Rumors had spread on the Sx Coast, and the lines of applicants had vanished. To keep up the strength in the Chitin Corps, the warbands now made press-gang raids into Elefelas and Love Beach. As a consequence, the walkways emptied at nights and a lot of folk were carrying guns, determined to fight and die on the coast rather than be inducted.

In the highlands, despite the massive effort, only six percent of the nests had been brought into production. A few individuals, armed with the accumulated wisdom of the syndicate quacks, had managed to uncover an inkling of the process of chitin talking. They'd discovered the sexual aspect of the process, the power of emotive love, which if used properly could bring a whole nest to the point where it would throb with pleasure at the contact between Vizier Mass and human, a phenomenon referred to by clan talkers as "purring."

To get just that six percent of renewed production had cost hundreds of human lives. Many nests had tasted human flesh and gone unrebuked. They were now feral and a deadly trap for anyone to approach.

But there was an even worse development—at least to Admiral Enkov and the High Command. Faced with the hysterical demand for longevity drugs that was manifesting itself on the coasts, the Chitin Corps commanders were sneaking out to dynamite as many nests as they dared, looting the Vizier Mass and shipping it to the black market.

Matters had degenerated so far that Enkov might soon be forced to deploy the Space Marines permanently, to oversee the whole operation. The dynamiting was destroying the future productivity of the valleys; the careful work of generations of clan talkers was being destroyed. And still the demoralized Chitin Corps' knowledge of the arts of building communication with the chitin was at best rudimentary.

Ira Ganweek was not surprised when the summons came, but he was surprised to be summoned to his own conference room atop the Bablon Dome. Admiral Enkov and an escort of fifty Space Marines in full armor dropped planetward in the pinnace and turned up at the dome after leaping in formation down the walkways, scattering the terrified population before them.

The marines fanned out to seize control of all key points in the dome, forcing angry syndicate security guards to back off.

Enkov removed his helmet and took a seat among the Bablon Syndicate magnates. He was very angry indeed and blunter than usual. "The failure of your Chitin Corps is absolutely intolerable. I've ordered the whole wretched mess dissolved, and I'm going to pack the lot on those planes and send them back to you. They're more trouble than they're worth. I can see I was gravely mistaken in trusting your word on this matter. This whole damn city is nothing but a pit of slime and bribery. Those goddamn corps commanders are just looting the chitin nests whenever we turn our backs."

Ira was patient; he groveled. "I'm so sorry, Admiral. We have done our best. You forget that we offered no miracles, we merely said we would try to raise an army of people to train as chitin talkers. We did, but few of them had the skill. You must remember that the highlanders recruit *children* for their chitin schools. They weed out those who are psychologically unsuited by the age of twelve and train the survivors most intensely. Obviously we cannot imitate their methods right away, but given time perhaps we can replace them."

Enkov ground his teeth. He felt he was slipping into a morass, a quagmire of corruption and deceit where nothing could ever be accomplished. His instincts told him to blast a hole through it and charge for the heights.

"However," Ganweek continued smoothly, "we must find some supply of chitin soon. The market panic is destroying the cities."

"So what?" Enkov snapped. "Why should I care about these cities? Why shouldn't you be left to your own devices?" The admiral's blunt anger took the starch out of the others at the table. Quermwyere turned a shade closer to green.

Enkov waited a minute, shook his head slowly, and reconsidered. "Well, perhaps that is too harsh. We shall have to consider your problems here, but these cities are long overdue for a transformation. I intend to impose martial law throughout the human-occupied zones of this planet. The policing of the cities will be supervised by Military Intelligence and certain offenses—looting, firing of a weapon, subversion—will be punished by immediate execution."

A buzz started around the table as everyone began to make plans for extended trips.

Ira Ganweek pressed his palms together and forced a smile onto his face. "Come, let us not talk of martial law. That is surely a side issue, an administrative detail that can be taken care of later. Our real problem is the lack of chitin talkers. Why don't we discuss that and try and figure out a solution?"

Enkov simply stared at them. They had failed him. They would not be given a second chance. "I have made plans already. We are searching for the highlanders."

Ganweek chuckled indulgently. "Isn't that a little like looking for the proverbial needle in a haystack?"

"Of course not. Aboard *Gagarin* we have imaging technology that could count the hairs on top of your head from our orbit—if you had any." Enkov looked around sourly. All these syndicate chiefs were bald, all old, all dependent on Pharamol—illegal, incredibly expensive Pharamol.

"I see," Ganweek said. "And what will you do when you find the clans?"

"Demand their chitin talkers; they can return to their nests and production can resume."

"Of course, they will resist." Ganweek suppressed a giggle.

"We have bested them before; they fled to avoid further battle. They will know better than to resist."

By the volcanic crags of Mahr, the Fundan Clan was coming together for the last time. In a matter of a few days the entire clan was dividing into small groups, a family of fein and a squad of humans with families, if they had such. At Mahr Fair Fundan reviewed each unit, from chitin talker teams to Impis, sept by sept. It was an exhausting schedule. She left but an hour every eight or so for sleep, and her staff was sleeping on their feet most of the time. Yet Fair ignored the fatigue. It was possibly the last time the clan would be together.

The other clans had split already. Many were widely dispersed in the deep forest. Soon the Fundans would be spread out in small groups over hundreds of thousands of square kilometers of jungle.

But Fair intended to take advantage of her guerrilla status. Several crack Ghotaw units were hidden in the forest near the mountains. Camouflaged transports floated on secret lakes. She had removed her pieces from the board and now she could watch the pressure build on the other players. The chitin market had gone crazy, prices doubling and redoubling. When that news rippled out at last to the black hole transmitting station at AO 4411, the admiral's strings would be jerked. The home system would convulse, just like the coastal cities.

It happened that on the third day of her clan inspection, she was visiting the Abzen forces who were about to splinter and head onto the plateau.

They were at luncheon when a message was received from the space forces.

Clan Fundan was targeted for immediate assault unless all Fundan chitin talkers were assembled for induction into the Space Navy. Fair ordered instant dispersal of all Fundan forces. With her staff she mounted specially trained nachri and disappeared into the trees.

Orbital fighters paced overhead, their bombs bursting balls

of orange fire beneath the trees. Black columns of smoke arose, fires crackled in the underbrush.

A scream of rage arose from the woodwose wherever they were all across the Hokkkh.

Six klicks west of Mahr Pinnacles, the group to which Fleur and Armada had been assigned jogged down the path.

Crumping detonations shook the trail ahead. A fireball erupted 200 meters away. More followed, a line of bursts up the trail toward them. Then it was past. They regained their feet and saw the parachutes of the Space Marines floating down through newly blasted holes in the canopy.

The marines dropped from clear skies without obstruction or ground fire, but landed in terrain unlike anything they'd ever met with before. On the dimly lit forest floor they found a nightmare tangle of vines that formed a jungle ten meters tall. This was difficult stuff to jump through, even more difficult to land in. No sooner had they formed up, though, than they encountered another problem, one that had been left out of the briefings.

Enraged by the havoc wrought in their trees, the woodwose now strode upon the marines.

Captain Lico Rodrique had barely had time to get his platoon in line and stifle complaints about the terrain, the trees, and the tangle-vine jungle, when a shout caused him to look over his shoulder. A forest animal, an incredible thing like a gargantuan stork crossed with an ape twenty meters tall, was bearing down on him with enormous strides of its spindly legs. Rodrique's daisy chain spun, the assault rifle came up and he watched puffs of dust, fiber, and blood jump from the impacts of .9-mm automatic rounds. To Rodrique's amazement the thing absorbed a full clip then grabbed him between hands the size of doors. With a howl of disbelief he pitched his suit to jump on the ham-springs, pitting the 800-horsepower Graatchen 250s against the thing's grip. It merely grabbed him tighter, cradling him like a football against its blood-streaked belly. Then it swung him, a ton of armor suit and motors, so hard against a tree trunk that the suit shorted out. As he was raised for another blow, Rodrique's last conscious thought was that he knew what it was like to die as an insect, crushed by a human foot.

The rest of the platoon turned heavier fire upon the creature.

Twenty-millimeter cannon shell and armor-piercing grenades finally brought it down. Awed, they gathered around the smoking, twitching remains.

"What in the name of hell is that?"

"I put an entire clip of nine-oh-nines into that thing, it didn't notice a damn."

"Didja see what it did to the captain?"

Lieutenant Marion Klipps assumed command. She moved quickly to break things up. "C'mon, everybody, let's move it out. We're already behind schedule."

"What about Rodrique?"

"He's dead, leave him."

They jumped and burst their way through the entangling vines. Every so often the vines got so bad they had to stop and use power tools and flamethrowers to cut through. The jungle ahead seemed even thicker.

Klipps told Action Command of her difficulties. She was told to move westward to get around the region of satursine infestation. There was clearer ground, with fein trails to the west.

Soon they ran into small groups of fein. Klipps had seen what happened to Rodrique and had felt an ancient primordial fear rise up in her guts, which disgusted her. She was eager to kill something now, the anger was bright and hard.

The marines fired, but the fein were like shadows, will-o'-the-wisps that appeared briefly then vanished again in the jungle.

Corporal LeBlanc pushed into a thicket of purplish glob glob fronds and was blown head over heels in a bright orange flash as he tripped a mine. Abruptly, incoming rifle fire began to slap the vines and ricochet loudly from their suits.

Two rounds slammed into Klipps' side, sending her tumbling, gyros whirling. When she came up she was still struggling to get her breath back. She continued forward but more cautiously. Bullets continued to hum around them, occasionally striking hard enough to stagger a power suit.

The marines were way behind schedule and some were low on ammo when they broke out of the vines and found a fein trail. Now they made much better speed, loping ahead on extended leaps.

They rounded a corner and found a small group of men and

women in combat fatigues marching along the trail. There was a moment's hesitation and then a girl with red hair swung up a handgun in a two-hand stance and accurately hit Lieutenant Klipps' visor, rocking her head with a stunning blow. The other humans scattered.

The marines leaped after them, running some down in the brush away from the trail and losing others in the tangled growths. The red-haired girl ran from Klipps, who overshot on the first lunge and with a curse found herself tangled up in a glob glob patch. The second time Marion was ready for the darting, sideways movement that the girl had employed so well. Marion jumped short and the girl turned right into her arms and rebounded. In a flash Marion threw her catch net over the girl's head and shoulders. With a jerk she tightened the net and toppled the girl, then stuffed her into the net, swung her over her shoulder, and clipped the net to her retaining stud.

The platoon reformed. Half of them had similar bundles, cursing but helpless, slung over their shoulders. They continued on the path. At one point they had to jump over another of the huge forest creatures, which stalked out from under the trees. Eventually they reached the grouping point with a dozen prisoners. They had taken three casualties.

Other units at the grouping point had different tales to tell. Bogged down by the vines and elusive fein soliders, they'd been attacked again and again by the woodwose. Few would ever be able to forget the sight of screaming marines being ripped out of their suits and thrust into those gaping mouths. With haunted eyes the survivors fought to get on the next shuttle.

Aboard the *Gagarin*, the prisoners were isolated, one to a cell, and immediately interrogated. But there were only five chitin talkers among them and they were defiantly uncooperative. Armada Butte was questioned. Her hair and looks had already aroused comment. When her identity was revealed, Admiral Enkov himself was informed. He immediately had her brought to his quarters.

Armada was not a passive prisoner. In the elevator she tried to kick the female guard in the stomach and had to be forcibly restrained. The officer thanked her makers she was biologically strengthened as she struggled to get the girl under control. When the guard finally dragged Armada in, hands bound behind her back, hair disheveled, still covered in mud from the jungle, the girl's face wasn't the only one red with exertion and rage.

Armada was locked into a seat. The officer dumped the prisoner's possessions, pack, gun and ammo separately packed, and left.

The admiral chuckled. "You might as well take it easy. There's nowhere to escape to from here unless you want to fly home in the pinnace."

She glared.

He chuckled again. "Come, come. I wanted to meet you in person—I've had precious little opportunity to meet many of you highlanders. They told me not to pass up the chance of seeing you. They told me you were wild, but they didn't tell me how beautiful you were."

Armada spat at him then hissed, "I demand to be returned to the surface. You have no right to detain me like this."

He grinned at her but the humor was hollow.

"On the contrary, I have every right. This is my ship and with it I hold responsibility for the entire system. I can hold that system, too—against anything. *I* am the ultimate arbiter of disputes and the ultimate authority in this system. In fact, you now tread in my world; the time of the chitin lords is done with. Now comes the era of the emperor."

She stared at him. He had to be the Admiral Enkov that Fleur had spoken of.

"Those of you who see the light in time will be rewarded with fiefdoms. You, for instance—if you were important to me for any reason, I would make more important than Fair Fundan. You could go far, but only if I allow you to."

"You're out of your mind. Return me to the ground. Every second I'm away is a violation of my oath. You have no—"

Enkov cut her off with an angry gesture. "You'll be returned soon enough if you don't cooperate."

"Then kill me if that's what you're threatening. I'd prefer to die than serve you or anything like you. You're not even human—deathbringer, killer of trees, enemy of Fenrille."

Not even human. It rang in his ears. He considered her, but he refused to weaken. Later he could indulge his whims. For now he must use every advantage.

He grinned again, eyes lying, the red nodules above them twitching. "Such wonderful nonsense you people spout. I was talking to Fair Fundan just now. She was begging me to spare the trees and to negotiate a peace settlement. You should have heard her howling about a lot of trees." He got out of the senso crib and pushed himself over to a cabinet where he removed a chilled drink container and snapped the straw.

She watched the red nodules dance on his skin and the inhuman bunching of muscles at the neck. Her mouth screwed up in disgust. "What did they do to make you look like that?"

He frowned; his voice turned ugly. "Of course you hate me. Every one of you hates me, and that's that. I see it well, but you cannot halt my path to victory. I will triumph. Do not doubt me. I will bring my power to bear upon your people until they know they must bend and serve me."

"So you say, but you'll have to find them first and you'll have to torture the chitin talkers to get any information—and they'll tell you nothing but lies; they're the best liars in the world. And you'll never win. You'll have no chitin production for years and by then your masters will have removed you."

He had to admit to himself that she was magnificent. He was half inclined to damn the diplomacy and force her into sexual relations. He could take her right there. But he pushed the idea aside. He would leave her to the coastal scum; he would relieve his needs later and not by force.

"There you're wrong, my pretty. Long before then I will persuade the fein to see sense and come to the table for themselves. They'll give up the clans, and that will soon bring the chitin talkers to discuss terms. I can be generous, too."

Yes, he had their secret now, that desperation in Fair Fundan's voice—"Do not damage the trees. Let us negotiate by all means, but don't harm any more trees." "Yes," he said expansively, "I've discovered your little secret. It won't take much."

"You're crazy, the fein will never betray us."

He laughed. "We shall see, we shall see." Then he had her removed with her grimy pack, but he kept the gun as a memento. As she was hustled away, he put in a call to Ira Ganweek down at the Bablon Dome.

Ganweek's image soon appeared on the screen. They discussed the situation—things were getting bad on the Sx Coast. To supply the market, private caches of chitin drugs were now a tempting target for warband officers and their men, acting either in uniform or as plain bandits. Break-ins and killings were proliferating in the wealthy neighborhoods

Ira did his best to press the admiral to negotiate with the clans. Enkov brushed such consideration aside and revealed his new scheme. "They're so concerned about their trees that they plead with me to avoid harming them. There are millions upon millions of trees, so why is Fair Fundan so anxious when a few hundred are damaged?"

Ganweek shrugged, pulled his robe around him. The security sirens were wailing on Fun Isle again. Law and order was close to total collapse.

"Tree worship is an important part of the fein mythology," the admiral said triumphantly. "The fein identify the trees with their ancestor spirits."

"Indeed they do," Ganweek agreed. He rubbed his temples. He was getting another headache. If only the damned space admiral weren't such a fool. "Indeed, I believe primitive men did much the same sort of thing in the Pleistocene. Remember we once crept into dark caves to paint magical reindeer."

"Indeed?" Sigimir Enkov snickered. "Magical reindeer . . . Well, well — the fein are hunter-gatherers whether they worship the trees or just their ancestors, but Fair Fundan's no primitive. Why should she plead for the trees unless she was afraid of losing the allegiance of the fein?"

Ganweek considered the data. Maybe the admiral had a point.

Then Enkov adopted a roguish smile, a confidential tone of voice. "There's another point I wanted to raise with you. It has been brought to my attention that we have taken prisoner a certain red-headed highland girl, a real little spitfire, that I'm told your syndicate now has a price of five hundred thousand credits on."

Ira's eyes bulged. Incredulous, he leaned toward the set. "You have her?"

Enkov's smile was infuriating and insulting, but Ganweek swallowed his rage. His mouth was dry with anticipation.

"Yes, indeed I do. A young female named Armada Butte. One point seven eight meters and 60 kilos of sheer fury. I swear she never stopped hissing at me the entire time I spoke with her. So I decided to let you have her, but at a price."

"How much?" The response was too fast — instantaneous —

and, recalling the contents of the kuilowee pouch, Enkov suppressed a guffaw of mirth.

"A considerable amount—something like two and a half quintals of Optimol, let's say. Enough to buy me the time I need to rebuild production in the valleys."

"Done," Ganweek said in a whisper, his eyes no longer seeing the screen.

22

FLEUR STUMBLED ALONG THE NARROW PATH, EYES AND EARS
straining for signs of life around her. The dim green light of
late afternoon showed her only trees festooned with high-grow-
ing vines, their trunks holding up the sky of leaves. Far away
on her left somewhere an unknown animal loosed a long, sobbing cry that echoed through the gloom.

For hours, ever since she'd escaped the clutches of a Space
Marine in a glob glob thicket, Fleur had followed the path,
unsure in what direction it led but convinced that it must connect
to another path somewhere and somehow bring her back into
contact with Fundan forces.

But the path seemed to lead nowhere. It wound on through
the trees. In places it was a tunnel through the lyissa vines,
obviously worn by the passage of many animals. The thought
that it might lead to the lair of some carnivorous beast, perhaps
even a pride of nachri, terrified her and almost inclined her to
turn and go back the way she'd come. But an even more
unpleasant prospect lurked at the back of her mind—what if
she were discovered by a woodwose?

As the light was fading and she reached for her flashlight, she discovered that in her efforts to escape the marine she'd lost her revolver. All she had left were two boxes of ammo. With the light on low power she padded down the path, ears straining for sounds ahead.

After dark she would have to climb a tree, but she had yet to spy one that carried a fein mark. To climb an unmarked tree would be to risk the attention of the woodwose, and that thought kept her feet moving quickly.

Once Beni had sunk below the horizon, the sarmer mackees began screaming and the trees echoed with the long, wailing cries. She knew that a hundred nocturnal predators would soon be stirring in their dens, sniffing the evening air and preparing for the hunt.

Her eyes ached from squinting into the shadows, her quick steps were slowing to stumbles. The gloom was utterly stifling. Every avenue in the dismal infinity of the forest seemed blocked by threatening shadows and crouching shapes. In the dark her imagination fed her frights until it was all she could do to keep from screaming in hysteria.

Fleur felt more than saw a massive root rise up ahead of her and pulled herself against it. It would be too dark to go on soon, but she dared not climb the tree. To stay where she was invited unknown dangers, to climb might summon the wood-wose. Fleur recalled Jane Fundin-22 and stifled a moan.

A light blinked on almost beside her and she jumped with fright. A little shriek, pale and wan, escaped, however, and then she saw the graycowl robes and the old yellow eyes of the adept squatting atop the root.

The ancient, muzzle whitened by the years and front teeth gone, extended a withered paw. "Come, lady, this way." To her surprise he spoke perfect Interenglish. "The path grows dangerous here, the wood trembles with the anger of the wood-wose. Follow me." He re-covered the glopod with his robe and she hurried close behind him as he floated away along the path.

At one point he detoured, climbing onto a low-slung root and using it to traverse a mound of vines that rustled with unseen lifeforms. They clambered over a knot and around another huge trunk and came upon a guard detail of eight fein with the white ear flashes of Ghotaw. The fein urged them to climb the pitons sunk in the bark of the tree they guarded.

"Climb quickly, the woodwose rage tonight." Fleur needed no encouragement, and she followed the pitons as they wound around the tree like a staircase. They were well into the climb, halfway to the first great branch, when the graycowl called her to halt. Lights were advancing up the trunk, straight up and very quickly. Fleur watched as a trio of great nachri, claws digging into the bark for purchase, climbed past them. Her eyes widened at the sight of Fair Funda and two security fein riding the nachri. Fair was seated on a small shoulder saddle and controlled her beast with reins and stirrups. The security fein rode their beasts bareback, but held reins for ease of control of their bad-tempered but high-speed mounts.

Fleur and Fair exchanged glances, then Fair was gone, the nachri scrambling up the tree like gigantic monkeys. With a renewed sense of wonder, Fleur resumed her climb.

Eventually she reached a branch and was given some food and a place to sleep. She asked around her if anybody knew where the Abzen Impis were. But the Ghotaw chitin talkers who shared the branch with her had no idea. They suggested she wait until morning then check with the communications group on the next higher branch. Then they went back to their game of Lift-a-leaf.

Fleur had barely laid down her head when she was fast asleep. She was soon tossed in dark dreams of rain, jungle, and unseen horrors that reached for her from the dark. Then her shoulder was shaken gently; she came awake with a small sob.

Two graycowl fein, seemingly even older than the one who had guided her on the trail, crouched beside her. It was dark, but some time had passed since she'd laid down. The sarmer mackees had ceased their screams. The air was cool and the humidity had lessened considerably.

"Come with us," the adepts said. "You are wanted by the Mother Fair."

The Mother Fair? Fleur pulled her clothes together around her, certain that she looked a mess but unable to do much about that. She followed the adepts and climbed with them to a larger branch high above. It was studded with glopods and the scene of intense activity. Dozens of men and women in Fundan greens were bent over tables with maps spread over them. Others worked with hand computers.

Beyond all those groups were more glopods and a large tent that, as they passed, Fleur saw to be a stall for three great nachri, now curled up in sleep like great tabby cats.

Fair Fundan awaited her on a red cushion. Around Fair a group of planners was talking animatedly with several graycowl fein. Behind Fair stood a pair of tall security fein with kifket, rifle, and full bandolier.

Fair saw her and greeted her immediately. "Welcome, Deputy Ambassador Fleur Kevilla, welcome to our forest retreat, and please tell me why it is that I find you, of all the people on our troubled planet, climbing into my tree for the night."

Other eyes were on her by then, so Fleur composed herself to reply. "I'm afraid that it is a very long story, but the fact is that I got lost after the fighting yesterday. A marine chased me into a thicket of glob glob and I hid there and waited until the firing stopped. Then I took the first path I found but it led me here instead of back to the people I was with."

"Indeed?" Fair said. She wore Fundan greens like any trooper but was wrapped against the chill of the morning with a black velvet shawl. "And what people were these?"

"The medical team of Doctor Olanther, from Cracked Rock Fortress. I've been with them since we left the valley weeks ago."

Fair's dark eyebrows rose at this. "And what could possibly have brought you to join my family on this long, arduous march? Why aren't you on the Sx Coast, trying to get some negotiations started?" Fair seemed genuinely angry.

"I'm sorry, Madam. Due to a strange combination of circumstances and bad judgment, I'm afraid I'm no longer part of the Earth Diplomatic Mission here. In fact, I'm pretty sure that the mission itself is virtually defunct. Certainly its useful role is ended. I was forced to escape from the Sx Coast at some risk to my life, a bizarre chain of events which even now I can scarcely believe overtook me."

Fleur was unable to stand Fair's concentrated gaze and so looked away from her along the row of people sitting around a low table to the left. One of them, a young woman in her twenties with corn-color hair tied up in a bun, triggered a partial memory. She stared and then broke into a gasp of amazement.

"Excuse me, but that young woman, where did you find

her? Isn't she named Debby? She was Termas Hith's girlfriend. I was looking everywhere for her."

Fair was rocked with surprise. "And how did you come to know about Mr. Hith, Ms. Ambassador?"

"She came to me, for help. But I was too busy to really spend the time, it was just before the summit meeting at Stroins' Rock. However, she left me a film clip and some pictures. Of course as soon as I saw the film clip I tried to get in touch, but by then he was dead and she'd vanished."

Fair called the young blonde away from the table where she was working. Debby broke into a smile. "Ambassador, why—"

"I know, I know, this is amazing. What *are* you doing here?"

"Well, Ambassador, you see, I never had a chance to come back after that morning when you were kind enough to see me. Things happened so fast after that. I had to leave the Sx Coast— they killed Termas"—her eyes fell—"but I guess you know that."

"I'm so sorry, Debby. I was just so busy, too damned busy. I suppose if I'd done my job properly this would never have happened."

"No, Madam Ambassador, it wasn't your fault." Debby extended a hand to her. "We just didn't have any time. Termas was determined to go to them. I begged him not to, but he comes from a proud family—the Hiths all go by the old-colony rules."

And for lack of a little time . . . Fleur continued her self-recrimination.

She looked to Fair Fundan. "So you know what Termas Hith gave the Bablon Syndicate?" Fair gave her a barely perceptible nod. Fleur turned back to Debby. "But how did you get here?"

Debby broke into a smile. "I hid out at Coast City where my folks live, but soon the Bablon people were all over the place so I had to get out. A family friend put me in touch with an agent for the Fundans. He took me in and helped me escape to Ghotaw Mountain. I've been under Fair's protection ever since."

So Fair's legendary spy network had caught the big fish . . . Fleur returned her attention to Fair Fundan. She knew; did she have more?

"My question is, why hasn't the Bablon syndicate released the formula, or started to use it? If they have a formula for a self-replicating catalyst, they can increase tenfold the production of Optimol."

Fair pressed her palms together. "I share your concern. The panic on the markets is tearing those cities up, so I'm positive they'd use it if they had it. In the hopes of finding it, I had drawn up plans for a commando assault on the Bablon Dome itself, but now I've changed my mind—they can't have it. Except that I know from my sources that it was Ira Ganweek who had Termas killed. There's a piece missing but I can't trace it no matter what."

She sighed, rested her hands in her lap.

"If only Termas had made more than two copies." Debby sighed, too.

"Two copies of what?" Fleur asked.

"Termas put the whole program—the formula and his results—on a memory chip. Then he made a copy and took that to Ira Ganweek. Ganweek had stuck by Termas through a lot of lean years. In fact, he funded the lab for seven years, and there were times when Termas was ready to give up but Ira kept encouraging him. So, what with his Hith pride and all, he wouldn't do the sensible thing. There was just that copy and the one he left in the laboratory safe. After they killed him, they totally destroyed the lab. Nothing was found. You know they never found his body either? His parents were just devastated by that."

But Fleur was staring at her suddenly, her breath caught in her throat. "On a memory chip? A white-bordered memory chip, about this big?" She held up thumb and forefinger.

Debby nodded. "That's right, it was a white one."

"Oh, my . . ." Fleur felt weak in the knees. She knew that chip—she'd held it in her own hand many times. Now it all fell into place. "I know where that chip is, or where it was anyway."

Fair looked up sharply. Her dark eyes seemed to pin Fleur to the night like a chitin specimen to the velvet of the collection box. "What?"

"Yes, I'm sure—it explains everything. That chip was in Ganweek's safe. He must've put in the most secure spot he could think of, and guess what else he kept there? Right, a batch of Pharamol. Well, Armada Butte, a ward of one of your valley commanders—"

Fair broke in. "Yes, yes—Lavin Fundin takes care of the child. She has enemies in her own family—but what of her?"

"She had that chip. The very same day that Termas was killed, Armada broke into Ganweek's private quarters and gelded him. It was an act of revenge, I should add, and she has very strong views concerning her honor."

"Understandable, considering her family history. But go on."

"Well, she also took a vault tube containing about 30 grams of Pharamol in little plastic packs. On top of the Pharamol there was a memory chip with a white border. I know because we used that Pharamol in lieu of food while we were escaping together."

Fair's eyebrows rose at that but all she said was "Where is the chip, then? Does she still have it?" She leaned forward.

"Yes, she still had the canister, anyway, yesterday. We were separated during the fighting, but I presume she still has the chip."

Fair was already out of her seat and heading for the radio. "Get me Lavin Fundin."

In less than twenty seconds, Lavin's voice, fatigued, blurry from recent sleep, but recognizable nonetheless, was audible on the speakers. But Fleur's smile was wiped away moments later when she heard the news—Armada captured or dead. The greater likelihood being capture. There were eyewitness reports.

The enormous hope that had blazed in the darkness just as suddenly imploded and disappeared. Fleur gave a little sob, then suddenly came to her senses. "Well, we can still call the admiral, tell him what she's carrying. Tell the whole world. Maybe we can save something from all this."

Fair, her head tilted to one side slightly, as if she were listening to a hidden voice, then paused a moment and then shook her head and muttered, "No, no, nonsensical . . ."

Fleur was shocked. Did Fair mean to refuse?

Then Fair straightened and smiled. "Of course, of course you're right." Fair was nodding. "No other course is reasonable. However, we shan't contact them from here. Such prolonged communication would allow them to pinpoint our position. You mustn't forget that we're still at war. We'll ride to the bald tree transmitter and communicate from there."

Ride? Fleur questioned silently. Fair signaled the nachri handlers and soon enough they were mounted on the backs of the great baboonlike beasts as they climbed the trees. Fleur thanked her lucky stars she'd always been a good horse-woman—a long-term member of her bureau's riding club—as she wrapped her legs tightly around the nachri's barrel chest and hung on while it accelerated up the tree. It seemed the work of only a minute or so before they reached the upper branches and the nachri ran nimbly along the canopy highways, scattering the smaller animals, which leaped away through the foliage with a fusillade of cracking twigs and shaking leaves.

At some point Fleur realized that the gait of the nachri as they crossed from tree to tree was predictable and only hard to ride during the occasional leaps to new branches. The nachri followed an invisible trail through the branches. They seemed to know very well where they were going. Then, abruptly, they stepped onto a dead tree, a giant not yet ready to fall but long dead from fungus. Bare of leaves, the branches were like claws reaching toward the stars. Above their heads the Milky Way blazed down. The Red Moon was visible just above the horizon of leaves in the west.

A communications center had been set up with a number of portable devices. The techs tracked the space forces above and monitored ship-to-ship communications. They also served as a redirection center for all the other Fundan groups, helping to preserve security.

It took no time at all to raise Admiral Enkov. "You have decided to accept my terms then? You will surrender the chitin talkers?"

"By no means. I am not calling to surrender. However, there is a new factor in the situation which you must consider."

"Indeed? And what might that be? Or do I, perhaps, already know? Your fein are mutinous because of the damage to their sacred trees. It's a good thing you decided to call now because in a few hours I was going to really demonstrate our strength. You are making a grave error by not agreeing to our terms now."

Fleur broke in to cut this sterile circle. "Admiral, this is

248

Fleur Kevilla—you remember, of the Earth Diplomatic Mission."

A momentary pause followed. "Yes, yes, of course, but what are you doing there? Have you joined forces with the Fundans? Ambassador Blake did report that you'd turned to banditry or something, but it sounded too fantastic to believe. That man lives in a drug-induced daze. Now I'm not so sure."

"Admiral, I haven't become a bandit and someday I promise to tell you all my adventures—goodness knows there've been enough of them. But something so much more important's come up that we really must pursue it immediately. It bears vitally upon this whole question."

"Really?"

"You took some prisoners yesterday?"

"We did."

"Among them was there a girl of twenty with red hair?"

He laughed. "By the void, there was—a little witch named Armada Butte. Why does everyone in this goddamned system want her so much? Or, should I say, why do *you* want her?"

Fleur's heart sank. "Did she have her pack, her shoulder pack? Do *you* have the pack?"

"I fail to see what this has to do with anything."

"There's a vital piece of data in her pack. A datachip that could end this crisis."

Enkov checked with Security, then frowned. "I'm sorry. Whatever it is you're trying to do, it's pointless. The girl was sent to the Sx Coast. She fetched a tremendous quantity of Optimol which I am in the process of dispatching to the home system. Her belongings went with her to the Bablon Dome."

Fleur groaned in dismay. The admiral knew why they would want her! He deserved the ultimate penalty. Then she clutched convulsively at the microphone. "Admiral, listen to me! The datachip held the formula for employing a certain catalyst to expand the supply of chitin proteins by a factor of ten. It represents an enormous breakthrough. Don't you see, we have to get that chip!"

The admiral's frown deepened into a scowl. "Of all the nonsense! If you had this microchip, which I'm sure is just some damn red herring, why the hell didn't you tell us about it before?"

Fleur tried to explain, but the story was confusing. Enkov

was irritable and refused to listen. "This is preposterous, get to the point."

"Will you at least call Ira Ganweek and ask him if he has that chip?"

"Yes, except that he doesn't have the girl yet. She's due to land in about ten seconds. But I will call in a little while."

"Thank you, Admiral."

Enkov called for Fair to take the microphone. "Madame Fundan, I repeat my demand for the surrender of the Fundan Clan chitin talkers. Gather them together and make them ready for transport to the valleys. If you fail to comply I will be forced to take extreme measures."

Fair bristled. "You will never defeat us—never, do you hear? We will melt into the forest beyond your reach and within a few years you'll be swept away on a tide of unrest. The tyranny you dream of is built on sand. You will see."

Enkov was unmoved. "To the contrary, you will be penned and captured, haughty lady, and your family's grotesque, feudalistic power will be broken forever. Surrender while you still can."

Impatiently Fair broke the contact. Immediately she turned to the radio technicians and ordered a message sent north on a secure channel. She spent a moment punching out the code for the signal and then turned back to Fleur.

"Every moment now is precious. Miss Armada is in great danger, but more important, she may still have the chip. So I will act at once. We were prepared already for this operation, one stroke of good fortune that may yet help us to redress the situation."

When they returned to Fair's headquarters Lavin Fundin was waiting, with Bg Rva beside him. Fair went over the details of the mission with him. The plans was virtually unchanged. When the adepts were ready, Lavin and Rva said good-bye.

Surprising herself with an unexpected desire for more personal danger, Fleur volunteered to go on the mission.

Fair immediately quashed the idea. "Nonsense, you're not trained for this sort of thing. Besides, I have another use for you, my dear. Near here lies the southern Fidnemed, the hall of grandeur. If I can get you to understand, my dear, then perhaps you will be able to explain how things are to the space admiral and save us all."

Before leaving, Lavin turned to Fleur, but something caught in her voice when she bade him be careful. He smiled. "Don't worry, we'll bring her back. And if she's got that chip we'll bring that, too." He shook his head ruefully. "To think that I had that thing in my safe, too, for days."

"Good-bye," Fleur whispered.

The commando saluted Fair and turned away. Not long afterward the sun tinged the eastern skies turquoise and the day began.

23

FOR SECURITY REASONS ARMADA HAD BEEN DROPPED FROM
orbit under heavy sedation and so she was unconscious when
the marines brought her in and the Bablon men surrounded the
stretcher table. Ira Ganweek was positively glowing as he gloated
over her. He had such exquisite plans for her! Then he ripped
anxiously through her miserable belongings until he found the
steel canister. With trembling hands he opened it. The Pharamol
was half gone! He cursed.

Then he spied the chip. It sat beside other chips, small ones
with blue borders in a plastic box. Eagerly he dug it out and
kissed it. This would give them the trump card in any negotiations. And to think that Admiral Enkov had let it slip through
his fingers for a mere two and a half quintals of Optimol.
Ganweek roared with glee.

"We have it." He slipped the chip into a slot in his hand-
held computer and flicked for a data printout on the big screen.

There was a moment's hesitation, then the computer displayed the music and words to "Pulz Time in Lowlight," switched

on the audio system, and played a few bars of the number-three tune in the Sx Coast Hot Hundred that week.

Horrified, Ganweek stabbed at the buttons, but the chip revealed only dozens of pulz dance tunes, each more thunderously vigorous than the last.

With an inarticulate howl of rage, Ira flung the computer module at the wall. "Bring her around," he snarled.

Ganweek wanted to scream from frustration, but he restrained himself. However, he promised himself that she would become the gentlest housepet there had ever been, a willing slave, once he had finished with her.

The medics attached tubes, began to flush the sedative from her blood. She was injected with a stimulant. Her eyes flew open. A ring of fat male faces burst into smiles, some chuckled.

"Now for the fun," a deep voice said.

With a snarl of hate she sat up and jammed two fingers directly into the ogling eyes of Asgood Wythe, who screamed and stumbled back, clutching his face. She was off the stretcher and running.

"F-fools, grab her!" Ganweek was nearly incoherent. He would not lose everything twice!

Armada was surrounded. She threw a karate kick at one man's belly and they fell back. The old men were hard of heart but soft of flesh. They waited until the security guards shouldered through, rope and restraints in their hands.

Armada saw the delight on Ganweek's face and decided she would not die at his hands or scream any more at his whim. Instead she charged through the senators on the far side of the ring and ran full tilt for the windows. They were fourteen levels up. This way they'd get nothing from her.

Ganweek chortled as the guards pursued her. The windows would never break. Then Armada dove at what she thought was glass and caromed off the window, pitching head over heels and slamming headfirst into the floor.

Ganweek's smile vanished. Fully alarmed, he bellowed for the medics and ran toward the unmoving body.

In the thick jik forest at the southern margins of Ghotaw reserve, Fair Fundan's call stirred a hidden unit. Men and fein moved to uncover hidden jet transports bobbing on floats in a reach of the Luther River. The planes were fueled and airborne shortly afterward.

By midmorning the long-range transports were over the Irurupup. Three were serving as tankers, and they circled while the others swooped in to land on the still patch of water near the Mahr Pinnacles. Lavin Fundin led a troop of volunteers from Umpiil's Effertelli Heroes on board the planes.

Within hours they were thousands of kilometers south of the Irurupup bend, and by nightfall they were close to the Sx Coast. Four planes throttled back and crept in low over the Dinge, to get under the radar at the airport, and landed in the brackish waters of the tidal swamp. A fifth passed on out to sea before curving around to fly parallel with the Sx Coast. It dropped parachutists and inflatible rafts and then drew off to the south and joined the others, kicking up ripples across the sullen waters of the Dinge.

The pilots huddled together and broke out bottles of Moka while pensively examining the dismal scenery, a nightmare of quaking shimsoil quicksands and small islets tufted with scrub and swamp trees. Not far away the *Esperm gigans* forest reared massive leafy heads into the sky. They looked south and east. Somewhere out there toward Spurn Head, Lavin Fundin and the fein commando stalked the woodwose. The pilots shivered at the thought.

When they strained their eyes looking south and west, they could see the lights of the Sx Coast, a chain of tiny baubles on the horizon.

Hours passed. The pilots drank Moka and discussed the war. They were edgy and none was prepared to consider sleep. Yet it was well past midnight when a hoot and a sobbing whistle told them the fein were back.

Lavin Fundin was eager to be on the move. "We have forty minutes to be in position. Everything will begin when the Pale Moon rises."

Privately Lavin wondered if it was possible that Armada still lived. She'd been in the syndicate's hands for an entire day. Once they'd brainprobed her or taken the chip, they would surely have killed her. He tried not to think of torture or what death Ira Ganweek would have given her, but resolved to make the syndicate pay in equal measure.

* * *

When Admiral Enkov finally got through to Ira Ganweek that night, after battering through layers of flunkies on the phone, he found the senator shaken, trembling.

"Then the chip is useless?" Enkov said after a moment.

Ganweek gave the barest of nods.

"Lucky for you. If your scheme had worked, I would have had to arrest you. That chip would properly belong to the Space Forces. We captured the girl."

Ganweek stared back stonily into the viewscreen. "Nonsense, the chip was my property in the first place. Why should I advertise its existence? Not that it matters anyway, now." He clutched convulsively on the small pouch he held in his hands, the kuilowee jui-jui. It was dangerous, bad for his heart, to allow such depth of emotions to overwhelm him, but his rage struggled to find release.

"Well, you have the girl, but she's in a coma. I guess you can't even torture someone in a coma—such a pity for you. The chip is blank, and you have proved useless to me. I don't know whether to arrest you all and throw you in the brig up here or to forget this whole farrago about microchips with magical formulas. I'm sending a team of medics and security men to oversee this. I want to be sure you're not lying."

Eyes like bullets, Ganweek wore a sour expression. "I wouldn't lie about this. If I had that formula we'd use it immediately to save the markets, you know that."

"Bah, I know nothing. This planet is a morass of lies and witches. I return to my own plans." Enkov broke the contact.

Fleur was asleep on her feet when summoned at sunrise to see Fair. Fair extended the golden Pharamol egg. "Come refresh yourself, my dear, we ride north this morning."

Fleur stared at the drug, Doctor Olanther's words in her ears. Then she succumbed and once more felt that surge of strength and acuity as the Fundankristal took affect.

They again rode nachri back. However, their progress through the treetops went on for hours and she was beginning to tire when at last they halted.

"We are very close," Fair announced with a strange look in her eyes. "The sacred grove is just beyond the rise."

"I thought all the trees were sacred," Fleur said in surprise.

"Indeed they are, but not to the fein. It is the trees of the Fidnemed that are theirs."

They rode to the bottom of the first tree then proceeded on foot.

"The nachri may not enter the esoteric membrane. Their minds are too short." They crossed a slight rise in the ground and entered another valley of trees that seeemed much the same as the giants everywhere else. Except that no animal cries broke the stillness.

"This is like walking into a library. Why is it so quiet?"

Fair stopped, waiting in a pool of shadow. The security fein waited nearby with arms folded.

"Tell me, my dear, how well do you understand the fein mythology?"

Fleur shrugged. "I've read Burrup and Horson. Of course I studied Xiang-piao on the early contacts with the fein culture. On the starcruiser, I read Emme Goldberg's *Buddhist Reflections on Fein Mystery*. Have you ever seen that? It's really beautiful."

"No." Fair shook her head. "But I have read your dreadful Burrup and Horson. Those gentlemen had no idea what they were talking about. But enough, you have read about the subject, you understand that the myths are very old."

Fleur nodded.

"In fact, is is totally degenerate mythology—it is all so old that the fein have no clear idea any more what the finer points mean." Fair caught Fleur's expression of shock. "No, it is true, the mythology is senile, like the fein—they are so old, you see. This ecosystem has persisted for fifty million years now without change."

"Burrup and Horson dispute that," Fleur said.

"Fools, they understand nothing. Pay attention. This place around us, for example, has been special to the fein for a mere five million years. Places like this are special, but they are temporary features. Every so often they shift, perhaps with the magnetic pole—no one is sure exactly—and the old ones lose their power and new ones emerge to take their place."

"What happens here?"

"A concentration of energies, peculiar forms. Come, I can show you the most obvious effect. Prepare yourself for unusual

256

perceptions, but remember this: Nothing that happens will harm you."

They walked down a path so well trod that in places it was as hard as stone. It broadened and they walked beneath the eaves of the Fidnemed. Fleur immediately felt a prickling sensation and a lightheadedness that made her want to laugh or cry out loud for no real reason.

The path opened into a series of circles bare of arble. "The first nodes of the far-flung *activistes*." Fair waved Fleur on into the circles. As Fleur's foot fell on the surface of the circle's center, there came a pulsation in her blood and a momentary flicker of half-glimpsed visions. Inexplicable shapes and forms flashed across her eyes. She looked back to Fair.

"What is this?" Fair flickered under crazy yellow streamers with black rectangles.

"What's happening to me?"

"Tread farther upon the nodes. It will reveal itself."

Fleur took another step. The world blinked away and instead she stared over a wide desert of green sand beneath a sky streaked with orange. Then it was gone and the trees returned. She took another step and was floating in space, a world turned below, hidden in scarlet clouds.

Each step produced a different vision. Some were inexplicable. One produced nothing but a darkness, a dreadful sinking sensation and an odor of terrible halitosis.

She'd crossed the circle.

"All right, explain. What is this?"

"Can you not see? Each vision is of a different place, no two in succession are ever the same. Feel the energy in this place. This is a nexus for a billion energy transfers. Here the ay fein can come if they have the wish to see the marvels revealed to the Arizel tki Fenrille during their great search."

"Who are the Arizel? What do they search for?" Fleur was confused. In Burrup and Horson's definitive text, *Fein Myths and Magic*, the Arizel were discussed as ancestor spirits, active around the hearth. They searched the heavens for the Creator. The search was endless, of course, and was thought to be primarily symbolic of the hunt.

"The Arizel, my dear, are the shapers of this world. Come walk on the central path in the full current, tread the nodes of the Expansionist cluster. You will see further."

Fleur looked at the trees, so silent, trapped in their impregnable vegetable solidity. She walked on into a larger circle, bare and smooth.

Snap—with a sound like hot frying food she stood on the shore of a boiling sea of ochre sulfur. She did not need to breathe the leaden, superheated air to know that no human life could survive there outside of a pressure chamber, and then it was gone and she had survived. Her skin wasn't even warmed.

A twinge, almost a chill—no more—and she looked out over an icefield to a curved horizon and a sky filled with a gas giant whose colorful ribbing striped the sky with green, orange, and yellow.

And then she trod fully onto the node of the Expansionists and a shuddering stroboscopic play of worlds and places began that led to a fugue of wide galactic visions, each a panorama of a different galaxy—spirals, ellipticals, irregulars—all viewed from various angles. She stepped out of the node at last and almost collapsed on the arble. Fair held her close. Fleur was too amazed and shaken to be embarrassed by such intimacy with the matriarch of Clan Fundan.

"How do those visions appear here? Why here in this place?"

Fair stood her up straight. "Wherever the distant Arizel wander, traversing the millions of universes that float within the Halls of All, they record these sights. Here the recordings mingle, a peculiarity of the energy fields the Arizel employ."

"Then they are alive? The Gods of this planet are alive?"

"Not in the way we are. They take whatever physical form pleases them. They subsist on the energy of the trees." Fair gestured. "These trees, all the great trees, these are their power sources."

"You mean to say that all this, the forest of Fenrille, grows to give energy to the ancestor spirits?"

"They traverse the patterns of universes, pass between universes on just this subtle energy. It is weak in comparison to the physical energies that we command—electromagnetism, nuclear forces—but when employed by the skilled adepts of Fenrille, it transcends all other powers."

"But what purpose is there to all this?"

"They seek the Creator. Look, consider the disposition of the landmass on this world. In the song of the Mahgara the fein speak of, 'four thousand bhalkwan that were taken to

258

refashion the world, to move north south and south north.' A single bhalkwan is around six thousand years, and what the fein describe is nothing less than the deliberate, controlled movement of the continents to join them in the stable ring continent. The whole thing coalesced within a million years."

Fleur trembled. Controlled continental drift! . . . "Even if this were possible, why would they bother? What was wrong with the continents as they were before?"

"In the equatorial ring, the climate was simplified and the forest they encouraged thrived. They created optimum conditions for the growth of *Esperm gigans*. Around the trees they organized an ecosystem that is tremendously self-sustaining, which resists mutation and any kind of alien intrusion."

"The woodwose, of course." Fleur mopped her forehead.

"There are millions of universes. New ones are constantly being opened by the Creator, whoever or whatever that entity is. Each universe sits within all the other universes, folded over inside the skins of all the others, but the space each occupies is vast and the matter filling it is tenuous. It has to be because if too 'heavy' it will immediately collapse into black holes and emerge elsewhere in the universe system. The universes are all unique — they're like flowers, blooming within endless emptiness, and like flowers they cannot last forever. Even the matter they're composed of finally withers and fades when the protons die."

Fleur was silent a moment, numbed by the torrent of visions, galaxies, worlds, and universes. "Why has this remained a secret? Why haven't Earth's scientists been here?"

"A good question since I know that Judith Spreak, among others, has sent any number of reports to Earth concerning this subject. Perhaps they discount her scientific credentials, although I must add that Spreak family science is of a high order. More likely, it all just seems too fantastic to the savants of Earth, the ravings of an exotic female colonist."

"Has anyone tried to communicate with these beings?"

Fair shrugged, a sad expression came into her eyes. "I'm afraid we have for many years. We send them the hairs of the dead we lose in battle. Our existence is stamped on the hairs, the fein say, so they have known of us for many years, but we have not troubled their preserves. Until now. Now the admiral destroys trees. He knows not what he does."

"That's why you brought me here." Fleur said it knowing that it might just be the most vital thing for the human race in its entire history.

Fair spread her hands. Without fingernails they seemed curiously weak and vulnerable. "I must explain it to the space admiral, but I fear that we do not communicate well. I doubt that he would listen to me. If you can capture his attention, possibly even persuade him to come here . . . If he would tread the nodes, he would surely understand."

Fleur heard the new desperation in Fair's voice. She who had everything, including everlasting life, now faced the abyss.

Later, back in the camp, with warm gwassa to drink, Fleur asked Fair how she'd discovered the Fidnemed.

"When I was a little girl my father, Luther Fundan, took me to the ceremony of the hairs of the dead. I never forgot that day at Ghotaw shrine. I became a student of the mysteries. In time I traveled to the Oracle Rock with an adept who tolerated my presence because I would carry a supply of food up the rock for him."

"That's the magical rock that answers questions in windsong? It is said to be a legend, lost for thousands of years."

Fair smiled. "Not lost, but it is hidden and not easily found. But it, too, is a manifestation of the Arizel. I should add that the popular conception is incorrect. The Oracle Rock not only answers questions, it also poses them.

"Then as I grew older and better versed in feiner, I asked the adepts in the wind shrines for word of the Fidnemed. But I still could not penetrate the veils—the adepts are gentle, but they approach a frame of mind more similar to that of the Arizel or their mutual ancestor than to that of the fein. They become aloof, opaque to human questions. Ambiguity creeps into their love of the world. They prepare for death with a happy heart.

"Many years later I returned to the search, and that time I knew enough to decipher the adepts' responses. I found this place and walked upon the nodes. But that was hundreds of years later, I'm afraid, and by then it was too late to be of any help."

There was no mistaking the bitterness in Fair's voice.

Fleur found it hard to sleep, questions pounded in her thoughts. Eventually the Pale Moon rose in the west and cast its coppery light over the forest. Fleur slipped into an uneasy dreamsleep.

24

WHEN RUMORS ABOUT MASS SHOOTINGS IN THE SYNDICATE Chitin Corps swept the slums of Death Wish, Tan Ubu took careful stock of his situation. It occurred to him that the syndicates, desperate for more recruits, might send press-gangs into the slums.

One night he took himself to the roof of the ramshackle three-story structure that housed the cheap Sex Bar where he worked as bookkeeper and bartender. The building also contained dozens of squalid apartments that looked out on the narrow street of cheap neons and flophouses skirting the massive foundations of the looming wosewall.

That was Hellbreath Row, a pestilential alleyway with the cheapest whores and drinks in all Death Wish. Dominating the two- and three-story buildings was the wall, 150 meters high, constructed for the most part of concrete slabs pegged together with steel beams. The outline of the wall was irregular, and many patches were visible where extensive repairs had been made. Splints of ferroconcrete, patches of brick and mortar, all gave the wall an almost organic appearance.

Tan found himself drawn to explore the wall itself. It was easily climbed. The numerous gaps between shifting concrete slabs had created chimneys a meter or more across, interrupted every twenty meters with good footholds and narrow ledges. As he climbed higher, he found that irregularities increased. The lower part of the wall had been built in one piece when Elefelas was first colonized. Since then many further initiatives had added a section here and a section there to raise the height. It was a maze of patches, and some sections on the heights were hollow, mere facades of brick providing for public display by their magnate constructors but allowing little real security.

From a vantage point atop the wall, excellent views extended in every direction. To the west, the domes of the peninsula crowded together in the foreground. Far away, under the stars, the dark ocean curved. In the south, were the lights of Fun and Sx Isles. To the north lay the mires of the delta of the great Irurupup, thousands of square kilometers of gray-tussocked swamp known as the Dinge.

The eastern view was blocked out by the remainder of the wosewall, a series of walls and traps and barbed-wire entanglements, several hundred meters deep.

When squads of warband soldiers began to appear in Death Wish on recruitment drives for the Chitin Corps, Tan invested one night's take at the Sex Bar in canned food and a watertrap and moved into the labyrinth of the wosewall himself.

On the innermost face of the high wall he'd found a small, roomlike space with the equivalent of slit windows at either end. To approach it one had to climb thirty paces along a ledge of broken bricks only as wide as a human foot. From above, on the top of the high wall, the place was hidden behind a curved, cracked parapet.

Tan spent his days thereafter exploring the intricacies of the wosewall and at night made forays across the high wall to get news and food.

Events on the Sx Coast moved precipitously. To preempt the imposition of martial law by the Space Forces, the syndicates had turned the warbands into a formally constituted police force. Now the entire population was to be photographed and filed by computer. Unrest and sedition, it was announced, were now punishable by execution.

One evening soon afterward Tan happened to be exploring

the outerwall, a honeycomb of ruined walls that had been rebuilt and reruined many times. Tumbled heaps of rubble, often with tormented steel beams projecting like gigantic spines, broke up the space between the walls into a series of irregular openings.

He was moving cautiously through a gallery of concrete T-forms that buttressed flat ferroconcrete slabs when he heard a noise ahead. Tan crept forward through a zone of rubble piled under the T-forms. In the open space below dark figures crouched over the sand.

Tan's eyes widened. The squat figures were too bulky to be anything but fein. They operated radio-controlled mine detectors. When a mine was discovered the fein dug delicately with their long knives to find the device and deactivate it. They seemed absorbed in their work, and Tan could see no lookouts posted.

A dozen questions leaped to mind. Why were fein digging for mines there? Were they running low on war materiel?

At the edge of the rubble another figure appeared, slender, a bantam beside the burly fein, clearly a human officer. In the fading light Tan could see that they all wore bits and pieces of green camouflage uniform, so he knew they were either Chung or Fundan fein.

They had cleared the space between the walls and Tan shifted, thinking to get back into deeper shadow lest they look up. Something sharp and cold pricked against his neck. "Peegaz," came a harsh whisper in his ear. There was a reek of oranges.

He was handcuffed and then unceremoniously slung over a massive shoulder covered in brown fur and carried on a swift, hair-raising descent of the wall.

They stood him up against a fragment of concrete that resembled nothing so much as a grandiose tombstone. The man in fatigues pushed forward, eyes tight, lips compressed.

"A snooper, eh? Out for an evening's crawl."

Tan saw the man, recognized his face instantly. "Lavin Fundin, isn't it? Abzen Valley commander?"

Lavin's eyes narrowed. "That could be your death warrant, my man. Who are you? How do you know me?"

Tan swallowed. The fein surrounded him in a virtual palisade of muscle and hot, yellow eyes. It would at least be a quick death. "We met at Stroins' Rock. I was with the Earth

264

Diplomatic Mission. You conversed with my former superior officer, Deputy Ambassador Fleur Kevilla."

Recognition bloomed in Lavin's expression, then he recalled Armada's story. "And you—you were the one who was with them during their escape from the syndicate. Tan Ubu, I believe, is the name." Lavin smiled then clapped Tan on the shoulder. "Congratulations on staying alive. They both expressed the hope that you'd survive."

Tan was thunderstruck. "You mean to tell me that they made it? That crazy plan of hers came off? Well, I'll be . . ." His surprise was instant and authentic.

Lavin chuckled. "They certainly beat the odds. But they had good weather all the way, and their navigation was letter perfect." He sighed, his face grew grim. "However, we are ill met—their efforts were all for nothing. My ward, Armada, was captured by the Space Marines and handed over to the Bablon Syndicate in exchange for a hoard of Optimol. Tonight we move to recover her or exact revenge. When the Pale Moon rises the wosewall will blow. In the confusion that will engender, we will strike."

"You're going to let those creatures get into the wall? The slaughter will be terrible! Hundreds of innocent people will die."

"They occupy our planet, to us they have no right to live here. However, we did intend to minimize the loss of life. I instructed the adepts to plead with the woodwose to be merciful. They will strike the buildings in preference to killing the people.

Tan was perplexed. Woodwose, so he had learned, were known to attack anything that moved. No human being could approach one closely without sustaining immediate assault. Moreover, if Armada was once more in the hands of Ira Ganweek, it was unlikely that she could still be alive.

"Who approaches the woodwose? How do they communicate? This is incredible."

"The adepts, of course, they who can speak with the trees. The trees recognize them and allow them to plead with the woodwose."

Tan gulped. "I think I heard you say that the trees recognize them and then allow them to plead with the woodwose. How does a tree allow anybody to do anything? Trees are passive lifeforms, mere vegetation."

Lavin wore a grim smile, a ghostly pale face in the darkness of the wall. "The pitcher plants feed upon insects, both here and on Earth. Such aggressive plants are a universal phenomenon and hardly evidence that plants are passive. But I haven't the time to discuss such things with you right now. Perhaps someday, if we live, we can walk together in the deep forest. Believe me, many wonderful things may be seen there. However, for now time is short, and I must decide what to do with you. If I let you loose you may raise an alarm, which will not only condemn Armada to certain death but also give Ganweek the means by which to dominate the world. It is that important."

Tan Ubu watched the fein fitting explosive charges in wall crevices. What they proposed to do was monstrous. Hundreds would die, even if the woodwose had been asked to spare lives—which Tan found hard to believe. Besides, he sensed that a wrong answer might yet earn him the kifket blade he'd feared earlier. They were serious.

"I wish I didn't have to decide this, if I can't I presume you will kill me."

Lavin looked back at him, enigmatic, silent.

After a moment Tan surrendered. "I won't give the alarm, I'll just save my own hide." He hung his head. It would not be wise to stay in his little room or anywhere on the peninsula. Security checks or no security checks, he'd have to take the Mass-drive Transit over to Fun Isle. He'd be safe there. Maybe he could work out a way to contact Fleur, wherever she was.

"We would not do this if there were another way and if our need was not so great. There is just no other way." Lavin turned away, dismissing the Earthman.

The fein melted away. In a moment they were gone. Tan stood immobile for a second, a crazy idea stirring in his mind. His normal, cautious self was doing its utmost to shout down the crazy idea but it would not go away.

He ran back to his hidden room and quickly grabbed something to eat, washed it down with a cup of brackish water from his watertrap, and then loaded and checked his gun before leaving the wosewall.

The plane's engines slowly faded away, leaving the commando bobbing on the ocean swell. With a smooth stroke the fein breasted the water and soon reached the waiting inflatables.

Lavin wriggled over the side and checked the time. They had near-perfect maintenance of the schedule. The moon would rise in less than a minute. He checked the TV monitor in the boat. Quiz shows dominated the channels at that hour, although there was a division championship All-Ball contest on the sports channel. Lavin noted sourly that on any other night, with time to spare, he'd happily have watched the game. But the fein had unshipped the paddles and with efficient strokes moved them inshore.

A few kilometers away, the Sx Coast thrust its domes into the sky under an umbrella of flaring lights, magenta, viridian, bright purple and blue, a glowing strand of alien jewels set against the implacable darkness of the Belt Continent.

The Pale Moon rolled a limb over the ocean, tawny light shed a path of shimmering arcs toward them. From far away sounded a series of booming explosions, muffled in the humid air. They paddled in toward the surf.

In Death Wish the blasts rocked buildings and shattered glass. Virtually the entire population ran out into the streets. Tons of rubble crashed into Hellbreath but fell short of the houses and hovels. A great gaping rent in the wall about half-way up became visible through the smoke and dust.

Panic soon reverberated into Love Beach, even into Ele-felas, several kilometers up the peninsula, and people crowded their balconies peering eastward. When the distant screams began to swell, they moved to the elevators. The footway to the west was jammed with people heading for the Mass-drive Transit stations. The screaming from behind became more pronounced, and there came the sounds of destruction on the wind. The crowds pressed nervously forward, someone started to run, shouting "They're coming," and in moments a great stampede of terrified humanity was charging for the stations.

Tan Ubu watched the TV with anxious eyes and nursed a bottle of cold Moka. He was resplendent in a new dark-brown body suit that he'd taken at gunpoint from a stroller in the garden of Nebuchadnezzar. It didn't quite fit, being a little tight under the arms and in the crotch, but it was smart, unlike his own clothes, and he was in the Oceanview Bar, a Bablon Syndicate joint.

The Pale Moon had risen, something he could attest to with

a glance out the window over the beach. The news should be breaking soon; he was sure they wouldn't dare to suppress it.

He looked back out. Two hundred meters up the beach sat the Bablon Dome, the glittering lights of the Hanging Gardens Club projected purple and gold onto the sand.

When the newsflash hit, everyone in the bar sat up and stared at the screen. A reporter appeared, the camera cut away to the domes of Elefelas, smoke rising, flames licking up in the distance. A closer camera angle, more smoke, hundreds of people running with terror on their faces. The camera jumped and wobbled. For a moment nothing was seen, and then there was too much. Frozen on the screen was a woodwose, twenty meters tall, swinging a length of steel-reinforced girder like a tennis racket and smashing holes in the outer wall of a dome as if it were cracking open an enormous egg.

The thing was so alien, with a spider's eyes and a pelican's mouthparts, it seemed impossible. How could anything like that have evolved? Yet Tan found it hard to look away, and when he did he saw that the beach had suddenly sprouted running figures, shifting dark shapes that flowed rapidly over the sands.

Of course!

Tan whistled in respect for Lavin's plan. They'd waited just off the beach until they picked up the newflash themselves. Now, while every eye was riveted to a set, they landed.

He jerked to life; it was time to go. He hefted the reassuring weight of his revolver in the shoulder bag and after paying for his drink slipped out the door.

No more than a hundred lunging bounds carried the fein over the curve of white sand in front of the Bablon Dome. A delivery way down an alley that passed below the Hanging Gardens Club gave them access to the warehouse level. The door gave easily to the shoulders of Bg Rva and Umpiil, and they tumbled swiftly into a dimly lit passage. Ventilation ducts spread across the ceiling and a large laundry room lay to one side. Lavin peered through the door—a pair of female drudges worked over rotating washing machines. Silently the fein tip-toed past the door. They reached an elevator bank unchallenged but then the doors opened and four security guards appeared at the far end.

Lavin waved the fein back to the washroom. Hearing movement, the ladies by the machines looked up to find seven-foot-tall fein with fiery eyes standing over them. One fainted and the other was soon immobilized with a stun bulb.

There were a dozen laundry carts, stout wicker carriers that held bulk deliveries from the restaurants of the dome. Fein laid the two unconscious washerwomen beneath piles of clothing and climbed into the baskets themselves. While Lavin Fundin kept a lookout until all the others were hidden, the security guards approached. He hid himself. The guards gave the room a cursory inspection, the machines continued to thrub, they passed on.

When the guards left the floor, the commandos clambered out and packed into an elevator that deposited them in a twelfth-level, yellow-tiled service corridor along which busboys pushed carts of dirty dishes from the tables of the Blue Parakeet. In the kitchen of the Parakeet, the cooks looked up from the trussed form of an enconthoderm from the southern ocean, a rare delicacy. Perplexity and astonishment filled their faces as they backed against the wall with their hands in the air. Lavin slipped through the press of wide-shouldered fein and applied stun bulbs to the cooks' necks. Fein caught the men as they slumped and tidily stacked them beneath their preparation tables.

For a long moment the fein eyed the spiny enconthoderm, bound to a rack with herbs knotted around its joints. It waved its last remaining free appendages, the long dorsal feelers that the chefs had been about to remove with kitchen shears. The fein had never seen such a creature and its degree of edibility immediately sparked a lively argument. Umpiil gave a snort of disgust and ended the dispute by taking his knife to the creature's bonds and releasing it.

"Maybe it'll find its way back to the ocean where it belongs," Neilk Lissiom said as the enconthoderm scuttled weakly away down the service corridor.

"Why anybody would want to eat such a thing is beyond me," Umpiil said.

Lavin returned from scouting the Blue Parakeet to find the fein clustered in the service door peering after the released enconthoderm.

Bg Rva grunted. They whirled and their heads hung sheepishly for a moment as they met Lavin's gaze. He saw the empty rack, the discarded herbs, and rolled his eyes.

The Blue Parakeet was a late-evening place. As yet no customers waited in the red and brown leather interior. They slipped to the door. Lavin described once more the layout ahead; a series of radial passages led inward to the hub and the main elevator banks. Concentric ring passages intersected the radial passages at three points. Then, with Lavin in the lead, they moved quickly and quietly down the carpeted passage.

They passed a tiled corridor leading to washrooms. As Lavin turned the next corner, he saw a patrol of five security guards approaching slowly along the ringway. He ducked back the way he'd come. With the fein he retreated into the tiled access way to the washrooms.

The security guards appeared, chaffering with each other goodhumoredly as they sauntered toward the access way. Lavin signaled the fein to retreat into the washroom, and they climbed into the stalls. Lavin secreted himself behind a diagnostics cabinet.

Seconds ticked by and then the door opened and the security guards entered and headed for the urinals. Lavin held his breath, happened to glance down and saw at the bottom the stalls were cut away a foot from the floor. Stocky calves and furry fein feet were clearly visible.

The men finished and washed their hands and rearranged their hair before replacing their guard caps. They were jocularly discussing an upcoming All-Ball contest as they began to leave, and one had actually gone out into the hall when the last man turned and dropped his comb. He bent to pick it up and gave a faint, almost comical, scream.

The fein erupted from the stalls and seized the four guards still in the washroom. But one had got away. The alarm would be raised in a moment. In despair, knowing the odds against their being able to fight their way in if the dome was aroused, Lavin jerked the door back and jumped out gun in hand.

The security guard was running down the accessway. He reached the corner before Lavin could fire. Then, strangely, he stopped and retreated back into the corridor with his hands in the air, before turning and walking slowly back toward the washroom. Someone slipped in behind him.

270

Tan Ubu kept his revolver tight against the short-cropped brown hair on the guard's neck. He waved to Lavin.

"I thought I ought to see if you needed any backup. I didn't really intend to get involved, but I came in through the Blue Parakeet, too, and then I saw this joker jump out of there and run like he had the devil on his heels so I figured it was time to act."

"You have our thanks, Earthman." Lavin solemnly applied a stun bulb to the guard, then turned to appraise the African. He extended a hand and they shook on it.

"You must get to the fourteenth floor, I take it," Tan said.

"That's where Senator Ganweek's quarters are, and we're pretty sure that's where Armada will be, too."

"The elevators are guarded. I counted fifteen men."

Lavin's lips were set in a grim line. "Fifteen it is then. We cannot remain here for long without detection."

Tan nodded. "But I have a plan, inspired I should say by Armada's tactics during our attempts to get away from the syndies."

Lavin flicked up a floor plan of the dome, and the wrist computer projected it on the wall. Tan outlined his idea and received wide-eyed approval from the fein. Even Lavin grudgingly admitted that it made sense.

They retraced their steps through the Blue Parakeet to the service elevators, and Lavin summoned a car. Fortunately it was empty. They piled in once more and rode down to the warehouse level. There they transferred to a utility elevator that rode in a shaft at one end of the main bank of express elevators.

Since a special alert was on, the security guards were posted at the corners of each elevator bank, but there had been alerts galore the last three weeks and thus their attention to detailed surveillance was not as keen as it might have been. When the utility elevator opened unexpectedly—it was rarely used on the 12th floor—they failed to turn their heads.

Only a screech of alarm from a nurse who was waiting for an elevator alerted the guards, and by then Bg Rva was virtually on top of them. The guards had time only to look up in astonishment as 300 pounds of fighting fein cannoned into them, knocking them aside like bowling pins. Umpiil, Pepaz, and the rest were right behind.

Utterly bewildered office workers, servants, and messengers waiting for other elevators crowded back into the corners as the fein scuffled with the security guards and rendered them unconscious without a shot. There wasn't time for weapons. The only sounds were of blows, harsh grunts, and bodies being thrown against walls and elevator doors.

Tan summoned an elevator from the fourteenth floor and they jammed into it. The fein were breathing slightly harder than normal, eyes were wide and ear tufts standing tall. In a moment their perspiration had turned the elevator into an orange grove.

They hit the fourteenth floor as the alarms went off.

The security guards by the elevator were reaching for their guns and one even got off three shots into the ceiling before Lavin shot him. Then the Effertelli and Rva were standing over the rest.

The alarm klaxon wailed. They sprang down the turquoise-carpeted hallway.

A fat little man, bald and wearing a gold robe tied loosely over his stomach, came out of a side door. His mouth open in a silent O of horror, he tried to retreat but Lavin none too gently laid the barrel of his gun against the man's head.

"Mirus Splasteen," Tan Ubu said. "Chief Honcho of the Teoklitan Syndicate. They work for Bablon most of the time."

"Good," Lavin grated, "then he will know the details." He turned upon the chubby syndicate don, a look of fearsome intensity spread over his features.

"Where is she?"

Splasteen's eyes rolled, he struggled to find his voice. "D-d-d-down the corridor," he stammered at last. "In the m-m-m-medical section."

"Medical, you say—then she still lives?"

Splasteen gulped a yes.

"Has she been tortured?"

"No, she's been treated well—" He cut off with a hissed intake of breath as Lavin rapped him lightly on the side of the head with the gunbarrel.

"Lie to me, insect, and I will personally kill you."

"I tell no lie, she has the very best in medical care. No torture, *really*—she is unconscious, in a coma. She knocked

272

herself out trying to commit suicide." The rotund little man was clearly sincere. Sweat beaded his forehead.

Lavin wanted to shoot him then and there, with no further compunction. "Coma. The best in medical care, I'll bet she has—can't brainprobe someone in a coma, can't torture them either."

"Why do you charge us with torture? We aren't torturers, there has been no torture. All we want is the information. Your attitudes are those of simpleminded, barbarian hostility."

"Really?" Lavin said, uninterested in Mirus Splasteen's opinions. "Where is the chip? Who has that?"

Splasteen's face crinkled into a study of dismay. "Alas, we have it, but it's worthless. She wiped it and recorded pop music on it. Of course there is just the chance that she retained the information somewhere else, but only she can know that, and she remains in a coma. It is our last hope of recovering the formula."

Umpiil suddenly towered over them. "More guards approach."

"Right, we move. To the medical section." Lavin thrust Mirus Splasteen ahead of him. "Run, rodent, you're with the fighting Abzen First Impi now, and we don't have time to waste."

They sprinted down the passage and erupted through swing doors and a senso haze into a large anteroom filled with magnates from every syndicate on the coast. The magnates' jaws dropped at the sight of fein, at Mirus Splasteen, face red from exertion, at the heavy .90-caliber assault rifles the fein carried.

A pair of white doors evidently led to the medical section. Lavin ordered the magnates to form a line across the room. The fein, standing behind, aimed weapons over the magnates as if they were a stone wall.

The onrushing pack of security guards shuddered to a halt. Their masters called on them feverishly to retreat and hold their fire.

Lavin and Bg Rva slammed into the medical section. Two doctors looked up in feigned amazement. Behind them on a stretcher bed lay Armada, a battery of medical electronics in place around her.

Lavin sensed it first and pushed Rva away and dove to one side. A shot echoed and Rva, shoulder singed by the bullet,

273

threw himself into a forward roll. Lavin knelt, steadied, and fired twice. A security guard fell from concealment in a tall white cabinet. Lavin aimed directly at the doctors. "Next one's for you . . ."

"There are three more," the younger doctor said quickly. He gestured with a raised finger behind his head. "In the supplies cupboard."

Rva signaled that he was unhurt, so Lavin fired into the lock on the cupboard and kicked the door in.

"All right, throw your weapons out and then come out with your hands on your heads. Do not hesitate. You'll not be asked a second time."

A series of curses came from inside the dark cupboard, then two guns were thrown out. Two guards emerged, hands on head. Lavin ordered them to lie on the floor.

Something stirred in the dark. Rva fished inside with a long arm and yanked on something fleshy that howled. It turned out to be Ira Ganweek's pale, plump calf. The senator was dragged out bawling for mercy.

They brought him into the other room, and Lavin bopped him lightly with his revolver to stifle the moans and cries.

He noticed the brainprobe equipment dangling on an L-bar trolley. Other equipment included handcuffs and a black metal electroprod. The "medical" section was well equipped indeed. He wondered how many foes of Ganweek had ended their lives there, strapped down, screaming for mercy.

Adrift somewhere between life and death, Armada had the peaceful look common to coma patients. However, the bandages all down one side of her face brought an angry twitch to his lips. So, girl, all that crazy heroism for your honor had been for nothing.

Life seemed incredibly bitter to Lavin just then. "What is her precise condition?" he demanded suddenly of the doctors.

The medics looked to Senator Ganweek.

"Answer me, or by the Spirit this old goat is dead. This is very simple. Can you understand?"

They could; so could Ganweek.

"She has a concussion, inflicted when she struck her head against a reinforced window. There are several contusions. However, we have only found microfractures in the skull, and no major physiological damage is evident. But the coma has

274

persisted for fourteen hours. There have been a few mild fluc-
tuations but the EDB readings continue at a low level. Brain
activity is minimal."

"Is her brain dead? Quickly now."

"No, I don't think so," one doctor said. The other shrugged.

"Your prognosis?"

They waved their hands diffidently. "We were discussing
that when you, aah, joined us."

Lavin pursed his lips, kept the gunbarrel tight against Ganweek's bald skull. Both doctors were torturers and execution-
ers; in justice he should kill all of them.

"The girl is young, tough, and blessed with a very hard
head. She's in good health, if perhaps a little underweight. We
both believe she would normally make a complete recovery
with just rest and good care. However, the coma is a worsening
negative sign. We have detected no serious brain damage, no
blood clots as yet, but our equipment is limited. Perhaps if we
took her to the hospital we could determine more. One thing
is clear: The longer the coma lasts, the less likely it is that she
will recover from it."

"Can she be moved safely?"

The doctors indicated reluctance to answer. Lavin growled
softly to Bg Rva, who carefully placed the blade of his kifket
alongside the younger medic's neck.

"I repeat my question."

"S-she should not be moved," the medic stammered. "She
should not be moved at all. In the normal course of events I
would recommend it only to get her to a hospital."

"Is there anything else wrong with her aside from the coma?"

The medics stirred nervously. Rva flicked the blade up again.

"Well no, not really," one of them mumbled.

Lavin thought hard. To stay risked everything, including
his fein. To take Armada risked her life and the possible re-
tention of the data. To leave her was unthinkable. He looked
down at her. She was already in the death that was not death.

He grabbed Ganweek by the front of his gown. "Senator,
if she dies from these injuries, I will return for your head. For
the moment, I'm sure the loss of the memory chip's contents,
through your own greed as much as anything else, is enough
for you to savor. But remember my words and know this for

275

truth: There is nowhere on this planet where you can be safe from me. If she dies . . ."

Using a screen of magnates as hostages, they made the return trip to the beach and then into the surf with the boats.

A large crowd had gathered by that time, with TV cameras and lights. Units of the New Police were unsure of what to do, so they attempted to restrain the cameras. But there were too many people, and to open fire on the reporters might provoke the fein who were holding the magnates with gun and kifket. From insanely close proximity, the crowd stared at the fein commando as it pushed out its boats and loaded up.

Umpiil and Bg Rva took Armada's stretcher out into the surf and held it steady over their heads until a boat was launched beyond the breaking point of the waves and she could be put aboard with the minimum of disturbance.

Not until the last VTOL jet splashed down on its floats and loaded Lavin and Rva did they release the magnates. Lavin threw a paddle out to Ganweek and indicated the throng waiting on the shore. "Go explain to them, tell them how you threw away their chance of eternity. And remember, all of you, you fat parasites—if she dies we will be back and none of you will escape."

The jet shuddered briefly as Pilot Gruness kicked in the boosters, then they rose smoothly into the air and turned away after the other planes.

25

FAIR FUNDAN HAD BEEN ASLEEP WHEN THE NEWS CAME. SHE read the brief strip of code and dismissed her staff to their rest. She kept the despair she felt clasped hard inside her.

Old Fy'pupe had not yet left. He tamped out his pipe, taking care to keep live embers from touching the bark of the tree.

"The young female is dead?" His low, gentle throb broke the spell.

"No, not dead." She couldn't keep the bitterness from her voice. "But she lies in a coma, a sleep that is not sleep but from which she cannot awake. The information we seek was either destroyed by or put in a special place by her."

"And she cannot be woken."

Fair nodded.

"You will have to bargain with the enemy then?"

"You know our extremity." *And we must grow, Clan Fundan must go on, we are essential to human evolution. Out here in the starfields lies the next step and Clan Fundan shall be it. We are destined to grow.*

And eventually the empathic node would swell among her

own flesh, her cloned descendants. They would have telepathy. Of course, by then the body of Fair Fundan might have passed on. Fair had no fear of thinking in the long term, planning for the next 25,000 years if need be. And that represented but a fraction of the Pharamol she herself possessed.

If only we can get beyond the grasp of that pullulating, polluting horde that will never let us alone . . . And leave the fein behind? Clan Fundan would have to. The fein would never leave Fenrille willingly.

"You will try and obtain a ship from him then?" Fy'pupe saw clearly what Fair would try to do.

"Yes, there is no other way."

"You would leave Fenrille?" Fy'pupe's eyes were troubled.

"I-I don't know. It would not be easy, Mzsee."

A breeze had picked up, branches shifted slightly, the timbers creaked, leaves rustled, the Pale Moon lit the western clouds, and for a moment she ached for the beauty of that world.

"But the Clan Fundan must. Our enemies will only grow stronger, they will not be able to rest until they seize the chitin for themselves. The clan must leave while it can, before they destroy us and plow us back into the genetic muck we have risen from."

She put her hands together. Fy'pupe waited; he knew.

"And if we must leave, to survive, would then the ay fein come with us?"

His old tail, liberally salted white, went into stiff-kinked shirrithee. Fy'pupe swallowed slowly and stared off, ears rigid, into the trees. "Such desolation is hard to bear. We are taught to accept the loss of things dear, the sting of bitterness in the sweetness of the world, but this is hard, very hard. . . . You know we could never leave. We aren't like you humans, young, preposterous, boistering across the stars. That is all long behind for us, lost in the times before the Mahgara. Nor would the Arizel allow it. They would return."

Indeed, exactly so had Fair long since surmised. And to arouse the interest of the Arizel tki Fenrille might be exceedingly unwise. *We are mice,* she thought, *nibbla in the granaries of a race of giants. So far we have not troubled them.* She rested her chin in her hands and closed her eyes.

Fy'pupe broke into her gloomy self-absorption. "The Fidnemed lies close by. We could take the girl and call upon the fein friends. Often a fein with an incurable complaint will go to the sacred place and perform the rites. Then the fein is either cured or given an easy death. I myself once knew of a fein with sawworms in his eyes who went to the Fidnemed with his cubs to walk him. However, I don't recall if he ever came back."

Hope stirred in the darkness. It was slight, but perhaps that might lead to something. "But she's a human being. And besides, coma is a mysterious affliction, a sort of brain shock. An indefinite unconsciousness following brain trauma. Why should the spirits of the Fidnemed care for a human, and, even then, how would they know what to do? They have no knowledge of the human brain."

"If they are of the Expansionist Tendency they will help if they can. They are generous of their time and respectful of the 'little' people. If they are of the Exclusionist Tendency, then they will not respond. We can call on the Mountain Spirits that are our special friends. They will answer."

She considered for a moment. At the most it would take up time and give her something to hope for. The hope was worth pursuing. The data on that chip, if it still existed, offered the only way of escaping the net that she felt falling into place around her.

At dawn she sent for Fleur Kevilla to be brought to the radio station. A microwave relay had been set up to link them undetectably to the distant transmitter on the bare tree.

Fleur, still groggy from sleep, rubbed her eyes and pinched her cheeks to wake up.

Fair Fundan wore a grave expression. As Fleur yawned, she frowned. "My dear, I need you to be fully alert. We must try and get more time from the admiral. Here." She extended the golden egg. The grain of purple rose in a tiny spoon that extended on a hidden mechanism from a slot in the egg's smooth surface.

Fleur wanted to refuse, to push it away, yet Fair obviously had a point. She was desperately tired, it would be silly to stop now. She took the grain on her tongue, bending forward as if to kiss Fair's hand, and she reflected on the manner in which giving Pharamol to others had become a facet of hierarchical manners in the clans.

In olden times we'd have bent the knee ...

The familiar energy of the drug surged in her body. Fleur felt her shoulders go back and her head come up.

Fair gave her an approving glance. "First, I should tell you that Miss Armada has been successfully recaptured from the Bablon Syndicate."

Fleur was stunned at the speed with which the mission had been accomplished. Then her joy broke through. "Oh, that's, that's simply wonderful. When will she be back? I can't wait to see her." And my, Mother Fair, how swift and sure your aim has become.

Fair's eyes betrayed her dismay, however. A somber frown formed. "Unfortunately the chip has been blanked. Armada did it, and she is unconscious from a concussion. She apparently tried to kill herself but was prevented by a bullet-proof plastic window."

Fleur's soaring hopes crashed to the ground. Suddenly she understood the air of desperation that wrapped Fair Fundan like a cloud on a mountain peak. The monarch was cornered. She saw the grim lines that'd formed around Fair's mouth. She has faced the abyss now.

Fair explained her view of the situation and, in a remote voice, as if forcing the words out, she described her worst-case plan. She would surrender control of chitin supplies, in exchange for survival for Clan Fundan.

In her heart, Fleur felt despair thicken even as she heard Fair explain. An immense sorrow rose within her. Poor Lady. She has reconsidered her position, she sees that it's hopeless. She believes this is the worst case imaginable, but she mistakes her enemies. Clan Fundan has stood against the rest of the race many times, and such defiance would not be allowed again.

A young woman in Fundan greens confirmed a contact with the Space Forces. Admiral Enkov's face appeared on the portable monitor.

"So, at last, you've come to your senses," he said and hunched forward into the camera.

"I have fresh proposals to make," Fair said. She held up her hand as if to ward him off, a demonic talking head. "And some new and important information."

The strangely angled eyebrows on Admiral Enkov's face tilted slightly. "Explain, please."

"Our forces have recaptured the young lady, Armada Butte, about whom we spoke not long ago."

Enkov smiled, red nodules jumped on the seams of his face. "Oh ho! That must have been something worth seeing. My friend Senator Ganweek must be in an interesting mood right now. But you must realize that I know perfectly well that the girl is in a coma, the chip turned out to be blank, and we have nothing to look forward to there but further chimeras."

Fleur let out a breath. Of course he knew, it would've been foolish not to expect him to, but it was interesting to discover how close communication between the admiral and the Bablon Syndicate had become. They would make good partners for the dictatorship that she sensed lay down the road once Enkov had dealt with the clans.

As it was up to her to expand a role as a go-between she broke in. The mechanics between Fair and the admiral were not good. If she could just get Enkov to agree to sit down and negotiate seriously.

"If I might say something in the name of diplomacy, this appears to be an excellent time to begin the negotiating process. Don't you agree, Admiral?"

"Perhaps."

"Both sides here have discovered limitations and difficulties in their original positions; I believe strongly that the potential for a breakthrough exists. Without any further bloodshed. Don't you think so, Admiral?"

Enkov's expression didn't flicker. "We have perfect awareness of the relative positions, thank you, Ms. Kevilla. I hold the upper hand—in fact, I have all the cards. Nothing is to be negotiated except the timing of an unconditional surrender."

"This is hardly the stuff of negotiations, Admiral. Why bring out controversy when discussion can be enjoined later?"

"I see little need for discussion."

"We do have some new proposals," Fair said.

"Indeed?" Enkov sounded almost bored. "What are these proposals? Please elaborate."

Fair pressed her palms together; composure, composure. She struggled to filter the rage from her voice.

"The choices before us are the surrender you demand, a negotiated peace, or a prolonged guerrilla war, which can only lead to the complete deterioration of every aspect of the problem. Since you've completely ruled out any notion of allowing us to retain our ancestral land rights and position in our valleys, we must either fight to the death or accept dissolution inside the corruption of the coastal society. However, there is one other choice.

"If we offer to help you restart the chitin schools, allow our talkers to resume their trade—those who would be willing to work for you, that is—we would want in exchange a space vessel, preferably a cruiser of the *Crecy* class. A ship that can take us far, far from the human hegemony. We will found a new world of our own once again, free of human oppression. This time, however, we will be able to put many, many years between ourselves and the rest of the race."

Enkov's expression had frozen as she spoke.

"Bah!" He pushed himself away from the camera. "You are incurably romantic. You must realize your true position. I am not empowered to give away my spacecraft. Who do you think I am, some blessed bureaucrat?

"Nor can I see any reason why your family should not surrender its pride and its private armies. Rejoin the human race, give up this endless quest for imperial purples. This is an age of enlightenment, not one of feudalistic nobility. Families like yours have soared but to fall many, many times before. Few have soared farther or higher than yours, but now you must humble yourselves before the tide of history."

Besides, Enkov reasoned to himself, he was the new power. Where you were the Queen of Fenrille, I will be the Emperor. Sigimir saw his way clear before him. Either they surrendered to him then or they would be forced to do so in a few more hours. The new operation was already planned, sketched, and being fed through the computers of the *Gagarin*. After this blow, the fein would revolt and the chitin talkers would be offered up to him whether the old crone willed it or not.

Forced patience dripped from her voice as Fair spoke. "I offer you an end to hostilities with no further loss of life, for the price of just one old ship from your command. Surely this is not 'nonsense.' Do you think you can destroy us so easily? I repeat that once we disperse you will never find us again in the forest. If we disperse, all other families will do so, too. Already many have done so."

"So you've said before." The angular head tilted to one

282

side. "But I have divined your great weakness and taken steps to exploit it to the full. I now repeat my offer. Surrender, accept the vouchers for the new lands that will be opened up, and I shall be merciful. Refuse now and you enter into enormous peril."

He folded his arms, evidently satisfied with the prospect.

"Admiral," Fleur said hastily, "the information that the girl might yet carry may change the situation drastically. Shouldn't we at least adjourn hostilities until it can be determined if she has that information?"

"This red herring was waved around before; I'm not going to chase it any farther. How much of this nonsense do you think I'm prepared to take? First the girl was supposed to have the all-important chip. Then it turned out to be blank. Conveniently, the girl is allowed to nearly kill herself by that fool Ganweek. Was there ever any information on that chip? Only the girl knows, but of course we don't know if she'll ever recover. No, the question to be answered now is whether the Fundan Clan will save itself and surrender to my forces now or in about five hours time. Surrender and I'll turn the girl over to my specialists aboard *Gagarin*.

"However, even if we do discover this magical formula, you must not imagine that the basic situation will be changed. The World Government will still insist on control of the production of chitin proteins."

Fair felt her heart sinking into ice. No way out of the trap existed except the most arduous of all—total dispersal in the forest. For years, if necessary. Even her offer to surrender in exchange for the means to escape the system had not moved the man. Nothing would work, there was nothing but the hardest path.

Fleur was trying mightily to prolong things with liquid phrases about "early negotiation postures" when Enkov reached the end of his patience. "Enough. I want this business finished with. We have overwhelming military superiority. Surrender now or suffer the consequences. In six hours you'll be broken. I intend to make an example of the Fundan family for all the others."

The contact was terminated.

Fair looked up. Her face was ashen. "We have no choices left." She seemed to have shrunken, to have grown old all of a sudden.

"What about Armada?" Fleur asked to change the subject.

Fair motioned with her hands in circles then shrugged. "Yes, you're right, there is that one chance. They will still want that formula. Come, we must hurry. Before they attack again."

She began to issue a stream of orders initiating a massive dispersal of the thousands of Fundans, fein and humans, still concentrated in the nearby forest. All septs and tech brigades would break up into small groups. Long-term radio codes and lists of future rendezvous points were distributed. Teams of planners and logisticians were hard at work.

A message with fresh instructions was sent to the returning rescue force.

Some hours later Fair, Fleur, and a medical team accompanied by Fair's guards and old Fy'pupe set out to meet the commando. The nachri bounded through the treetops in a line, their riders crouched low to avoid branches and leaves.

26

THE MORNING MIST STILL CLUNG TO THE TREES, FORMING WISPY
pennons that waved from branch and twig as sinuous snakes
of vapor coiled over the forest floor. Fleur wondered how
Fy'pupe read the trail when almost every distinguishing mark
was hidden, but the nachri sprang unhesitatingly along the
branches in their usual swift patterns. Up ahead, Fair rode
alone, lost in a remote melancholy.

Beni climbed into the sky, changing the blue of morning
into the aquamarine of day. The mist dissolved under his rays.
It was another beautiful day, without a cloud in the sky.

They reached the rendezvous point and found Lavin Fundin
waiting for them. Bg Rva squatted beside a stretcher bearing
Armada and other fein formed a ring about them. Fair dismounted and embraced Lavin. "Our hopes have been most
gloriously fulfilled. Your mission will go down forever in the
history of the clan." She turned to Bg Rva and Fleur noted
with wonder the tears in Fair's eyes. "And never, never shall
we forget the Hero of Brelkilk and the brave fein of Abzen."
She vanished into a huge fein hug.

Fleur shyly stepped forward. "I'm so glad you made it safely," she began, but her eyes fell on Armada and she choked. Lavin took her hands and for a moment they looked into each other's eyes. A current quickened then in Fleur and with a nervous duck of the head and a little smile she turned away but he held her.

"No, wait a minute." He indicated another human who'd stepped into sight.

She gasped in surprise. "Tan Ubu! Is that really you behind that great ugly beard? Oh, I can't believe it!" The two diplomats embraced and wept happily on each other's shoulders. "I was sure they'd killed you."

"You thought I was dead? Listen, boss, I was the one that walked away, you were the one who was going to fly."

"Yes, of course, nobody should've expected us to get through, but we did. And you, how did you survive?"

"In a word"—he tugged his beard—"camouflage. I hid out in Death Wish. It's another world down there."

The medics ran a series of swift tests on Armada and reported to Fair that though the girl remained in the coma, her vital signs were otherwise positive. Fair absorbed the news with the same somber expression she'd worn all morning. She gave a vast sigh and turned to Fy'pupe. "Then let us try the Fidnemed, old Mzsee. Better to bring on the Arizel's interest on a small matter, but the damage already is unforgivable." Fair's misgivings rattled in her heart, for now Clan Fundan and everything she had fought so long to preserve hung in a droplet of the All from the lip of destiny. In the Fidnemed they might succeed too well and trigger a response that would tear down the very skies.

They went forward on foot. Fleur and Tan fell in together, and Fleur heard of the breaking of the wosewall and the subsequent invasion of Love Beach by the woodwose. She shuddered and told Tan of her own experience with the woodwose.

Tan pressed her for more details about her adventures and Fleur hesitated, not knowing where to start. So much had happened since that morning on Spurn Head. Before she could begin, though, Nekoosa, leading the nachri behind him by their bridles, gave a sharp cry and pointed up through the topmost canopy. Several bright objects were passing swiftly overhead

286

"Those are very high up," Tan said. "Must be orbital aerodynams."

"Admiral Enkov threatened further attacks."

"Well, they're not Fundan planes—much too fast," Tan replied. "Look at them move." Then sonic booms struck across the forest, and the bright pinpoints receded into the distance.

A minute or so later, when no one was looking up at the sky, the first flash flung the world into negative vision. Everything flopped from black to white, and they all screamed— nachri, human, and fein alike—and dropped to huddle on the trail. Fleur whimpered as she buried seared eyes into her elbow. Then she heard the blasts.

A shattering roar, distant but closing, growled through the forest. The trees shook. A great wind was coming. An immense cloud rose. Beside it was another and another and another— a line of them leading into the distance like pillars of fire struck by an angry God. Vast mushroom lentils grew swiftly to roof in this temple of furious energies.

"Will the blast reach us?" Fleur asked, half in wonder, half in horror.

Lavin and Rva worked furiously with the battlecomputer as a wind began to blow through the forest bearing a strange stench. It grew furious and then the roar filled the world, a titan's rumbling that brought darkness and a taste of salt in Fleur's mouth while the wind rose to a sobbing shriek.

"No, we're safe," Lavin shouted, and even as he said that the wind began to die down a little. But the sky was darkening as immense clouds built in the east over great carpets of flame.

They were all back on their feet except Fair Fundan.

"The rain will be radioactive," Fleur said.

"But not too terribly," Tan said. "Space Fleet ordinance, clean warheads." Then he scowled and shouted, "But why? Why nuclear weapons? Why?" His voice broke.

Lavin turned, something furious on his lips, his eyes harsh and hard. He saw Fleur then and, instead of speaking, just looked into her eyes, resting on the strength he found there.

She saw the trapped expression, like some mighty animal, finally worn down to the finish. *Is that how it is? Is there no way out now?* Not even great Clan Fundan had been able to beat the system and buck the rest of the human race.

Fair Fundan tore off her silky wig and ripped her finely

pressed suit of greens. She cried aloud in feiner, kneeling still, and with her all the fein howled in chorus. A fresh wind was picking up, blowing inward to the firestorm.

A vast wall of cloud was topping out in enormous thunderheads of pepper and salt. An ocean of flames licked over the husks of millions of trees.

Fair Fundan caught Fleur's hand; her face was ashen, lips pale. "They have rung the judgment bell, our fate is no longer in our own hands."

The first drops were already spattering down.

Under dark, lowering skies they dragged themselves on. The stench of the burning grew stronger for a while and a tide of animals overtook them. Nachri ran in the midst of herds of skep. Were, nibbla, brightly colored skrin, all raced past.

Fleur became aware of another sound, a deep basso profundo, a rumbling note that rolled on and on and on, as if the God of the great fire had struck out a piano chord that reverberated forever at the lower edge of perception.

"The trees are singing" was all Fair would say to Fleur's urgent question. Then Fair wrapped her shawl around her head and got to her feet. "If we take enough Pharamol we can defeat the effects of the radiation, but it will be costly." She turned away, seemingly absorbed in some private conversation.

When they reached the outskirts of the Fidnemed they were soaked, slippery with the warm mud that was coming down in the rain. In the gloom the forest seemed to Fleur more elemental than ever. Nor did the strange rumbling bass notes fade away. If anything they grew stronger.

Something exploded with a sharp report off to their left. Fleur froze, everyone else turned, fein raising rifles. They waited but no further sounds followed, so they went on, nervously, heads up, the mud streaking fur and faces.

In the Fidnemed itself, another sharp crack cut the stillness and the rain. Fleur thought it might be closer than the first. Perhaps something stalking them? Then tiny orange bubbles began to appear in the air at a point about six feet off the ground. They came from nowhere, floated downward for a moment, and then burst. They ceased.

Energy hummed in the air around them. The hairs on Fleur's neck rose, her spine tingled. Snaps and prickles were going off like oddly accented firecrackers in many directions. Loud cracks sounded, like fat electric sparks.

The trees were visibly energized, lustrous spots glowing in nachreous glory. Veins like streaks of pearl were visible in the bark.

At the nodes Fy'pupe and Fair Fundan approached and began the ceremony to call on the Spirit of the Abzen glade.

Fleur steadied herself then drew closer to a great root that overhung the path. She touched the tree and with wrenching suddeness was elsewhere, confronted by paradoxical geometry, shifting forms, an elsewhere that her mind could not comprehend. She cried out and pulled her hand back. There was a pop, she felt a force release her, and Lavin Fundin was holding her.

"You felt the power here."

"Felt it? It's overwhelming. What is happening here?"

Fy'pupe uttered the calls to the Spirit and at one point he got up on his feet and performed a little dance, a jig step, shuffling forward and back, tucking his arms in front and behind. Then he lay down, right upon the node, and repeated a long incantation.

The air continued to pop and squeak with inexplicable energy, but the sound of the storm receded. The air grew heavy, then heavier still and quite calm. The wind ceased. Fleur felt a sudden strong sense of a nearby presence, as if somebody invisible but enormous were standing close beside her. A sense of expectancy, rising as the air dulled, started a tremor that plucked in the darkness on the strings of a tonal scale that teased her mind in ways she'd never known before. Something seemed to rumble through her being, speaking to her gut, to her belly and womb, to the center of her self.

"What is it?" she said in sudden terror.

Lavin put an arm about her shoulders, holding her close. "The Spirit comes."

Now came wafted sounds, uneasy twisted tones that fled hauntingly from human analysis. Her lips puckered and she knew not why, her hands twitched and she suddenly felt a primordial terror, a huge fear that made her want to jump like a startled rabbit and run for her life. *Get away, get away!* screamed a voice deep within her. *Something terrible comes.*

And then she found she was struggling in Lavin's grasp and

sobbing for breath. "Easy now"—his arms were around her—"there's nowhere to run to. Besides, this is a gentle Spirit, it will not harm us."

Tan was staring straight ahead as he tried to identify the presence he felt shimmering above the figures of Fair and Fy'pupe, who were kneeling on the bare ground of the node.

The presence around them grew, the humidity rose, and sweat trickled down Fleur's face, mingling with the rain and mud already there. A dance of light and power was in process. Minute gleams, sparkling blue, appeared momentarily as if some invisible entity were flickering in and out of reality. Fleur gained the impression of some immense choreography of parts, a movement as of huge pistons laboring in cyclopean engine mounts. Now Fair rose to her feet and raised her arms beseechingly. With a snap, her body stiffened and remained frozen for a long, silent moment. Then she spun away and crumpled to the ground.

Fy'pupe remained prone to the ground, his body cradled over the node.

Fleur felt something, something enormous to her perception, tap at the doorways to the innermost part of her mind.

It was impossible! Instinctively she cried out, a long involuntary scream of terror. Something evil touched her in her most private part, in a place where no one but she had ever been. She shuddered with a nameless revulsion. The violation was unimaginable.

The tapping grew more insistent, demanding access, attempting to force communication upon her through the center of consciousness. All of her would be exposed to its greedy knowing. Her skin crawled; her mind was being raped by an alien being, a thing of limitless power. She felt it wrap around her mind, squeezing until she thought her eyes would pop from her head. And then, with disgusting ease, as if it'd simply found a doorknob and turned it, the thing opened the doors of her mind and rolled through them.

Her scream cut off with a choke. She stared down and saw herself staring up. A kaleidoscopic whirl spun by, a discharge of sparks in green, purple, and gold blocked her vision. Then she was looking at herself through other eyes and there was gold, glowing in sluggish drops through the veins of her sight.

Fair had raised herself on one elbow. Now she stared gauntly at Fleur.

"Greetings, little one," something said in her thoughts, and an image of a girlish Fleur bloomed. Fair was talking inside her head, but not with words, more a form of complete image transfer.

"These are the glyphs of the Arizel path. I am primed with them by the Spirit that has responded to our call. It is the Spirit-that-preferred-to-move-softly, the guardian of Abzen Vale. It will speak directly now, within you."

But Fleur's fear had risen again like a cloud. The alien gripped her mind and inhuman imagery chased across internal horizons. Without warning her belly heaved and she vomited and scarcely noticed the act. Indeed her flesh felt unreal, as if she were wasting away to nothingness. *Perhaps I'm suffering the onset of radiation sickness, an early form of delirium,* she thought, comfortingly.

Then the presence within her "spoke," the glyphs whispering into the mind's view like vast balloons floating up from the center of consciousness. "You are Fleur." There was a scattershot of flower images and she sensed a compliment, even a kindliness, which made the presence within of the alien less alarming. Less alien perhaps. The shuddering revulsion was gone.

Instead she felt/saw snapshots from her past, dozens of younger Fleurs who walked, ran, sat in classrooms, made love, dreamed impossible dreams, built a telescope. "You can never be the same again. All futures are canceled and will be rearranged. Accept this now."

The glyphs were silvery, powdered with meaning, shining bright. "You are young, still locked within the boundaries of universal matter. Once I was as you are. Once, but that was long ago."

Everything else was lost in the throb of gray static, only the glyphs shone out. They followed each other at a slowly accelerating rate forming a pattern that communicated some parts of the history of the search for the Creator of universes undertaken by the Spirit-that-preferred-to-move-softly. The search had been long indeed. "I move softly but I move longly," the final glyph pulsed.

Again Fleur heard a "voice" weakly glyphed from Fair Fundan and again she had that sense of mingling minds with Fair that offered startling vistas into Fair's private thought, vistas that astounded her. Fleur turned, even while Fair's small glyphs rose into her mind, and gazed with mouth open at Lavin Fundin.

"Yes, Fleur, you have seen into me, to my deep secrets," Fair glyphed. "But this is a time for courage and composure. We must put aside all personal matters. We need you. Your love must wait and with it all the questions and answers that you seek. I hold only half the story, and you must give up the other half—the Arizel awaits."

Somehow, unbidden, Fleur glyphed, "Does he know?" The question rose like a tombstone into the sky.

"No. Not yet." Fleur just had time to absorb the response before the Spirit adjusted within her and a nauseating sensation of being drained began. Giddiness came with it. Something was reading her memories in a totally unselective way, but with the effortless speed of a huge computer. When it was done there was a release, as if a spring had been triggered. The alien presence faded, and she bounced back. A surge of memories, many sharper than they'd been in years, flooded through her thoughts.

A moment later the "voice" resumed the whisper of glyphs. "The situation is becoming clearer to me now. There is great peril in this, the tree damage is dreadful." And the glyph for tree damage burned horribly bright.

"The Exclusionist Tendency will be eager for a judgment and will call upon the experience of bhalkwan nine hundred to prejudice the case. One expungement would have served to prevent the reinfestation. The Exterminators are too eager these eons, I'm afraid."

Expungement?

"It will be up to the Pragmatixt Endeavor to establish an entirely novel solution which will call for no extinctions whatever. One avenue lies open. We might, for instance, call for an extra shell of defenses for the Knuckle of Delight."

Fleur sensed that there was a hope.

"However, the truth must be faced. The Pragmatixts are a small group with little influence among the elite. The Exclusionist Tendency is much greater today than it was; some spirits grow too vengeful in their great antiquity. Within the Exclusionists lurks the Expungement Faction, and they grow more powerful, a swelling node of influence that will call for harsh action.

"It is unfortunate that this problem should arise from an aspect of the Expansionist Compromise solution to the Great Problem of bhalkwan nine hundred. The Divider will lead the Exclusionists, and it was the Divider that was denied in the previous vote on expungement."

"The Divider?" Fleur said aloud, wondering if she'd understood the glyph correctly. An odd glyph followed.

"The cruel farmer is the good farmer." And there was an ominous note of respect, a coloration of worry, and an image of a pair of Dividers, rendering down the universe for exact judgments.

Fleur realized what it was that Fair Fundan had hinted at but which she had never properly understood before. The Arizel glyphed terms such as "expungement" with unmistakable overtones of "ridding the warehouse of beetles." And that glyph for "tree damage" was unbearably fierce. Then a new glyph series arose.

"A specific needs to be addressed here, a young human female with a condition of brain shock, a physical trauma resulting in a deathlike trance. I understand this now. The physiology is similar to that of our ancestors, the problem clear. Let us see what can be done."

The glyphs ceased, a silence held in the glade. Fleur exchanged glances with Lavin.

There is something you don't know, my Lavin, she thought, *something that may destroy you. I pray it will not, nor come between us.* And yet Fleur could feel it now. To Fair he was already wed, a component in her insane dreams. The magnitude of Fair's legendary experiments in her family was clear to Fleur now. Could there ever be room in the Fundan dream for any outsider?

"You see, I told you the Spirit would not harm us," Lavin said.

"The glyphs fill me with dread. There will be a judgment? What might that mean?"

"Look, Armada is moving."

In fact, Armada was shaking her head and crying out something, and then her eyes flew open and she tried to raise herself on one elbow and speak. The girl's eyes were wide with fright, shocked rigid, but she held to the Spirit as it moved within her as if she were a child clinging to an adult in deep water, trusting, helpless. The coma was gone.

"Her memories are intact, she has suffered no permanent damage," said the glyph. Fair, crouched beside Armada, exclaimed, "She has it. Oh, thank the Spirit, she has it. Oh, you wonderful girl!" The matriarch of the Fundans clasped Armada to her and planted a kiss on her forehead.

"Mother Fair," Armada said at last, "what happened? How did I get here?"

Fair laughed, a deep-seated chuckle of indulgence. "That, my dear, is a rather long story and I will gladly tell it to you— but for now just accept that we got you back and the Spirit brought back your mind. And because of that wonderful highland upbringing you've had, you kept alive our last chance. Never throw anything away: you never know when you might need it, eh? Isn't that what they teach at Butte Manor?"

"But I blanked the chip. The data is at Cracked Rock in the main memory."

"Yes, you wonderful girl, that's what you did. The main memory from Cracked Rock, it's all in cache, is it not?" Fair looked to Lavin, who nodded.

"Good. The odds improve slightly, but the judgment approaches nonetheless."

27

THE SPIRIT-THAT-PREFERRED-TO-MOVE-SOFTLY STILL HOVERED above and within them. Then it moved again and Fleur felt as if she were filling with light, emptying of thought and memory until her consciousness alone danced on a sea of dark, still liquid.

"I am the sea beneath ye," read the glyph that rose and passed through her essence and ascended beyond, toward the distant stars.

"I am the stars above ye," another glyph said, and the stars expanded in luminosity until they blazed across the sky like so many suns.

"What am I (in this scheme of things)?" Fleur glyphed, without meaning to, the glyph being drawn from her unbidden.

"You are Fleur," and the reply was followed by a glyph tail of images plucked from her memories. Those blended into other images that swiftly depicted the human race with considerable detail.

Now she became intensely aware of other minds hovering close by. They became visible to her as more stars, small stars,

295

glistening orange ones and hot white ones. There was motion, apparent motion. She moved toward an orange star and knew that it was a fein mind-star.

"The orange ones are fein?" she glyphed again without thinking consciously.

"They are an old folk with little fire left. Ye are yet young," the great central sun glyphed.

Fleur was in orbit like the others, and as she looked at each mind-star she received an impression of whoever it was. One in particular caught her attention and within it she suddenly found Lavin's eyes, and her eyes within them, and his within hers, and they caromed off each other into infinity.

The vision was gone, but they were still together, under the overhang of the root. The glyph rose unbidden from her heart, like a bubble, and she almost wanted to trap it and hold it down but in the instant that she hesitated it escaped. She felt a dread embarrassment that almost turned her away, but she held firm long enough to find the same glyph rising from him.

"I love you," it read in warm ways, golden with esteem. Then another glyph floated, and it was difficult to decipher as if incomplete or hidden behind a mask, "Harlequin minx."

She laughed with him, a lovely sound.

Somewhere both below and above them they felt the Spirit laughing, too.

"I love you, love," she glyphed with Lavin, then questioned, "but how do we know this, how do we know where we are?"

He shrugged, smiled. "We don't seem to have much choice about it. Why worry?"

She laughed and thought of how unbearably sweet it was, and how she and he might lose that precious thing, which brought tears to her eyes. But she continued to face him without flinching.

"How pleasurable it is to dally occasionally among a young race," came a calm glyph that rose above them in a cloud of benevolence.

"Once I knew the glory of love, but such things are only feasible for creatures of gross material structure. Pursuit of the Mahgara renders such glories to the dust, yet I sense much beauty in this urge of your species to love and nurturement. Of course, this elevation of the sexual role is not unique to your kind. I've seen it on a thousand worlds under a thousand suns, yet in this we perceive the gentleness of the Creator, too."

A glyph of buddhalike peace, smile curling enigmatically in emptiness, glyphed through their minds.

Fleur looked to Lavin. Poor love, he still did not know Fair's secret. Would it fall to her to tell him? She couldn't hide her knowledge from him.

Then all thought was constricted to dark holes by a shriek of agony, a white glyph-flare that obliterated all else. Fleur felt the Spirit's scream. It withdrew, and she saw the Fidnemed once more, but starkly lit by a distant nuclear flash.

"Oh, no," she whispered.

"Farther away this time," Lavin said quietly behind her.

"I counted ten bursts, Lord," Bg Rva said in a harsh whisper.

"How far away?" They checked the computer.

Fleur turned to look. "Ninety-five kilometers, another line of them." The distant rumble was getting louder and louder.

"That's on the other side of Mahr then."

"They're trying to box in the Fundans around Mahr."

The Spirit was back. "This is intolerable!" The glyph was harsh and black, hot with anger. "Such activity, such tree damage, must cease immediately." The glyph for "tree damage" literally dripped with blood in Fleur's consciousness. She sensed a ferocity in the alien being that made her think of a raptor, eyes flaming, talons at the ready, in defense of a nest of young.

"We must convince the space admiral to stop his bombing. He doesn't know, you see."

"He must be told then, or there will be a very intense reaction among the Arizel tki Fenrille."

"THIS IS TRUE," said a "voice" in a plangent twanging glyph.

"We are no longer alone," glyphed the Spirit-that-preferred-to-move-softly.

"TRUE ALSO."

Fleur sensed another presence, something shimmering in the air.

"I AM ADDRESSED AS SLEUTH. I AM FORERUNNER FOR GREAT TSHAK 404040." The newcomer's glyphs were strident, bull voices roaring in a marble chamber.

"COMPOSE YOURSELVES. INSPECTION. I AM THE SCRUTATOR. I MUST EXAMINE ALL. THERE IS DISTURBANCE. TREE DAMAGE.

297

TREE DAMAGE. TREE DAMAGE. . . ." The glyph for tree damage was so strident that Fleur felt shaken by the force of the crime it described.

"ALL EVIL INDECIPHERABLE STAINS WILL BE CLEANSED. HOLD UP THE MARKS OF GREED. NOTHING MAY BE HIDDEN. ALL EVIL INDECIPHERABLE."

The Arizel mind reached toward them. Fleur felt its *touch*. It was heavy and cold, a truncheon mind, wrapped in cold leather.

Then a glyph interposed. "Hold. There is no need for this. I have all the data you will require. Your master will be content."

"WHAT? DO YOU INTERPOSE BETWEEN THE AGENT OF GREAT TSHAK 404040 AND THESE TRANSGRESSOR/INDECIPHERABLE/ PLANET LICE? IMPUDENT BEYOND PATIENCE. YOU ARE NOTHING BUT A MOUNTAIN SPRITE. GO BACK TO YOUR FREEZING MEAD-OWS. MEDITATE ON THE GREATNESS OF GREAT TSHAK 404040 AND HIS NINETEEN-LEVEL ANALYSIS. AWAY NOW, I MUST SCRUTATE THE CREATURES."

A new grip wrapped around their minds. Fleur felt as if a great hand had descended on her skull. It sought the entrance-ways. She felt a return of that elemental panic, of being taken unawares in an impossible place. Hard cold fingers probed for her. She shrank away and they came after. Soon they would find it, soon she would be lost. Then another force welled up within her and slammed defensive walls around her hurling back the dark probes.

"Hold," came the glyph once more.

They contested for her, the cold weight of the bull-voiced Arizel pitted against the Spirit-that-preferred-to-move-softly. Fleur had an impression at one point of many levels of struggle, of a dance, almost like a game of chess played at computer calculation speeds and of moves that had to be made in many other places than there and even in many other times. With that impression came the sense of how small and unimportant might the affairs of men and fein seem to such entities.

Burrup and Horson's authoritative tome on Fenrille would have to be revised, Fleur decided.

By then the struggle had ceased. The other power backed away. She saw a hint of physical form, shifting surfaces on the horizon of perceptibility. Great knottings and windings, glimpsed in flickers.

298

"ENOUGH THEN, MOUNTAIN SPRITE. SO THESE INDECIPHERA-BLE/CREATURES ARE YOURS? I SHALL TELL GREAT TSHAK 404040 OF YOUR CLAIM. PERHAPS HE WILL TAKE THEM FROM YOU. FOR NOW YOU MAY KEEP THEM. YOU HAVE SURRENDERED THE NEC-ESSARY INFORMATION."

"As you say," wafted from the Spirit with subtle overtones that stressed indulgence, as of a perturbed child.

"A MORE RIGOROUS EXAMINATION COMES LATER. AND I SHALL HAVE THE MARK PUT UPON YOU IN THE EXCLUSIONIST TEN-DENCY. THERE MUST BE A JUDGMENT. YOU REALIZE THAT, DON'T YOU?"

"Yes," replied the Spirit's glyph.

"THEN SOON TO THE DOOM."

The bull voices were gone. There was a loud pop, and air rushed into the glade.

"We are alone again," whispered the glyph of the Spirit. After the raw power of the Arizel argument, the glyph from Fair Fundan seemed a small thing. "Must the Arizel return?"

"Yes, the tree damage is too terrible."

"And the judgment?"

"All will depend on the nature of the case. Evidence must be supplied, the reasons for the outrages examined, the danger of further damage eliminated. The last precedent, indeed the only previous case of this kind took place thirty-three million, three hundred and forty-one thousand, eight hundred and six planetary years ago. That return was sparked by the activity here of the chitin insect, which at the time was a technologically advanced species from a home star eight hundred light-years away, toward the inner edge of our local stellar association, closer to the major arm. The chitin colony here pursued an extreme process. All native lifeforms were to be eliminated as inessential. The Arizel attempted to reason with the colonizing hives and the home world hives as well."

"What happened?" Fleur blurted out in crude speech.

There was a moment's silence, then "There were certain adjustments, and the chitin were reduced in scope. Here on the Knuckle of Delight the chitin were incorporated into the eco-system. Today their nests are found here and there on the forest floor where the insect plays a useful rose in recycling carrion and culling tree pests."

Fleur saw Tan's face; shock showed there. Thirty-three million years! What were the adjustments? She opened her mouth to speak again but the Spirit suddenly signaled that it was withdrawing.

"I must examine the other elements in the current situation. Time is now precious. Please remain here for the duration."

Quite abruptly the presence that had lain around her thoughts like a riverbed hugging a river was gone. The air around them was stirring, a breeze came up, the rain came down harder than before, and the nuke-generated clouds roiled overhead. In less than half an hour, the afternoon had been shattered and, along with it, Fleur's conception of the universe.

28

A NUCLEAR STRIKE WAS A RARE THING TO WITNESS, EVEN FOR the bridge personnel of the *Gagarin*. They watched in rapt attention as the video reran the bursts. They took it in with almost a greed for it in their eyes.

"Reminds me of the end of Barbuncle," said Three.

"What nonsense—you could hardly see anything in the Neptune campaign. It was all hidden in clouds."

"Anyway these are tiny warheads, these Mark IXs—nothing like the ordnance we had in the old days."

Admiral Enkov expressed satisfaction with the placements and the penning in of the Fundan Clan in a wall of fire and smoke. Now he had them trapped. "How long before we can get some kind of radio communication with the ground?" he chimed to Communications. The admiral was webbed in, his pad raised on hydrajacks to place him up close to the sphere screen in the bridge center.

"By our next pass, sir," said Communication Three.

"All right then, let's relax, get ready for the surrender ceremonies. Unwebbing now." He began unzipping himself from the myriad human–machine interface connections that made the link to the cranial interface that he wore like some huge exoskeletal skull while on the webpad. The bridge unwebbed as well.

"At last this program is moving on some sort of schedule," Sigimir said with satisfaction while pulling microplugs from the tiny input holes in his skull. "I think this calls for a little celebration. Somebody get some champagne."

"Rightaway, sir," One said, disappearing toward the galley freight tube.

Enkov chinned into the shipboard PA. "Okay, folks, it looks like we've got things under control now, and in my opinion that means we're finally going to get some shore leave. So we're going to get that surrender and end our little fracas on this oddly beautiful little world—and then we're going into that Red Moon and we're going to raise some hell. I've been wanting to see those Red Moon bordellos now for a few years too many."

The ship was full of high spirits after that.

The celebrations began. In fact, the first cork was out of a bottle of Space Colony Blancs de Blancs and glasses were raised high when an alarm blared throughout the ship.

"What the hell is that?" Enkov snarled as the alarm escalated through condition yellow to red.

"Computer's going crazy, sir. Says something is invading it."

"What?" Enkov turned to the nearest monitor. The screen blanked, wobbled an image, blanked again.

"I'm getting very bizarre readings from engineering levels, something's messing with the fusion drives."

Enkov felt his heart freeze. He and One exchanged looks of surprise, then anxiety.

"Computer is blanking its memory banks, we're losing control."

One tried to get something onto his monitor.

"Systematic data degradation. We've been invaded by some kind of alien presence."

"You're out of your mind," Enkov snarled. He pushed One aside and stared at the image that finally froze on the monitor: A series of circles forming one within the other, dissolving and reforming.

"If we lose control of the drive, we could lose the ship."
One's voice was tight, ominous.

Admiral Enkov looked at him. "You mean?" They both
swallowed. Then in a voice like gravel crunching under a
steamroller, Enkov ordered the fusion drives armed for self-
destruction. "We'll blow the ship if we have to."

Everyone on the bridge paused for a sick moment, and then
they redoubled their efforts to discover the cause of the chaos.

But all the monitors showed the same image. The Computer
ran down to imbecility. The alarms continued to scream. The
champagne went flat and the *Gagarin* staggered on, blinded,
memory base deteriorating, in the grip of the unknown.

In the glade of the Fidnemed there was a long silence. No
one cared to be the first to project speech into the absence of
glyphs. The fein were in a rigid state of near ecstasy, trans-
ported by the presence of the Spirit of Abzen Vale.

Fleur looked to Fair, but Fair had pulled her shawl over her
head and was sunk in deep meditation. And when she turned
to Lavin his eyes were there, as she'd known they would be.
"Oh, my dear, my love, how can this have happened to us?
And we so young." She touched his face with her hands.

"When you say 'us' do you mean just you and I or the
human race?" Lavin asked.

"Just you and I, thou and I."

"How long have you known?"

"For what seems an age but in reality is just a few hours.
Since I realized that you were going to try to break Armada
out of the Bablon. I thought you were sure to die. I never
imagined that ten fein and Lavin Fundin could just walk into
the Sx Coast and walk out again with the syndicate's prize
prisoner. And so I thought you were dead and I was so sad.
Then, when I heard you'd done it, I knew. I knew again."

He grinned for a second, rubbed the two-day stubble on his
chin.

"And you," she said, "how long has it been for you?"

"Oh, hard to say. But more than a few hours."

"Not since Mimi Zimi's goddamn raunch party on that boat?"
she asked accusingly. He grinned and ducked to kiss her.

"And we have no time, isn't that right? That's what the
Spirit said. There will be a judgment." She pressed against

him, seeking some comfort from the fear. "Would they do that? Are they that powerful?"

"I think so," he said.

They had strolled some distance from the others, leaning together under an overhang that kept off the rain. She felt wet through, was coated with mud, and her hair was a mass of snakes. And through her thoughts rang the glyphs, over and over... "The cruel farmer is the good farmer... Expungement... the chitin adjustments..."

And she felt a surge of desire so strong, so primal that it would not be restrained, so that in the face of the death of everything or everyone, she would snatch a last moment of love. She turned to him and he was already waiting. "You're always just ahead of me," she said wonderingly.

"Yes, of course, I went to Ghotaw Academy. But, why not? While we still can." He took her hand and led her into a warm, dry area beneath the roots. The space was empty—the normal inhabitants of the forest avoided the Fidnemed entirely.

They made love as if they were going to light a last lamp for humanity with the fire newfound between them. A flare of love, bravado against the gathering dark.

Later they sat together in the dark with their backs against one root and their feet against another. Fleur was filthy, coated with bark fibers and dirt. Yet the slick of love's water that trailed down her thigh filled her with satisfaction.

If they were to die, then at least their love had not perished before one chance of realization. Slowly the satisfaction faded, however, and the world forced its way back into her thoughts. She moved restlessly.

"Try not to, it isn't up to us."

"I can't stop myself thinking about it, I'll go crazy."

"Don't."

"Easier said than done."

"I know," he said wearily.

She tried to sound a bright note. "Well, did we do all that much damage anyway? I mean in terms of the area that was destroyed."

"We?"

"I mean the Space Forces, of course."

"Our best estimate would be at least eight hundred square kilometers. A lot depends on the residual radiation."

"Well, that sounds like a lot except that this continent is one hundred and forty million square kilometers in extent. So what's a few hundred compared to all that? Surely that's not enough damage to merit a war between the Arizel and the Earth. Especially as the human forces didn't understand, they didn't know. I mean, they weren't attacking the Arizel, were they? That can't be enough of a reason to destroy us."

"To us perhaps but everything indicates that it may not be so for them."

She shook her head, hugged closer to him in the womblike darkness. She had faced death a number of times since that mad day when she'd decided to track down the red-haired girl. But facing death at the hands of the woodwose was one thing, facing the extermination of the human race was another—it made an emptiness that she could not fill, a pit too deep to see the bottom. There was nothing to be done, though; the decision was not theirs to make. Fleur tried to blot it out, to think of other things. "How would you describe it then?"

"Describe what?"

"What we just did in here, silly."

"Desperate but wonderful." His voice did not betray the doom he felt growing upon them.

She frowned. "Desperate" was all too accurate, but it wasn't what she wanted to hear. "Then I'm not too skinny?"

He chuckled. "Perhaps Bg Rva will have to take care of you. Once he starts on you you'll be eating gzan liver twice a day and drinking more herbal potion than you could imagine."

"Liver, ugh! I don't think I could ever eat that."

"He can be very persuasive."

She sighed, then wiped a trickle of perspiration from her brow. The air was stifling, it was oppressively humid.

The first glyph came as a complete surprise. She jumped with fright and Lavin sat upright, cracking his head on the root above.

"Pardon," said the glyph. Fleur felt the presence of the Spirit once again, but this time it had crept up on her so subtly that she'd never detected it. How long had it been there?

"Pardon once again. We have intruded upon you, but time is so short and I must fashion a number of 'weapons' for the coming conflict. Furthermore my companion could only join me to observe you for a very short time."

They'd been watching them! Fleur felt a deep flush building on her skin under the bark and the dirt.

"Pardon, but we observed you for longer than I had at first contemplated. It was initially inadvertent but my companion hadn't witnessed such a tender undertaking in so long that it begged me not to interrupt you."

"If you're going to exterminate us, do you have to play voyeurs with us as well?" Fleur's anger was loud and harsh to her own ears.

The glyph was tinged in apology. "I would not vote for your extermination, not for anything. Others of my kind would feel less compunction. That is why I am here."

Then another glyph consciousness became apparent, the hidden companion now moved. Fleur felt it and initially her sense of size, the sheer scale of the other, terrified her. The thing was so huge it loomed larger than a planet in her mind. Lying on her back beneath the roots, she could think only of a colossus that was rolling over her, a weight that would extinguish her completely as the dark extinguishes light.

There were no cold probes, no hands groped for hidden doors. The big Arizel intended to roll through the doors, collapsing them and every other barrier. But the doors gave way in an instant and her panic ceased in the next. She recovered her control, her breath coming in hard gasps.

"This is the Steadfast-in-Pursuit Spirit." The glyph rose easily in their minds. "Now you will learn, this is an exchange to benefit us both."

Fleur received a number of descriptive glyphs, many indecipherable, that emanated in a stream from the new Arizel, and with them came a feeling of almost indescribable ecstasy, as if she were suddenly privileged to be allowed to sit in the cockpit of an incredibly advanced machine and drive it herself.

Steadfast-in-Pursuit was very different from the Spirit-that-preferred-to-move-softly, and Fleur was amazed by that. The sense of personality that she felt from the Abzen Spirit's glyphs was absent. Instead, the new Arizel seemed more like a vast machine without any characteristics other than devotion to its purpose. The portion of its consciousness that could be devoted to such affairs as theirs was minute, a mere gleam against the background blast of the power of its radiance.

"It withdraws now," glyphed the Spirit-that-preferred-to-

306

move-softly, and indeed she sensed that rolling progress again. Steadfast-in-Pursuit turned, as inexorably as Fenrille itself, and slipped away with a final glyph of farewell.

"Once again I beg your pardon for the intrusion upon your intimacy, but at the judgment we shall need every ally we can summon."

"Will Steadfast-in-Pursuit be a good ally?"

"None could be better; it is the oldest of all."

"Of the Arizel?"

"That is correct. But come, the judgment is at hand, the return begins."

"It has?" Fleur clutched at Lavin.

"Listen," he said. A throb had begun, above them, deep in the heart of the wood.

They scrambled from the root cave and brushed off as much of the mess as they could before putting their clothes back on.

The forest had come to life. An incessant crackling, almost a roar of sound, could be heard and the soft lights that had made the trees such traceries of beauty at night were bright and hard. Like scarlet and gold veins, they laced the trees, glowing within the bark. On the roots, the nodes and maculae were glistening in strange colors, oily sheens with occasional sparkles of green.

"They have returned," Lavin said, zipping up his greens. "All of them. So now all their power is concentrated in the forest, from which it emanates in the first place. You can feel it, it's almost like an electrical charge. In fact, there is a charge and metal objects will probably give you a shock from now on, so remember not to touch them. But the Arizel are weakest in the electromagnetic spectrum, or I should say they only have power over electromagnetism at the extremes."

"Why is that?"

"At Spreak Tower they say they've determined that the Arizel manage to manipulate all the four aspects of the creation force but that their control is greatest with gravity. In some way they use biological energy—weak electrical fields in sub-le patterns—to control gravity, to momentarily deflect it elsewhere. With the other forces, such as the nuclear forces and electromagnetism, their control is much less exact."

Fleur's clammy clothes were clinging to her, but the snap-ing and crackling in the air, the pulsing veins of light in the

307

trees made her forget her discomforts. It also made it hard to concentrate on the path, and she stumbled several times.

In the central glade the noise was loudest. The fein were waiting, in a supertense group with wide eyes and tails stiff and straight. Rva stepped forward; he had to raise his voice.

"They come, Lord, the Great Ones." Rva's eyes were slightly glassy; the fein was stunned by the turn of events. For the Arizel to return in any fein's lifetime was a miracle, but for it to be in his lifetime? That was more than the Hero of Brelkilk had ever dreamed of.

That faint basso chord that had been thrumming steadily had crept up in volume to provide a drone profundo that went on and on behind the short-lived aural crepitation.

Rva and Lavin clasped hands, his lean tanned wrist vanishing into a huge mitt of dark brindle fur. Their eyes locked, but they had no need for words.

Eventually Lavin noted old Fy'pupe lying to one side, Fair Fundan kneeling beside him.

"The old one?" Lavin said.

Umpiil turned his head. "He dies in a great moment. Never did I think that I might live to see this." The Effertelli were stiff, not even a tail was flickering. Their eyes and ears were alive to the evidence of the return.

The basso was altering, modulating just a little and jumping up the volume scale. A rhythmic tonal passage began, music of a sort, but extremely slow and stately music. As far as Fleur could tell, the phrases never repeated themselves and soon higher notes began to intrude, then harmonics and wafting echoes and faint chords. Then a sound with thrilling vibrato, akin to violin synthetics, began to slowly play a simple tune. The tune was completed and other voices joined it, first a few, then dozens, then hundreds until there were a multitude of such "instruments" and then it was in the millions and the sound filled the world, tore down the sky, rang from the rock of the continent itself.

They clapped their hands to their ears. Fleur felt herself forced down to a crouch by the power of the sound. It swelled to a point where she knew that removing her fingers from her ears would damage her hearing permanently, a sound so violently loud and glorious that it seemed more elemental than the monsoon itself.

The trees of the Fidnemed were pulsing with light, golden flashes sparkling in the bark, red and gold traceries aglow. The Arizel tki Fenrille, wanderers of the heavens, were returned to their ancient seat of glory. The trees rang out in trumpeting majesty, the ground trembled with the thunder of the power.

As the age-old associations were reknit so the Arizel combined for the great glyph sequence, the first cantos of the Yllblssa, the Ode to the Creator and the paean for the Mahgara.

The glyphs were overwhelming. Fleur felt them burst into her mind with trumpets and banners, enormous proclamations of joy and reverence and determination.

Now she understood Fair Fundan's forebodings. Truly were the Arizel tki Fenrille named "the mighty" by the ay fein.

As the glyphs continued so the music died away, and when the glyphs began to speed up, incorporating historical images that were largely indecipherable to Fleur, the sound calmed to almost nothing.

But the glyph paths were shuddering with a million glyphs a second as every individual Arizel contributed its own to the great tapestry they wove. Glistening shapes, inexplicable images, all flickered by madly while the humans dropped to their knees and held their heads and tried to block out the overload.

The torrent built to an unbearable level and then stopped abruptly with one last great glyph that seemed to roll on forever beneath and above, rising majestically out of the pit in the center of consciousness with the deliberation of the planet turning on its axis. Fleur realized that in a sense that's what it was, Fenrille—the planet's history laid out in one vast glyph. There, in such baffling detail that it defied human analysis, was the whole vast story of the world and its slow progression, culture to culture, to the world culture that had endured long enough to become the launching pad for the Arizel themselves. A history that stretched back to some point in the terrestrial Jurassic.

When that great glyph finally rolled past into nothingness, there was a silence. After the music and the glyph torrent it took them all a little while to pull themselves together. Fair Fundan was gray and haggard, Tan Ubu seemed stunned. Lavin was the first up. He helped Fleur regain her feet. The silence around them was eagerly expectant. Fleur had the distinct impression that a great multitude of very keen minds were watching her, waiting for her to speak.

A glyph rose easily into her mind. "The appointed Council of Inquisition has taken up the case. Now must all transgressions be exposed. Be advised that the judgment will be justly made and swiftly executed. In pursuit of justice we are merciless."

Fleur swallowed. Merciless? Lavin squeezed her hand; she turned to him. "We might as well hang on to each other now," he said, pulling her close. "We may not have very long."

She smiled, somehow, and fought back the tears. Their real lives had just begun. Everything that had gone before, she saw, had been incomplete, waiting for that moment. And soon it would be snatched away, along with everything else.

The Council's identifying glyphs now appeared in sequence. First came one that proclaimed itself to be the Migrant-of-the-Halls-of-All. A swift glyph, hard and steely and filled with strong energy. Then came the Inward-Migrator, a being that glyphed without emotional tones at all, as if utterly devoid of ego, a machine in pursuit of its goal.

The Migrator was followed by a vastly different spirit. The sparkling glyph of Endiclav the Finest fairly erupted into consciousness, alive with a sense of purpose and mission, but tinged with kindliness and even, somewhere, a sense of humor. Then came the graceful glyph of Far Wanderer, which hinted of sailing, a vessel on the oceans on the cosmos.

A momentary delay was followed by the almost crude glyph, slashed and ugly, of Humble Origins, and Fleur sensed a message calling for true humility before the All.

A glyph, unmistakably from Endiclav the Finest, announced, "These are the representatives of the Expansionist Tendency for this Council, and I am their prolocutor."

After a pause another glyph came; an incredibly detailed one that outlined some mathematical discovery by which the projector of the glyph was known, great Tshak 404040. That entity broadcast a cold determination and steely will to seek out tree damage and its perpetrators.

No sooner had Tshak 404040's great glyph disappeared than another replaced it. But it was virtually inexplicable. Fleur's impression she translated as "In excellent husbandry it is the cruel farmer that clips the creatures to divide well."

Another aspect seemed to suggest that "the cruel farmer clips the creatures and divides well." No human terms existed to describe the processes involved, but she perceived a principle of division, multiplied endlessly within a screed of mathematical symbols. A tao symbol that gradually shed the black, dividing it to a point of infinity, and then an identity seemed complete—the Divider. The name lingered for a moment.

Another delay ensued, but it was brief and ended with a short violent glyph that projected little more than vast, restless energy, an entity eager to be off and away and running for the edge of the galaxies. All that remained to name this being was an onomatopoeic form and a cluster of red suns, Brrrp-43 Red Suns.

Then a glyph with the unmistakable tone of the Divider announced, "These are the representatives of the Exclusionist Tendency for the Council and I am their prolocutor. Forward the glyphs."

Then came Endiclav the Finest. "A judgment must be made in respect to the tree damage."

Once again the frighteningly intense glyph for tree damage arose.

"Who understands the matter?" Endiclav questioned.

"I do," whispered a familiar glyph source, "the Spirit-that-preferred-to-move-softly."

"Inform us all then."

Swiftly the glyphs succeeded one another as the Spirit-that-preferred-to-move-softly described the causes of the crisis and the tree damage. When the narrative was completed, in a matter of moments, there was a hush. The Council seemed to be thinking it over, then Tshak 404040 erupted with angry glyphs, pulsing with rage.

"TREE DAMAGE, NUCLEAR WEAPONS, RADIATION, PERMANENT TREE DYSFUNCTION. EXTREME STEPS ARE NECESSARY. ON BEHALF OF THE EXPUNGEMENT FACTION, I MOVE FOR AN IMMEDIATE VOTE ON THE PREJUDICIAL TERMINATION OF THE INTRUDING ALIEN SPECIES."

Endiclav responded by calling for the vote. The tree damage from nuclear weapons was unpardonable; some retribution was essential. Arguments for exterminating the human race would be heard from Tshak 404040 and the Divider. A spokesperson for the humans was to be sought.

Fleur felt the passage of justice was moving awfully fast and in a dreadful direction. "Aren't we being a little quick about all this?" she stammered. For once she was not mortified by the sound of a human voice speaking to all those glorious glyphs.

"Justice is sure and justice can be swift, can it not?" Endiclav replied.

"But it ought to be sure as well. You ought to hear all the story before condemning us. The motivations of those who did the damage, for example."

Fair Fundan was nodding vigorously at her although Fair was obviously too overcome to speak herself.

"Indeed, the human has a point. We shall want to question the precise perpetrators of the deed," the Divider glyphed.

"There are other elements to the case as well," said the quiet glyph of the Spirit-that-preferred-to-move-softly.

"TOO MANY ELEMENTS CAN ONLY OBSTRUCT THE FOCUS OF OUR JUSTICE AND MOST NATURAL RETRIBUTION."

"We have hardly presented too many elements yet," the Spirit observed.

Tshak 404040 did not care to reply. The Spirit continued, "First we must send for the rash perpetrators of these deeds. And to do this most easily and effectively I think we should send for them with some of these humans here as couriers. They will be more easily understood than one of ourselves, at least initially. I have found that the humans are, to a great extent, unaware of our existence or even to the possibility that lifeforms might exist outside of their perceptional fields. They are a very young race."

Endiclav seconded this proposal with a commendation. "The idea has merit, Mountain Spirit. Long has it been since one of your tier spoke before this Council. Welcome."

Endiclav took a quick poll of the Council members then acted.

29

ABOARD THE *GAGARIN* THEY STARED AT THE MONITORS. THE ship was back under human control although the computer was still badly degraded. Fascinated, they watched as the outer atmosphere of the planet below flashed with aurorae, haloes, and huge ball-lightnings.

"Our ground-based probes are picking up something very strange, sir," Communications Three said. "Here, I'll put it up on your right-hand screen."

"There's a malfunction again. Get that contrast down, will you?"

"Sorry, sir, no malfunction, that's what we're getting from all our ground-based probes." The trees were glowing with unearthly energy. Gold veins throbbed.

"We've lost most of the auditory trackers, too. Something is making enough noise down there to shatter your eardrums. Well above one hundred decibels."

Enkov chinned the Inner Five for Command consultation. "All right, what are we facing? I'll listen to anyone with a bright idea."

313

Nobody had any ideas, bright or otherwise. But One spoke. "We're getting a slew of SOS calls from the coastal cities."

"What do they want?"

"Emergency evacuation."

"Bah!" Enkov snorted. "There are twenty million people down there. They're crazy. Even if we could lift them, where do they think we'd put them all?"

"Not on the Red Moon, that habitat is overcrowded as it is."

"The hell with that." Enkov was firm. "There's nothing we can do for them. Let them ride it out. They chose to live there. Anyway what's happening to them?"

"I can't make any sense out of that part of the message, sir."

One was about to try to intervene on behalf of the coastal masses when alarms crashed in and there was an abrupt popping sound, like a champagne cork magnified many times. Two human figures had appeared from nowhere and hung within the command module.

Security systems sprang into action, guns came up, men launched themselves toward the intruders.

Enkov recognized Fleur Kevilla, although she was so disheveled and filthy that she was literally shedding hundreds of particles of dirt, fibers, and grit into the surrounding air. Her companion was equally filthy but plainly male, a tall young man in partial Fundan uniform.

The security team waited for an order to fire since the intruders were not armed and had made no move. The men floating toward them were bounced aside by an invisible hand.

"There is not time enough for this," said something that seemed to open like a flower in their consciousnesses. Enkov, eyes wide in amazement, saw that the others had all heard it, too.

"What is that?" he spluttered.

A glyph arose in their minds. "Do not fire. It is pointless to try to harm our ambassadors to you. Open your minds to enlightenment."

Fleur spoke. "Admiral Enkov, we've been sent here by the Arizel Spirits. They request your presence at the judgment. I know this sounds crazy, but it's also very real—they're conducting a trial for the human race, and you are a witness,

314

believe. An important witness. It's very important. You must come with us."

"She's mad, quite mad," Enkov said. The two intruders continued to hang together shedding matter from the forest floor into the central command module.

"But how in the blue-fired hells of Orion did they get in here?"

Lavin fixed Command Two with his eyes. "Your use of nuclear weapons has caused the Arizel to return. Now they judge humanity on the matter of tree damage. To them nothing is more important."

"The Arizel tki Fenrille, where have I heard of that? Isn't that the name of the ancestor gods that the fein worship?" Two laughed.

"They are no gods."

"Funny, I thought they were. In Burrup and Horson it says clearly that they are worshipped as the ancestors of the fein."

"Burrup and Horson are wrong about a great many things."

"Hold it just there! What is going on here?" Enkov said in exasperation.

"You must come with us, Admiral," Lavin said, "because of the damage to the trees, you see. The forest is the source of the power that is employed by the Arizel. They demand an accounting from you."

"Good grief," Enkov said. "Mad people! I'm surrounded by the crazed. But I still don't understand how you got in here. Anyway, Security, seize these two and take 'em to sick bay. I want them cleaned and examined for dangerous parasites before I interrogate them personally. Void alone knows what they might be harboring."

"Hold," came the glyph, urgent, hot for attention.

"Look, we have met before, have we not?" And the glyph carried with it a representation of a monitor screen on which odd circular patterns formed and dissolved. The glyph split to become dozens of identical monitors, all bearing the circles.

"Oh, wow," Three gurgled.

Two choked. "But this doesn't make any sense. How do these people get in here?"

Another glyph swiftly replied. "They were moved by the Council of Inquisition which sits and awaits the admiral. Now that it has been explained to you, he will be moved as well."

315

With loud slaps, as if a giant had clapped his hands, Enkov disappeared along with the two intruders.

"Sensors, scan this. Computer, for void's sake get me a reading. Where did they go?" One shouted as he frantically stabbed at the module's control studs.

On the fourteenth floor of the Bablon Dome, Ira Ganweek crouched low and scuttled over to the kitchenette. Something smacked into a sandbag at the end of the suite, and he threw himself to the floor expecting another clip's worth of automatic fire from the sniper in the gutted Teoklitan Dome. The Apache Warband had seized control there. Now only the Flanians stood between the Apaches and the Bablon. Already there was fighting in the gardens of Nebuchadnezzar. Things were breaking down.

Ira had barricaded himself into a small corner of his suite along with a stock of food and water and plenty of ammunition. He'd moved first, beating his security guards to the punch on the day that the Teoklitan went down. Now their bodies were stuffed in with the sandbags they'd so laboriously put in place.

The *ripping* of 50-mm slugs through the room didn't take place, however. Instead there was just a single report and it sounded as if it came from inside the room.

"You can get up off the floor now," a voice said. It rang a little too resonantly in his memory.

Ganweek lifted his head and shuddered. If the voice was a hallucination, it was awfully good. If it was a holo, then his enemies had him at their mercy. Either way, he felt the breath freeze in his throat.

Then it moved toward him and he knew it was real, it was really her! With an inarticulate roar he went for his gun. Hallucination or not, he would kill her. Nothing else seemed reasonable.

His finger froze on the trigger.

"Hold," said something that shone, that tricked and picked its way into his mind. With silvery gleams and crystal clarity it bubbled up to the surface of thought. "You may not fire your weapon. She brings you grave news."

"To hell with that." Ganweek giggled, aimed, and pressed the trigger. But it wouldn't budge. He wrapped another finger

316

around it and strained furiously, but it would not fire. "Damn thing's jammed, but I've got others."

"All your weapons are now inoperable."

"Listen well, you old toad," Armada snapped. "You're summoned to the judgment now being undertaken by the Arizel. The great Spirits have returned because of the nuclear attack. Now they have placed the human race on trial."

"The Arizel? Spirits? What are you babbling about? How can ancestor totems return? Return to *where*, anyway?"

"They live, can't you feel the power? The whole continent is shaking with them now."

"You mean they're responsible for all this..." His voice trailed off. "But—"

"No buts. Come." She reached out, caught him by the hand, and drew him through a door that opened out of nowhere and into utter darkness.

His mouth was still framed in a round O of astonishment when, in the next moment, he stood on the floor of the Fidnemed. The great trees loomed above, lit up from within as brilliantly as if they were inlaid with neon tubes. Surging in his mind were echoes and traces of the myriads of glyphs passing among the Arizel at that moment. The place resounded with poltergeistic audio effects. He shook himself, pinched his cheek hard but the scene remained the same.

"What is this?" Nearby stood a small group of fein and some humans. Armada Butte was looking at him. "The end of the world, Senator, that's all."

He couldn't kill her, his gun *was* inoperable.

"How did I get here?" he howled, tears starting from his eyes.

"Silence!" snapped a crisp glyph from Endiclav the Finest.

"We are the Council of Inquisition, appointed from the dominant tendencies among the Arizel tki Fenrille. Before us lies a motion calling for the extermination of the human race. The motion is made by the Exclusionist Tendency. Their representatives will question you, if they so desire, when I have finished my interrogation. My name is Endiclav the Finest, so called for obvious reasons, and I question you on behalf of the Expansionist Tendency.

"We are interested primarily in any light you may be able to throw upon the synthesis process. You possessed a memory chip. All we require of you is that you think over your own memories and we will probe for the details ourselves."

Ganweek noticed that Admiral Enkov had appeared out of thin air nearby. The admiral wore a look that mirrored his own astonishment.

More glyphs arose, directed at Enkov but washing into Ganweek's mind as well. The Council, wherever they were, announced their purpose.

"I have a question," Ganweek said at length. He saw Fair Fundan, without a wig, wrapped in a shawl standing alone at the edge of the clearing. "Where are you? I understand the voices you project into my head, but who or what are you? I can't see you."

"Look into the trees, there you will see us."

And Ganweek looked into the trees, into the tracery of gold and red and shimmering there, as pale as ghosts. He saw faces, alien faces. Like hawks, they were cold and austere, with large fein eyes set widely apart, with ears that were small cups set high on the sides of the bulging crania.

"You are not the fein?"

"Of course not. Have they not told you? They are the ay fein, those who were left behind. For their own reasons, many of our people chose to remain here on Fenrille rather than seek out the grace of the Creator. They were modified so as to fit comfortably into the new ecosystem that we established."

Then a glyph crashed out, the great historical glyph of Fenrille, but with a difference, an accentuation that conjured up in human minds pictures of the last days of the High Planetary Culture.

Graceful onion domes towered over cities laid out like parks. Aircraft, dirigible balloons, moved continually through the air. Limited space exploration had been carried out. Small probes had been fired to the other worlds of Beni's system. An orbital telescope had operated for a century to map out the heavens in crystal clarity. At length the glyph faded.

"This was our world. The endtime of our culture. When it was becoming apparent that there was only one task left for us to perform."

Again the glyph for the Mahgara crashed out, ringing with glory and reverence.

When it faded at last the questioning began in earnest.

Ganweek, Fair, and Fleur were selected to answer. From them the nuances of the problem of longevity drugs were soon absorbed by the Council.

Seizing on a moment's hesitation, Fair Fundan spoke up, her voice sounding thin and reedy. "Great Lords of Fenrille, in light of what you now know about the supply of longevity proteins, you can see that it is a small thing, really, that the humans need to take from your mountains. The biosphere is hardly affected."

"ALL VERY WELL BUT THERE HAS BEEN TREE DAMAGE," the immediate glyph thundered.

"The tree damage will not happen again," Fair replied. "It must be remembered that the damage occurred more from ignorance than malice."

"I will allow that this is very likely," Endiclav's glyph said.

"Then is it truly necessary to destroy the human race? If chitin proteins can be synthesized and extended then even the struggle which precipitated the crisis here will end. Peace will return to Fenrille."

"Indeed," Endiclav glyphed rapidly, "this does seem a reasonable conjecture. Therefore I put it to my colleagues on the panel of Inquisition. What do they say?"

"THE WOMAN IS EVIL, UNNATURAL, SUNK IN HER EUGENICAL SCHEMES. SHE MUST BE PURGED. THE HUMANS, TOO. THEY ARE INSATIABLY GREEDY AND DESTRUCTIVE. OBSERVE." Tshak 404040 now interrogated Ganweek, a process that sent old Ira's eyeballs rolling into his head as his brain was forcibly probed and his secrets exposed.

"THIS CREATURE STINKS OF DEPRAVITY AND MURDER," Tshak 404040 announced. "THE CHEMICAL SYNTHESIS THAT HE POSSESSED WAS OBTAINED BY THE CALCULATED MURDER OF ITS INVENTOR, A SCIENTIST. THE CREATURE HAS MURDERED A SCIENTIST FOR GREED. THIS IS A GREAT EVIL, THE MURDER OF INVENTION, THE TRAMPLING UPON THE SACRED RIGHTS OF SCIENTIFIC INQUIRY." Tshak 404040 was almost beside itself, the glyphs so hot and angry they were painfully bright.

"SO THESE THINGS MUST BE BALANCED. THE CREATURES ARE INSATIABLE AND DESTRUCTIVE. THEIR HOMESTAR IS NEAR ENOUGH TO ALLOW THE FAMILIARITY OF INTERSTELLAR SPACE TRAVEL. EITHER WE MUST MOVE FENRILLE FROM ITS SACRED

319

ORBIT OR DESTROY THEM TO END THEIR INFESTATION OF OUR WORLD."

Now it was Admiral Enkov's turn to grimace and scream as Tshak 404040 bore down on him.

"FROM THIS CREATURE'S MIND I READ A DESIRE FOR A WORLD EMPIRE UNDER HIS OWN COMMAND. HE DESIRES TO TURN HIS OWN RACE INTO HIS SLAVES. NOTHING BUT IMPERIAL DOMINATION WILL SATISFY HIM. HE IS DESPERATE FOR REVENGE UPON THOSE WHO SENT HIM HERE, UPON ALL THE NORMAL HUMANS. HE HATES THEM. A THOUSAND SMALL SLIGHTS AND INSULTS FUEL HIS RAGE. HE HATES THEM, HE HATES EVERYTHING, BECAUSE HE IS DIFFERENT. HIS HATE BOILS WITHIN HIM LIKE VAPOR OVER THE LAVA OF A VOLCANO. IT SEEKS ESCAPE THROUGH ANNIHILATION OF ALL WHO OPPOSE HIM. EVEN NOW HE CALCULATES THE POSSIBILITY OF USING HIS SHIP TO LAY NUCLEAR WEAPONS UPON US TO DESTROY THE ARIZEL TKI FENRILLE.

"THE CONTENTS OF THESE TWO MINDS, WHEN PUT TOGETHER WITH THE STRANGE ECSTASIES AND HORRIBLE GENETIC EXPERIMENTS OF THE OLD WOMAN FUNDAN, MAKE A VIVID EXHIBIT FOR THE NEED TO EFFECT TOTAL EXPUNGEMENT OF THIS DISGUSTING RACE OF PLANETARY PARASITES. THEY HAVE EVOLVED WRONGLY. TOO SOON THEY TREAD THE SPACE LANES. THEY MUST BE REMOVED."

Fleur shook from the power of the glyphs. Tshak 404040 was nothing if not wholeheartedly for his idea. And yet she had to smile at the thought of an Arizel terming Fair Fundan old.

Now the Divider glyphed, "We have long divided to divine."

Fleur felt again that eery sense of detachment, a didactic extreme, aloof and cold.

"In such dividing of things, we have proposed the hypothesis that per galaxy there can be but one intelligent and dominant species. Our researches in other galaxies have given us evidence to support this view as being close to a pure universal principle. Thus we must either eliminate other potentially troublesome species or inhibit their progress to star travel and space empire. Since we have abandoned the pursuit of the control of gross matter, we have no interest in becoming the dominant space-going species in this galaxy. By this reckoning it is hard to avoid reaching the conclusion that we must either take extreme action or some form of inhibiting action against the humans."

320

"What form of inhibiting action would you propose?" Endiclav the Finest questioned.

"While not wanting to be too specific, I would focus on their spacegoing capacity. We might have to shatter their technological culture."

"The means?"

"There are many. For instance, it is easy to divine that they are a warlike species. As with all young sentient species, they have yet to master their animal natures. They could be induced to fight among themselves."

"I RECOMMEND THE TRANSFER OF A BLACK-HOLE SINGULARITY OF AT LEAST TWICE SOLAR MASS TO WITHIN FIVE SOLAR RADII FOR LONG ENOUGH TO TURN THE STAR NOVA. THIS WILL CLEAN THE ENTIRE SYSTEM OF THESE DANGEROUS CREATURES."

"That might be a little extreme," Endiclav countered.

"Possibly not," the Divider replied.

Endiclav hesitated a moment then agreed. His glyph carried overtones of slight reluctance. "I will put both of your recommendations on the list for the vote."

With a sinking feeling Fleur realized that things were proceeding swiftly and in the same inexorable way. The Arizel could vote in the matter of a few seconds on any motion put before them. The sentence might be carried out equally swiftly.

"Are there any other views that should be heard?" Endiclav asked.

The Spirit-that-preferred-to-move-softly glyphed with uncharacteristic speed and determination, "I would present an idea conceived by the Pragmatixts."

"Indeed?" Endiclav glyphed, with overtones of surprise and slight condescension.

"HOW WIDE IS THE SUPPORT OF THIS FACTION?" Tshak 404040 trumpeted.

"Somewhat limited," the Spirit-that-preferred-to-move-softly admitted.

"WHY IS IT THAT THE EXPUNGEMENT FACTION IS NOT ALLOWED TIME TO AIR ITS VIEWS AND YET WE WILL ALLOW THIS GROUP OF PRAGMATIXTS TO DO SO?"

"Would you prefer equal time?"

"OF COURSE NOT. LET US GET ON WITH THIS MATTER. THERE ARE MORE IMPORTANT THINGS TO BE ATTENDED TO."

"Let us now Divide to Rule," the Divider glyphed. "Shall we hear the argument of the Pragmatixts?"

Endiclav put it to the assembled Arizel and it was rejected within seconds. The Spirit-that-preferred-to-move-softly had been turned away, the Pragmatixt Endeavor was simply too small a group to win the attention of the majority of Arizel. That majority continued to thirst for a democratically simple, straightforward solution, and a dreadful doom for humanity.

The surprise would be total and there would be no time to save anyone in the inner system. A black-hole singularity so close to the sun would churn the interior of old Sol to a nova state. So great a flash would ensure that Earth would be seared in a matter of minutes, hours at most, her oceans boiled away. The Solar System's space habitats would also be scorched or destroyed in the great outflow of solar material that would follow the flash.

Without the home planet and the inner system, the outer system, populated thinly by specialist groups, would be hard pressed to survive, even if the flash didn't burn them out. And the radiation would be lethal; only thick shielding would offer any hope.

Endiclav now put the case of the Expansionist Tendency. "There are now two motions from the Exclusionist Tendency on the tally. Before we vote on them, let us heed the teachings of the Expansionist Viewpoint. It is unwise to tamper with the materials of the Creator. These young lifeforms are soon to become more numerous. Our galaxy approaches its great fruit-ful period. The contending races are already beginning their march down the space lanes. Are we to obliterate them all, to sterilize the rest of our galaxy, to keep our world safe? This is a question we must face now. After the humans will come the others, the natural children of the yellow-star worlds.

"These humans are so young, so fast moving, that they contain astonishing conflicts of impulse. However, we must decide to do something about them. They cannot be left as before. They thirst for the longevity drugs derived from chitin. Thus they will not leave willingly. We would have to post a watch to prevent their return. They have mastered the electro-magnetic force and are learning to master the nuclear forces. They have traveled a long way down the road to the life of power, glued to material illusion. They do not know the golden road and may never discover it now they are launched so firmly on the road to the other.

"To control them would require technology, which we do not have. We were never so technologically organized; our kind found the golden road early and never sought for the stars. Instead we seek the Creator of the Stars.

"So we must act now. Of course, in the Expansionist Tendency, we prefer to find alternatives to violence and exterminations. Thus we must choose to support the idea of an Expulsion. The humans will be expelled and a rota will be set up and all Arizel will contribute some part of their time to keep watch over our world. Indeed, such a watch will become necessary soon anyway; the humans have just precipitated it. The galaxy wakes and more space travelers will come. They must all be kept away."

Rumbling dissent glyphed up in storms from the masses of Arizel. A rota of space patrol, having to shed mass and waste time and, even worse, having to return to Fenrille, that was unpopular. It was evident that the Expansionist Tendency's call for guard duty was on poor political ground.

Even Endiclav seemed torn. "Such a rota would be burdensome, I know, but I am opposed to the idea of burning another race. This is not the chitin and what we did to the chitin home world was a great crime against life. The song of the great Hives of Herxx was cut off in a scream of hate directed toward us. A death curse from a whole world—do you not think the Creator would have heard? Who among us will wish to discuss the matter with It?

"I remember that death scream, how it shakes in the glyphing." And Endiclav put forth the glyph itself, etched in black rage on the bleakness of the void. The sun leaping out to the intruding mass, the flash, the heat storm, and the shriveling of the hive cities. The dying, the burning of continents, the sunside scorched down to basalt and the fire slaying all inexorably as the perimeter advanced with radiation. The last cry of the Hives of Herxx before final obliteration.

"This is what Tshak 404040 calls for again. It is simple, it is crude, and it is too great a punishment. It represents the easy way out and we must not take that way."

Endiclav finished, but the death of the chitin home world was a memory tinged with a certain grim satisfaction among the Arizel. The obdurate chitin had pursued its objectives with an insectal singlemindedness that had shattered the patience of the Arizel. The insect had tried to destroy them and eventually they had acted to save themselves. Let all other races know that an assault on Fenrille would bring down their own doom. Now the Arizel expressed bleak anger about the tree damage and thirsted for retribution.

"Before us then are three possibilities. First, the obvious one—the Expansionist Tendency calls for the Expulsion of the humans and the creation of the guard rota. Let us vote."

The guard rota was unpopular; barely forty percent of the Arizel voted on the measure, most against.

With tones of gloom Endiclav continued, "Let us vote on the motion from the Divider, to inhibit their culture by fomenting war among them or by otherwise tampering with their home system."

The Divider's motion gained acceptance widely. Seventy-five percent voted, and the vote was two to one in favor.

"Finally, we have that solution proposed by Tshak 404040, the use of a black-hole singularity, which will rid us forever of the human threat."

And Fleur knew it would be close. Enough of the Spirits would vote it through. They would do it because they refused to take the time to consider the human race significant. Their inward-directed saga was all that mattered.

"Those in favor of the motion from Tshak 404040—"

"Hold," came a new glyph, a glyph that unfolded within everyone's mind as if it welled up from some deeper place, deeper than any yet opened among the Arizel. Fleur instantly recalled the feeling, the sense of scale and purpose that accompanied it.

"Steadfast-in-Pursuit will break the silence of eight thousand bahlkwan in order to speak for the young race. I have observed them. They are still capable of love, something many of us have forgotten. Love is of the finer natures, if not the finest. Shall we crush such beauty so casually? Do we dare to modify the Creator's universes so freely that we can burn out a young race without giving the matter just a little more time? Let us give the Pragmatixt Endeavor a hearing. A little time is not much, and the extinction of a socially advanced race is a heavy step to take. Our galaxy may birth only ten such species in all its time within the Halls of All. We are the firstborn, and it is perhaps our responsibility to take care of those who come after."

A shift in opinion had occurred, spurred by respect for the oldest and wisest of all and some shame that stung those who had earlier favored extermination.

"You may present your views," Endiclav glyphed quickly, "unless the Exclusionists wish to object?"

Not even Tshak 404040 wished to clash with Steadfast-in-Pursuit.

"But be brief," Endiclav continued. "No extravagant rhetoric, no exhortations or chanting, please."

"I thank the assembled for their indulgence of a new trend." The Spirit-that-preferred-to-move-softly now took center stage.

"Once again Fenrille and our sacred forest are under assault. Great ships of space orbit the world and rain down destruction. We all remember the previous such occasion."

The insolence of the chitin was indeed on many minds.

"Furthermore, in this instance there is a terrible difference— nuclear weapons have been employed. This will mean a slight but permanent loss in the forest. We have lost a small percentage of our powerload."

The glyph for powerload kicked off a strange little automatic response from the Arizel, and Fleur was left wondering why as a simple glyph was repeated over and over: "the golden road to the powerload, the golden road to the powerload."

When it finally faded, the Spirit continued, "In both of these instances our recall has been forced by the action of an aggressive spacegoing species seeking colony worlds—alien species, pursuing their own interests here. Now for good reason we do not advertise our presence, and we wish our world to remain a secret. Our ecosystem was designed to repulse alien colonizers and to resist change or mutation. It has worked well—it has certainly proved itself exceptionally stable. We have been maintained upon our quest now for many times the original period we imagined when we set out. In all that time the forest has withstood change. So it is successful, yet still it remains that we have been forced to return twice to protect it.

"This suggests something to the Pragmatixts."

Opinions among the Arizel were in flux. It was a problem, no doubt about it.

"Furthermore, we of the Pragmatixt Endeavor do not want to have to admit to the Creator someday that we have obliterated a single species of Its creation."

Again there were unmistakable impressions of shifting opinions.

"The humans have also developed a unique form of colony here. They occupy only the marginal areas that do not grow the *ayeirl*. They have failed in their major colonizing thrust. What they want from our world now is the drug they are dependent on and which they obtain from our highland areas. The supply of the drug is vital to them, and we, in the final resort, control it. Thus the humans can be easily persuaded to avoid any further tree damage.

"We believe the humans can be easily made to understand these things and that they will be cooperative as a result. Therefore, we propose to employ them rather than exterminate them or expel them. Since we have been invaded twice by alien spacegoing colonizers, evidence suggests that we will be again. The galaxy wakes with life and only now are the appropriate star groups maturing fully. Thus we suggest that we invest the humans with the responsibility for preserving our world and our forest from harm. We will simply add them to the woodwose as guardians of our trees.

"In return for this service, they will be allowed to continue harvesting the chitin for longevity drugs.

"Incorporating the humans into our system in this way will add a shell of necessary technology to our defenses. Our interests will be equally served. We will be freed of these returns, which draw us away from our vital search. They will be assured of their longevity drug, and at the same time we would be free of the onerous responsibility for further extinctions of young, sentient races."

A definite pause followed, a sense of widespread approval. Then a slow-building susurration of positive glyphs. It was cut short.

"THERE IS ANOTHER POINT TO CONSIDER," roared the glyph from Tshak 404040. "THE HUMANS HAVE NUCLEAR WEAPON TECHNOLOGY, EASILY ENOUGH TO DESTROY FENRILLE BY SURPRISE ATTACK. WHAT IF THEY TURN UPON US AND DESTROY OUR FOREST?"

326

The shift in opinion stopped dead. Fleur could feel the dread and the hesitation.

But the Spirit-that-preferred-to-move-softly swiftly glyphed, "It is unlikely that such an attack would be countenanced considering that it would be certain to end the supply of longevity drugs. However, we could also set the highland clans to serve as human watchfein for us. Their interests are obviously allied with this solution so they will make staunch allies for us. They will serve us by being in charge of the defense forces around Fenrille. That way they will work to ensure there is no treachery."

Again a tide of agreement pulsed through the Arizel.

"Does the Divider wish to speak against the motion of the Spirit-that-preferred-to-move-softly?"

All waited a moment on that didactic aloofness, and many were surprised when the Divider's glyph arose.

"No, indeed we find the idea has merit. The humans are easily divided and controlled. They are utterly dependent on the longevity drug. It can only be refined from Fenrille chitin, thus the humans are ours just as the chitin are the humans'.

"However, the humans are a young, fairly lowly order of life. What guarantees do we have of their ability to protect our world? Are their space crews efficient? Are their ships well constructed?"

"I have tested, them," glyphed the Spirit-that-preferred-to-move-softly. "The admiral and his ship were faced with an impossible enemy." With the glyph came the sense of the short encounter between the *Gagarin* and the alien. A strange sensation rippled through the trees; the Arizel were laughing!

"Yet our struggle came to a point and at the moment of greatest danger I found they were prepared to destroy themselves by detonating their fusion drive. Such ferocity of purpose seems ideal for the task. Furthermore, the crews are eugenically altered to withstand high acceleration, the ships are powerful, the crews practiced. On the whole, they are very capable of protecting our world."

Seeing the way things were moving, Tshak 404040 burst out, "HOWEVER, THE COMMANDER OF THE FLEET IS TOTALLY UNACCEPTABLE TO US. HE CANNOT BE ALLOWED TO REMAIN. THE EXPUNGEMENT FACTION WILL DEMAND NOTHING LESS THAN HIS

327

LIFE. THE TREE DAMAGE HE CAUSED DEMANDS IT. LIFE MUST BE TAKEN TO QUENCH THE AGONY OF THE TORTURED ROOTS."

"Must there be the taking of life?" Endiclav's glyph queried.

"SO IT IS STATED IN THE 9TH CANTO OF THE YLLBLLSA. WE MUST QUENCH THE DAMAGE WITH LIFE. AGAIN WE WILL REQUIRE A LIFE FOR THE RENEWAL OF THE MAHGARA. REMEMBER WE ARE ALL HERE, EVEN STEADFAST-IN-PURSUIT IS HERE. THUS WE HAVE NO ONE AHEAD TO PULL ON IN THE HOLES OF VOID."

"Yes, you're correct about that," Endiclav admitted.

"OF COURSE," Tshak's glyph replied, dripping condescension.

Enkov took in a shuddering gasp. They were going to kill him, just for damaging some trees? He hadn't even been aware of the existence of these beings a few minutes ago and now he was going to be sacrificed by them!

"This raises a problem," glyphed the Spirit-that-preferred-to-move-softly. "The admiral will have to be spared, even if he did cause the tree damage."

"NONSENSE. HE MUST DIE AND WITH HIS DEATH HE WILL PAY AMENDS FOR THE TREE DAMAGE."

"Except that we will need him to send back to the humans' home world. He is the only one that superior leaders there will listen to. Anyone else would be dismissed as a fantasist and treated as mentally unwell. And because we will return him, we will demonstrate most directly our power. They will be forced to listen."

The silence that followed was pregnant with possibilities. The Divider broke in. "This seems an interesting divination. Delve further."

Fleur noticed that glyphs from the Divider seemed to splash into the front of consciousness, tingeing all thought in a way that was unique.

"We must get the human leadership to formally agree to serve us in return for our continued indulgence of their need for the longevity drugs. We can improve communications between Fenrille and Earth if we move a black-hole singularity closer to their system. They have mastered the technology needed for rapid-line communications but are hampered by the lack of a nearby black-hole singularity."

"INDEED, AND SUCH A BLACK-HOLE SINGULARITY WOULD THEN

BE HANDY IF IT WAS EVER NEEDED FOR EXTERMINATING THE HUMANS."

Nobody cared to comment on that.

"Furthermore, I believe that we should request some additional space vessels for the Fenrille fleet. Another ship of the *Gagarin* class and several smaller ones. We want to be sure of good protection. The galaxy quickens and new space runners will soon come."

"Of course," agreed Endiclav the Finest. "If we're going to employ the humans in this way we may as well have good protection. We can't stay hidden any longer, it seems, so the fleet must be well equipped." Endiclav had taken to the idea of the Pragmatixts with enthusiasm.

The winds of opinion were blowing once more.

"Again then, shall we take a vote on the motion put forward by the Exclusionist Tendency?"

They did and then the Divider announced in a somber glyph, "Our motion has been defeated. We are ruled by the division, as always."

The Divider withdrew.

Now Admiral Enkov became the center of a keen scrutiny.

"We have read your thoughts, there can be no possible deceptions," Endiclav glyphed. "You know this as you know us now."

Enkov was still reeling, revolted by the idea of his mind being invaded.

"We shall return you to Earth, to Chairman Wei, and you will explain what has happened to him and how things must be from now on."

"He won't believe."

"You will have to convince him. We will send Senator Ganweek with you. He will be an informative exhibit for the chairman, don't you see. And there will be an Arizel emissary as well. We must examine your culture. By all accounts it is very large and exceptionally vigorous. To have expanded so far on the gross material plane while remaining so innocent on the higher planes is an indication of great vigor in a race. There has not been time for lasting evils to have set in, yet we can see how youthful a kind you are, veritably ye are children. Only six hundred bahlkwan ago did you form from the creatures of your world."

"Who will command *Gagarin*?" Enkov said, clutching at the last pillar remaining in his dreams. Only minutes before it seemed he'd been contemplating final victory and the beginning of his march to Imperium. It was hard to settle his mind, to think through the daze.

"The second in command, Officer Ursk, will do very well. I see that you believe him to be a better officer than yourself. His career has been blighted politically while yours has swollen. He will make an able commander. Now you must remember to impress upon the chairman the urgency of our demands for more spaceships. He will understand our desires, of course, and the news concerning the synthesis of chitin protein."

"How will I get to Earth?" Enkov wailed. "If you keep my ship, I'm stuck here."

"Nonsense, everything has been arranged. Are we the Masters of the One Force or not? Remember, ye are before the Council of the High Arizel. Comport yourself accordingly."

Enkov struggled with the new ideas for a moment, then ceased resisting. His shoulders sagged. "What will I tell Chairman Wei?"

"That the continued existence of the human race is now contingent upon a rigorous defense of this Solar System from outside interference. We note that the problem of undersupply of chitin drugs will be considerably alleviated by application of the Hith formula. Of course, the problem will never go away, not until humans learn to live without such drugs, but in our judgment that will be a very long time indeed.

"The fleet here is to be strengthened as we mentioned and the commanders and crew will be vetted by the highland clans. We appoint the clans our guardians."

"The clans?" Shock and outrage radiated from Enkov and Ganweek.

"Of course, they are the true humans of Fenrille. We accept them into our ecosystem."

"What about the coastal cities?" Ganweek shouted, almost in tears.

"They are too heavily populated, the people will be encouraged to emigrate. Or be incorporated into the clan structures. We want an end to the warbands and the greedy syndicate operations. The outerplanets of this Solar System are largely unexploited. Your race has the technology to adapt them or to construct space habitats from them. However, the population allowed on Fenrille shall henceforth be smaller than it is now, and the clan leadership shall enforce the prohibition."

"Don't you think this is a rather harsh sentence?" Ganweek implored.

"No."

"Why am I singled out to be sent to Earth? How can I survive there?"

"You'll find a way. And you make an ideal spokesperson for us."

Perplexed, Ganweek let further pleas die in his throat. By comparison with racial annihilation, which had hung over them only a few moments before, it was a light sentence. And yet the cities would be uprooted and millions displaced.

Once more Endiclav moved the judgment along briskly to vote on the proposals and they were accepted by a wide majority, despite a strong note of dissent from Tshak 404040 and the Expungement Faction.

Stung by two straight Expansionist Tendency victories, the Expungement purists shifted their attention. "THERE IS STILL THE MATTER OF A PAYMENT IN LIFE. FOR THE TREE DAMAGE."

"Of course, there is the principle; it must be attended to, alas. The canto prescribes that a single life, if volunteered, will suffice."

"OUR LAST RETURN ENDED WITH THE EXTINCTION OF THE AGGRESSIVE CHITIN HOMEWORLD. THE TREE DAMAGE WAS PAID FOR IN JUST RETURN. THE BLASTED AND DESTROYED ROOTS WERE WATERED."

"What will it take this time?" Endiclav glyphed.

"HUMAN LIFE, OF COURSE."

"The coastal cities?" Ganweek quavered. "Are you saying you're going to kill them?"

Fleur shook a little at that. The Arizel were quite capable of it. Would they seal the agreement with the lives of millions? And then calmly order humanity to protect their planet for them?

"ON REFLECTION, THE CITIES' POPULATION WOULD SUFFICE TO PAY FOR THE TREE DAMAGE."

"But there are millions of people in those cities, millions. You can't slaughter them all, surely?" Ganweek asked.

"OF COURSE WE CAN. THE PALE MOON CAN BE SHIFTED CLOSE

ENOUGH TO RAISE A TIDAL WAVE TO CLEANSE OUR COASTS OF THE HUMAN HABITATIONS."

"But isn't it wrong to take life like that?"

"IN EXAMINING YOUR BRAIN, I FOUND LITTLE INDICATION THAT YOU HAVE EVER HESITATED TO TAKE ANOTHER'S LIFE IF IT SUITED YOUR PURPOSES."

"But—" Ganweek's face fell.

"Well, then volunteer," Endiclav said. "One volunteered life will be enough. We of the dominant tendency would be satisfied with that."

Ganweek paused. He would be on Earth, light-years away and probably doomed to stay there. Why should he care about the coastals' plight. Let the wave take them. He shrugged.

"So . . ." Endiclav's glyph was unmistakably cool. "If there's no further business, let's get on with it."

Fleur felt herself step forward as if she were in a dream. It was not something that she rationalized or even made a decision upon, it was just something she did. As if it was the duty her parents had spoken of so often in the little apartment in New Souk where she'd learned to read and type the word "diplomat" on the house computer. "I will volunteer then; it seems someone must. And at least I can claim to represent the Earth in this matter."

The Arizel paused and turned their attention to her. The intensity of such study almost caused her knees to wilt, but she held herself up until Lavin came up behind her and smothered her in his arms and clapped a hand over her mouth.

"Enough of this, she can't be the one to go. She's much too important a link between Earth and Fenrille, a diplomat who understands the real situation, an Earth representative that has met the Arizel tki Fenrille. Don't you see?"

The Arizel continued to observe silently.

"Instead I will go. My purpose in life has been restricted to fighting wars. As there will be no more wars, my function is lost. Take me."

Fleur struggled but Lavin was far too strong.

"My darling, it's true," he whispered. "It has to be this way."

"Thy death will be swift and painless," Endiclav's shining glyph pronounced. "And thy spirit will enter our service. The

332

life you now lead will come to seem pale and meaningless in comparison with what lies before you."

The ritual incantation of the death canto was beginning. The glyphs from the Arizel were hard, austere, sharp and cold.

But another glyph then broke in upon them, a different kind of glyph, one with unmistakable human characteristics. The Arizel halted the death glyphs, astonished.

"Hold," said the glyph from Fair Fundan. "These matters should be the concern of the adept, and these young people have but begun their lives. The death of either would be a grievous waste. And now I know that all I have striven for is accomplished, Clan Fundan's future is assured. My task is completed, and now I, too, will go on forever for I will die in thy great service. No other deed—except to die for the Creator itself—would be more fitting. Besides, these youngsters are of my flesh. Thus I will survive here among the living, too. Truly this will be the best of times to leave the mortal world."

Fair caught Fleur's wide-eyed stare and smiled a quiet smile.

"No . . . my dear, it is quite right. Believe me, I think I can understand it now, at last." Her eyes seemed to fix upon some remote horizon.

"I have done all that I ever intended to do. There is nothing left of my world. But there is a new world for you to build in. You see, my dear, I think I've discovered at last that people are meant to die, that after a while you lose your perspective, you begin to mistake your career for your self. I fell into that trap so deeply I recreated myself to ensure continuity. Now my successor will be my own flesh, my success is complete. What more could I want?

"And if I stay? I can only decline and continue petty feuds with such as Ervil Spreak and Young Proud. No, and besides, I would only be in your way because Lavin shall soon take over from me. He will take charge because he's like me, restless unless things are done right, the way I would want them. And you will help him, my dear Fleur, you with your practical genius will be at his side. What better hands could take over the reins of Clan Fundan? You will help, won't you, Fleur?"

"Of course, Mother Fair, of course." Fleur felt her own tears welling up.

Everyone else was staring at them in amazement. Fair, the

matriarch of Clan Fundan, going willingly into death? After only 309 years of life?

But they were all young—even Ira Ganweek was a mere child—they knew nothing, nothing of the golden road. And Fair knew what the death offered there by the Arizel would bring.

Fair saw that her great task had been to shepherd Clan Fundan through this last crisis. That realization had cleared the path to the next—that it was time to die. And this moment offered the greatest opportunity.

"Mother Fair," Lavin whispered, reaching out to touch her eyes, his fingers on her face. And into his mind came her glyph, pulsing on the powerload that she had learned the first secrets of.

"Follow the golden road, Lavin. Investigate the secrets of the mystery. Consult with the old ones always, and know that I am thee and thou art I. We are one flesh. What I could never tell you before I must relate now. Thou art me, my flesh reborn in eternal remarriage of the genes. To the end that I strove for, the eternal safety of Clan Fundan and the new higher form to come of it someday, I made you."

And Lavin understood with total clarity. True-genes Fundan, she had said! He was Fair Fundan herself, only in the experiment he had turned out a male instead of a female. True-genes! He was staggered! The mystery of his parentage was vanished. Revealed was a truth he never considered. He doubted that he could accept it; he rebelled against it.

"But you are much more than just a repetition, my Lavin." Her glyph came quickly before revulsion could set in. "On the battlefields of Abzen you proved that; your own genius came to the fore. You will go on and take the instruments I have given you to higher levels that I cannot even imagine. So do not grieve for me or hate me. Remember only that I gave you life, and now I give you Clan Fundan. It will be yours to manage in my absence; be sure to care for it well. Remember also to tread the golden road. It leads to the powerload."

And now her glyph sought out old Fy'pupe, who lay dying by the side of the glade. "Farewell, old one, well did thou teach me."

But the Spirit-that-preferred-to-move-softly intervened with a quiet glyph. "I shall soon take up the hair from the adept Fy'pupe. His time has come."

"We shall journey together then in death as we have in life."

From Fy'pupe's dying consciousness a flash of contentment fluttered up.

"Once more then," glyphed Endiclav the Finest. The Arizel turned their attention to the deeds to be performed.

With loud slaps of air Admiral Enkov and Ira Ganweek disappeared into nothingness.

"The distance is great and the load is light. Exercise great care," said the glyph of Endiclav.

Then: "It is done. Now they will learn of their new purpose."

"And I volunteer to serve as the observer of the humans. To assist them in understanding," the Spirit-that-preferred-to-move-softly announced.

"Your offer is accepted by the Council," Endiclav glyphed.

The Arizel turned once more upon the figure of Fair Fundan. Her face frozen and intent, she moved to the center of the glade.

Fleur clung to Lavin and shook a little as she felt the power rising around them.

"The return is ended," Endiclav the Finest announced. "Once again we vault forth upon the sacred trail."

With the great glyph of the Mahgara thundering forth, the Arizel focused on Fair, and her body began to glow from within with a golden light. The light grew brighter and brighter until it was hard to look directly upon her, and her flesh luminesced and became transparent. Then, with a flash so bright it was as if a small sun had been ignited in the glade, she vanished.

And with her went the Arizel tki Fenrille.

The thunderclap of their passing faded, and with its echoes died the energies in the trees. The veins ceased to glow, the glisters and nodes became bits of bark once more. The Fidnemed, recently scene of such awesome events, was quiet once more. The trees loomed as before, silent giants blocking out the sky.

Lavin looked up, saw Tan Ubu staring up into the vault of the trees. Nothing would ever be the same again for the human race. The new knowlege would take a lot of adjustment; many would find it hard to accept.

Bg Rva was politely waiting for Lavin. The Effertelli were coming out of their trance state. It was time to be moving.

Fleur squeezed Lavin's arm. Her slender body felt good beside his. There was the extra part that he had always needed o complete the life in Abzen Vale.

"A lot to do, my love, isn't there?"

"More than we'll ever manage to finish, much more."

"I think I'm very glad about that," she replied.

Postscript

IN THE HANGING GARDENS ABOVE THE CHAIRMAN'S PALACE IN New Baghdad, Chairman Wei pruned his fig trees at the end of the day. Something slapped the air behind him like a firecracker.

He whirled, with surprising agility for a double nonagenarian, ready for the assassin he always expected. Instead he found Sigimir Enkov, wide eyed, mouth tense, accompanied by a bald, potbellied little man with a similar expression of shock. Chairman Wei refrained from executing the killing stroke that he had intended with his pruning shears.

Enkov took stock of his surroundings and sat with an odd groan on the edge of a tree tub in red marble.

"What are you doing here?" the chairman said.

Enkov's eyes searched wildly, he spread his hands. "That's a story that will take a while to tell. Prepare yourself for a surprise. . . ."